PENDANT OF DRAGONS BOOK ONE

THE ALDRICH LEGACY

K. Isabella Frost

Printed in Australia
First Printing, 2019
ISBN: 978-0-6484641-8-1

White Light Publishing
Melton, VIC, Australia 3337
whitelightpublishing.com.au

In memory of Elizabeth (Betty) Webster and Frederick (Fred) Webster. Thank you for always believing in me and for teaching me to enjoy my imagination, Grandma and Grandad.

Acknowledgements

Ever since the day the idea of this story came to me as a child from an image of a girl riding a dragon there have been many people who have helped me to organise my thoughts, to learn the skills needed to write, and who have encouraged me on this path. Without them this story would not have become what it has today and would still just be a bunch of childishly scribbled drawings and ideas in my head.

First I would like to thank my Mum and Dad, Lynne and Kevin, for encouraging me to read and to follow artistic pursuits like drawing and writing. Both being avid readers they have set me on a great path of learning and given me a powerful love of the written word. I would also like to thank my grandmother, Betty, and my grandfather, Fred, for reading to me and adding to the knowledge that my parents already gave to me. Grandma was also very encouraging and a great listener to my ideas as I came up with them. And while Grandad wasn't with me for very long he was a great influence on my life.

To my sister Jessie and my brothers Patrick and David, thank you for all the games of imagination as kids and our shared love of fantasy in some form or another whether it be fairies, dragons, superheroes or science fiction heroes. In addition, a big thanks to David for his sound business and financial support and guidance, and for serving as the witness to signing the contract that has brought this work to the pages of a printed published book.

To all those who have inspired some of the characters that appear in these pages and added to the depth of the story. To Kade for giving me the inspiration for Carden Highever and the Guardians. To Emma who gave me great advice on how to edit my work and the name Tibain which perfectly fits the character. There are many others, but to thank you all would be a book in itself on this subject.

A big thank you to all of my teachers and mentors including Charles R. Slucki, Bettina Spivakovski, Chris Ray, Peter Hudson, Jennifer Valente, Amanda Godfrey and Brooke Kelly for all of their support and knowledge ranging from the practical aspects of writing, acting and reading to the more metaphysical, supernatural and psychic arts. You have all been a wonderful help and inspiration to me.

To Lauren Kelly and everyone at White Light Publishing House. Thank you so much for taking a chance on me and on my story. I am so grateful for all of the help and support you have given me as well as for welcoming me into the WLPH family. I hope this is just the first of many further journeys we take as Pendant of Dragons is brought to the world of published literature.

Lastly, to everyone I haven't mentioned but who I would love to thank, and to all of you who are yet to join the Princess and her friends as you now open these pages to embark on this adventure, thank you so much. I hope you enjoy your trip to Aldegaad and the rest of High-Realm.

Contents

Preface

I never realised how much I still had to lose, even after everything I already had. My grief had blinded me from really noticing, but in that moment, it was all too clear to me. My friends didn't know what was coming, but I did, that knowledge too painful to ignore.

The monster stood before me; his glowing green eyes coldly victorious as that cruel, sinister smile spread over his pale lips. The fear I felt was too real, too tangible as I truly came to understand what he had just said to me.

In that moment I felt an overwhelming warmth and I looked down at my chest. The stone in the core of my pendant was pulsating with violet light, heat radiating out from its centre across my skin and clothing.

I looked to the Shadow Lord, wide eyed as he smirked and began to laugh. I knew what was coming, turning towards my friends with a sudden desperate need to rush forward and save them...

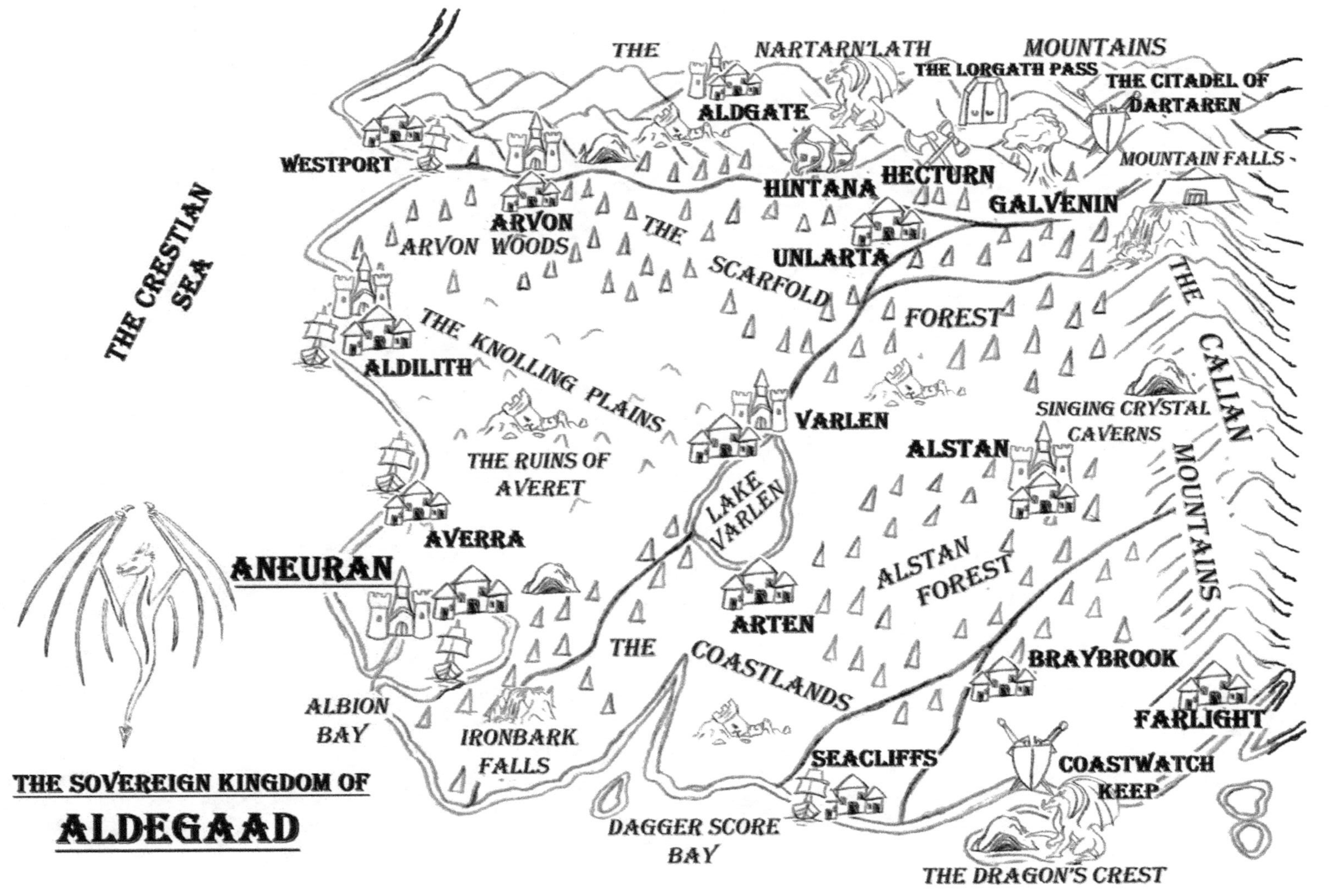

THE NARTARN'LATH MOUNTAINS
THE LORGATH PASS
THE CITADEL OF DARTAREN
ALDGATE
MOUNTAIN FALLS
WESTPORT
HINTANA
HECTURN
GALVENIN
ARVON
ARVON WOODS
THE SCARFOLD
UNLARTA
FOREST
THE CRESTIAN SEA
THE KNOLLING PLAINS
ALDILITH
VARLEN
SINGING CRYSTAL CAVERNS
ALSTAN
THE CALIAN MOUNTAINS
THE RUINS OF AVERET
LAKE VARLEN
AVERRA
ANEURAN
ALSTAN FOREST
ARTEN
THE COASTLANDS
BRAYBROOK
ALBION BAY
IRONBARK FALLS
FARLIGHT
SEACLIFFS
COASTWATCH KEEP
DAGGER SCORE BAY
THE DRAGON'S CREST
THE SOVEREIGN KINGDOM OF
ALDEGAAD

Chapter One
The Guardians

Early morning was my favourite time to walk the castle battlements and under crofts, the cold air coming down from the Nartarn'lath Mountains so soothing after awakening from my sleep. The dawn had broken the horizon and now laced the grey clouded sky with golden rays of light and tints of orange hues.

I passed through the walkways around the keep's exterior, the guard walls only meters from where I finally came to a stop. I stood overlooking the gardens and their unbridled beauty. Verdant greens filled the courtyard below the archways, the many colours of flowers beginning to open breaching my senses as the new day broke the sky with its warming light.

I couldn't think of a better place to find the solace I needed, my title of "Princess of Aldegaad" often making me feel stifled, and for a girl of only seventeen winters that was a lot to endure.

I pulled the dark blue velvet folds of my hooded cloak further around my neck and shoulders, fighting the cold coming off the mountain winds. There were only really a few seasons in our home country of Aldegaad: clear skies, cloudy cold, torrential rain and deepest winter snow, summer heat a true rarity.

I let my eyes wander across the early morning light drenched walls and gardens, trying to lose myself from the nagging thoughts in my head.

Today my elder sister was to leave us, to depart with her husband, Prince Sten Brander, eldest son of the Balganian King, Einar. My heart ached at the thought of this goodbye that was swiftly approaching.

I wished Aislinn the best for her new life with her true love, but I felt cold tears for the emptiness that would come with her leaving. My sister and I had been together since I was born, and she was the one who had truly watched over me and guided me. Now with her leaving I felt like a ship with no compass, lost in a deep, dark fog.

Looking at my hands where they rested on the stone barrier of the walkway, I gathered my strength to face this challenge.

I have to be strong. I must show Aislinn that I am happy for her. After all, marrying Sten now means that she will one day be Queen of Balganis at his side when he becomes King.

A small laugh escaped my lips.

Truly, I don't envy her that.

"Princess Leander?" a voice broke me from my deep thoughts, drawing my steel blue eyes towards its owner.

My handmaiden, Cara, stood before me, her chestnut hair pulled back and hidden beneath a sheer veil, her grey eyes soft and clear.

"Yes Cara?" I asked softly.

"Your Highness," she said with a tiny bow of her head, "your mother asked me to find you. Your sister is to depart soon."

Without another word, I followed Cara from my place overlooking the gardens, my cloak and skirts flowing around me like purple, blue and gold mists drifting in deep clear water.

We left the north wing and passed through into the keep, making for the Great Hall. We made our way down the wide staircase, entering the hall, which was designed in stone walls with high ceilings of wood supported by mahogany columns.

I had always loved the dragon carvings in the columns, reminding me of the creature that Aldegaad was known for and of a time of High-Realm's darker past. Even our banners carried the Dragon, a golden winged form with a coiling tail, its head to its right, belching flame against a cobalt field.

I would love to see a dragon one day. If only they weren't extinct.

We came to the main entry hall of the keep which led to the front courtyard. It was here that Cara left me and I made my way alone. As I walked down the stone steps from the keep I turned my attention to the gathering of figures before me. One group were dressed in the same blue cloaks with golden trims that I wore, the others in green with silver. They were surrounded by knights and soldiers wearing the two colours as well.

My eyes instantly fell to my parents, my two uncles, two aunts, cousin and sister.

My mother and father stood before the Balganians, Mother fighting tears as she was saying goodbye to my sister. Father was trying to smile through his neat grey tinted brown beard, his jaw length hair waving lightly in the wind.

Aislinn wore a blue and gold gown similar to mine, though her sleeves and under dress were a pure white while mine were a deep purple. Her dark auburn hair hung to her hips, a few strands splitting away in the cold breeze on their own, her shoulders shielded beneath her blue cloak.

My sister and I shared many features: our greyish blue eyes, our dark auburn hair, our fair white skin, but we were also very different. Aislinn took after Mother's side of the family, more petite and standing at five foot seven with smaller shoulders. I took after Father and was taller at just over five feet eight, my shoulders a little broader, my curvy shape stronger to look at, but that was our Aldrich blood, common in the women of his line.

"Ah, Leander, my youngest, there you are," Father smiled, glad of the shift in focus. "I worried that you would not be here."

"I wouldn't miss seeing my sister off on her new life, Father," I smiled at him, turning my gaze to Aislinn.

King Einar was saying his goodbyes to Uncle Aric as Sten and Aislinn stood together, saddened by this parting from our family; her first ever in her entire life, and it would be an almost permanent one.

"Mother," she wrapped her arms around our mother, fighting back tears.

"Be brave, Aislinn," Mother tried not to sob, hugging her tightly. "You're married to a fine young man and you shall be a wonderful queen and mother one day."

"I do not wish to say goodbye, Mother," Aislinn struggled not to cry. "I've never been away from Arvon or from you."

"It will be alright, my dear," Mother tried to be strong as she reassured her with a smile. "We will see each other again. You'll see."

Aislinn nodded sadly, then turned to Father. "Oh, how I will miss you, Father."

"And I you, my brave daughter," Father told her, fighting back his own tears. He then put his hands on her shoulders, smiling warmly. "I am so very proud of you, my Aislinn. Truly, I am."

"You have my love, Father," Aislinn kissed him on the cheek and forced a smile. "Always."

"Sten," Father turned to his new son-in-law sternly, but there was only care in his voice and eyes. "I want you to take care of my Aislinn. You love her and treat her right. Do you hear me?"

"I swear my oath as both a prince and as my father's son that I shall, Lord Ewan," Sten assured him with a nod. "By the honour of my homeland, I shall treat Aislinn with the love and respect she deserves."

Father smiled and hugged the young man, both of them patting each other on the back with closed fists, smiling respectfully as they stepped apart.

Aislinn turned to me.

I was standing close to Father, my hair hanging freely over my shoulders, my eyes more sorrowful than I had intended them to be.

"So, this is it?" I asked softly, my voice wavering a little.

"I suppose it is," Aislinn nodded solemnly.

She reached out and hugged me, the two of us struggling not to cry at the thought of this farewell.

"I am going to miss you most of all, little sister," Aislinn said softly and sadly. "Though, you are not so little anymore."

"I'm taller than you," I managed a weak laugh over her shoulder.

"Truly though, Leander, I *will* miss you."

"I'll miss you too," I replied, feeling a tear trickle down my cheek, cursing it silently.

Aislinn pulled back, studying my face for the last time and brushing my traitorous tear away with her thumb: "Remember, if you need me, simply call. I will come. I promise."

"I will, Aislinn," I agreed.

"Goodbye, little sister," Aislinn sighed, fighting back tears of her own.

"Goodbye," I returned sadly.

"My Princess," Sten offered Aislinn his arm. "Our honeymoon awaits."

"So it does," she nodded, taking his arm.

As they walked down the steps from the main doors they passed our knight-commander, Ser Mithras, and several knights. The men and women stood dressed in their chainmail and tunics, their dark blue cloaks hanging across their shoulders, swords either at their hips or across their backs.

"My Lady Aislinn," Mithras bowed his greying haired head solemnly. "Fair winds to you."

"Thank you, Ser Mithras," Aislinn smiled warmly at him. "Watch over my sister."

"I will, Princess," he nodded then turned respectfully to Sten. "My Lord, it has been an honour."

"The honour is all mine," Sten replied gratefully and the two men bowed their heads to each other.

"Well, we too should be off," King Einar said to Uncle Aric and Father. "We have a ship waiting for us in West Port."

Uncle Aric nodded, smiling respectfully. "And you have a kingdom to rule, Einar. You cannot keep your people without their king for too long, my friend."

"I am thankful for the joining of our two houses, Aric," Einar told him. "I think Aldrich and Brander are now stronger for it."

"I know my niece and your son most certainly are for their union," Uncle Aric agreed and placed his forearm to his chest, bowing his head. "Fair winds, my friend."

"And easy travels to you," Einar responded. "Now, my advisers will be waiting and I cannot have that."

Uncle Aric laughed. "Certainly not."

Einar turned to his younger sons. "Geir. Hakon. Come, lads, it is time to leave," then to his wife, "Astrid, my love."

She smiled and took his hand, the two of them walking towards their horses.

Their two handsome, blonde haired, younger sons walked from the steps, Geir turning to me and kissing my hand, my need to suppress my tears suddenly overwhelming.

"It was nice to see you again, Princess Leander," he told me, obviously infatuated with me.

"And you, Prince Geir," I replied, smiling at him, but secretly uncertain about his signals.

As Einar, Astrid and their sons walked down the steps and mounted their horses, my eyes fell on Aislinn for the last time. My sister sat on the white steed that Sten had ridden to our castle on, her husband sitting behind her in the saddle with his arms around her.

As Mother started to cry and clung to Father's arm, I waved one last time to my sister. Aislinn waved back and Sten nodded his farewell to us.

The Balganian entourage turned their mounts and swiftly left the courtyard, trotting out across the bridge towards Arvon itself. Aislinn looked past Sten from beneath her hood, taking one last glimpse of us, tears streaking her face.

As a final sign of respect to the departing newlyweds, Mithras and the knights formed a line facing their departure, and, in unison, held their forearms and fists to their chests, bowing their heads.

I kept my tear-filled eyes on Aislinn until the very end, watching my sister disappear from our home for the last time as an Aldrich and the first as a Brander.

I'll miss you, Aislinn...

* * * * *

Once again I found myself seeking the solitude of the gardens in the hours that followed my sister's departure. I took my favourite book to read, a blue hard cover entitled **Tales of Dragons**, and returned to my place overlooking the hedges and flowers.

I sat with my back to the stone wall of one of the arches above the west courtyard which linked into the north gardens, relaxing with the feeling of cold stone against my shoulders. Mother had often worried about me sitting so precariously over the ten-foot drop to the gardens, but I had never listened. She could be too strict when it came to my role as a princess and a woman, which led me to hide away even more that day.

I can't endure such things right now. I need to be alone, not playing the part of a princess. Not now.

As I had countless times before, I curled my knees up and rested the book against them, my hands pressed to the thick, rough pages. I could feel the raised edges of the inked words, touching them with my fingers as much as reading them with my eyes.

I loved reading. It was my one escape beyond the castle walls without an escort, unlike all of my trips into the surrounding provinces of Arvon. When I read a book I could travel anywhere on my own without needing protection, though in reality I hadn't yet needed to be defended. No one had ever threatened me or my sister in our lives, and I doubted that anyone ever would.

After two hours of reading from my last place I had come to the part of the story where the wizard, Ranzel, the Elf warrior, Corbya, and the last Guardian, Dartaren, had entered the Lorgath Pass in search of the great Ice Dragon, Kelapas. This tale – which covered four chapters of the book – was my most favourite because it contained the rarest dragon of all and the last of the original defenders of High-Realm. Both were quite a strong fascination of mine.

"What's this?" a scathing voice asked. "Little Leander's buried herself in a book? Again?"

I cringed at the mocking tone my cousin used, a little shocked that I hadn't noticed his approach.

"What do you want, Farah?" I asked without looking up.

"Maybe I'm bored and I'm looking for some fun," he replied, his haphazard balancing on the wall in front of me finally drawing my gaze. "So, I thought I'd look for you."

"Mother won't be happy if you fall," I warned him, turning my gaze back to my book.

He shrugged. "Neither will my mother, but I'm an adult and I have no need to really listen to her anymore. Unlike you."

"I'm nearly an adult too, you know," I pointed out quietly.

"Seventeen winters doesn't make you an adult, little cousin," he retorted.

"I'm eighteen in less than a week," I countered.

"Talk to me once you reach your twenty-first year," he sounded so smug that I just couldn't look up at him at all. "That's when you're really an adult you know."

I sighed and shrugged, keeping my eyes on the book, trying to ignore him.

"Hey!" I exclaimed as he snatched the book out of my hands and threw himself down to sit beside me.

He handled it roughly, mocking me with his childishly stupid actions, turning it upside down and letting the pages flap freely. I tried to grasp it back, but he pulled it away, staring straight at me as my desperation grew in my chest to my throat.

"Why do you read this one so much anyway?" Farah asked almost with disgust, eyeing the pages. "I mean, why the fascination with ancient stories about dragons?"

"Please, Farah, give it back," I pleaded, reaching for it, my fingers grazing the hard cover as he pulled it from my grasp again.

"You're always reading," he smirked at me, holding my book over the edge of the walkway. "Someone needs to pull you out of the pages and back to reality."

"No, Farah! Don't!" I begged frantically, trying to force my voice to be calm. "Please! Grandfather gave me that book!"

He paused, frowning at me, hesitating.

"Please. It was the first he ever gave me. I've had it since I was only five winters old," I continued to plead.

"Alright," he said in a more serious tone, slowly handing it back to me. "I'm sorry. I was only teasing."

I took the book back, clutching it to my chest as if it were my precious child, the relief pushing the panic away. It was so old now that to drop it from that height would destroy it and I would be devastated if that happened.

"You must really love it," Farah observed, watching me as I cradled it like a fragile newborn.

"It was my first book of my own," I replied, looking up at him after staring at its cover for a moment. "My sister used to read it to me until I was old enough to read on my own. As did Grandfather."

"I... I didn't know..." he trailed off quietly.

I looked him in the eye coldly: "Why do you do these things to me, Farah? Why do you tease me so?"

He shrugged and scratched the back of his neck. "I don't know. I don't mean to hurt you, cousin, I just... I don't really think," he sighed. "Maybe it's because of the way my mother and father treat me."

He pulled his feet up onto the wall with mine, leaning his back against the opposite pillar facing me.

"I just feel like there is so much they expect of me," he confessed, staring up aimlessly at a single spot in the stone ceiling. "I don't want to be my father's perfect copy, but it seems that I can't avoid it."

I let out a short half-hearted laugh. "My mother is the same. She has such high ambitions for me without ever asking me what I want. I mean, isn't it important that I have a say in how I want my life to turn out?"

"I completely agree," Farah looked to me, smiling faintly and crossing his arms. "It's like our parents can't allow us the choice, as if they think we won't choose well enough or something like that."

"You're right," I shrugged lightly. "That's exactly how Mother treats me."

"I feel sorry for you, Leander," he said earnestly with a sigh. "Of all of us you have it the worst, considering who you're named for."

I tried to suppress the involuntary twinge that cracked through my shoulders and spine, forcing it to a slight quiver rather than a full-on cringe. Of course, I knew who he was talking about. I had only known my whole life.

Why did my parents have to name me after her? Gods, why?

"I wish everyone would stop reminding me of that," I grumbled, staring at my knees and pinning the book to my chest with my crossed arms. "I'm not her."

"I don't think anyone expects you to be," Farah replied, trying – in his way – to reassure me. "After all, you're far too soft to be like the Great Heroine."

I threw him a hard stare: "Thanks."

He grinned at me and patted my knee. "Oh cheer up."

"I'm sorry," I said quietly, shrugging. "It's just that saying goodbye to Aislinn today was harder than I thought."

"I'll be honest that I don't really understand what it is to say goodbye to a sibling since I don't have any," he admitted, drawing my eyes to his face, kindness – which I didn't expect to see – lingering in his blue eyes. "But if you need to talk, I'll listen."

I was surprised. *Nearly eighteen years with him and he has never been so nice just for the sake of being nice. Amazing...*

"You know, you're not really as much like your father as people think," I told him, smiling softly.

He seemed relieved. "I'm glad someone thinks so. I agree with him in a lot of ways, but... his stubbornness and his selfishness makes me wish I wasn't his son sometimes. He's nothing like Uncle Aric and Uncle Ewan."

"Uncle Fane is just unhappy because he's the youngest," I reasoned. "I'm the youngest too, but I don't complain like he does."

Farah laughed. "I know. Remember the last mid-summer festival when he got drunk and went on about preferential treatment from Grandfather?"

"Right. I remember. He spent an hour complaining about how he was always 'the Bronze Child'," I giggled.

We both laughed.

"I feel like he sort of deserves it," he slowly eased off his laugher and we sat in silence for a few moments.

"Seriously though, Farah," I said, "thank you for what you said. I'm glad you're not the pigheaded jerk you were pretending to be."

He shrugged and waved a vague hand. "Ah, don't worry about that. I just tease because I care. You know that."

I smiled and nodded. "Yes. I know."

"Well, you two seem to be getting along better," my mother's voice startled me and my near loss of balance prompted her to scold me: "Oh, really, Leander! What have I told you about sitting on that partition?! You'll fall and break your neck!"

"Sorry, Mother," I nodded, Farah and I both standing up quickly from our precarious perches.

Mother stood with Aunt Patrice and Aunt Evangeline, all three without their cloaks as Farah and I were. They were likely just coming from having tea in the drawing room, but I was surprised to see them out on the garden and courtyard walkways.

Patrice turned her cold gaze towards her son severely, shaking her covered head. "Farah, you are the elder. You should know better. And what are you doing anyway?"

Farah answered: "Keeping Leander company, Mother. I thought Aislinn's departure might have left her feeling a little lonely."

I threw him an appreciative gaze.

"That's very thoughtful of you, Farah," Mother smiled at him.

He changed the subject: "What brings you, Mother and Aunt Evangeline to the gardens, Aunt Caralyn?"

"We were looking for the two of you, actually," Aunt Evangeline answered in her heavenly sweet voice, smiling angelically.

"Us?" I raised a curious eyebrow.

"Yes," Mother said, standing with her hands clasped in front of her hips. "There are courtly duties to attend to and I need your help, my dear daughter."

No... I don't want to be dragged into courtly duties at the moment. Why does she insist on making me such a public figure?

I groaned without meaning to, immediately gaining a severe glare from her.

"Now, Leander, we've had this discussion before," she reminded me sternly. "You *are* a princess and the daughter of this castle's and province's lord. You have certain duties you *must* attend to..."

"Why must you draw me into these courtside encounters, Mother?" I complained, looking at her tiredly. "Aislinn has been gone only a few hours and already you want to throw me to the wolves again?"

"That's an ungrateful tone to take with your mother, Leander," Patrice turned on me lowly, glaring at me with those frozen daggers she called eyes. "I'd have thought a young woman such as you would know discipline and courtesy like my son does," she turned those icy embers towards Farah expectantly: "Isn't that right, Farah?"

His body becoming instantly rigid, Farah nodded and responded: "Yes Mother."

Is it respect or fear which my cousin shows to his mother? I wondered as I glanced between them. *She has never seemed warm or kind for as long as I've known her.*

My aunt turned her chilled gaze back to me: "Perhaps you should learn to be a little more grateful, girl..."

"Patrice, really, there's no need," Aunt Evangeline stepped between us, almost shielding me from my harsher aunt.

"You don't have children, Evangeline, so don't presume to know anything about raising them," came Patrice's scathing remark.

My heart lurched in my chest and I locked my gaze on Evangeline. She just stared with haunted eyes for a moment, the hurt at Patrice's words so strong. She turned away from Patrice as my mother threw the harsh woman a severe glare.

Oh, you horrid woman!

Evangeline contained herself then faced me with that heavenly sweet smile she was so well known for.

"Leander, dear," she said softly, "Your mother and I need your help hosting some honoured guests who are coming here. And I *know* that you *will* be interested to meet them."

I raised a curious eyebrow. "Who are they?"

Mother smiled knowingly. "Three Guardians are to be staying with us for a time."

I felt my jaw drop and my eyes widen. "Really?"

"Guardians are coming here?" Farah was just as surprised as I was. "Why?"

"They have business with Aric and your fathers," Evangeline expressed evenly between us. "It is the reason why we have not yet departed back to Aneuran."

"When are they coming?" I asked, feeling that I might have appeared too eager, but not caring.

"The tower sentries have already spotted them coming up the main road from Arvon," Mother explained. "We're going to meet them now. Farah, could you fetch your father and uncles and have them come to the main courtyard?"

"Of course, Aunt Caralyn," he confirmed and hurried off.

Mother turned back to me as we heard horns from the battlements signalling riders approaching. "Leander, darling?"

"Of course," I agreed, falling into step beside her as we started off along the north-west walkway. "I've never met a Guardian before."

"Normally I would not encourage such meetings given your less than... ahem... acceptable interests," she told me, her eyes ahead, "but given the magnitude of such a visit and the prestige of our visitors it is your duty to make an appearance."

"For once I won't argue, Mother," I said softly.

We made our way from the garden walks, turning through the walkways towards the main courtyard where the Balganian Royal Family and my sister had departed only hours ago. I could already hear the hurried calls of the soldiers guarding our home, shouts of approaching riders being sighted echoing through the grey stone walls.

"What business could Guardians have here in Castle Arvon?" I wondered aloud, looking more to my mother and Evangeline rather than my other aunt, who I was now ignoring. "Aren't they High-Realm's peacekeepers and protectors?"

"Yes, they are, my girl," Mother answered as we turned into view of the central courtyard. "And I'm not certain what business they have here, but I can only assume that it is to do with your father and uncles."

I studied her face for a moment, frowning as that tell of hers began to show. Whenever she was hiding something, my mother's expression became more solemn with the hint of a smile tugging at the corner of her mouth.

"What aren't you telling me, Mother?" I probed with one raised slender eyebrow.

She turned her eyes my way, their greyish hue darkening for a moment as she studied my younger, softer features. She glanced to my aunts in turn then faced me again, her long, delicate hands grasping the edges of her wide cuffed sleeves.

"What makes you think I'm not telling you something, my girl?" she asked casually, another sign.

"I'm your daughter," I reasoned. "I can always tell when there's something on your mind."

"It is something you'd best discuss with your father," was her quick response.

"But..."

"I can say no more, Leander. Talk to your father."

That was always how Mother escaped a conversation she didn't want to be a part of with me. Deflecting me to my father was one of her classic moves and I had become so used to it that I knew there was no point in arguing further.

We came to the courtyard, entering from the northern side – to the left of the main gates. The guards and knights were readying themselves as the portcullis gate was rising, the wall archers watching the surrounding hills and woods with great diligence.

From the gates and the bridge beyond came the clattering of hooves, three horses trotting through with black hooded and cloaked riders upon their backs. The riders' cloaks were lined with silver designs, their horses bearing the symbol of the Guardians on their saddles and harnesses: a shield with two crossed swords behind it, the points down. The three horses – one chestnut, one black and one paint – slowed as they came to a stop in the cobblestone courtyard, their hooded riders tugging on the reins and making them ease their stamping.

"It seems our guests have arrived," Aunt Evangeline smiled as we stood at the stone barrier of the walkway.

I rested my hands on the cold stone, my book pinned by my palms as I stared long at the figures before me. I was instantly entranced, the stories and legends paling in comparison to the reality of these great heroes.

Gods... they truly are Guardians...

The one on the chestnut horse and in the lead threw back his hood, revealing his long dark hair and his thickly bearded face. He had brown eyes and an aged face that still held the youth of a man in his late forties or early fifties, though it was hard to tell if that was his real age. He carried a strong oaken staff in his right hand, a blue crystal set into its top. Beneath his cloak he was dressed in the robes of a mage, but they were short to reveal his dark grey leg coverings and black boots. He wore a sleeveless overcoat of deepest black with silver detailing, a satchel hung across his shoulder and down to his left hip where there also sat a sword. Despite his severity he held a kindness in his dark eyes that said he could not be harsh or cold.

On the white and brown paint horse was a beautiful woman with tanned skin and long golden hair. The strands shimmered with the colour of the sun, her hazel eyes stern, but underneath there seemed to be a youthful inexperience as well. She wore very simple, but neat clothing, corsetry in the front to tighten the pale emerald green shirt she wore under a black and silver sleeveless tunic. She carried with her a sword identical to the Mage's, an elegant bow of foreign design across her back with a quiver full of hawk feathered steel arrows.

I knew enough of the peoples of High-Realm to recognise her as a Ranger from Dorvana, one of the northern nations past the Nartarn'lath Mountains. The colour of her eyes and hair, as well as the blue and silver armband with the symbol of a wolf she wore on her left upper arm the clearest indicators of this. She couldn't have been older than twenty-eight winters.

The third of the trio was a handsome young man no more than twenty-three winters old. He had sharply defined features, his pointed cheekbones and smoothly angled jaw standing out strongly. He had the most amazing jade green eyes, his hair as black as night, cut to just below his jaw and sweeping back to his neck, just off his broad shoulders.

He wore a dark teal shirt laced up under a buttoned up, silver detailed, black leather tunic that was bound by a belt at his waist. His collars were left open enough to reveal the fine details of his subtly defined muscles that met his neck, my eyes inadvertently following the line down to his athletic chest. At his hip he carried a triplet sword to the ones his companions held, one broad hand reaching for the pommel subconsciously as his eyes surveyed the walls around him. He also wore throwing daggers on his belt.

It was this man that drew my gaze the strongest, something in me urging my eyes to stay locked on his perfectly shaped and sculpted face. I couldn't decide what it was about him, only that there was something that held my attentions and kept them.

Who is he? He's... he's so... gods... I don't even have words...

The young man's eyes drifted to where I stood and locked onto me. I felt a gasp escape my lips, slipping up through my throat to freedom. My heart fluttered as our gazes met and I wondered: *What is it about him that draws me so strongly? I've never been so entranced by a man before.*

He stared at me with a strange look I couldn't even begin to explain, a depth in his eyes that seemed to appear from nowhere. Even as he dismounted from his black steed he didn't take his eyes off me just as I didn't take mine off him.

"Leander, dear, come along," Mother broke me from my trance gently, my dazed expression drawing a raised eyebrow from her.

I obediently followed her, the four of us making our way along the walkway towards the steps that rounded nearer the keep's entrance. My eyes kept darting back to the young Guardian, his green gaze inexorably frozen on me. I felt myself blush, looking down at my feet and hiding beneath my dark hair.

He keeps watching me. Gods, why am I blushing?

I looked back up to the doorway of the keep to find my father and uncles walking out with Farah close behind. To my father's right was Mithras, the Knight-Commander dressed in his silvery plate armour. He turned his gaze to me, smiling faintly, his hand moving to his sword pommel as his eyes returned to the three Guardians now striding to face the five men as we reached the steps.

Uncle Aric took charge – as a good King should – opening his arms wide to our guests and smiling.

"Welcome friends," he beamed from behind his ever whitening beard. "It is an honour to meet you and have you in our ancestral home."

The three Guardians dropped to one knee and bowed their heads as their horses were tended to, the Mage central and forward of the other two. He looked up after a moment as I came to stand near my father and Aunt Evangeline moved to Uncle Aric's side.

"Your Majesties, King Aric and Queen Evangeline," the Guardian Mage addressed them respectfully, "it is an honour to be called upon by your family as our order once was in centuries past by your great ancestor."

They stood slowly at my uncle's bequest, the Mage grasping his staff with both hands and leaning on it for support or perhaps just out of habit.

"It is not every day that we are welcomed to Castle Arvon," he continued.

"This castle is under my brother's command," Uncle Aric gestured to Father. "He has kindly offered his home as our meeting place."

"Given the reasons for our meeting I could think of no better place, brother," Father agreed, gesturing to my mother and I. "Please, allow me to introduce my wife, Caralyn..."

"Your Ladyship," the Guardian bowed his head with a warm smile to her.

Father put his arm around my shoulders: "And my youngest daughter, Leander."

"Princess," the Guardian bowed with great reverence to me, "it is the highest pleasure to meet you."

"You're really Guardians?" I asked without managing to control myself, certain of my parents' shocked stares.

The Guardian chuckled lightly and nodded. "Yes your Highness, we are."

"From the Citadel of Dartaren?" I urged on excitedly.

"You must forgive my daughter's eagerness," Father smiled brightly at me, then turned to our guests. "She has often expressed her fascination of the Guardian Order."

"It is quite alright, your Lordship," the Guardian responded politely. "May I introduce myself and my juniors? I am Aldwyn Draken, Mage of the University of Safferan and Master Guardian," he gestured then to the woman: "This is Tallinn Landrace, a Ranger of Dorvana and my first junior."

"A pleasure your Majesties and Highnesses," Tallinn bowed her head gently, her stern expression doing nothing to hide her overall beauty.

Aldwyn turned to the young man: "And my youngest charge and Guardian apprentice, Carden Highever from Gorvenna."

The young man smiled and bowed his head subtly, his eyes locking with mine again.

Carden? So that's his name. I felt myself blush once more as he smiled lopsidedly at me. *He is so incredibly attractive. Gods, stop blushing, Leander!*

"We know who you all are," Aldwyn continued to my family, "and we have been sent by the High Council to be their emissaries, and to serve you as best we can."

"We have much to discuss in private, Master Guardian," Uncle Aric said respectfully to Aldwyn. "But that would be best done once we have you situated in accommodations."

"Ser Mithras," Father turned to the Knight," would you be so kind as to lead our visitors to the guest wing?"

Mithras nodded. "Of course, my Lord."

"We shall discuss everything later in the privacy of my study," Father told the Guardians. "In the meantime, please make yourselves comfortable and welcome to Castle Arvon."

As the three Guardians were led away, I wanted to ask so many questions, but something told me to stay my tongue.

I wonder what it is that they must discuss with Father and my uncles.

My father turned to me as the rest of our family, aside from Mother, returned to the keep's warmth.

"A little eager, Leander?" he grinned at me.

"I'm sorry; I just have a lot of questions," I admitted softly.

"There will be time enough for those later, my girl. For now, there is much your uncles and I must discuss."

"Can I just ask one question?"

"And what is that?"

"Why are there Guardians here?" I asked softly.

Father raised an eyebrow at me, folding his arms firmly. Immediately I knew I wouldn't get an answer as soon as he had locked his hands beneath his shoulders.

"There are reasons which I am not yet ready to explain to you at this time," he explained evenly. "I realise this is not an answer that will satisfy you but understand that there are necessities for this visit."

"But Guardians don't just go somewhere for no reason," I pointed out. "And I doubt this is a social visit since they only come when there is someone in danger."

"There are issues that you need not concern yourself with, Leander," Father said calmly, keeping his tone even and cool. "Don't obsess over any of this and just try to find something to occupy yourself with. You will get your chance to speak with the Guardians soon, you have my word."

He reached out to me, stroking my hair back from my forehead and over my ear. I just stared back sternly.

"Now, my sweet girl, it is far too cold for you to stand around out here," he expressed. "Go warm up and find another way to entertain yourself."

"Just don't bother you or your guests, right?" I asked coldly.

"We'll talk later, Leander," he said, glossing over my words. "I promise."

I nodded and watched as he walked away, Mother smiling at me then following him.

I stood for a few moments staring after them, clutching my book to my chest, almost having forgotten I was carrying it still. Knowing there was no way to break my father's iron will, I sighed and made my way into the keep, my skirts trailing behind me as my hair and sleeves caught in the icy breeze.

Chapter Two
A King's Proposition

With the Guardians settled into their quarters in the castle's guest wing, rumours soon began to spread as to why they were visiting us. I can't even count the number of stories I heard in passing from guards and servants. They ranged from tales of conspiracy against my family to outrageous claims of monsters hiding in the towers.

I didn't believe any of them, of course, but I was just as curious about our visitors as anyone else in Arvon was. Despite all of my efforts, however, I couldn't get a moment to speak with the Guardians. Even my status as a princess didn't help me to achieve this desire. My father and uncles had cloistered themselves away in Father's study with the Guardians to discuss their secret intentions. Aside from a few glancing encounters, I almost never even saw them.

My name day was fast approaching, and I was finding it difficult to occupy myself. Finally, the monotony became so much that I had to do something. So, I went to the training rooms. When I arrived I found Mithras with a young squire I had sparred with before, a dark haired boy a little older than me named Baldric.

"I expected to see you today, Princess," the aging knight smiled knowingly as I entered, gesturing to an armour rack, then a weapons rack. "You'd best put on some armour and choose a sword. I think a sparring session is appropriate for both you and Baldric here."

I followed his instructions and took up my position in the training circle opposite Baldric, trying not to laugh at the squire's arrogance as he faced me.

Dressed in the simple training armour provided with my hair tied back, I readied myself, the chainmail rattling as I moved slowly with the sword held up in both hands. My blue eyes remained on the squire in front of me, his own gaze locked on me as he mirrored my movements.

Mithras leaned against the wall near the weapon racks watching us as we faced off with our swords raised at each other. He crossed his arms casually, his mail armour rattling over his sleeves, his dark eyes locked squarely on us. He seemed amused.

I watched my opponent carefully, trying to judge how he would move and how the next strike would come at me. After two hours I could see that Baldric was getting tired just as I was, but I had been trying to heighten my stamina in a fight for the last few months.

Suddenly, Baldric lunged, forcing me to block with my sword, the two blades clanging loudly. I ran my sword across his, thrusting him back then taking two swings to throw him off balance. He panicked at the second blow but managed to block it regardless.

Again he attacked, the two swords clanging together as we moved against each other. I spun around, wielding my sword swiftly to block another strike before tripping and staggering, but I regained my footing in time to throw him back once more.

"Always be mindful of your footing," Mithras called to me.

I nodded, focused, then attacked again, striking with three strong blows against the squire, who blocked them easily. He swung his sword and I just barely managed to catch it with my blade before being assaulted with a flurry of strikes.

I moved to attack with an underarm strike, Baldric slamming his sword towards the ground and knocking mine from my hand. The force pushed me to my knees and he easily pointed his sword at my throat.

Breathing heavily, I froze, my eyes locking with his, my heart racing in my chest from the effort, sweat beading my forehead despite the chill in the room.

Baldric smirked with arrogance, his eyes blazing, his every movement showing how highly he thought of himself. Even though I was at his mercy I was still amused by him and had to hold back my own smirk.

"Yield," he grinned smugly.

I glared up at him, my teeth set and my lips pressed in a grim line on my face, my hands at my sides.

"Now then, let's review," Mithras said, drawing our gazes. "Baldric has bested you, Leander, because you sacrificed your footing for fancy moves."

Baldric's arrogant grin broadened and he looked to Mithras proudly as I silently cursed my mistake.

Mithras then smirked at Baldric: "But Baldric's mistake is taking his eyes *off* his opponent when he *thinks* he has her beaten."

I allowed myself a wry smile.

"What?!" Baldric turned back to me just in time to receive a boot to the gut.

He dropped his sword, staggering backwards as I rolled up, grabbing my own sword and elbowing him in the back in one fluid sweep. I kicked his legs out from under him, dropping him hard to the floor, and with both hands on the hilt of my sword I aimed the point of the blade at his chest, my feet set firmly apart.

"You yield," I growled with a small smile, satisfaction filling me at his brash ignorance and now his bewildered stare.

Mithras clapped lightly, walking over to the two of us. "Yes, well done, Leander. Well done, indeed."

The greying haired knight rounded up on my left as I stood over Baldric unflinchingly, never once taking my eyes off him.

"Now then," Mithras lectured casually as he observed us, "in this situation, the opponent who was originally at the mercy of the other is now the one with all the power. And this is due to the previous power holder's inability to focus and his blatant arrogance in the fight."

Baldric didn't take his eyes off my sword, too nervous to move just in case I decided to gut him where he lay. I remained very focused, though I was breathing heavily, my sword steady in my hands.

"Aha," Mithras crouched down to look at Baldric, observing his body language. "Now that you are at her mercy you pay attention to her. Just because she is a girl do not believe for one moment that she is weak," he nodded to me. "You can let him up now."

I withdrew my sword, stepping back and lowering the blade's point towards the floor as I brought my feet together, looking down at Baldric all the while. Baldric very warily got to his feet, glaring at me the whole time, almost as though he didn't trust that I would let him up.

"Observation is of great importance to any warrior, awareness even more so. Without awareness we trip, we fall," Mithras looked to us both with a wry smile, "we die very bloodily and violently at the hands of an enemy. Awareness is one of the fundamentals of combat and forgetting it is what leads to failure."

"And what about cheating, Ser Mithras?" Baldric demanded, glaring at me.

"Cheating?" Mithras raised an eyebrow, glancing between the two of us before settling on Baldric.

"She cheated," Baldric accused sourly, still eyeing me off.

Oh, wonderful. Must he be so childish?

"Did she?" Mithras looked a little amused. "And how did she do that?"

"Kicking me and striking me with her limbs," Baldric whined angrily, turning to Mithras. "There is no honour in that."

Mithras nodded, pacing around us as he spoke, his hands behind his back. "In duelling circles, you're quite right; it is only with weapon and shield that we fight. But on the battlefield it is a *very* different story."

"It wasn't a fair fight!" Baldric griped more obviously, his eyes locked on Mithras.

"Wake up, boy!" Mithras rounded on him ferociously. "When you're fighting for your life against an enemy knight or, gods forbid, against some horrible monster, you aren't going to be playing by any rules! You'll kick your foe in the stones the first chance you get and lop his head off so he doesn't take yours!" he then smiled at me and said: "Don't quote me on that, however."

I smiled against a laugh, looking down at the floor to contain myself. I found Mithras so amusing whenever we trained with the squires, his attitude towards them so much harsher than it was towards me. His way of speaking was certainly... *colourful*.

"But..." the squire tried to argue.

Mithras slapped Baldric across the back of the head and I stifled another laugh. "You won't be fencing with barbarians as a knight, Baldric! You'll be killing them so they don't kill you!"

"It's not barbarians I was facing here, now was it?" Baldric grumbled, rubbing his head.

Mithras turned to me with a mocking look of surprise, then back to Baldric. "Then it is just young women you cannot tolerate in battle? You prefer to bed them rather than fight alongside them? Eh?"

Baldric looked at Mithras sheepishly, not sure what to say as he turned his eyes down so as not to look at me. Again I fought the urge to smile at his foolish arrogance.

"And that says everything," Mithras smacked Baldric again, making him face him. "A man is not measured by how many women he beds or how many enemies he slays. A true man recognises that he must do what is right and show his worth through his behaviour and actions," he snorted and shook his head. "And your actions scream petty child."

"I am a knight! She is just a girl!" Baldric exclaimed, outraged, trying to tower over both Mithras and I.

"You're wrong again," Mithras countered sternly. "You are *not* a knight. You are a squire training to *become* a knight. And she *is* a princess, daughter to a prince and niece to a king. *And* she is also a hell of a lot better with a sword than you are!"

"I shall tell Ser Garvin about this!" Baldric growled furiously, his posturing reminiscent of a child's tantrum.

"He may be training you as his squire, but I trained him as mine," Mithras warned him. "You'd do better to run home to mummy and hide behind her apron!"

Baldric groaned loudly, then glared at me. "And you! Just because you're Prince Ewan's daughter and the King's niece don't think that you're any better than me! You're not!"

"Actually, I think you'll find she is," Mithras told him smugly. "She certainly has a better personality and is a much better fighter than you."

"Humph!" Baldric snarled then stormed out of the room, flinging open the door and striking out up the stairs.

"Well," Mithras smirked, turning to me, "squires and their precious little feelings, huh?"

I nodded, taking my sword and putting it back on the rack, giggling a little.

"Maybe I was a little opportunistic with my strikes," I admitted, turning over my shoulder to him.

"Nonsense," he responded, crossing to stand beside me. "You're fighting exactly as I taught you, although, your footing *does need* work."

"I know. I keep forgetting," I acknowledged in all seriousness, picking up the other sword and crossing back to the weapon racks. "I think I get a little overzealous when I'm fighting."

"That can be dangerous, girl," Mithras warned me, his hands at the small of his back again. "Combat is not fun. I keep telling you this."

"I know, but training can be," I replied, untying my hair and letting it flow past my shoulders. "I can't help enjoying myself knowing that I'm not in any real danger."

"True, but you must treat our sessions as if they were real battles, just lacking of the killing blows, obviously."

I shrugged, crossing my grey sleeved arms and leaning against a stone partition in the centre of the room: "Obviously."

He was watching me, that deeply penetrating observant gaze of his as obvious as the stone walls surrounding us. I knew what he was thinking, not wanting to really talk about my reasons for being in the dark of the training rooms. But I also knew that he would pull it out of me without much effort, though I would resist.

"Is something bothering you, Leander?" he asked quietly and evenly.

"What makes you think something's bothering me?" I tried to sound aloof.

"Experience," was his answer as he came up beside me on my left, standing very close.

I tried not to look at him at first, staring with crossed arms at the stone floor, his gaze never budging from my face. I could feel his attention as if he were touching me, though his hands were firmly on his belt.

"Come child," he urged me gently, "speak of what vexes your young mind."

"Father," I replied with a reluctant shrug.

He arched a thick eyebrow at me. "Your father?"

I shook my head, submitting. "He keeps telling me that my eighteenth year means that I will be allowed to know more about things that happen in Aldegaad, that there won't be so many secrets. "I sighed glumly, shaking my head and staring at the far wall: "But this visit from the Guardians... he, Uncle Aric and Uncle Fane hiding with them in his study," I shrugged. "It just feels that no matter how much older I get that my parents are going to continue keeping secrets from me."

An amused smirk appeared on his face: "Such is the mystery that we call parents."

"I'm not trying to gripe or anything," I clarified, meeting his gaze, "I'm just wondering why everyone is acting so... *strange* around me lately. I mean... when I was little Father and I used to talk about everything. He never hid anything from me, nor did Mother. But now that I'm a teenager Mother's only interest is in finding me a suitor, and Father has taken to hiding himself away with these secret conferences with strange visitors. And then there are the rumours..."

Mithras nodded thoughtfully. "Ah yes, I've heard many rumours amongst the garrison and the servants. It seems that a visit from the Guardians has caused quite a stir in the town and the castle."

Staring forward again I chewed my bottom lip in thought: "The Guardians are High-Realm's peacekeepers. If not to defend someone who is in danger or to stop something terrible from happening then why have they come to Arvon?"

"I agree with your musings, child," Mithras said, considering everything. "Taking into account that one Guardian is often enough to handle the smallest of trials, we must consider that there are *three* visiting us," he glanced at me, almost hinting: "And while the King is here, nonetheless..."

I narrowed my eyes up at him suspiciously. "You know something, don't you, Mithras?"

"Do I?" he gave me a small half-grin.

"You're our Knight-Commander. I really doubt Father or Uncle Aric would keep much from you," I reasoned.

"You're right, of course, but you realize that I can't tell you anything. Don't you?" he asked in all seriousness.

I sighed and nodded. "Yes, I know."

He placed a hand on my back gently, drawing my gaze by touching two fingers under my chin and turning my face to his. Were that it was anyone else doing this I would have been expected – and maybe even self-influenced – to pull away and be offended, but Mithras was like an uncle, even a father to me. I trusted no one like I trusted him.

"Do not be disheartened, Leander," he said softly, meeting my eyes. "Some secrets you are ready for, others you are not."

"I just think that I should be the one to make that decision for myself," I replied quietly.

"Such things are never decided by those to hear the secrets, but by those who hold them," he said wisely like an old sage. "Give it time. Your father will entrust you with what you must know. Sooner than you think."

I could tell that he was hinting to me that whatever it was my father, uncles and our visitors were discussing was about me. That left me both uneasy and curious, but I knew that Mithras was right.

"Alright Mithras," I nodded. "I won't ask again."

He smiled warmly at me, almost admiringly. "You have such a curious way, Leander. Do not forsake your willingness to ask 'why', for it is the one thing that will ensure that you continue to learn."

I nodded, smiling at him. "You know, I like that you refer to me by my name, not just my title. I wish more people would do that."

"Names are the great equalisers," Mithras commented coolly, almost philosophically. "Though I am a knight and you a princess we are still the same, still human and still given names. Titles are but formalities as far as I am concerned."

I smiled again, shaking my head thoughtfully. "I think my mother may have something to say to that."

"Between you and me," he leaned in towards me, pretending to whisper, "I think your mother could do with a good fight against you. You could certainly teach her a thing or two. Eh?"

The two of us started to laugh at his joke. I shook my head at him as he straightened up and tilted his head back, letting out his laugher.

"Now then," he said, patting my shoulder, still smiling, "why don't you go rest after our session? I have no desire to take a lashing from your mother because you can't walk or lift your arms in the morning."

"I will," I nodded, slipping out of the light armour and handing it to him. "Thank you, Mithras."

"You're very welcome, Leander," he replied.

I left him to attend to his other duties, making my way up from the sublevels of the castle and back to my rooms. I had to pass through the Great Hall, narrowly avoiding my mother as she was entertaining guests, knowing that she would scold me for my "less than lady-like attire" as she called it.

I entered the stone walled, wooden panelled confines of my rooms, closing the door gratefully and sealing myself away from the castle's activities. I closed my eyes and took in a short, slow breath, relaxing my aching muscles.

Mithras' advice played over and over in my head, settling my disquieted heart enough that I could take my leave of my uneasy thoughts.

Slowly, I made my way through the room, my boots scraping on the stone floor, the only section carpeted at all being around and under the large double bed. I walked towards it, flicking my hair back across my shoulders and letting the dark auburn strands fall past my shoulder blades.

With a soft exhaling groan, I lay down on the soft, plump mattress, my hands above my head, my hair splaying out in a halo behind my shoulders on the covers. I gazed up at the blue velvet curtains that hung at each corner of the bed, tied back to let the light shining in from the balcony's double glass doors reach me. Through the top of the bed I could see the wood panels of the ceiling arching towards the bed's right; large crossbeams piercing through the stone sections of the walls highest up.

I closed my eyes and drew in another breath, letting myself release the tension in my limbs. Stretching my arms helped, the cool fabric of my close fitting grey shirt's sleeves spreading with them against my skin.

I wish I could see more of the world, I thought, studying the girl in my mind that I could only imagine to be the adventurer within me. *I wish I could have an adventure like in my books, not just sit in a castle my whole life.* A tiny smile crept over my soft face. *Maybe I will one day...*

There came a gentle knock at the door, bringing me back to reality from my silent musings.

I stood from the bed and crossed back to the door, opening it slowly. I nearly double stepped backwards and dropped a breath as I faced the person waiting outside.

Standing about six inches taller than me was the young Guardian man, his black hair hanging in a neatly unkempt manner, his green eyes focused on my face. There was a gleam in them that lasted only a moment as he first saw me, but quickly faded as his focus on duty returned.

"Princess," he bowed his head respectfully, "forgive my intrusion. I was instructed to find you."

I just stared for a moment, then responded: "Um... it's... it's Carden, isn't it?"

"Yes, your Highness," he nodded, "it is."

There were so many things I wanted to say, so many questions I could ask him. This was the first time in the two days since their arrival that I had gotten the chance to speak with one of the Guardians alone. And of course it had to be him. I fought the blushing heat that was rising in my cheeks, hoping he would just think it was from the exertion of my training exercises.

"May I ask why you were sent to find me?" I enquired gently, my eyes locked on his.

"Your father has requested your presence," he answered evenly. "I'm to take you to him."

"Um... I think I'm capable of finding my own way."

"I mean no disrespect, your Highness, but I was told to accompany you by the King."

Well, there's no arguing then. I nodded thoughtfully for a moment, resting both hands on the door.

"Alright," I agreed with a slight shrug. "Just let me clean myself up and we'll go."

"I will wait out here, your Highness," Carden said, turning back into the corridor, his cloak swaying at his ankles as he moved.

I closed the door, frowning at the thought of being summoned by my father and uncle.

Oh yeah. Mithras definitely knew more than he was telling me.

I shed my training clothes and threw them into the hamper, then drew myself a bath. I wasn't in for very long, cleaning myself as quickly as I could then drying my hair and skin with one of the fluffy white towels.

Returning to my bedroom from the en-suite, I crossed to the dresser and chose some small clothes, putting them on then selecting a new set of leggings. I took a blue velvet dress lined with teal silk from the wardrobe and slipped on the pale mauve dress under it. I fastened the front with the black cord weaved through the eyelets of the bodice and took a quick glance in the mirror to make sure I was presentable.

With my boots on underneath the dresses' folds, I opened the door and nodded to Carden, who hadn't left the corridor the whole time. I had to admit that his conviction was as impressive as his behaviour as a gentleman.

We walked the corridors together, Carden's eyes ahead of him, his face set with a mask of great focus. I silently wondered if it were at all possible to lift such a mask from a dedicated Guardian like him.

There were no words between us, my nerves stopping me from starting a conversation while he was just so silent anyway. It didn't matter though as it was only one flight of stairs up the keep from my family's quarters later and we were entering the corridor that led to my father's study.

Carden stopped at the door, his left hand on the pommel of his sword at his hip. He stared at the door then glanced back at me with a frown. I listened, voices arguing on the other side within the room.

"It seems that they are still arguing," he commented more to himself than to me.

"How long has this been going on?" I asked him.

"Some hours now," he answered, throwing me a soft half smile. "I don't envy you going in there, Princess."

"There's no way I'm going in there while they're arguing," I crossed my arms, my wide over sleeves swaying from my elbows and against my hips.

I listened more closely to the words being said, their volume lessened by the heavy wood of the door. The loudest was Fane, but I didn't find that to be a surprise at all. I recognised Uncle Aric's voice as well, the only other loudest one, my father's the quietest of the three.

"It's ridiculous, Aric!" Fane was raging relentlessly. "How can you seriously think that this is a good decision?!"

"Because it is a decision that cannot be made rashly, brother," Aric responded calmly, but loudly, matching his brother's volume without screaming.

"If you follow this choice of yours then it *is* rashly made!" Fane snapped. "She's too young and she's a girl!"

"Is your prejudice because of her age, because of her gender, or because she is *my* daughter?" came my father's quietly frustrated retort.

"If it is not me then why not my son?!" Fane barked. "Why place so much responsibility on the youngest Aldrich left to us, let alone a female?!"

"I would not entrust such an important inheritance to Farah," Aric explained coldly. "The boy has a good heart but it is his head that concerns me. He has a mind for conflict, much like you, Fane. Leander does not."

"Leander is only seventeen! She could never shoulder such responsibilities!"

"She is more capable than you think!" Aric retorted harshly, his frustration reaching breaking point.

"Tradition..." Fane started.

"Do not speak to me of tradition!" Aric cut him off. "Our ancestor did away with such narrow minded thinking as what you are insisting that we adhere to! I will *not* return to such bigoted ways as yours!"

"Would you argue with your King, Lord Fane?"Aldwyn's voice chimed in lowly and collectedly.

"Do not speak to me, Guardian!" Fane howled at him furiously. "You and your charges have come here to rob me of my birthright and hand it to some stupid little girl!"

"That's my daughter you're talking about, Fane!" Father roared.

I glanced at Carden, nervously knitting my fingers together in front of my stomach. He was shaking his head as he looked to me and reached for the door with one large hand.

"Enough of this," he muttered and opened it.

As soon as the door opened the arguing stopped and all eyes in the room were set on us. I twisted my hands together nervously, my unease only growing as I met their gazes.

Fane looked as if steam was about to shoot from his ears, his face red with pure rage, his hands balled up into fists. Father stood at the right side of the oaken desk, his back to the large arched window with Aric standing up from sitting at the desk by his side.

Aldwyn had his back to us, turning from the fight to acknowledge us with a vague nod, Tallinn on guard to my right as I stepped through the door.

To my far right of entering the room there stood a man with long white hair streaming down his shoulders, his hands clasped at the small of his back. He was dressed in green and brown robes that looked thick and well-travelled, a cloak, staff and wide brimmed hat set nearby in one of the chairs. He didn't turn to us, his focus on the crackling logs burning in the fireplace. But there was something about him that drew me in, that left me with a strange sense of familiarity.

"Forgive the interruption, my Lords," Carden spoke clearly, braver than me as we faced my quarrelling family, "but I have brought the Princess as requested."

"Thank you, young Guardian," Uncle Aric acknowledged him with a slight nod, then looked to Fane. "This conversation is over, Fane. Understood?"

"Then Patrice, Farah and I will be returning to Aldilith. *Tonight,*" Fane growled angrily.

"Do as you will, brother," Aric replied tiredly, sitting back down in the chair behind the desk.

Fane stormed towards the door, stopping beside me and staring me down. I met his gaze uncertainly, feeling very closed in by his intimidating proximity.

"Always the favourite, aren't you, Leander?" he snorted contemptuously at me, then stormed out of the room.

"What was that about?" I asked, looking to my father.

"Hurt egos and selfish ambitions. That's all, Leander," Father responded. "Come in."

I walked forward into the room, glancing over my shoulder at the strange man studying the fireplace. Deciding not to make any note of it until I needed to, I faced my uncle evenly.

"You wanted to see me, Uncle Aric?"

"Yes Leander. Have a seat," he gestured with one hand.

I sat down in one of the two cushiony armchairs set in front of the desk, folding my hands in my lap nervously and glancing across at my uncle.

"That will be all, young Guardians," Aric addressed Carden and Tallinn.

"As you wish, your Majesty," Tallinn said respectfully, and I heard her and Carden leave with the soft thud of boots and the swish of cloaks.

"I will take my leave also, King Aric," a wizened voice spoke up from behind me to my right.

I didn't turn towards the man behind me, something stopping me as if in warning or by magic, I couldn't decide which. I felt a warm, comforting gaze on my back, something inside me telling me that this mysterious stranger was nothing to fear.

"Are you certain?"Uncle Aric asked, looking past me towards him.

"I believe I have taken up enough of your valuable time, my Lord," came the man's response, his voice sounding old and experienced, holding so much power.

I heard the click of a staff hitting the floor and the rustling of a cloak being picked up. Out of the corner of my eye I caught a glimpse of him as he put on his hat, but all I really saw was shape and colour.

"As it is I have a long journey to embark on and an item to acquire as we have discussed," he went on. "I trust that my guidance has been of some help to you."

"It has, my friend," Uncle Aric responded, "as ever it has in the past. Safe journeys."

"Goodbye King Aric, Prince Ewan," the man farewelled, then added: "Princess Leander."

I turned around in my seat just as he faced away from me, his hat and hair concealing his face. I caught the glimpsed gleam of a golden pendant around his neck with an emerald at its centre as he turned, the man pulling his cloak on and hiding it from view.

He paused and tipped the brim of his hat down to Aldwyn, who nodded in respectful response, then the stranger left the room, sweeping the door shut behind him.

I turned to my uncle curiously: "Who was that?"

"A friend whose counsel I have long trusted," Aric responded, clasping his hands together and resting them on the table as he leaned forward. "Now, I'm certain that you are wondering what all of this is about, Leander."

I just nodded, not certain what to say.

"I assume that you heard much of that argument at the door. Did you not, Princess?"Aldwyn asked me.

I nodded to him. "Enough to know that it involves me and that Uncle Fane isn't happy about your decision. Whatever that may be."

Aric cleared his throat, thinking for a moment as I looked back to him uncertainly. He turned his blue eyes to me and studied me for a few seconds before finally speaking.

"There are... certain requirements that I have had to meet as king. Requirements that I have failed to accomplish."

"Don't say that. You're a great King, Uncle Aric," I assured him earnestly. "The people love you and you have been nothing but just and kind."

"It is kind of you to say, child," Aric nodded faintly, staring at his hands for a moment.

I watched him as he stood and walked over to the fireplace. I could see how he was beginning to age now, his walk filled with time's ravages. He was starting to fade and I knew it as he himself did. He was nearly seventy, after all.

"To see the turmoils of our past arising once more as my days grow dimmer is not something I hoped for in this life, or the next," he murmured, almost to himself as he stared into the fire again.

"Uncle Aric, what is this about?" I asked softly, watching him from my seat.

"You know the history of the feud between Ivansten and Aldegaad, do you not?" he spoke quietly, glancing over his shoulder at me.

I nodded, my confusion obvious. "Aldegaad and Ivansten warred for two hundred years across the Nartarn'lath Mountains. Tens of thousands gave their lives to defend the borders, on both sides."

"Do you know why that war started?"

"Ivanstenian Forces invaded the northern parts of Aldegaad to take territory from us," I answered, recalling my history lessons. "They took what is now the Aldegaadian side of the mountains and spread all the way to the Knolling Plains. They captured Arvon in that attack and this castle was taken as a position for their garrison. There was a battle here twenty years later that freed Arvon and pushed the invaders back over the mountains."

"You've learned your history well," he applauded softly, still facing the fire.

I frowned, looking at him uncertainly. "But we've been at peace with them for the last three hundred years."

"An uneasy peace," Father corrected, drawing my gaze for a moment.

Aric turned to me, trying to determine whether I was capable of comprehending what he had to tell me. I knew this, seeing it in his eyes and in the way he held himself. He was assessing me for something.

"As I told your father," he admitted, "there may be a new war between Ivansten and Aldegaad looming on the horizon."

I stared at him in disbelief. "How can that be?"

"There has been growing activity on Ivansten's borders over the past few weeks," Father explained calmly. "Their gate city of Ivanstead is seeing far more military presence than it has in previous years."

"I have bolstered our garrison at Aldgate in preparation for an assault from Ivanstead, however I am uncertain if we are facing another attack," Aric explained gravely.

I sat silently, digesting this carefully.

"Is there no way to find out why they are so active without resorting to violence?" I asked hopefully, turning my gaze back to my uncle.

"I have sent messengers to Ivansten's capital to ascertain the truth," he replied gravely. "They have not yet returned, but I am certain they will with some ridiculous excuse as to why the Ivanstenians are enacting such movements," he moved to me, crouching in front of me and placing his hands on mine, drawing my attention to his face. "It is why I am concerned for my failures as King."

"I don't understand," I stared at him. "What failures?"

"I have no heir, Leander," Aric told me gently. "You know this."

"Yes," I confirmed with an uncertain nod.

"As King, it was one of my responsibilities to produce an heir to the throne; someone to take on my duties when I reach the end of my days and to rule Aldegaad bravely and justly after my passing," he explained softly. "I have not been able to achieve this requirement and I am now too old to do so."

I frowned. "Are... are you asking me what I think you are?"

"I want *you* to be my heir," he proposed earnestly. "I want *you* to take my place and become Queen of Aldegaad."

"Queen?!" I froze, terrified of that notion. "You want me to be Queen of Aldegaad?!"

Aric nodded enthusiastically. "Yes. Upon my death I want you to take my place as sovereign ruler of Aldegaad."

"Why not my father?" I suggested, staggered by this offer.

"Your father's days are numbered only slightly greater than my own," he told me. "I need someone young to take the throne."

"Then, what about Farah?" I asked, almost frantic as I realised my heart was pounding in my chest faster than a horse's hooves at a gallop. "He's older than me and he's a male. Would a king not be better?"

Aric winced at that thought. "No. Farah may be a capable warrior, just as your Uncle Fane is, but he is just that: a warrior. He would take Aldegaad to war rather than keep peace."

"But... I-I mean..." I stuttered, not sure what to say or do. "This is all... s-so much."

"I would not offer it if I did not believe you could handle it, my girl," he assured me, squeezing my hands gently. "I know it is a frightening prospect, but you are worthy of such a birthright. This stands with your namesake, after all."

"My name..." I murmured, knowing what he meant, resent filling me instantly.

"You are Leander Idona Aldrich the Second," Father stated proudly as he moved closer, "named for the first Leander Idona Aldrich, the Great Heroine of High-Realm who slew the Darkest Shadow and defeated the Dominion. She was the first Queen of Aldegaad, the architect of the land we call home. She lived here in Arvon, this castle built by her eleven hundred and fifty years ago to be the new home of our family line. Our line is the blood of a new kingdom born from the ashes of an old one."

Aric placed his hands on my shoulders, smiling warmly. "You, Leander, are her descendant, holding that same fire and passion that she was known to possess. Your future holds so many bright opportunities. You have the strength in you that she too once had. That is why I have chosen you as heir to the throne."

"Do not take this the wrong way, Uncle Aric," I said respectfully, standing from my seat. "But I will be eighteen in another day, and even though I share the same day of birth and name as our ancestor, I am my own person. I want to live my own life before I am a ruler or anything of that nature."

Seeing the near look of despair on his face, I put my hand on his shoulder, looking into his eyes.

"I am not refusing you, Uncle Aric," I began to hate myself for the words that now fell from my mouth with such strange grace. "I'm just asking that I be allowed to have some sort of a life first."

"It is not something that will occur yet, my daughter," Father said, stepping closer to us, now at my side. "You cannot take the throne until your twenty-first year as per the laws of our country. Should the unthinkable occur and your uncle pass before then, I will stand as Regent of Aldegaad until you come of age. You still have time to enjoy a life before you take on your new duties."

I sighed and shrugged reluctantly but knowing this was right. "Well... then, I will be your heir, Uncle Aric. I will become Aldegaad's next Queen."

"Thank you, my girl," Aric said, standing and moving to the fireplace again. "I will be publically naming you as my heir next week in Aneuran. Sadly, I have my concerns that there are those amongst our people who would like nothing more than to usurp the throne from our family, and that could place you in danger."

I frowned. "Is that why the Guardians are here?"

"It is, your Highness," Aldwyn spoke calmly, his hands clasped in front of his belt. "Because of this and the turmoils building between Aldegaad and Ivansten, your uncle saw fit to bring us here to ensure Castle Arvon's security and your personal safety."

"So, I have three Guardians to protect me from a threat that probably isn't even real?" I observed with a curiously raised eyebrow. "Really?"

"It is a precaution, Leander," Aric said, turning from the mantelpiece with a small mahogany box in his hands.

I just nodded, absorbing all of this.

"Now," he said as he turned to me again, "as Evangeline and I are departing for Aneuran tomorrow morning I will not have the chance to see you for your name day. So, I thought I'd give you your gift now."

He offered me the box with a small, knowing smile. I frowned at him and took it, unlatching and opening it, gasping at what lay inside.

Nestled amongst the purple folds there lay a necklace. It was a small silver pendant, oval shaped with a slender, delicate silver chain. Inlaid into its centre was a beautiful purple stone that resembled an amethyst, the gem seeming to dance with its own internal glow. Around the stone the pendant branched out into coils like the vines of plants, flowery leaves reaching from the longest sides in silver bloom.

"Oh my gods," I breathed slowly through a gasp, running my right hand's fingers over the smooth pendant. "I've never seen anything like this."

"It's a family heirloom," Father explained with a smile. "Your uncle and I have discussed giving it to you in depth since you were five winters old."

"We agreed that you should receive it for your eighteenth name day," Aric added, smiling. "Do you like it?"

"Oh, Uncle Aric, I love it!" I exclaimed, taking it in my fingers and lifting it from the box.

The pendant was small enough to hold in my palm, not much bigger than a simple broach, its shape cool to the touch, yet its stone was strangely warm.

"This was the pendant worn by your ancestor," Aric explained. "She wore it throughout her life from the age of thirteen, a gift from her mother. It has been passed down and kept by our line for generations, but never once given to another Aldrich since her."

He took the pendant from my hand, allowing me to set the box down and pull my hair up in my hands as he stepped behind me. He unclasped the chain, placing it around my neck and fastening it again. It fell softly to my skin, the pendant itself hanging just below my collar bones.

Letting my hair down, I held the pendant in my hands, looking down at the amazing purple stone as a strange shimmer flickered through it again.

"It is said that while she wore this pendant she was protected by the power of the dragons," he told me, watching me over my shoulder with a proud smile. "It seems fitting to me that this pendant should pass to you."

"It's so beautiful," I turned to him, smiling brightly. "Thank you, Uncle Aric. I love it."

I hugged him, Aric laughing brightly and looking down at me as we separated just enough, his hands on my shoulders.

"I am glad," he said. "I thought that only you should carry this pendant. It has never felt like it could belong to anyone else, and your father agrees."

"Thank you so much, Uncle Aric. I promise I will always take care of it," I smiled brightly.

"I know you will, my dear niece," he said with certainty.

"Sweetheart," Father drew my gaze, "would you mind now if your uncle and I discuss some things with Aldwyn in private?"

"Of course, Father," I nodded, letting the pendant fall to my chest. "I'll take my leave."

"Thank you, Leander," Father smiled, giving me a hug. "Now, run along and I'll see you tonight at dinner."

I nodded, smiling at them both then leaving the room. I stepped out into the corridor feeling relieved now that I knew what was happening. And while the concept of one day being Queen and the one to carry the Aldrich Family legacy was so daunting to think about, I felt that I was alright with everything that we had discussed.

It won't be so bad, I figured as I made my way towards the stairs. *Maybe I could handle being Queen one day... Who knows, maybe I will be a good queen...*

Chapter Three
Dark Intentions

The sudden ice cold and the crack of thunder startled me, bringing me out of the sleep that I had fallen into. I felt the harsh slap of a strange frigid air hitting me in the face and of hard gravelly ground beneath me. I opened my eyes, shocked to find myself lying on the firm ground of a desolate vale, a storm raging in the sky above me. I was cold, my long dark hair falling around my shoulders and neck to provide the only warmth my body had. I wore only my mauve nightgown, not even having a robe to shield my skin from the icy air.

Slowly, I got to my feet, the hard ground and the cold air chilling my skin. I looked around, shivering as I clutched my arms around me, trying to regain some warmth and a hint of how I had gotten there.

What's going on? Where am I? Is... Is this a dream? But it feels so real.

I thought back to all that had taken place before I had gotten there, recalling having dinner with my parents before retiring to my room for the evening. Nothing unusual had happened and I felt that the night had been normal, yet my surroundings said otherwise. My mind led me to the only logical conclusion that was left: this was a nightmare.

The howling winds were so loud that I could barely hear myself think, my hair and clothes thrashing around me violently. I had never experienced a nightmare like this, but somehow I knew it too well, as if I'd had a dream like it before.

"Where am I?" I asked myself.

My words seemed to echo around me as though I were standing in a deep, underground cavern, but there were no walls, no mountains, nothing for the echo to have come from.

I wandered for what felt like hours until I came upon a strange light in the distance. It was an eerie turquoise colour, something that reminded me of ghosts and evil. Then, I felt as though I was suddenly thrown forward and I saw where I was.

Terrified, I stood in a dead vale full of black rocks, grey stone and twisting black peaks surrounding it. The sky above me was dark with a dry storm that held no rain, just flashing green lightning. I stared up at the gigantic black stone and iron fortress that took the central point in the haunted vale with a deep dread in my stomach.

It was a twisted, frightening structure towering high into the sky, accessible only via a long black stone bridge across a deep chasm that surrounded it, that same eerie supernatural light glowing up from beneath in the darkness that lurked below. From the base of the structure rose two towers, one taller than the other, their malicious looking spined shapes tipped by a flat roof with five gigantic towering spikes. The tallest tower was the main fortress keep itself, the other tower and rock imbedded structures connected to it via various stone, steel and iron bridge walkways.

I stared up at this malicious structure, absolutely petrified by its sheer mass and dominating presence. I had never seen anything so terrifying in all my life and hoped now that this truly was just some awful nightmare.

At that moment I heard a horrible, piercing roar and dropped to my knees, cowering in the dirt. I looked up as a gigantic black and crimson dragon flew up out of the crevice, its eyes seeming to be a burning molten orange, its scales tinted with blue and violet. Its long jaws opened as it flew higher into the sky, letting out a rock shattering roar.

It flew to the very top of the fortress, clinging with its large clawed hands and feet to the side of the tower, its wings spreading out to show their purple and red colouring on their underside. Then it roared again, turning its mouth up and sending a blast of purplish-blue flame into the darkened sky.

I staggered backwards from the fortress and the monster atop its spire crowned peak, just wanting to run as fast as I could from this nightmare. As I moved away, my eyes fell to the spiked battlements of the fortress. I could see the dead patrolling there, each figure a horrible corpse-like guard lumbering around with bony arms and skeletal visages.

The monster's roars drew my gaze back up and I realised that the beast could see me. That was when I heard it, my head beginning to ache. It wasn't even like it was speaking in any language that I knew, but I could feel its dark intentions. This wasn't a peaceful dragon like I had read about in stories or in the histories of High-Realm. This was perhaps not even a true dragon, but a daemon masquerading as one to frighten me.

I could sense its mind and hear its thoughts, and they frightened me. This thing wanted so much more than just to scare me. It was telling me how badly it wanted to hurt me and everything else in the world.

Suddenly, I felt the pain subsiding, a strange purple glow drawing my gaze down to my pendant. It was shimmering brightly, the stone shining with a protective purple light that the monster seemed to despise.

"Princess..." a cold, calculating voice mewed.

Slowly, I looked up from the pendant, freezing then as I saw *him*; a towering black shape that seemed to appear through the mists like a shadow. I couldn't see his face, but I knew that he was a monster of purest evil cloaked in deepest, darkest shadow.

"Who... Who are you?" I managed to stammer, stumbling back from him. "What do you want from me?"

I could have sworn that I saw the curling of pale, thin lips behind the shadows of his cowl as well as the gleam of two demonic green eyes.

"Who are you?!" I demanded again, terrified as the cowled figure moved towards me without answering my question. "Please! Leave me alone!"

The figure laughed coldly, stalking me slowly, forcing me back towards the fortress and the dragon watching from its pinnacle. I could barely keep myself from screaming as the dead began rising around me like wraiths from the earth, surrounding me. The dragon's roars drew my gaze again and I stared into the face of the truly evil beast helplessly.

Just as I was certain that I would be stuck in that nightmare forever, my pendant glowed even brighter, enveloping me in a protective purple shield of light. The dead shrunk away from it as the hooded figure continued towards me which left me sure that the light would not deflect him.

There came another roar and I turned over my shoulder to look at the dragon. Suddenly, a sweeping shape appeared; a second, smaller dragon flying towards me, this one mostly purple, silver and blue. It swept down, orange eyes locking on the hooded figure as it landed in front of me, shielding me from him.

The dragon had two prominent horns on its head, a sort of wing-like crest reaching from its skull beneath each of them, and three smaller horns set between the larger ones and the crests. Its tail was tipped with a scaly arrowhead that it whipped in preparation to fight.

The dragon seemed to be glowing, wreathed in the same purple light that my pendant was shining with and surrounding me in. Its presence was a welcoming and protecting thing in that dark place.

The sinister figure stepped back as the dragon roared at him, his hand up in front of his cowled face. He staggered, pulling away as the dragon snapped at him furiously, turning his hidden gaze frantically between me and it.

He turned towards me again, his rage and desperation clear. I saw his hands glow with an eerie green flame, but before he could strike, the dragon let loose a powerful breath. Purplish blue flame engulfed the demonic figure, causing him to scream horribly as he thrashed around, finally evaporating as if he had never existed.

The dragon looked to me then, and I could feel that it was telling me that I would be alright the way a dear friend would...

I woke with a start, sitting up in bed, breathing heavily. My heart was racing and I felt so scared that I was even beginning to worry that the shadows around me were monsters from my nightmare. It took me a few minutes to realise that I was alright, safe inside my bedroom in Castle Arvon; the familiar wood panelled stone walls and ceiling comforting me. I sighed, looking around my room, relieved that I was home, not in that sinister vale.

Curiously, I put my hand to the pendant around my neck, grasping at it and gazing down at its purple stone with a deep frown.

Are these nightmares simply just that, nightmares? Or do they hold some greater meaning I don't yet see? Or are they my mind conjuring some great imagining of what this pendant can do based on its legends? I don't know...

In any case, I hoped that it was a dream and nothing more, though I was definitely disturbed.

Lying back again I watched the greyish daylight fade in and out as the clouds gave way to the sun for sporadic periods, the brighter illumination giving the world a warmer feel after my nightmares. My body ached a little from the night spent thrashing around, my eyes still full of sleep as I lay amongst the pillows, savouring the feeling of the cool sheets on my skin.

That comfort and peacefulness was disturbed though when there was the click of the door opening, causing me to turn and see Mother enter. She immediately frowned at me.

"Still in bed?" she scolded, shaking her head with her arms crossed.

Oh... just perfect! I turned onto my side, burying my face into my elbow, my hands under the pillows as I let out an agitated moan.

"Being eighteen years old does not give you the right to simply lie about, Leander," Mother lectured me as she stood over the bed.

"But it gives me the right to my own privacy and having people knock on my door before they invade it," I retorted through my arm, not looking up.

Mother sounded unimpressed. "A smart mouthed attitude will not take you very far as Queen, my dear daughter."

I pretended that I didn't hear that, remaining where I was.

"Now, get up and get dressed," she ordered, pulling the covers off me and causing me to make a whining sound in frustration. "Lord and Lady Seward are arriving soon and you must put in an appearance. Their son, Tibain, has been asking about you again."

"Oh, Mother, not Tibain," I groaned. "He is insufferable..."

"He is interested in your hand in marriage," she replied.

I scowled. "Precisely what I mean."

"Leander, it simply will not do for you to keep refusing so many suitors, and Tibain has been the most resolute to show an interest," she smiled thoughtfully. "It is endearing."

"It is infuriating," I responded through my messy dark hair.

"Now, that is not true," she replied with her arms crossed, the common sign that she was becoming annoyed. "He is very persistent and quite charming..."

"He is rude, arrogant, selfish and apparently unaccustomed to being told no," I retorted coldly. "He has no respect..."

"Well, respect is exactly what you will show to him and to his parents. Renton and Angora are dear friends and you will not offend them by refusing to speak with their son," she scolded me sternly.

"But Mother..." I tried only to be cut off.

"Get up, get dressed, come downstairs," she stated finitely. "There will be no more arguments about this, young lady. You are a princess, now act like it."

With that, Mother left, closing the door as I sat up on my side, glaring after her. I groaned and slumped onto my back, pressing my hands to my face and shaking my head.

Why do I have to do more of these meet and greets? Can't I just be abducted by mercenaries and sold as a slave girl in the Blackfelds? That would actually be a pleasant change...

Despite this, I dragged myself out of bed and went to the wardrobe, taking out the clothes I had chosen for the day.

I slid out of my nightgown, dressing in a slip and a lilac long sleeved gown before my velvet over dress. This gown was a gentle cobalt blue with golden detailing, just like most of my other gowns. With my boots on over dark leggings to shield against the cold and hidden under my skirts' long hems, I straightened myself up, then made my way out and down the corridors to the main hall.

When I arrived, I could already hear both of my parents talking with someone. Taking a deep, slow breath, I made my way down the stairs, my dresses' long hems trailing behind me. I could see my parents speaking with a slightly older couple; he with short grey hair combed back from an aging face, she with icy white hair and adorned with many jewels to empathise her station. Behind them stood a tall, handsome, dark haired young man at least seven years my senior. His eyes immediately locked onto me the moment I entered the room and I had to struggle to contain my disgust.

Tibain... Wonderful. I managed not to glower.

"Ah, there you are sweetheart," Father held up his arm, inviting me to his side.

I took his cue and let him put his arm around me in a hug.

Turning to his guests, Father spoke warmly and proudly: "Renton, Angora, you remember my youngest daughter."

Lord Renton Seward nodded and smiled; his hands clasped behind him. "Yes, indeed I do," he turned his attention to me. "So wonderful to see you again, Princess."

"Thank you, Lord Seward," I returned his greeting with a courteous smile. "You're both looking well."

"And you," Lord Seward commented, "Eighteen now, is it? My, how you have grown."

"Into a very beautiful woman," Lady Seward added, turning to hold out a hand to her son. "Your Highness, you remember our son, Tibain. Yes?"

"I do," I confirmed, suppressing my contempt for this vile man. "It is nice to see you again, Tibain."

"And you, Princess Leander," Tibain greeted me, smiling with a clear intention of what he wanted. "You surely are more and more beautiful every time I see you."

"Oh, he is such a *nice* young man," Mother looked to me with an almost boasting attitude, then turned her eyes to Tibain. "You've become quite the hunter, is that not so, Tibain?"

"Indeed it is, Duchess Caralyn," he confirmed, mirroring his father's body language as he clasped his hands behind him. "Why, just last week I slew a mountain lion with a single arrow."

"Really? How very impressive," Mother eyed me suggestively again.

I knew what Mother was getting at. She wanted me to be impressed, to fall all over this poor excuse for a suitor and swoon. She wanted both daughters married and under the care of an able bodied man who would not allow us to be independent or travel, just sit in the courts of the kingdom and act all fey and doughy. It was something I couldn't stand. Still, I had to forbear and smile at my mother's attempts to marry me off to the first pompous dimwit that came along, though I refused to swoon.

"I'm sure it was no challenge for you, my Lord," I responded, pretending to be interested.

"Oh, I can assure you, Princess, that it was *some* challenge," Tibain bragged, a failed attempt to appear modest. "Of course, I overcame it."

And there's that hubris I've seen so many times, I thought sourly, but kept forcing myself to smile.

"Perhaps you can take Tibain for a walk around the grounds and he can tell you the story, dear," Mother suggested, her motives obvious to me.

I glanced at my father, seeing the knowing smile on his face, then turned back to my mother.

"Of course, Mother. I would be happy to," I said with false enthusiasm, then gestured for Tibain to follow and led him towards the west side of the castle.

I looked happy, but I was secretly fuming at the prospect of being stuck with this lout for the afternoon and the days his family would stay at the castle. I threw a look at my father, seeing him crack a smile and quickly hide it behind his hand as he turned to the Lord and Lady, Mother already playing the grand hostess, as she was so practiced at.

"Perhaps there may be another marriage soon, Angora," Mother was saying.

"Oh, that would be wonderful, Caralyn," Lady Seward prided.

I cringed.

* * * * *

We walked the outer walkways of Castle Arvon for a couple of hours as Tibain related the story of his *"heroic"* defeat of the mountain lion in detail. I played the simpering girl and catered to his ego, knowing that to not do so would draw the wrath of both his parents and my mother.

We were passing through the training courtyard as he was bringing his story to the end. Seeing the weapons on racks made me think that if I'd had a sword at that moment that I would have clubbed him in the head with the pommel.

A girl can only dream.

The squires and guard recruits were hard at work training, practicing with swords, pikes and bows. Mithras was pacing through the ranks as he usually did along with Ser Garvin, barking orders at the young men and women. He gave me an amused smirk as he saw me passing by with my *"guest"*.

I looked behind Tibain at him, mouthing the words "help me".

Mithras laughed, shaking his head and continuing with his students' lessons. He knew my distaste for the young lord better than anyone.

I led Tibain up onto the wall, the view of the Great River Arvon spectacular from here, the sea visible as it met the river and the mountains in the West.

"... and so I took my sword and cut the beast's head from its shoulders, thus earning my greatest trophy," Tibain was ending his story as we moved to stand at the edge of the battlements.

He leaned one elbow on the wall as I rested both arms against the stone near the battlement, my eyes on the distant sea, the wind blowing through my hair. Both of us were wearing our cloaks to guard against the mountain chill, but I was used to it.

"It sits now on our trophy wall in Castle Alstan," he bragged, his expression that of a blatantly arrogant man. "A true monument to my skills as both a warrior and a man."

I nodded, my eyes still on the sea ahead of me, my hands clasped together. I was calm on the outside but cringing on the inside.

"That was a very... *interesting* story," I lied as convincingly as I could manage.

I knew he was too infatuated with me to notice. I could already feel his gaze running the length of my body, his eyes taking in my shape and his mind undressing me even as we stood there.

How I despise you, Tibain, you disgusting letch.

"You know, you truly are the most beautiful woman I have ever known, Princess," he told me, moving to mirror my pose, his eyes never leaving my body.

I didn't answer, but kept my eyes forward, glad of the presence of several wall guards, which meant that there was someone there to assist me if I needed them to. Then again, I knew I could probably cripple him with one sharp jab of my knee to his loins. The thought almost stole a smile onto my face, but I managed to hide it.

"How is it that you have not yet married as your sister has?"Tibain asked, staring at me with an unsettling longing.

I shrugged. "My sister is twenty-six; I am only eighteen as of yesterday. I feel that I am far too young for marriage," I looked at him. "Besides, I don't yet know love."

"Your parents have guarded your virtue well, Princess," Tibain looked aroused at the thought of me still being a virgin. "Perhaps there will be a time when a man worthy of such an honour shall..."

"Don't," I placed my fingers on his lips as he tried to lean closer to kiss me. "It isn't something that I'm ready for and I won't give it so easily to just *any* man."

"Perhaps one who can kill a lion with his bare hands?"Tibain tried to impress me, putting his hands on my hips.

I pulled away, staring at him. "I thought you killed it with a single arrow," I said a little cockily.

He suddenly looked uneasy and I had to try not to smile again. "Uh... yes... I did. That was *another* lion."

"Kill a sea serpent, a mountain troll and bring me a unicorn, then we will talk," I rolled my eyes facetiously, trying to be a smart mouth.

"You jest, Princess," he chuckled, leaning over me again, drawing my most intense gaze. "So much for your touch? It seems like an impossible task."

"You misunderstand. That was only the price to speak about it. You'll have to do even better for the rest," I laughed to myself and turned to the north wall, walking away from him and shaking my head.

Dunce!

I glanced back, amused by the confused look on his face. I really did think he was the lowest of the low despite his social stature.

As I walked, I heard the call of a falcon from above. I looked up to see the bird circling the castle, which was not an uncommon occurrence. I preferred this beautiful bird's gaze to my current attempted suitor's.

"Princess," Tibain called to me, rushing up after me and slowing at my side. "I believe that you are a woman of great humour. I enjoy your mirth."

"Great. I'm glad you do," I replied, secretly wanting to throw him from the battlements.

As we continued along the walkway, I turned my gaze up towards the bird in curiosity again. The falcon seemed to be circling over us in a very odd way that I felt was less like a normal bird's behaviours. I frowned as I followed it with my eyes, seeing it swoop towards the mountains that were now on my left.

Pulling my cloak further around me against the wind, I frowned again, stopping in my steps to gaze across the distance between the castle and the mountains. I could have sworn that I had seen a figure standing there amongst the rocks. A second glance confirmed my suspicions and my heart began to race.

I saw the flickering of a cloak and the waving of fur as I caught the flow of dark hair on the figure. I felt cold eyes locked on me and I found myself staring back across the river at the figure as a deep sense of unease hit me.

"Princess?" Tibain's voice was a welcome distraction for once, drawing me back to reality. "Are you alright?"

"Huh?" I looked up at him, feeling as though I had just blinked myself out of a deep trance.

Tibain raised an eyebrow at me, standing still at my side. "I asked if you were alright, your Highness. Does something vex you?"

I turned and looked to the mountains again. "I saw someone on the cliffs overlooking the castle."

"Where?" Tibain asked.

I grasped his shoulder and angled him to look where I pointed with one finger. I felt his gaze lazily drift from me to the cliffs as I looked again myself.

The space where the figure had been was empty, leaving the cliffs uninhabited. I frowned, searching the skies for any sign of the falcon I had seen, but there was nothing. The bird was nowhere to be seen, the dark clouds crushing overhead with a severe rumbling that spoke of a storm yet to come.

"I see nothing, Princess," Tibain turned his gaze back to me. "Are you certain you saw someone out there?"

You smarmy bastard!

"I'm certain," I said sternly, more to myself than to him.

"It is nothing to be concerned about, my beautiful Princess," he moved to touch my face, but I ducked away and started striding quickly along the battlements.

I didn't care anymore if he was insulted by my behaviour, my concerns now overwhelming all my other impulses as my dreams began to push back on me.

"Guard!" I called, sighting one of the blue surcoat clad soldiers passing through an archway. "Guard!"

"Yes, Your Highness?" the guard bowed his head to me respectfully, standing quite a bit taller than me.

"I think I saw something out in the mountains," I explained, ignoring Tibain as he rushed up to me. "It looked like a man standing on the cliffs watching the castle."

"A man, Princess?" the guard questioned me severely, his duty to protect me taking over with his now stern tone. "Are you certain?"

"Your Highness, is everything alright?" Tallinn asked as she approached, her black and silver cloak swirling around her in the breeze, her blonde hair tied back neatly.

"The Princess says she saw a man watching her from the cliffs, Lady Guardian," the guard explained.

"I only saw him for a moment," I clarified, twisting my hands together in unease.

Footsteps drew my attention and I looked over my shoulder to see Mithras and several guards approaching us. Relief flooded my senses at seeing him.

"Princess Leander," Mithras spoke respectfully, stopping right beside me and throwing Tibain a warning glance. "Is there a problem?"

"The Princess says she has seen someone in the mountains," Tallinn responded to the Knight-Commander's query, blinking her blonde locks from her eyes.

Mithras nodded and turned back to me. "What did you see exactly, Your Highness?"

I shrugged and shook my head. "I'm not sure, just a man in the cliffs across the river, his eyes set on the castle. Seeing him gave me a very bad feeling, Mithras."

Tibain snorted. "It is probably just a villager from Arvon walking out in the woods. It isn't anything sinister, I am sure..."

I glared at him as he said that, wanting to tell him what I really thought. I chose instead to focus on the situation.

"The man was standing there," I pointed out the place to the Knight, Guardian and guardsmen, looking to Mithras uneasily.

The guard I had first approached frowned. "People generally do not walk along those cliffs. They are too treacherous to find safe footing. Anyone from Arvon would know that."

Mithras nodded, not hesitating as he turned to the soldiers with him. "Alright, you lot go out there and take a good look around. Report back to me."

"Yes, Knight-Commander," the lead soldier nodded and led the other five soldiers back along the battlements.

"I will find Aldwyn and Carden at once," Tallinn rushed off, taking this all very seriously.

Mithras turned back to me and nodded. "Do not fret, Princess. I'm certain it is nothing to be concerned about, but I will not take the risk."

I just nodded, relieved that he always took me so seriously.

He threw a sideways glance at Tibain, then raised an eyebrow at me, trying not to smile.

"Is there... anything *else* I can assist you with?" he enquired.

I glanced at Tibain – who was completely oblivious to our conversation – then back to Mithras. I sighed and shook my head, but his smile told me that he knew my desperation to escape.

"No... that is all, Mithras."

"Alright," Mithras struggled to contain his mirth, "I will let you know what the soldiers find. Just do not leave the castle grounds."

"I won't," I assured him, and he nodded his goodbye to me.

I felt a hand touch my shoulder and once again suppressed the urge to dry reach. Tibain turned me to face him, smiling and gesturing to continue our walk.

"Shall we, my beautiful princess?" he asked, his false charm repellent.

"Yes," I sighed and nodded. "Of course."

"I have a great many more stories of my bravery and skills as a warrior that I am certain you will enjoy hearing," he said arrogantly.

I swallowed back my disgust and followed on, hating him with every fibre of my being, desperate for this day to end and hopeful that what I had seen truly was nothing as Mithras had said.

Chapter Four
The Mercenaries' Prisoner

As evening approached, I found myself wishing more and more intently that Tibain would leave soon, though the Sewards wouldn't be travelling back to Alstan for two days. I couldn't stand his irritating presence much longer and had begun to fear that I would inevitably take a sword to him. Still, I remained calm and allowed him his narcissistic ramblings.

We ate with our parents, which left me suffering the whole time as I was purposely sat with Tibain. That was my mother's doing and I was beginning to resent her for this. I even wondered if saddling me with this moron was some form of amusement to my parents.

At last, dinner came to its end and my parents invited our guests to join them in the parlour for tea. Tibain insisted that he wanted to go into the town for a while with his entourage who had accompanied him, Angora willingly permitting him to go. I took the opportunity to excuse myself and go to my rooms, stating that I was tired.

Glad that my father permitted me to leave, I turned and started along the halls to the north staircase, silently cursing my mother for this *distraction*. I soon entered the corridor leading to my family's quarters, surprised to see Mithras there. The Knight walked towards me, a large grin on his face as he saw me.

"Your dinner with the Sewards has ended, I see," he said, a knowing tone in his voice laced with amusement.

"Amused, Mithras?" I crossed my arms, eyeing him as I stopped short of his position.

He chuckled and shook his head. "I have to admit that your demeanour in the training yard was reminiscent of one of adamant repulsion to Lord Tibain."

"I think the title *'lord'* is a little too generous," I rolled my eyes, annoyed at the thought of Tibain. "Just knowing that he will be staying here for the next two days makes my skin crawl."

"Is this annoyance I detect in your voice, Leander?" Mithras raised an eyebrow, his smile broadening.

"Ugh!" I threw my gaze to the wood beamed ceiling, shaking my head in frustration. "He is the most... the most... self-absorbed... irritating... *man* I have ever known," I looked back to him; my frustration clear. "He kept changing his story about the lion he killed. First it was with one arrow, then his bare hands, and then it just keeled over when it saw him," I rolled my eyes, exasperated by all of this. "Honestly, it was all just to get me to lie with him, I'm sure of it."

"Then your virtue remains intact, safe from a lying lord," Mithras smirked. "Let us hope that the next suitor your mother sends your way is of better character."

"That's the other problem," I complained. "It's all my mother's doing. She just wants me to marry a rich lord and settle into a life in court," I shook my head, my voice quieter as I spoke. "Ever since Uncle Aric named me as his successor Mother has been far too insistent on me doing things her way. She seems to care more for social status than for me."

Mithras looked to me sympathetically, touching two fingers to my chin and turning my eyes to his.

"Your mother does not value society and status above you, Leander," he told me. "She hopes for a better life for you than you already have."

"If I were starving in a gutter, I might understand that, but I'm not. I'm a princess living in a castle," I shrugged helplessly. "I doubt my needs could be catered to any more than they already are."

"And yet, you despise such things," he chuckled again. "I have never known anyone of a noble line to be so resistant to having others serve them."

I met his gaze with certainty. "I know who I am. And being served isn't me."

"You'd rather serve than be served," Mithras nodded, understanding me. "How strong willed you are. You know, Leander, you could have been a Guardian. Perhaps you could still be."

"Not anymore," I shrugged. "I have to be a queen in the future. That is my fate," then, a thought occurred to me. "Speaking of which, have the Guardians returned yet?"

He shook his head. "Not yet. I do not think that we will see them again until the morning."

"Alright. Goodnight, Mithras," I turned and started away from him, heading towards my room.

"Goodnight, Princess," he called after me before turning towards the stairs.

I reached my bedroom, entering the doorway and closing the arched wooden door, feeling more secure in my privacy as I had now separated myself from the rest of the castle. I took a moment, savouring the quiet of that room before moving to the balcony doors to look out at the night. As I stepped onto the balcony, tossing my purple cloak onto the chair in the corner, I heard a sound in the night air.

My steel blue eyes sought it out, finding the source. A falcon was perched on the barrier of the balcony, its sharp golden eyes staring directly at me. It squawked at me again, letting out a shrilled sound as its taloned feet held it in place.

"Go on," I urged it gently, feeling uneasy by the way it was staring at me. "Go. Go home."

The bird flapped its wings and screeched at me again. This time I simply closed the doors over and locked them, keeping the bird outside. I could still see it through the glass, its gaze unshifting, almost as if...as if it was stalking me.

"Strange," I murmured to myself, walking away from the doors.

I crossed to the vanity, looking into the mirror at my reflection. The pendant drew my gaze again and I found myself wondering about my ancestor, the woman I was named after.

I wonder if she had to put up with any of these trivial pursuits. Like meeting suitors...

Feeling tense from the day's visit with the Sewards, I unfastened the pendant from my neck, setting it back in its case, then went to the bathroom, turning to the basin.

This is something they didn't have in my ancestor's day, I thought to myself, highly aware that plumbing was a new addition to the world along with clockwork.

I washed my face, drying my skin before moving back into my room. I became aware that the falcon was still watching me as a new storm began to blow up with a harsh, dry wind. I chose to ignore the eerie bird and walked over to the vanity table where I began brushing my hair, untying the knots the winds had put in the mahogany strands.

A squawking drew my attention back to the balcony doors. I narrowed my eyes as I peered through the glass, my sights locking on the falcon again, the bird still sitting there. Unnerved by it, I drew the drapes then returned to brushing my hair.

When I was finished with the mirror, I crossed from my vanity table to the bookshelf, selecting a book and turning it over in my hands to look at the cover: **The Wandering Prince**. As I opened the book, turning to the bed and reading from the last place I had left off, I heard the door open.

Ugh. What now?

"Mother, please, just give me some time to my..." I turned, expecting to see Mother and freezing as I lost my words.

The masked man stared at me, his sword ready as another man moved in behind him, blonde hair hanging out of his hood. I backed away, staring at them as they entered my room, their gazes locked on me. Fear crushed me and I started to shake, but I knew I had to find my strength. Still, I couldn't help my body's most basic responses.

"Who... Who are you?" I managed to ask with a weak, little voice. "How did you get in here?"

"Princess Leander," the leader spoke through his mask, a smile appearing, hidden from me save for the movements of the cloth. "You *will* be coming with us tonight."

A chill of fear spiked down my spine as he said this.

"W-Why?" I asked, frightened, my hands touching the bedside table, the book still in my right.

"We're being paid a rather ridiculous sum for your capture," he replied honestly, the other man moving in behind him. "So, be a good girl and you needn't be harmed."

I couldn't take my eyes off the sword in his hand, my breath catching in my throat, my heart pounding like a drum beneath my breast. There was only one thing I could think to do.

I threw the book as hard as I could, hitting the lead man in the face and knocking him backwards into his cohort. While they were distracted I ran to the closest, reaching for the sword I kept there. With a loud metallic grinding, I drew my sword and turned to face them, pointing my weapon at the leader and glaring him down.

He turned his gaze back to me, amusement in his pale eyes.

"I am *not* going anywhere with you," I growled, standing ready to fight, conscious of my footing and the squaring of my shoulders.

"Now this was unexpected," he chuckled, pointing his blade at me. "I did not know you could fight."

"Maybe you should learn more about your intended target before approaching them," I told him icily, courage growing within me.

"He didn't say anything about her being a fighter," the blonde man pointed out, looking over his mask at his leader.

"It's not an issue," the leader replied, his eyes locked on me. "I've got this. Keep watch."

As the blonde man left the room the leader and I circled each other, ready with our swords. As I expected, he made the first move, allowing me to parry him easily. Then the fight began.

I parried and brought my blade to meet his, swinging away and stepping backwards, conscious of my footwork, but also watching for any weakness he showed. My boots gave me a better grip than slippers would have, allowing me to move easily despite the length of my skirt hems.

Our swords rang clearly as we fought, all other things forgotten as I battled to save myself from this abductor. I dodged another strike, continuing my assault, trying to force him back. I needed to buy myself time and give the guards a chance to reach me.

We swung at the same time, grabbing at each other's sword arms with our free hands, a struggle ensuing. I felt my arms weakening already, much smaller than my attacker's, but still I kept fighting, determined to beat him back.

Finding an opening, I lashed out with one foot, kicking him in the stomach, then elbowing him in the chest, forcing him back. I quickly regained my defensive stance, ready with my sword as he turned to face me again.

"You're not just some spoiled child with a little fencing training, are you?" he looked to me, quietly amused. "You know how to fight. But it will not save you, girl."

I didn't answer, ready for the next strike. I blocked the following blows, determined to keep him away from me by whatever means necessary. I swung my blade twice, meeting his sword each time with a resounding clang, then lunged and cut his shoulder with the tearing of cloth and the squelch of bloodied skin.

That's right. I am not some simpering girl that you can just take, criminal.

He glanced at the wound then continued to fight me with more fury. He started pressing his attack and I was beginning to stagger a little. I now found myself desperately trying to fight him off, my years of training since I was eight perhaps not as much of a match for his skills as I had first thought.

I made a few more sweeps with my sword, but he kept coming, striking harder and harder, forcing me to back away. Still, I tried to hold my ground, before seeing an opening and taking it.

I lunged at him, but he side stepped me, grabbing my arm and knocking my sword away. He spun me around into his arms before I could recover, my back pressing to his chest as his sword rose to hang its sharp edge just before my throat. I froze instinctively, terror filling me as I realised my situation. The blade was cold on my skin and I whimpered without being able to stop myself, breathing hard now.

"Well done, girl. I have never had a child cut me like that," he said into my ear as I stared anxiously at the blade. "You've got some skills, but not enough to best me."

He lowered his face close to my right ear, his breath hot on my neck as I glanced worriedly up at him, my eyes hurting with the threat of tears.

"You should never go for such an obvious strike. It is often a trap," he whispered coldly, a smirk in his voice.

The blonde man entered again, his eyes lighting up as he saw me at his leader's mercy.

"You've got her!" he said breathlessly, but with delight. "Let's get out of here!"

"Grab that cloak off the chair," the leader instructed as I began struggling in his arms, whimpering as he jolted me back, bringing his sword even closer to my neck. "We can't have her freeze out there."

The blonde man grabbed the cloak, the leader dragging me to the door.

We stepped into the hallway as I tried to struggle free, but the man jerked me back against him, the sword pressing lightly into my neck. I froze again as if by some ice conjuring magic, only without the chill, his left arm pinning my arms to my body.

They led me through the corridors' stone and wood worked surrounds, both men searching diligently for any guards that might be approaching. When two guards were pacing a corridor ahead, my abductors forced me into a darkened room to hide from them.

I was hurled against one of the walls, turning around just as the leader lunged towards me. I tried to scream but his hand slammed down over my mouth, stifling my cries, his fingers crushing my cheekbone. His other hand brought the sword to my throat again as I struggled to hold back the tears that were burning hot in my eyes.

The blonde was hovering near the door, watching through it from the dark room into the torch lit corridor beyond.

The leader locked his eyes on me and came closer, my desperate struggles and helpless cries doing nothing against him.

"Now listen here, girl," he hissed lowly, his hot breath hitting my face through his mask, "you need to be quiet and stop struggling. I don't want to draw attention to us and your noise will do exactly that."

I tried to be defiant, to scream again and struggle to hit him with my fists or my knees, but that sword was a constant threatening reminder that I just couldn't escape.

"If the guards hear you," he warned me in a quietly vicious tone, "then they'll find us and we will have to kill them. You don't want people to die, do you?"

I tried to compose myself, to stop myself from crying, knowing that he was right.

"Do you?" he demanded coldly.

I shook my head, unable to control the heaving of my chest or the sniffing sobs that escaped my nose and mouth. He just nodded and looked over to his companion. The other man gave us the signal and we were out of the door moving along the corridors again.

I had to suck in deeper breaths just to hold my tears back, my desperation not to cry overwhelming me.

They took me down one flight of stairs in the back of the keep to avoid the grand staircase and the Great Hall, bringing me to the library doors. I couldn't help frowning as they forced me inside, the blonde slamming the doors shut.

I was tossed to the floor, hitting it hard and lying still for a moment. I kept my face down, trembling in terror as I waited for what would come next.

"What the Void happened here?" the leader demanded, concern deep in his voice.

I risked a glance up towards him, seeing the room around me. Bookcases surrounded us like giant wooden sentinels of ancient knowledge, a large table set in the middle of the room with several armchairs placed around the space. A chandelier hung above with its candles burning brightly, a few tall floor standing candelabras dotted strategically in place.

That was when I came face-to-face with the most terrifying creature I had ever seen at that moment. He looked like a man, yet he was anything but, towering above me at maybe over eight feet tall, his harsh violet eyes gleaming from beneath a mammoth hood made of hide. He had a prominent jaw that was set hard, each hand large enough to engulf my head entirely.

His skin was a strange purplish-blue colour, taking on a greying tint in the faded candlelight. Long black hair streamed down his shoulders, braided strands gliding down from behind his ears. His massively muscled arms were folded firmly across his chest, looking as strong as steel. And across his back he carried two large, curved blades unlike anything I had ever seen one of our smiths make.

The giant glowered down at me, the only one there to not wear a mask.

There were two others in the room, both dark haired, one with his mask and hood off, blood drenching his shirt and jacket, his skin a deep brown. He was Harredi, a man from the land of the same name in the south-east. The other was pacing wildly, as frantic as a frightened beast cornered by a predator.

On the ground there lay four guards dressed in the castle's colours, all dead with pools of blood surrounding them. I gagged at the smell, feeling as if I were about to be sick.

"Morgan's hit," the pacing man told the leader worriedly. "These soldiers tried to kill us, but we got them."

"You deserve it!" I spat without thinking, letting out a scream as the giant's right hand closed tightly around my entire neck and lifted me from the ground.

"Shut your mouth, girl," the leader hissed at me before turning to the dark-haired man. "Davis, open the door. Then help Jarvis and get Morgan out of here."

Davis hurried to do as he was instructed, the door opening in the wall behind the tapestry that hung there, a hidden passage suddenly clear. I had heard of this secret passage, an escape route that our family would use if absolutely necessary.

How did these men know about it?

Davis then moved to Jarvis and Morgan, helping to get his wounded companion to his feet, Morgan's mask hanging off to reveal his face.

The giant dumped me to the ground and the leader towered over me.

"And you, Princess," he snarled down at me as I looked up at him in fear, "are going to learn that things aren't as simple in the real world as they are in your protected little life. Bad men often take what we want and young girls like you do as they are told. Now, move."

He dragged me to my feet then shoved me into the passage, keeping his sword at my throat. The giant followed last, closing the passageway again with a lever on the wall, the escape route sealed once more with the heavy clinking of gears.

I was dragged down a stone spiral staircase and into the dark tunnels of the escape passage. The smell was dank and damp, the air frigid and I could hear the river rushing somewhere nearby, echoing in the caverns.

Terrified by these men, I kept my mouth shut, complying with their orders as they fled with me through the natural rock bowels of the castle. After a few minutes we emerged on the river's banks, the castle's bells chiming furiously and deeply as the garrisoned soldiers and knights hurried out into the night, searching already for our escape route.

I wanted to scream for help, to be rescued from these monsters, but my fear was stronger than my resolve and the winds were too strong for my voice to be heard.

"If you scream," the leader growled into my ear, reading my mind, "I'll stab you and leave you to suffer all the way to the meeting place. Understand?"

"Uh-huh," I whimpered, nodding meekly and breathing heavily as I met his gaze over my shoulder, blinking against my hair catching in the wind.

"Good," he snarled, then forced me forward again.

We moved as quickly as we could, Morgan and I being dragged like heavy sacks, only with me struggling to keep my footing while Morgan had fallen limp in his allies' arms. I could hear horns echoing from the castle walls, shouts rising up from the battlements as the soldiers frantically mobilised for a rescue. But this man had obviously planned this out too well. He acted like a man who had been to Arvon before and had come to know the terrain.

The thought of this horrible nightmare was starting to hurt me so greatly, my desire to cry held back only by my resolve.

I won't cry; I won't give them the satisfaction of seeing me weak. Monsters like this always love preying on girls like me, more so if we cry. So I won't.

Moving as quickly as they could, the men climbed into the cliffs, dragging their wounded companion and I with them.

The giant stopped suddenly, turning to gaze down at the windy hills below, torches dotting the land in the deep darkness. There also came the sound of dogs, bloodhounds trained to seek out scents.

"What is it?" the leader asked him, still holding me by my shoulders as I turned my attention to the giant as well.

I had never seen anyone so big in my life. The sheer size of his cloak was terrifying, but not as terrifying as he himself. I felt so insignificant beside him, fearing that he would break me in half if I tried to move without permission.

"These humans have bloodhounds," the giant told the leader sternly. "They are tracking her scent."

"Then we need to deal with that," the man pushed me to the ground abruptly.

I grunted as I hit the dirt, looking over my shoulder at him. The impact hurt enough to make me softly cry out, but not enough to cause serious harm. Again, he pointed his sword at me, glaring at me over his black mask. I stared up at him, my eyes flicking to the sword uneasily then back to him as he suddenly lurched towards me.

"No! Don't!" I screamed and tried to wriggle away.

My efforts were wasted, the man able to grasp me by my arm with ease. He took his sword and tore a section of the hem of my blue dress away. I stared up at him, suddenly very afraid and strangely confused. I feared his intimate touch and trembled, the need to cry becoming ever more overwhelming as I imagined him tearing more of my dress off me.

He turned and handed the scrap of blue fabric to the giant.

"Throw those mongrels off the scent," he instructed him evenly. "Then meet us in camp."

The giant nodded, taking the scrap and striding away with it. Now I understood why he had taken it from me.

The leader grabbed my upper arm, dragging me to my feet and forcing me to walk beside him as he nodded to the others to continue. We made our way through the hills and the cliffs, passing close to a small woodland area in the foothills, the mountains standing over us like great black arrow shaped towers in the night. After another hour we reached their campsite, everything they had with them set up just inside a shallow cave and outcropping of rocks.

Jarvis and Davis moved Morgan to an area of the camp where they had laid out furs and padding for a place to sleep, laying the groaning, injured man down. They were immediately looking at his wounds, Jarvis possessing healing skills clearly, though nowhere near those of a doctor or mage.

Their leader dragged me into the camp as I struggled to stay on my feet, his grip hurting my arm.

"Davis," he called clearly to the skinny, brown haired man. "Keep watch until Joran gets back."

Joran. So that's the giant's name.

It was little comfort knowing all of their names, but it would help me identify them.

"But, Fawkner, it's cold and there's a storm blowing up," Davis complained, the wind billowing through the trees outside the shelter.

"Stop complaining and do your damned job," the leader, Fawkner, ordered.

Begrudgingly, Davis did as he was told, getting to his feet and trudging back into the cold night, his crossbow in hand. I was able to see all of the men's faces now as they had pushed their masks down.

"Now then," Fawkner turned to me to my horror as he pushed his hood back and pulled his mask off, showing me his face.

He was handsome, with dark ginger-brown hair and pale eyes, his face shortly bearded, a nasty scar running over his left cheek and forehead, his eye left in between.

"You come here, girl," he said to me severely.

He dragged me into the corner of the outcropping as I struggled against him. I fought his grasp as he spun me around, his hand suddenly burying its fingers into my long dark hair and pulling hard. The pain ripped through me as I squirmed desperately, his grip intensifying. I cried out as he pulled my hair again, grasping my wrist with his other strong, coarse hand.

"Do yourself a favour and stop struggling," he advised me. "You're more valuable to me unharmed."

"This is all about money, then?" I tried to glare over my shoulder at him, but his grasp made it impossible to move with my arm pinned into my back. "What are you? A bounty hunter? A mercenary?"

"A mercenary," Fawkner answered, letting go and allowing me to stand up straight again. "Do not move."

I obeyed uneasily as he moved to a bag he had left in the cave earlier. I glared forward at the wall of the cliff, trying to increase my anger to outweigh my fear. Even so, when I spoke my voice betrayed me.

"Why would anyone hire mercenaries to kidnap me?" I wondered aloud, trying to sound angry. "What possible reason could there be for someone to do this to me?"

"I didn't ask," Fawkner replied, retrieving a length of smooth rope from his bag and standing behind me again. "It's part of our work. Don't ask questions you don't need answers to. The client's motives are none of my concern."

"Client?" I asked then let out a startled yelp as he grabbed my arms, pulling them behind me. "What are you doing?!" I was panicking, struggling.

"Tying you up," came his answer as he began lashing my wrists together. "We can't risk you escaping."

I could feel the terror rising in me again as I knew that they weren't going to give me any opportunity to escape. I had to think of something, anything to help me get away from whatever vile tortures they were planning for me.

"The soldiers are looking for me out there," I threatened him, knowing it was a long shot. "They'll find me."

"No they won't," Fawkner said as he bound me, tugging on my arms to keep me close to him.

"Then the knights will," I retorted, looking over my shoulder at him. "You can't keep me prisoner forever. They'll save me... and catch you."

He finished binding my wrists then pressed a hand to my throat, leaning his face over my shoulder and glaring at me. I stared at him out of the corner of my eye, frightened and shaking against my will. I could feel his rough hands on my throat and upper arm, his breath on my neck as he eyed me with that pale gaze.

"You don't realise that you aren't a princess in our company, girl," he told me coldly. "You don't get special treatment and you aren't free to say or do what you wish. You *are* our prisoner and you'll learn to shut your mouth when you're told to. Understand?"

"I-" I closed my eyes, flinching as he jerked my body back again, glaring at me as tears started to form in my eyes.

"Do. You. Understand?" he asked slowly and harshly.

I opened my eyes, looking at him. I didn't speak, too afraid now to say anything. Instead I just nodded, showing my understanding.

"Good," he dragged me to a spot and pushed me to sit on the ground, my back to the wall. "Do as you're told, and you will be treated well. Behave like a spoiled brat and you get nothing," he informed me evenly. "As I said, you're worth far more to me intact and unharmed. So, do as I say. Any questions?"

Teary eyed, I nodded, a hard lump forming in my throat. I felt like I could start sobbing uncontrollably at any moment, my heart racing frantically in my chest.

Fawkner waved a hand to me. "Then let's hear them."

"A-are you... going to... to... to hurt me?" I asked, my voice shaking now.

"No," he shook his head, slightly amused by my change in attitude.

I stared at him, tears slipping free as my fears held me firmly.

"Are you going to... going to...?" I swallowed hard against the lump of fear in my throat, the thought almost too much to bear. "Are you going to... touch me?"

"Touch you?" Fawkner looked suddenly confused as he crouched in front of me.

I looked to him through terrified tears: "I mean, are you... going to make me... d-do... things?"

He realised what I meant and shook his head, leaning closer to me.

"No one is going to violate you," he promised me honestly. "I won't allow it. We may be many things, but *that* is *not* one of them."

I nodded, feeling a measure of relief, but I couldn't be sure they wouldn't do this to me all the same. I looked down at my knees silently, trying to be brave.

"What... what *are* you going to do with me?" I murmured.

"That is none of your concern for now," he replied lowly.

I just nodded softly, too scared to ask anything else.

"Now then," Fawkner drew my gaze back to him, "if those are all of the questions you have, keep quiet and sit here. Don't try anything or I may be tempted to hurt you. Got it?"

I nodded, turning my eyes down to my knees, my tears falling free hidden by my long hair.

He stood, glaring down at me as I stared up at him again, starting to struggle back sobs. He turned and walked over to where Morgan lay. I watched from where I sat against the rock face under the outcropping, looking over my shoulder at the men as they talked.

"How are you feeling, Morgan?" Fawkner asked his injured comrade, care in his voice now.

"Like I've been shot, and Jarvis has pulled the arrows out of me," Morgan answered as Jarvis was bandaging his wounds, his words accented with his painful winces and his Harredi tongue.

"Will he recover?" Fawkner asked Jarvis, stern, but genuinely concerned.

The blonde-haired man nodded, though half-heartedly, uncertainty in his eyes. "He might, but I don't have enough to help him here. He could still die."

"If he does," Fawkner decreed venomously, glaring at me," then *she* suffers for it."

I gasped, pressing myself back away from them, terrified.

But it's not my fault! I thought in horror. *I didn't do anything!*

Fawkner eyed me coldly, then turned around as Joran and Davis came walking back. The giant still had his hood over his grizzled head, his violet eyes turning to me where I sat trembling, his expression stern.

"Did you do it?" Fawkner asked.

Joran nodded, speaking stoically. "Indeed. I scattered the dress scrap into the river. It will draw the mongrels away from us for the next few days."

"Good, because we're going to need that time for Morgan to heal and to wait out the town guardsmen before we can move," Fawkner told him, moving to sit down and start a fire. "We'll head out in a few days to finish the job. For now, let's just rest and recuperate."

"I shall take watch," Joran volunteered – to Davis' delight – and walked away.

As the mercenaries settled in, I sat under the shelter of the outcropping, helpless, restrained and scared. I was shivering, my dress and leggings alone not heavy enough to keep me very warm out in the elements like this.

I watched the five men as Fawkner lit the fire, the illumination of the flames spreading over the cave around us. His eyes turned to me severely and I shuddered, sniffing back my sobs. He turned away from me and was back to working on his previous task as I tried to slow my breathing, briefly testing the ropes binding my slender wrists behind me. They were too tight, the knots perfect.

I had to be strong, to keep myself together no matter what happened. That they would violate me was still a heavy thought in my mind, a fear I couldn't shake free of, but nowhere near as terrible as the fear that filled me with their true unknown plans for me. I felt horrible, dreading what hell these men would put me through and what their mysterious nameless client could possibly want with me.

I closed my eyes and lay my head and shoulders back against the wall, starting to cry softly. *I wish this wasn't happening... Please... why can't it just be a horrible nightmare? Please...*

66

Chapter Five
The Knolling Plains

For three days we lay in hiding amidst the rocks to the east of Arvon. We wouldn't move until two things happened: one, Morgan was well enough to travel, and two, the patrols had moved off in another direction, clearing our path. I was hoping neither would occur, but on the fourth day the mercenaries' luck improved... and mine worsened.

It was early morning, the sun not even rising yet, when the coast was clear. Fawkner had sat up all night watching the passes and the roads, his sword in hand, the blade's tip to the ground.

I had laid there on my side the whole time, trying silently to free my wrists, but with no success. I had tried to sleep, but what little I had gotten had been restless.

Joran was on watch again as well, silent and still as always, his violet eyes surveying the early morning darkness carefully.

Fawkner nodded to him and the giant immediately began packing up for the journey. Fawkner then calmly crossed to where Morgan lay, crouching down beside him and pressing a hand to his shoulder. Morgan awoke easily, blinking away sleep to gaze at his leader.

"How are you feeling, my friend?" Fawkner asked gently.

"Well enough," Morgan groaned, shifting under the furs that covered him, his left side and shoulder bandaged heavily.

"Can you travel?" Fawkner enquired evenly.

Morgan nodded. "Yeah. I should be fine."

Fawkner nodded then shook Jarvis awake. "We're leaving now," he explained to the blonde-haired mercenary. "The path is clear down through the woods. Help Morgan."

"You got it," Jarvis nodded, pulling himself up then moving to help Morgan get to his feet.

Fawkner strode over to Davis, kicking him in the side roughly, snapping him awake and breaking his loud snoring.

"Huh?! Wha?! I'm up! I'm up!" Davis insisted, dazed as he sat up, his hair a mess.

"You snore far too loudly, Davis," Fawkner scolded, glaring at him. "I'm surprised we've lasted three days without the Arvon soldiers finding us."

"It's still dark," Davis whined, turning over to go back to sleep. "We're just gonna sit around again today. What's the point of waking me up?"

"Because we're moving out," Fawkner said through gritted teeth, kicking him again. "The patrols have gone west, now we move south-east. So, drag your arse out of bed and get moving, you lazy sack."

Davis started to get up with a glower, crouching over his sleeping area and packing it all up for the move.

Fawkner then strode over to where I lay on my side, my cloak thrown over me to keep me warm. Seeing him coming I closed my eyes and tried very hard to look like I was asleep. Glaring down at me, he nudged me with his foot. I pretended to start stirring and opened my eyes to look at him.

"We'll be leaving now, girl," he informed me, crouching down and removing the cloak from my body with an easy movement. "We've got a long journey ahead and you have to walk with us."

I didn't answer as he reached behind me, unbinding my hands. I didn't dare move, knowing that to do so would most likely enrage my captor and force him to hurt me. Instead, I waited for his orders, thinking to only obey and hopefully stay safe long enough to be rescued.

He got me to my feet and handed me the cloak. I pulled it on, glad for the extra warmth against the wind's icy chill, but I still glared at him coldly as I did.

"Hands out," Fawkner instructed me.

With only a small amount of hesitation and a great amount of fear, I complied, placing my hands out in front of me, allowing him to bind my wrists once more. He kept a length of the rope free, but tied me tightly so that I couldn't escape. He then dragged me forward with that free length, forcing me to walk like a dog on a leash.

"Is everything ready?" he asked the others.

Jarvis nodded, supporting Morgan, his arm around his companion's waist. "All packed up and ready to go, Fawkner."

"Good," Fawkner eyed me coldly, causing me to shrink back from him before he faced the others again. "We have a long journey ahead of us. Let us not linger any longer than we already have."

They nodded and followed as Fawkner led the way with me in tow.

We climbed down the hillsides carefully, Joran leading the way in the harder parts, lifting Morgan and I to the ground below each time. I staggered behind Fawkner as he forced me forward, my eyes darting to my right to where Arvon was. I couldn't see much of my home but recognised the ravine pass that led into the town. I desperately wanted to run back to the castle and safety.

Unable to use any of the bridges across the river, we were forced to find a shallower part and wade through, Joran carrying Morgan and I across one after the other. From there our path led into the nearby woods to the south, the sun beginning to peek over the horizon.

By the time the sun was in the sky and the moons had set behind the mountains our small group had already made its way several miles south, Arvon now far behind us. It was far enough, at least, that no patrols would find us. My stomach twisted and my heart sank at that thought.

For three days we travelled onwards, breaking to make camp every night, the mercenaries taking turns to watch for guards, bandits or beasts while the others slept, and to ensure I didn't manage to break free and escape. But with the falcon on their side they were assured safety from anyone running across them by chance.

I heard them discussing how Fawkner and the bird called Farsight could share sight between them. I realised that she was the same bird I had seen circling over the castle a few days ago. I cringed at the thought that he had been watching me in my rooms through this bird.

What private things has this man seen of me through his strange magic with the falcon?

With every day that passed I slipped further into hopelessness, my fear that I wouldn't be rescued nearly becoming certainty. Still, I held out hope, praying that the Guardians would find us, that I would be saved. I didn't speak of this hope, of course, knowing better than to reveal the truth to my abductors.

Only once did I become so desperate that I managed to trick Davis into freeing me under the pretence that I needed to relieve myself. The foolish man allowed me out of his sight, and I took the chance to run. But I didn't get far, Fawkner easily capturing me after about an hour and dragging me back to the camp. That was when I suffered a few sharp kicks to the side from Davis, Fawkner stopping him before he could do any more harm. The leader then warned me that such treatment would be what I could expect if I tried that again, and he tied my wrists once more.

After that failed escape attempt, I was watched by two men at any given time and left with aches and bruises to remind me not to try it again. I was back to praying that I would be rescued, fearful and helpless to save myself.

Less than a week after my abduction from Castle Arvon, we emerged from the Arvon Woods and onto the Knolling Plains. Still being led by the wrists, I staggered out into the bright sunlight, staring at the plains with awe.

The six of us stood on a hill looking out over the wide grassy expanse. There was nothing but plains of grass, everything a deep forest green colour mixed with dried yellow and brown grassy patches throughout the expanse. There were clumps of trees dotted all over the landscape, some areas barely a thicket of trees, some areas only having a few trees sparingly spread over distance while the rest was clear all together.

Then there was the reason for the plains' name. There were dozens of rocky knolls rising up all over the landscape, some no taller than a few feet, others as wide and tall as a great oak. Most of the knolls were dusted with dirt and grass, almost as though they were growing it from their tops like hair from a head. Others were untouched by plant life at all, the sun beating down on the bare, grey rock mercilessly despite the cold air.

The plains had a beautiful presence, yet they seemed almost barren due to their isolation.

"The Knolling Plains," Fawkner indicated, pulling me closer to him as his men gathered around. "One of the widest open spaces in High-Realm. We couldn't be farther from human influence if we tried."

"How far to the meeting place?" Morgan asked, now hobbling with a crutch they had fashioned from a branch.

"Another four days at most. Perhaps less," Fawkner answered, his piercing eyes surveying the landscape carefully.

He spotted a line of trees, jabbing a finger towards them.

"We'll head for those trees and make camp there," he directed evenly, completely in control. "We should arrive just after nightfall. Once we're there Jarvis is on first watch, then Davis, and no complaints."

The sun disappeared behind dark clouds, drawing our gazes. Fawkner watched the light turn grey as the cold wind blew up around us again. I kept my head down submissively, determined to keep myself safe at his side, the ropes itching on my wrists. I was glad that my hood was drawn, allowing me to hide my face from them if just for a little while at least.

"Let's move before it rains," he instructed, pulling on the rope and forcing me to follow him again.

For as long as we had daylight we travelled across the plains towards the small line of trees Fawkner had indicated, our progress swift as we feared the rains. The whole way I stumbled as I was dragged by my wrists, completely helpless against Fawkner and his impatience. I felt the wind slapping me hard, the uneven ground causing me to twist my ankles unsteadily as I tried to keep my footing, the wind chill worsening.

If this was the adventure I had asked for, that I had yearned so deeply for, then I was willing to give it back. This was anything but exciting.

Just after nightfall our group reached the trees, a very small pocket of foliage to hide amongst for the night. Immediately, the mercenaries got to work setting up as Fawkner took me to a tree in the clearing, sat me down and took out a second length of rope from his bag. He pushed my shoulders to the trunk of the tree and immediately lashed me to it, binding the rope around my upper arms and chest to hold me in place, my hands still bound in front of me. This was what he did now after my attempted escape.

As I threw him a hard glare, he stood and went to start the fire as Davis and Jarvis finished setting up the camp. They used tarps to shelter us from the rain that was beginning to patter to the ground, creating a makeshift tent top with the cloths and the trees. Then they set up the sleeping areas before Jarvis went and took first watch.

I watched the activity in silence, unwilling to say anything or make a sound, fearing what they would do to me if I did. I stayed as quiet as possible, only moving enough to relieve cramps in my arms, wrists and back where I could. I thought that trying to struggle would invite more punishment from the men, and that scared me.

The camp took shape in about twenty minutes and Fawkner soon had a fire lit, the flames engulfing all the twigs, bark, grass and logs that were tossed into it. Joran returned, having vanished nearly a half hour earlier, a dead deer across his shoulders. The giant tossed the animal's carcass to the ground then started to carve it up to roast it.

Soon enough the camp was at a peaceful state, the mercenaries eating the deer meat and drinking the water they carried in their packs. Morgan was resting comfortably as he ate, his bandages clearly visible beneath his shirt, his arm resting across his stomach.

Jarvis stood watching the surrounding landscape, food in hand as he ate, unbothered by the fact that he had to eat while standing watch. Davis scoffed into his own food, greedily shovelling it down and swallowing as much water as he could. It would have been easy to think that this whiny thug had never been fed properly in his life.

Joran ate only a little, which was surprising considering his size. Once he had eaten and had taken some water, he moved to his small section under the canvas and sat down on the furs, cross legged, hands on his knees. He closed his eyes and remained silent, staying as still as stone. He was frightening, but fascinating.

I stared at the fire quietly, feeling tears of hopelessness starting to fall again. I couldn't help wondering what fate lay in store for me when we reached our destination. I knew that there would be some horrible person or group waiting there to take possession of me to be their new slave or for whatever other dread purpose they had in mind for me. I didn't dare to think of it.

Fawkner approached me quietly, a small bowl in one hand and a skin water flask in the other. He looked down at me, his cloak and jacket removed, only his grey shirt, leg coverings and shin length crimson over tunic covering him now. He didn't carry his sword, but his knife was still at his right hip, gleaming in the firelight.

I knew he was there, but chose not to respond, continuing to stare blankly at the ground beside the fire.

"I brought you some food," the man offered me kindly, but quietly, his sharp eyes studying my tear-soaked face. "I thought you might like something to eat."

I glanced at his legs then turned my eyes back to the fire, still silent and shivering in the cold.

Fawkner crouched down, looking at me gently. "You need to keep up your strength."

"Why?" I looked to him savagely but spoke so softly. "Because I'm no good to you dead?"

He shook his head, no sense of cruelty in those hawk-like eyes. "Because you will become sick."

I turned my gaze from him, staring at the flames again. The thought of this man's concern for me was almost laughable.

How can he show me care when he's planning to do something unspeakable to me? If this is some attempt to gain my trust then he's failing miserably.

Fawkner watched me for a moment, then nodded.

"I understand your position, girl," he told me honestly, his eyes never leaving my face. "I know you are afraid, that you do not wish to be here. It is not something I envy."

I blinked against hot tears of anger and fear, trying to stay stoic as I kept my gaze on the fire. I wouldn't respond, I wouldn't answer him, although it did begin to occur to me that by remaining silent, I may influence him to harm me anyway.

He smiled faintly for a second, observing my silence. "What's this? Now you are quiet? Before I could not silence you, girl. Why is that?"

"I have a name," I murmured in annoyance.

"What?"

"You keep calling me '*girl*'," I said, looking up at him. "I *have* a name."

"Yes," Fawkner nodded. "Leander."

I nodded, sighing sadly as I turned back to the fire. I felt like I had given up, that I had no reason for fighting any more. It seemed now that after more than a week in their company that I wasn't going to escape on my own or be rescued by my father's men.

"Would you please eat?" he asked me gently, drawing my saddened gaze. "You've not eaten at all in two days. In fact, you've barely taken any water either."

"I'd rather die than be handed over to others who would hurt me," I answered with a false strength.

Fawkner shook his head. "You do not mean that."

I blinked, tears sliding free as I shook my head, my voice breaking from the dominating tone I had been taught to use in moments like this.

"No... I don't. I... I don't want to die," I whispered, tears sliding down my cheeks. "I don't..."

Fawkner pressed a hand to my cheek as I started to cry, stroking my hair gently.

"It's alright," he assured me. "You're not going to die."

"You don't know that," I sobbed, looking up at him sadly. "You don't know what these people you're taking me to are planning to do with me. What if that *is* what they're planning for me? You're not going to save me... You won't."

He looked back to the water flask; his face covered in guilt so thick that he could have worn it like a mask.

I closed my eyes, looking away from him and sobbing quietly, my fear now overtaking whatever resolve I had left. I had truly become just a frightened, fragile little girl.

Fawkner watched me for a moment then reached out for the ropes binding me to the tree. He loosened them, then withdrew them carefully, making sure he didn't hurt me. I looked up at him, surprised by this small act of kindness, despite the fact that my hands were still bound.

"I do not think that this rope is necessary," he said, setting the rope aside as he looked to me. "You won't try to escape again. Now will you?"

I shook my head, staring up at him through my tears, fear clutching at my heart and filling my breast.

He nodded. "Good. Perhaps now you feel like eating, Leander?"

I just nodded softly, gaining his faint smile.

I blinked away my tears, allowing him to place the small bowl in my hands. I set it on my knees and watched him as he retrieved his sword, then returned to sit beside me.

My eyes moved to a nearby low hanging tree limb, Farsight perched there. The falcon watched us silently, her sharp, golden eyes locked on both of us.

Starving, I picked at the deer meat in the small bowl, eating as slowly as I could, trying not to stuff my face like Davis had in front of me. It worried me a little that I had come to know my captors, no real bond forming with any of them, except perhaps Fawkner.

I didn't understand why, but something in him seemed to suggest that he cared for me. It was almost fatherly in some strange way. I spent the night wondering why he was so protective of me.

* * * * *

His cloak swirling around him with the early morning wind, Fawkner carried Farsight on his left arm's bracer, the falcon's talons digging into the leather harmlessly. Carefully, he walked up the sloping side of a knoll, the bird flapping her wings in anticipation. He looked to her, murmured something, then threw his arm up, the bird launching into the sky, screeching loudly as she gathered speed and height.

Climbing back down, he took the rope holding me from Jarvis, bringing me up beside him. I was watching him from beneath my cloak's dark purple hood, my steel eyes showing my uncertainty towards him.

We travelled farther south, the uneven ground almost too much for our wounded party member and I. As we walked at midday, I managed to gather enough courage to speak to Fawkner.

"Can I ask you a question?" I said, looking to him as I moved awkwardly beside him.

Fawkner glanced to me briefly. "I suppose. What's on your mind, girl?"

I watched my footing, nearly tripping over a few rocks, but managing to regain my balance.

"I was wondering why you've been so concerned about me," I told him, my eyes meeting his. "I mean, you've abducted me from my home at the point of a sword, killed some of the soldiers who were assigned to protect me, and tied me up and threatened me. Now you're taking me to give me to some dangerous person who is looking for me for some unknown reason..."

"And?" he asked emotionlessly.

I shrugged, glancing at my feet as I watched where I was going before turning my gaze back to him. "I'm just wondering, why are you being so kind to me?"

Fawkner remained silent for a few moments, his eyes straight ahead. It was like he was thinking, considering things carefully. He walked steadily, his hands still holding the rope firmly enough that I couldn't just pull myself away, though he clearly wasn't present.

I watched him, wondering what he was thinking.

"Fawkner?" my voice was soft and calm.

This startled him. "You know my name?"

I nodded. "I've travelled with you and your men for the last eight days. I've heard you talking, and I've learned all of your names."

He seemed a little impressed, turning his eyes forward again. I waited for him to speak, wondering whether he had an answer to my question for me or not.

Finally, he spoke, his eyes still ahead.

"Not one of my men would not show concern for you because they seek to claim their rewards," he explained, turning his eyes to me. "We were paid fifty gold sovereigns each in advance to capture you and shall receive fifty more when we deliver you to the client."

"Five hundred sovereigns?" I was startled by this confession. "Am I truly worth so much?"

"You are to someone," Fawkner answered, turning his gaze forward again.

"So, you protect me so that you can be paid?" I asked coldly, feeling disheartened at this thought.

"No," he shook his head, looking to me again. "The others would protect you for gold. *I* protect you because of what you are."

"A princess?" I murmured.

"I told you that you are no longer a princess as my captive," he reminded me, sighing. "No. I protect you because you are a young girl, a child."

"I'm eighteen," I pointed out. "Technically I'm an adult."

Fawkner nodded, granting this: "True. However, you are still a child compared to all of us. Regardless, you have no choice in this matter, whatever I think."

"Whatever you think?" I raised a curious eyebrow at him.

He looked almost ashamed as he spoke, shaking his head then bringing his eyes back to the way ahead.

"I do not kill innocents, especially children," he looked to me with an honest expression, his eyes saddened. "Were it up to me, I would let you go."

"You still could," I tried to convince him, meeting his gaze, almost turning my body front on to his left side. "You could let me go. I'll run away and... and you can say I escaped while you were sleeping. This client of yours doesn't need to know you helped me."

Fawkner smiled a faint expression of unease and confliction: "I cannot release you, Leander."

"Why not?" I asked, my hope returning and clinging to the thread that it hung by. "Why can't you let me go? Is it because of the money?"

"No, not the money."

"Then what?"

"Fear," Fawkner answered with the most honesty I had ever gotten from him at that point. "I fear this man who seeks you."

There was silence between us for a few moments, our march continuing with only the trampling of our feet and the gusting of the winds. Then I asked the question I feared more than any other.

"Who is he?" I murmured softly, my eyes still on Fawkner's face. "This man who wishes me brought to him... Who is he?"

Fawkner shook his head. "I am not sure. He never gave me his name. He simply hired us."

"Then why do you fear him so greatly?" I persisted, my eyes not deviating from his face.

Fawkner sighed, fighting back a deep sadness. He couldn't look at me for a few moments, but I could see his pain all too clearly.

"He did something to you," I realised. "Didn't he? He hurt you."

Fawkner faced me then, his eyes filled with deep grief. "He killed someone very close to me."

"Why?" I was almost afraid to ask.

Fawkner gave me a haunted look. "You wouldn't understand. You're just a young girl, a princess, the King's niece. What would you know of sorrow and suffering?"

I looked down silently, taking in a slow breath before glancing coldly to him again. There was nothing that I could say to that. Truly, I didn't understand the sorrow he surely spoke of. At least, not yet.

"This man... *thing*... whatever he is, will not take no for an answer," Fawkner went on, his eyes ahead of him once again. "Though my heart warns me against these actions that I take, I fear him far more than anything else. I have never known such evil in all my years on this earth, nor shall I ever again, I think," then he muttered lowly: "Besides, it is better not to anger a sorcerer..."

I said nothing, only staring coldly at him, though the mention of the word *"sorcerer"* certainly made my heart jump in fear and my chest tighten anxiously.

Fawkner glanced at me briefly, then turned his gaze from me once more, continuing forward. I was close to weeping again now, knowing the reason for Fawkner's actions and a little more about the man who hired him. I began to wish that I had never asked him any of it.

Suddenly, he paused, his eyes staring blankly into space as there came a loud shrieking from high up. It was the falcon.

I followed his gaze, trying to find the bird as we came to a stop. The other mercenaries halted beside us, their gazes on their leader, all of them very curious about what he was doing.

"Fawkner?" Jarvis came up behind me, his eyes on his leader. "What is it? What does she show you?"

"We're being tracked," Fawkner murmured, his eyes unfocused. "There are three of them."

I couldn't tell what he was seeing, but I knew that he was using the strange magic he held with the bird. A thrill of hope filled me. Perhaps it was soldiers from Arvon who had picked up our trail. I resisted the urge to smile, knowing I would take punishment from the men if they saw me show any signs of hope or joy.

Fawkner relayed what he saw to the rest of us: "Two men, one around my age, perhaps older, the other is more a boy. He couldn't be any older than twenty-three. The third is a woman, blonde haired. I think she's a Dorvan Ranger."

The Guardians! I realised, my heart filling with greater hope. *They've found me! Oh gods, the Guardians are following us! Please, let them catch up to us, let them reach me in time! Please!*

"A Dorvan?" Morgan asked, surprised, his voice drawing my attention back to the conversation. "Are you sure?"

Fawkner looked to him icily. "There are no other humans in High-Realm who can track a quarry over long distance as she is."

"Why would they be tracking us?" Davis asked, panic rising in his voice.

"Reason would state that they seek the girl," Joran suggested, eyeing me coldly, then turning to Fawkner again. "Perhaps they are mercenaries seeking to take our prize to another bidder?"

"Maybe she had something to do with this!" Davis pulled a knife and put it to my throat, a strangled scream escaping my lips. "You did, didn't you, girl?! What did you tell them?!"

"Nothing! How could I have?!" I cried out, terrified of the knife now aimed at my throat.

"Davis!" Fawkner snapped, Jarvis quickly pulling him aside. "She has been with us the entire time! Her hands are bound! How could she have told them anything?!"

"Maybe she's a witch!" Davis suggested, snarling at me as Jarvis held him back.

"I'm not! I swear I'm not!" I cried out defensively.

Me?! A witch?! Please! I haven't got a magical bone in my entire body!

Fawkner turned to me as Joran pinned my arms by my shoulders, glaring down at me menacingly. "You know who they are though. Don't you, girl?"

I swallowed hard as he drew closer, more threatening again as I pulled my shoulders back into the giant's midriff, twisting my hands in front of me against my bindings.

"Before you answer," he warned, "think *very* carefully about lying to me."

I knew I had no choice, finding a measure of satisfaction in uttering the truth: "They're Guardians."

"Guardians?" Jarvis went pale.

"They were at the castle to protect me," I told them, fighting a smile tugging at my lips while still feeling deep fear. "They're the ones following us and they won't stop until they get me back."

"Guardians, Fawkner! We're being tracked by Guardians!" Davis nearly screamed.

"No matter," Fawkner said, seriously considering this. "They're behind us now. Our only option is to push on towards the ruins."

"How far behind us are they?" Jarvis asked calmly.

"Two days, maybe a little less," Fawkner replied grimly, looking to me. "They're on horseback and gaining on us."

He studied me for a moment, considering the options they had. I looked at him, worried about what would happen now that they knew I was under the protection of the Guardians.

Fawkner finally decided what to do: "Joran, you carry the girl. We'll have to move faster."

I tried pulling away from the giant, but he held on to my arms, lifting me and settling me on his back, letting me cling to his neck. He supported my weight with his large arms, his violet eyes watching me as I frantically looked around, helpless to get back down from his eight-foot height. I was terrified I would fall.

"You just be silent and hold on, girl," Fawkner ordered me, then looked to the others. "Jarvis, help Morgan. Let's move!" he shouted the last two words, taking off at a brisk cross-country run.

As they ran I imagined what Fawkner could see through the falcon's eyes; the Guardians clear in my mind as though I could see them myself. They were just cloaked figures riding on horseback in my thoughts, but it offered me some ghost of hope.

The pursuit continued well up to nightfall, Farsight no longer able to see the men and the woman chasing us. We needed to rest, breaking to make camp.

The next morning was much the same, the mercenaries moving as swiftly as they could to get going, Joran once again throwing me over his back and carrying me like a sack of potatoes.

As they rushed forward, Farsight still watched the Guardians charging through the Knolling Plains, their goal clearly the mercenaries, their speed never faltering as they went. And so it continued like this for the next two days. The mercenaries would run with me securely held over Joran's back, the Guardians hot on their heels. Now the hunters had become the hunted.

* * * * *

The morning of the final day dawned. I lay on the furs provided for me, my eyes focused on the smouldering ashes of the campfire, its flames having gone out hours ago. I found myself wondering what this, the eleventh day of travelling, the fourteenth held by these men, would bring for me. I couldn't imagine it would be anything good.

Within the hour we were on the move again, the camp packed up and stowed in their packs. I looked to the sky, seeing Farsight flying overhead. I wondered if Fawkner could still see the Guardians pursuing us, if they were any closer. I could only hope they would reach us soon.

As the sun was drifting towards the horizon again after another long day, our group slowed at the top of a grassy rise, looking to a gathering hill much higher up, rocky slopes and paths leading to the top. Atop and throughout the knoll's cliffs and crags were the remains of an old fortress; a watchtower. It was in ruins, most of it crushed and destroyed already, but it was at least a shelter from the harsh, cold winds bombarding the landscape.

Fawkner stopped as Joran put me down, grabbing onto my shoulders as I glared up at him, so tiny in comparison. The other three mercenaries made their way up the smaller hill to join us where we stood.

"Here we are," Fawkner told us, his eyes on the ruins ahead. "This was the Watchtower of Averet. It was once an important outpost over a thousand years ago," he looked over his shoulder at us. "We'll go up to the top and wait for the client to collect the girl."

The mercenaries started down the hill at an easy walk, Joran forcing me to move against my struggles. They were no longer concerned about the Guardians pursuing us. It was too late now anyway. I would be handed over, the mercenaries paid and this whole ordeal would be a distant memory for them and a continuing nightmare for me.

Now I struggled and kicked at Joran, my fear intensifying as I was dragged towards the tower ruins. I screamed for help, terrified of what was going to happen to me. Joran didn't flinch as I lashed out at him, simply carrying me towards my fate.

We climbed the stairs inside the carved-out corridors of the tower within the knoll, the fading grey light filtering down through the ruined walls and the remaining windows. Fawkner led the way, his cloak flowing behind him as they forced me up the stairs towards the highest accessible point.

The space was a large round area of stone blocks and pillars, many of the arches and columns still intact, though the ceiling had long since been destroyed. A few central columns remained around the room, five out of eight in total. There were also some old torches remaining there.

"Light the torches," Fawkner directed, his hand on his sword's hilt as he looked at Joran. "Remove her cloak. Tie her to that pillar."

I was dragged struggling to the indicated pillar, thrashing as hard as I could. My cloak was removed, leaving me only in my blue over dress and my simple lilac dress beneath. Then I was forced to sit before the pillar, my back against it. I tried as hard as I could to get my bound hands away from Joran as he pulled the loose length attached to me towards the pillar.

"No! No, please!" I begged futilely, still fighting to free myself. "Stop! Let me go!"

The giant tied the rope to the pillar, pulling it up so that my arms were pressed to the stone, my wrists secured above my head. He took a second rope and bound it around my waist and hips, pinning me to the pillar more completely.

The giant turned and waited for more orders as I struggled and fought my restraints desperately, unable to free myself. I was far beyond terrified now, breathing rapidly and heavily, tears streaming down my cheeks.

"It's freezing up here," Davis whined, another complaint in his long list. "Can't we start a fire?"

"Fine," Fawkner agreed, turning to Joran. "Watch over her."

The giant nodded, remaining silent.

"Fawkner!" I pleaded through my sobs."Please, don't do this to me!"

"I am sorry for your fate," he said, standing over me, "but I cannot help you. We have half our payment already. If I were to help you, then it should have been back when we were given the contract."

"Please!" I sobbed desperately. "Let me go! Please! Please!"

"You need to be quiet, girl," Fawkner warned me severely, but sympathetically.

I tried one last desperate gamble: "Whatever this man has done to you please don't take it out on me!"

"Were that I had a choice, I would take it... but I do not," he said, crouching before me and gently placing a hand to my cheek, my eyes falling shut for a moment before meeting his again. "Truly, I am sorry for what I must do to you, Leander."

He stood and turned from me, shame in his pale eyes. I rested my head against my arms and let myself cry as Fawkner walked away, leaving me there as he and the other three humans settled in for a long wait.

I struggled for about an hour or so but wasn't able to free my arms from the ropes binding me to the pillar. I felt so completely defeated, my warrior training with Mithras now counting for nothing as I waited helplessly for the mercenaries' client to arrive.

Hours went by and darkness fell, but still there was no sign of horses or of any men approaching the tower. There was only the howling wind, cold air and the haunting shadows of the tower's ruins.

Fawkner stood at one of the outer arches, his back against it and his eyes on the darkened ground below. Only the faintest starlight was available, the moons in their dark phase now, the ground barely visible from that height.

"Are they running late or something?" Morgan asked, pulling his cloak around him, shivering. "I mean, we've been here for hours now. Where are they?"

"Maybe they backed out, changed their mind," Davis grumbled as he too huddled under his cloak.

"Don't be such a wimp," Jarvis advised him, sitting with one knee up, an arm resting over it. "You don't hear Joran complaining, do you?"

"That big oaf wouldn't complain if his arse was on fire," Davis griped, glaring at me. "I just think that it's stupid that we went through all that trouble to get this girl and he doesn't even come to collect her."

"Just shut up," Morgan glared at him. "You're really pissing me off now, Davis."

"I'm surprised you haven't had your way with her yet," Davis retorted, glaring at him. "You're the one always trying to bed every woman he sees.

"Well, firstly I'm injured, and secondly, she's the target, so no, I'm not gonna try to bed her," Morgan responded sourly. "Still, being over sexed is better than being a whiney little bastard like you."

"Whiney little bastard?!" Davis growled.

"Enough!" Fawkner barked, glaring over his shoulder at them. "You think we don't have enough problems to deal with? Shut up and keep warm. We'll just wait."

He looked towards me as they fell silent, sympathy showing on his bearded face.

I glanced at him, tears still in my eyes, my arms and shoulders shuddering uncontrollably as the cold affected me through my clothing, my arms aching from their tight position above my head. My long hair hung messily around my face and I was sure I looked weaker than before. I know I certainly felt it.

Slowly, I turned my eyes away from him, returning to my soft, terrified sobs, letting my chin drop to my chest. Fawkner did the same from me, suddenly seeing something that terrified him. I looked up at him as I noticed his expression, then I saw it too as I followed his gaze, fear crushing me.

There were shapes moving in the shadows of the ruins around us. My breath caught and my heart skipped a beat as I watched them with wide eyes.

"Boys. We've got company," Fawkner told the others in a low tone, eyes still on the shapes moving through the ruins.

Davis, Jarvis and Morgan got to their feet, gazing around at the figures that had surrounded us, only Joran remaining untouched by fear's icy grip.

I pushed myself further towards Joran as much as possible, my restraints only allowing me a few inches of lenience. I stared at the figures with wide, teary, frightened eyes, my shivering body now trembling with an entirely new fear.

They emerged from the darkness like ghosts; haunting visages that looked like men but were of a more frightening nature. They were clad in terrifying armour, horrible skull-like masks attached to the silvery helms they wore on their stiff-necked heads. Their armour clanked and groaned as if it was so ancient that it had come from centuries past, their hands rigid as they moved. They each carried a shield and a sword set across their backs, all looking rusted and old.

The figures almost seemed to be hunched as they moved forward, the eyeholes of their masks showing nothing but a deep blackness beneath their helms.

Then, rising out of the darkness like terrible wraiths amidst the haunting soldiers came two new figures. They were taller, each with a trailing, flowing black cloak, dressed in black robes and clad in black armour. Their shoulder plates rose up with a sharp spiked curve, adding height to their shoulders, their hands covered by clawed gauntlets. Their faces were shrouded behind terrifying knights' helmets, sharp featured and with snarling eyeholes, almost like more vicious and ornate versions of the masks the soldiers wore. But these helmets had sharp metal crests rising from them, adding to their ferocious appearance.

Fawkner backed away from them towards the other three humans as I started whimpering at the sight of these ghostly knights and their troops. I was beyond terrified, dreading what they wanted with me.

The two knights strode forward confidently, sharp breathing audible through their helmets, their heights more than human, but less than the giant's. They each carried a cruel looking sword sheathed at their left hips and a large heavy shield on their arm, their forms sweeping as if they were walking on air.

One knight eyed off the mercenaries while the other moved towards me. I stared up into those black eyeholes, trembling in terror as I felt the cold in the air deepen as if transmitted from the knights themselves.

I whimpered, shaking uncontrollably and turning my eyes back to my knees as I drew them closer to my chest. I didn't wish to look into that terrifying face, even if it was just a mask. What lingered beneath was sure to be far more terrifying, my mind racing with countless imagined horrors.

"She is the one," the creature hissed icily, its voice so harsh to my ears, the guttural sound of it drawing a hard, crying shudder through me.

I glanced up fearfully, watching the Knight, my arms straining above me.

The mercenaries stared at them in fear, waiting for the Knights to make the next move. But the two figures did nothing. They simply stood still, as if they had turned to stone, the dozen haunting soldiers standing around us silent as well, almost as though they were waiting for something.

"We have done this task asked of us, Knights," Fawkner addressed the two towering figures, a hint of yearning for this to end in his voice. "We ask only to be paid for our time and be allowed to leave freely."

"Of course you do," a low voice said coarsely.

I opened my eyes and followed the mercenaries' gazes to a space behind the Knights, the voice terrifyingly cold and easily pulling my gaze. My eyes widened as I saw a black shape forming from wispy, shadowy smoke that seemed to gather from nowhere.

The shape took on a human visage, then solidified, becoming a tall figure in dark robes and a black hooded cloak rimmed with crimson. I was terrified at the sight of him, seeing the icy, grey hands with their long fingers hanging at his sides beneath the wide sleeves of the robe, his face hidden in deep, relentless shadows.

The shadowy figure stepped forward, his cowled gaze locking onto us coldly. I could feel the penetrating eyes beneath his hood surveying us.

Now I knew for sure that I wasn't going to escape this mysterious sorcerer and his dark knights, but worst of all I recognised him. He was the monster from my nightmares...

Chapter Six
The Ruins of Averet

The shadowy sorcerer stood before us boldly, a power flowing off him that gave him easy cause for such a stance. His unseen eyes surveyed the six of us callously, the promise of terrible things to come visible in not only his presence, but in a voice whispering in my head. It was almost as though the sinister figure could invade my mind and take what he wanted from me without resistance on my part, even if I tried.

Flanked by the Knights, the Sorcerer turned his gaze around at the mercenaries, his eyes settling on Fawkner as he towered over him.

"You have done well, mercenary," the Sorcerer mewed with a cruel satisfaction. "You have achieved your goals as I had set out for you. I am impressed."

"I was not certain that we would see you here, my Lord," Fawkner approached, stopping a few feet away from the Sorcerer, hiding his fear behind a mask of courage.

"Indeed," the Sorcerer nodded his cowled head slowly. "I was not certain that you could accomplish such a task. And yet, here you are with the girl as I commanded."

I cringed at his mention of me, feeling tears heavy in my eyes, struggling not to cry.

"We nearly lost one of our men," Fawkner told the Sorcerer coldly. "He was wounded during the infiltration of Castle Arvon."

The Sorcerer looked past Fawkner, his unseen gaze falling on Morgan, who stood resting one arm on the crutch. The creature smirked beneath his hood, his lips a little more visible now with the torch lights.

"So I see," the Sorcerer nodded, still watching Morgan the way a lion would a deer. "Perhaps you would like me to... *end* his suffering?"

Morgan cringed, looking to Jarvis and Davis before hobbling behind them in fear. The two other men showed their own terror at that thought, too afraid now to do anything more than stay away from this figure.

"I would prefer that you not talk about my men in such a manner," Fawkner warned the Sorcerer coldly. "We are not simply mangy dogs to be put down."

"Oh, that's precisely what you mercenary filth are," the Sorcerer hissed coldly, staring at him. "The bottom feeders of this world, scrambling for scraps and barking about your unfair lot while you fight amongst yourselves. This is why *I* am so powerful, and *you* are merely in my employ."

The Sorcerer smiled at them, then turned his attention to me.

I was sobbing softly, my eyes wide with terror and pouring tears of panic. I felt a harsh cold coming off this creature, seeming to be emanating from deep within him. His mere presence terrified me beyond anything else in this world. Even the fear of these monstrous knights was nothing compared to him.

I pulled down on my restraints, trying to press myself as low as I could, almost as though I could disappear into the ground if I tried. But staring into that shadowy void beneath the hood told me that there was no escaping him, at least not on my own.

"Remarkable," the Sorcerer mused as he studied me. "I see that same strength and will, yet there is so much more innocence in her. How perfect she is."

Fawkner watched him as he took a few steps forward, the Sorcerer's attention only on me, my eyes darting to the man desperately before locking on the monster again. It was like he had forgotten about the mercenaries and the soldiers surrounding us, only he and I existing in his mind.

I cringed as I watched him approach me, whimpering and struggling against my bonds for a few moments before turning my face away into my left shoulder. I didn't want to look upon this monster, didn't want to see what he was about to do to me.

I thought of my parents and my sister, of my life back in Arvon, and I desperately wished for any chance to be taken home and away from this place. I silently prayed to the gods, hoping they would hear me and grant me some kind of reprieve from all of this.

"You understand that we have not completed our transaction," I looked up to the sound of Fawkner's voice, his hand in front of the monster, staying him from me.

"The girl..." the Sorcerer went to say.

"Is not yours," Fawkner interrupted, "until our business is complete."

"Yeah!" Davis shouted, greed taking over. "Where's our money?!"

"You speak out of turn, coward," the Sorcerer eyed him icily.

"Don't start that crap!" Davis shouted, drawing his sword. "You owe us for bringing this little bitch to you! Now, give us what we deserve!"

The Sorcerer eyed Davis icily, a strange shimmer of green appearing where his eyes were beneath the cowl's shadows. His body language had changed from his calm and imposing presence to an intensely violent and predatory one. He moved a few steps forward, his eyes locked on the dark haired, skinny mercenary, his jaw set into a cold snarl.

"You want your reward, do you?"the Sorcerer asked with a calm coldness.

Davis nodded furiously. "Yeah! Give me my reward!" he brandished his sword.

The Sorcerer smirked and straightened up. "As you wish."

He held up one long, grey hand and closed his fist. Eerie green flames erupted through his fingers, engulfing his hand, but not burning his skin, the Sorcerer suffering no pain. The faint details of the lower half of his face became visible as he sneered, his lips parting into a cruel smile.

Davis looked at him in terror as Fawkner's eyes widened.

"No!" Fawkner cried, turning to Davis, but it was too late.

Davis threw his head back, screaming in agony and wrenching his entire body helplessly. He dropped his sword to the ground with a loud clang, his body seizing and shaking violently. He howled out the most terrible sound I had ever heard, then that same green flame the Sorcerer held erupted from the man's eyes.

I screamed in horror as his anguished howls intensified. The two jets of flame tore from his skull, dropping him to his knees. Then flames erupted from his mouth as if his tongue had been engulfed, his screams cutting out with a sickening gurgle.

I turned away, closing my eyes and crying frantically, straining my outstretched arms as I tried to pull them down from where they were anchored. I didn't want to witness any more of this, but I felt compelled to take tiny glances. That was a mistake.

Fawkner backed away, his arm up to shield his face, Joran actually showing fear as he too staggered backwards. Morgan lay on the ground, scrambling away, yelling in terror as Jarvis had his back against the pillar of an archway, his eyes wide with fear.

Davis' hands were out to his sides, green flames starting to curl from his fingertips, coming up from beneath his fingernails. He was convulsing in agony, impossibly, still alive as he was being torched by the supernatural flames from the inside. I felt horribly sick seeing this, especially as his skin started to become ash.

The Sorcerer laughed and closed his fist. As he did, the flames erupted through Davis' skin in response to the gesture. All I saw was a bright green explosion of flames before squeezing my eyes shut and burying my face into my arm.

A strange billowing wind was sweeping around us as this nightmare continued, the men's screams echoing through the pillars. Then my sobs were the only sound in the silence that followed.

I opened my eyes and watched again, tears streaming down my face. All that remained of him were blackened bone fragments amidst smoking ashes.

"What was that?!" Morgan screamed, still scrambling backwards as the Sorcerer lowered his hand, the flames vanishing from his palm.

Jarvis was in tears, shaking in terror. He no longer resembled a mercenary, but now looked more like a frightened child. He slumped to his knees, crying in fear, hiding his face in his hands as he howled.

Joran stared blankly at the remains, his mouth open and his violet eyes wide. He didn't move any more than that as he stood beside me.

I cried helplessly; my fingers curled around my restraints with a need to cling to something for protection. Meanwhile, Fawkner stood over the smoking remains and turned to face the Sorcerer, eyeing him coldly.

"You've killed another person important to me!" he said, his voice shaking. "Davis was a friend!"

"He was a greedy fool," the Sorcerer said with deep indifference. "You cannot tell me that you would not prefer to live without the constant whining."

"He was my friend!" Fawkner shouted, tears in his pale eyes. "How many others will you kill?! How many?!"

"I will kill everyone you know if you keep what is mine from me any longer," the Sorcerer promised him coldly.

Abruptly, Fawkner snatched his sword from his hip and moved to me. I stared at him for only a second before realising what he was doing, trying to pull away as he almost leaped on me. I let out a short, strangled scream as his sword's blade pressed up under my jaw and against my throat, his other arm slipping around my back and hooking my waist tightly.

I glanced between the two men through my terrified tears, Fawkner's expression one of desperate fury, the Sorcerer's still unseen.

"None of you make a move," he bellowed at the monsters surrounding us, "or the girl dies!"

"No, no, no! Don't!" I pleaded in desperate terror.

The Sorcerer was watching on without moving even an inch, his hidden gaze locked on us. I couldn't tell if he was assessing the situation or just biding his time, but I didn't think that he was afraid even for one instant.

Fawkner jerked the sword to my throat again to make his point, a whimpering moan escaping my lips as I squeezed my eyes shut against the flooding onslaught of tears pouring down my face. I glanced past my arm at him, trembling as I wondered if he would really do as he had said.

"You will honour our deal, sorcerer," Fawkner dictated calmly and evenly, his hold tightening on me. "You will pay us, you will let us go, and you will never bother us again."

"And in exchange?" the Sorcerer questioned lowly.

"You'll get the girl, as promised."

"No, please... Don't..." I started, but he just jerked me back again. "Uhnh!"

The Sorcerer considered this for a moment, taking a step forward. I whimpered again as Fawkner threatened me even harder than before, his sword hand so steady. The monster stayed his feet, watching us coldly as the mercenaries around us found a new courage.

"We can come to an arrangement, my friend," the Sorcerer said, his palms out to his sides in a reassuring manner.

"Don't trust him," I murmured worriedly to Fawkner, knowing this man – this *thing* – was deceiving him. "He's going to betray you."

Fawkner throttled me mildly again and hissed into my ear: "Be quiet, girl," then he turned his gaze back to the Sorcerer. "What say you? You want her, do you not?"

I swallowed hard as I looked to the Sorcerer again, waiting for him to speak, fearing what nightmare would explode against us next. To my surprise he remained very calm.

"I have no desire to be dictated to by scum like you," he said in an almost bored way. "But I *did* promise you a reward, did I not?"

Fawkner eyed him numbly as the Sorcerer nodded to one of his knights. The Knight withdrew the promised bags of gold from his robes and tossed them to the ground before Fawkner.

The Sorcerer nodded his hooded head. "There is no need for us to be uncivilised, Fawkner."

"True. But, unfortunately," Fawkner nodded and gestured to me coldly, "the girl is right about your treachery."

I looked over my shoulder at him in shock. *Wait... What?* A horrible chill of dread spiked down my spine and I took in a shuddering, painful breath.

The Sorcerer glowered and I could see the glow of his inhuman green eyes.

"You know what I am capable of, Fawkner," he said warningly. "Now, give me the girl and you shall live."

Fawkner shook his head, taking his sword from my throat and pointing it towards the Sorcerer. "Gods know what you'll do to this girl! I will *not* give her to you!"

The Sorcerer nodded with a low sigh: "So, you have grown a conscience since last we met. Very well," he gestured towards us as the Knights drew their swords. "Kill him and his cohorts. Bring me the Princess."

"Can you run?" Fawkner asked me, eyes on the approaching monsters.

I stared over my shoulder at him in shock. "You're... you're helping me?"

"I am," was all he uttered as his eyes deepened with their focus.

As the soldiers drew their swords there was suddenly a whistling sound, two arrows striking two of the inhuman soldiers, throwing them backwards, one after the other. They fell to the ground hard, no longer moving as they slumped to the stone, their bodies giving up.

The Sorcerer looked up from Fawkner and I watched another arrow take down a third soldier, throwing him from the tower's edge. Three figures rushed through the main archway, the Guardians easily recognisable, their black cloaks swirling around them heroically.

Tallinn rushed forward, bow in hand, stringing arrows and firing swiftly as if she were moving with supernatural speeds. She dropped another two soldiers, three more avoiding her shots with their shields.

Aldwyn moved forward, pushing back his hood to reveal his long dark hair and neatly bearded face. His brown eyes surveyed the scene and he focused on two soldiers rushing him. A dazzling blue orb of light was launched from his left hand, slamming into one and throwing it backwards. He swung around, hitting the second soldier with his staff and beating the creature down as it screamed a horrible inhuman sound.

He turned, facing the hooded sorcerer, who was now retreating behind his knights, almost appearing afraid of the three newcomers, though I doubted that.

A soldier rushed at me, forcing me to close my eyes and wait for the blade to strike me. There was a loud yell and two swords clanged above me.

I looked up to see Carden now standing before me, his handsome face tense, his jaw set as his green eyes burned with rage. He pushed the soldier back, swinging his sword and fighting hard against him.

With one strong strike, he took the soldier's head from its shoulders, quickly slaying another and engaging a third. He delivered a swift kick, throwing the soldier from the tower's edge, the armoured body crunching loudly on the rocks below.

He took out a fourth, pulling his sword free and rushing towards me as Tallinn covered him against several incoming soldiers, her bow quicker than their feet. Behind them, Fawkner had engaged one of the knights, his sword clanging against its own in a desperate fight for his life.

Morgan threw down his crutch, drawing his sword, but took an arrow in the throat from one of the haunted soldiers. He dropped to the ground, dying instantly. Jarvis ran to his friend's aid as Joran was throwing soldiers down, the giant's sheer size enough to give him an advantage. His twin blades cut through the enemy, throwing them aside as his eight-foot shape gave him greater protection against their strikes.

Jarvis managed to dispatch two of the haunted soldiers easily, a third running him through just before he could reach Morgan. He cried out in agony and fell to his knees, swinging his sword around and taking the creature's legs out from under it. They died together, Jarvis' sword in its chest.

Carden ran to me, startling me as he dropped down beside me.

"Carden?!" I gasped out.

"Princess, are you alright?" he asked urgently.

"Please, just get me out of here!" I sobbed, tensing my arms against the restraints, terrified by this new battle.

"Don't worry," he told me, reaching for the ropes holding my wrists. "I'll get you out."

"Look out!" I cried, my eyes on the figure behind him.

The raven-haired boy rolled out of the way as the second of the knights swung its sword, the blade cracking the stones as it hit the floor. Carden was on his feet again, turning to face the armoured monstrosity, sword at the ready.

The Knight turned its frightening helm to him, bringing its sword up from the broken stones and attacking. Carden kept parrying, the Knight pushing him away from me, keeping him occupied. He desperately tried to get back to me, but I knew that he had to defeat this creature first in order to reach me.

He ducked past a pillar, the Knight's sword slicing through the stone and toppling it over. The pillar knocked two soldiers from the tower as it slammed into the floor, crashing through the stones and tumbling down to the rocks within the fortress.

Carden turned to face the creature, his cloak swirling around his body, his eyes focused as he fought. His sword rang loudly as it collided with the enemy's blade, his arms looking like they were aching as the creature struck with inhuman strength.

I tugged on my restraints desperately, fighting to free myself. Then, I froze, sensing a gaze locked on me. I looked up and my eyes widened in terror.

The cowled sorcerer stalked towards me, his path cleared, his robes and cloak flowing around him like black flames. He strode forward, suddenly towering over me and glaring down at me. He was a horrifyingly impressive figure this close, his imposing presence chilling the blood and freezing the soul itself.

I stared up into the hood he wore and came face-to-face with the real creature beneath. Now I could see what he really looked like, and he was beyond terrifying.

Suddenly, a bright ball of sapphire blue energy struck the Sorcerer in the side of his cowled head, shattering against him like it was made of water. He turned his glowing green eyes from me, roaring angrily as another orb hit him in the left shoulder, pushing him away from me.

I squinted against the light and looked up to see Aldwyn moving towards us, his staff held in his right hand, his left-hand glowing with blue energy. It looked like a shield of magic stood against his open palm, his staff's crystal glowing with sapphire light.

"You shall leave this girl alone, dark one," he growled through his teeth.

"You dare to come between a Shadow Lord and his prey, mage?" the hooded creature hissed.

Shadow Lord? I know that phrase. But how do I know it? It's... it's so familiar.

"Leave this girl be," Aldwyn commanded.

"You are truly ignorant to think you can command me, human," the Sorcerer growled.

He launched an emerald lightning storm from his fingertips, striking at the Mage. Aldwyn held up his left hand, the blue energy field absorbing the attack, glowing brighter with every bolt that hit it. When the strikes faded, he aimed his staff forward and attacked again.

I cringed back at the strikes, squinting against the blinding flashes of magical energy.

Three blue orbs of light launched from the staff's crystal, hurtling towards the creature. They hit him hard, one after another, pushing him backwards. They struck with a resounding, sickening thud as they hit him in the stomach, shoulder and face.

Aldwyn continued his assault just as Carden finally bested the Knight, throwing the armoured monster down and burying his sword into its chest.

"Carden!"Aldwyn shouted to him. "Get to the Princess!"

"No!" the Sorcerer howled, throwing a fireball at Carden to my horror.

Carden jumped out of the way as the Knight moved to attack again, taking the green fireball to the chest and thrown some seven feet away where it dropped to the ground, and remained unmoving.

Before he could attack again, the Sorcerer was struck repeatedly by several more blue energy blasts, grunting in pain and staggering backwards as he put his arms up to shield his eyes. Aldwyn pressed the attack, bombarding him again and again with sapphire energy, forcing him farther away from me.

Carden rushed to my side as I looked up at him in fear. He quickly untied me, then pulled me into his arms. I clung to him as we stumbled back to the ground, lying there together watching his companion fight the Sorcerer.

The remnants of the haunted soldiers were now dead, and Fawkner finished the final knight, taking its head off its shoulders and stabbing it through the heart with its own jagged, monstrous sword. It fell to the ground, crumpling into a pile as the mercenary turned to the fight that now remained. Like Joran and Tallinn, he watched on as the hooded figure faced Aldwyn, fighting him desperately for ownership of me.

I was almost on my side as I wrapped my arms around Carden's waist, my cheek to his shoulder as he kept one arm around me while he knelt on one knee, his sword in his other hand.

The creature roared, launching a few more fireballs at the Mage in anger, the green fire dispersing across the mystical shield that Aldwyn held in his left palm. In response, he threw three more blue energy strikes at the Sorcerer, forcing him even farther back.

The orbs broke against him, repelling him with a force that became harder and harder with each strike. He howled in anger, powering up another strike, but was hit in the arm with a blue orb, shattering his spell and throwing him down.

He turned to the Mage angrily, now on his feet and taking several more strikes. Five orbs struck him at once, only a small intermission between them as they hit their marks.

The Sorcerer stumbled backwards as Aldwyn walked forward, his eyes burning as he fought the monster. More orbs of light lanced out from the staff, pushing against the Sorcerer and forcing him towards the edge of the tower. The monster took a blow to the chest, falling to one knee to then be struck in the left shoulder and the top of his head.

He pushed himself to his feet, moving to strike again only to be hit three more times, the green energy he was about to launch fizzling out in his hand. He grasped at his chest, staggering backwards as more blasts hit him again and again.

He glared at me across the tower, then howled angrily as he was smacked in the side of the face by another blue blast, three more thundering into his right shoulder, hip and chest. Another hit him in the back as he spun, one final blow striking his chest before he suddenly evaporated into a bank of smoky black shadows. He dissolved into mists as two more orbs passed through where he had been standing harmlessly.

The smoky shadows pulled away, whipping into the air as if carried on the wind, disappearing into the night and the storm clouds overhead.

We were left amidst the corpses of the dead monsters, their bodies fading and leaving tattered robes and broken armour behind. Only the ashes of Davis' bones and the bodies of Jarvis and Morgan remained then. There was silence, the wind whispering through the night and the breathing of the survivors echoing through the ruins.

Aldwyn relaxed, lowering his left hand and righting his staff, the energy fading away from both. Tallinn lowered her bow in her left hand, her hazel eyes on the Mage as he turned to me.

"Princess Leander," he addressed me, his face calm and gentle. "Are you alright?"

I nodded as Carden helped me to my feet. "Yes. I am. I knew you'd come for me."

"Such is our duty, your Highness," Aldwyn assured me.

"Thank you," I said, looking around at the three of them, my eyes lingering on Carden.

Carden smiled at me as he sheathed his sword, his grin roguish and matching his youthful face. He was incredibly handsome and so unlike the other young men I had met in my life. I smiled to him thankfully then looked to Aldwyn again.

"What now?" I asked uncertainly.

"Considering what we have learned here tonight," Aldwyn said direly, "I think it may be prudent to contact the Guardian council when we return to Arvon and ask for their guidance."

"Anything you say," I agreed, looking up at the two men. "Just, please, take me home."

"And what about these two?" Tallinn asked, eyeing Joran and Fawkner as they stood over their fallen comrades.

"I would leave that decision to the Princess," Aldwyn responded and looked to me. "Whatever you command, we shall abide by."

I looked around at the three Guardians uncertainly, then turned my eyes to the two men. I watched Fawkner as he crouched over Jarvis' and Morgan's corpses, his grief clear. I couldn't help but feel for him, despite what he had done to me. I understood him more now as I stood there looking down at him and I felt no anger, only sympathy.

"We'll take them to Arvon with us," I decided, drawing Fawkner's teary gaze. "I won't let them get away with what they've done, but I won't make them suffer either."

"You would show us mercy?" Fawkner was surprised as he knelt before me, Carden close to my side, glaring at him, his hand on his sword's hilt.

I nodded. "Yes. You've done some terrible things, but I believe that you are a man of honour, and if I am to be a queen then I must show forgiveness and mercy. I see that you were coerced into your actions, so I will not punish you for that."

Fawkner stared at me, stunned by my words. He didn't say anything, too confounded by my decision.

"Child," Joran spoke, drawing my attention as he looked down at me, "you show mercy to those who showed you none. You are callow, yet you spared my life. Now, it is yours."

"Joran, are you serious?" Fawkner stared at the giant with increasing shock. "You're giving her a life debt?"

Joran nodded. "I am. She has shown me mercy and I have shamed myself through my actions against her. And so I must offer my life in service to her."

"I don't understand," I looked up at him, confused by his words.

"It is the way of my people," Joran told me stoically, his face maintaining its smooth calm. "You were within your rights to kill me for the wrongs I have committed against you. You have chosen to spare my life, and so I must now serve you for the rest of my days."

"No... I-I don't want that from you..." I started.

"It is a matter of honour," Joran insisted. "I must do this. Our traditions command it."

Reluctantly, I nodded. "Alright. Then, I guess, I accept your life debt."

"I shall serve you until my final breath leaves me," Joran pledged, bowing his head, his arms crossed in front of him, fists pressed to his shoulders. "My loyalty is to you and I am at your command."

I nodded uncertainly, this strange creature leaving me both stunned and confronted by his words.

"And what shall become of me?" Fawkner asked, looking up at me.

"You'll just come with us," I said simply.

He nodded, standing and placing his wrists out, his expression one of defeat: "Bind my wrists and I shall come quietly, then."

I shook my head. "No. You'll walk free."

"Are you certain, your Highness?" Tallinn asked apprehensively, walking up beside me. "He abducted you and brought you to these monsters for money. You cannot trust him."

I shrugged, studying Fawkner's face. "I am giving him a chance to prove himself to be better than his previous actions."

"You are possessed of a wisdom beyond your years, Princess," Aldwyn observed, leaning on his staff. "Very well. They come with us, unbound, but we will watch them carefully."

Fawkner lowered his hands.

"You are a better person than I could ever be, Leander," he told me softly, thankfully. "You are stronger than I would have believed."

I nodded, shivering with the cold. "Then there's just one thing left to do. We need to lay your friends to rest."

Fawkner stared at me in amazement. "You would do this for men who threatened and abducted you?"

"Yes," I said simply, nodding. "Everyone deserves a burial."

Fawkner started to sob softly and nodded his thanks.

A funeral pyre was constructed, Morgan and Jarvis wrapped in their cloaks and set atop the pile. It was lit and the six of us stood there watching as it burned slowly, engulfing the two bodies.

The three Guardians stood around me protectively, all under their own hoods, guarding me with deepest conviction. In front of us Fawkner and Joran gave their final farewells to their deceased friends, the two mercenaries silent as they too stood wrapped in their hoods and cloaks against the gently sprinkling rain that had begun to fall.

As I watched the fire from beneath my hood, I felt sympathy for Joran and Fawkner, but no resentment for what they had done to me. I only wished now to return home and put this whole ordeal behind me. But I felt a terrible dread deep within me. The Sorcerer - the Shadow Lord as he'd called himself - was still out there and I couldn't help feeling that this wasn't the last I would see of him...

Chapter Seven
Gifts and Warnings

The journey back to Arvon took twelve days. I rode with Carden, our horse central in the group with Aldwyn leading the way and Tallinn following on behind with Fawkner holding her waist. Joran travelled on foot beside our mounts, too big for a horse and constantly on guard for attack since his pledge to me.

As we approached the town from the fields, farmers looked up to see us, welcoming us warmly and bowing to me. I blushed and hid beneath my hood self-consciously, never liking this kind of attention.

Horns blew and we looked up as several riders galloped towards us on horseback from the castle. They carried swords and crossbows, their blue and gold cloaks swirling around them in the wind as their scale armour glistened in the sunlight, their helmets gleaming in kind.

"Your Highness," one of the riders bowed his head to me as they came to us. "Thank the gods you have been returned to us unharmed. We must go to Castle Arvon. Prince Ewan and Duchess Caralyn have been beside themselves without you."

I nodded. "Take us."

We followed on our horses with the riders around us and trotted on through Arvon towards the highest point of the river near the ravine, the castle standing tall above us. I felt an overwhelming relief rush through me to see the grey stone walls and the towers reaching above me. I had missed this place so much in my short absence.

The bridge across the river came into view and we rode across as guards shouted for the gates to be opened. With the last riders galloping through the gates, the heavy portcullis was shut as soldiers ran into flanking positions throughout the courtyard.

Carden brought his horse to a stop and dismounted.

"Your Highness," he spoke from my side, offering me his hand. "May I help you down?"

"Thank you, Guardian," I responded, allowing him to take my arm and lift me to the ground.

Mithras was walking down from the main doors flanked by knights, smiling brightly at the sight of me.

"Mithras!" I beamed brightly, looking past Carden as the Knight walked towards me. "I'm so happy to see you!"

"And I you, Princess," Mithras returned my smile as he came to me.

Forgetting my station, as I so often did, I threw my arms around him, hugging him closely and feeling the warmth that I had been missing over the past month. I pulled back, smiling up at him, so happy to be back with my old friend and mentor.

"Your parents are expecting you, Princess," Mithras told me gently, then looked to Aldwyn, Tallinn and Carden. "If you'll all follow me."

With that, we were led up the steps, Joran and Fawkner moving in behind us silently, all of us flanked by soldiers and knights. I glanced back at the giant and the man who I had spent a month trying to figure out.

I hope they will be alright.

The main doors opened onto the grand hall, my parents sitting in their minor thrones surrounded by guards and servants. My father's eyes widened, and a smile forged over his face.

"Leander," he gasped happily.

"Leander?" Mother looked up, tears swelling in her eyes as she saw me.

"Mother, Father!" I cried, rushing into my father's arms as he bounded down the steps of the dais to hold me.

"Gods be praised!" Father proclaimed, holding my shoulders and looking down at me happily. "Our daughter is returned to us! I prayed to Thringar that he would make this so, and behold how he has!"

"Leander!" Mother sobbed, pulling me into her arms and hugging me firmly, almost as though she intended to never let me go again. "Are you alright, my girl?! Did they hurt you?!"

"I'm alright, Mother," I assured her, feeling a presence behind me as Father turned his blue eyes to the Guardians.

I turned with him, Mother refusing to let go of me, both of us watching as my protectors approached.

Aldwyn took the lead, laying his staff down and genuflecting on one knee, Tallinn and Carden following his example. The three Guardians bowed their heads respectfully before my parents and I. Suddenly, I felt uncomfortable again.

"You need not bow to me, great Guardians," Father told them respectfully. "You have saved my youngest daughter, one of my most important treasures. You *must* be rewarded."

Aldwyn looked up to him, remaining where he knelt, peering up past a curtain of long brown hair.

"With respect, your Lordship, we do not require any rewards," he responded reverently. "We pledged an oath when we were initiates to defend and serve all the peoples of High-Realm. This we do without need of rewards, for it is our duty to not only the people, but to High-Realm itself."

"That your daughter is returned to you is reward enough, Sire," Tallinn added, her head still bowed.

I was impressed. These were such noble people, more noble than even the knights of our country. It was an ancient ideal that I saw before me and I felt a smile tug at my lips.

"But I must ask you not to kneel, my friends," Father urged them. "Please, stand."

Slowly, the three got to their feet, standing there proudly as honoured guests in Castle Arvon. They faced the three of us and I allowed a smile to appear on my face.

"I would at least like to extend the thanks of Arvon to you, my Guardian friends," Father declared to not only the three warriors but the entire room. "Though you ask for no reward, I would honour you for what you have done here for my family and our small town, as well as the Kingdom of Aldegaad itself in defending our heir to the throne."

Aldwyn looked to the other two, gaining their approval. I had learned that he always referred to them before deciding on a course of action, a strange practice for a master.

"With respects, your Lordship and Ladyship, any celebration will have to wait. We had thought that it would be prudent for us to contact the heads of our order, and to enhance the castle's security," Aldwyn told them calmly, but solemnly.

Father looked a little confused. "Why do I feel that there are graver concerns than I am aware of?"

"Some developments have come to our attention in recent weeks," Aldwyn explained cryptically, careful not to say too much in front of the court. "These have given us concerns for your daughter's continued safety."

Father nodded, crossing his arms. "Because of the mercenaries who abducted her?"

Aldwyn shook his head. "Rather the individual who hired them to abduct her. I fear that he is more than a simple enemy of the kingdom or a slaver seeking a unique prize."

I sucked in a sharp breath at the thought of the black cloaked figure.

The Shadow Lord... Isn't that what he called himself?

I glanced uneasily between Father and Aldwyn.

"We shall discuss this in my study," Father decided, looking to the three Guardians in turn.

That was to keep it from me, I knew. Father never liked discussing things such as this in front of me.

"Your Lordship," Mithras spoke up, drawing our attention as he addressed Father. "What is to be done with these men?" he indicated Joran and Fawkner.

Father considered the two, his eyes falling on Joran. It was clear to me that my father was surprised by the giant's presence. I could see the recognition in his blue eyes as he considered the black haired and violet skinned man, his expression not one of fear, but of intrigue.

Has he seen someone like Joran before?

"A Storvari," Father breathed, impressed as he gazed up at the towering, muscular figure, confirming my quiet suspicions. "You are of the Storvari people, are you not?"

Joran nodded. "I am."

"What brings you to High-Realm?"

"I served as a mercenary," Joran answered honestly.

Father's face dropped and his eyes darkened. "You were among those who invaded this castle and kidnapped my daughter?"

Again Joran nodded. "I was."

"And you admit this so freely? Why?" Father asked, surprised by the giant's forthcoming attitude.

Joran turned his violet eyes to Father. He seemed to be studying him, almost as though he was deciding what to tell him or what gesture to make, however I had my doubts that Joran was looking for a pardon.

I felt suddenly concerned, Father's gaze severe.

"I am ashamed," Joran admitted, dropping slowly to one knee and bowing his head, still taller than me even though I was standing on the small dais the thrones rested on. "I acted for the dark intentions of another in exchange for monetary recompense. My actions nearly ended the life of this woman-child."

"Your life is forfeit," Father glared at him angrily, but his voice was straight and calm. "Your actions condemn you."

That tone Father used scared me more than any other he possessed. That meant he was very angry, that tone often used on me when I had done something to really upset him as a child. I gulped back hard.

Joran nodded. "This is why I bowed before my Sarissi and offered my Saris to her."

"Sarissi?" Mithras looked stunned as he moved forward to stand beside me. "She is the holder of your Saris?"

Joran nodded again. "Indeed."

"Saris?" I looked to Mithras as I noted my father's look of shock.

"It is a Storvari word for life," Mithras explained aside to me softly. "You are his Sarissi."

"What's a Sarissi?" I asked softly.

"Roughly translated, it means "the One whom I shall serve to the end of my days, whose life is precious and to which I am custodian"," he looked to me knowingly. "Basically, he has pledged a life debt to you. It is the feminine form of the word, Sarassa being the masculine."

"Yes, he did say something about that back at the ruins," I agreed.

"You serve my daughter now?" Father asked the Storvari, having heard the exchange between Mithras and I. "Your life is hers?"

"I serve the Sarissi," Joran pledged again, head still down. "As demanded by the Carethanes and decreed in the Histories of Storvarkar, I am bound to she whom I have wronged. She shall be the holder of my Saris, the Sarissi I shall serve. The honour of my Jaaktar is hers and I will honour her with every breath I take. I will burn the sacred Celtcthu upon my flesh and I will enact the Ritual of Gekvar'tor. My Saris is hers and I will serve her to my final breath. As it is demanded by the Carethanes, so shall it be done."

"I didn't understand some of that," I whispered to Mithras.

"I'll explain later," Mithras told me.

Father looked down at the now silent giant kneeling before him, the Storvari's shoulders still high enough to be in line with my father's chest. There was no hatred in his eyes, only understanding.

"What is your name, Storvari?" he asked.

"I am Joran of the Vorash Jaaktar," Joran answered, still bowing.

"Then I accept your pledge, Joran of the Vorash Jaaktar," Father told him.

"Forgive me, human Prince," Joran turned his violet eyes to Father, "however, only the Sarissi can accept my Sarisil."

"Sarisil?" I glanced to Mithras again.

"His life pledge," Mithras responded.

Father turned to me then, all eyes in the room falling on me. I felt self-conscious again.

"What have you to say, my daughter?" Father asked.

I looked to Joran, the giant's eyes now on mine as he waited without emotion for my response. I liked him, strangely, his size less a threat to me now and more a comfort. I don't know why, but I suddenly felt that I could trust this unusual man.

"I accept," I said simply.

"Then arise, Joran of the Vorash Jaaktar," Father directed the giant.

"Forgiveness," Joran said, "but I cannot stand taller than the Karthesan of the Sarissi while in court."

"Karthesan means "Lord-Father"," Mithras translated, knowing that the Storvari words were confusing me.

Father nodded then looked to Fawkner. "And this man. Who is he?"

"I am the leader of the men that took your daughter," Fawkner said coldly as two soldiers forced him to his knees.

Mithras had his hand on my arm as if to keep me back and stop me from speaking, throwing a warning look to me. My mentor knew me too well.

"Do you also have a life debt with my child?" Father asked icily.

"I do not," Fawkner responded, glaring at him.

"Then why do you speak with an honest tongue?"

"Only that I be ended swiftly without further suffering, Sire," Fawkner answered honestly.

"You wish for death?" Father asked, surprised.

Fawkner nodded. "I seek only what punishment I deserve, Sire."

"Father," I moved to his side, looking up at him appealingly. "I promised that he would not be harmed."

"Amnesty is not yours to give, daughter," Father retorted calmly, eyeing me.

"If I am to be Queen..."

"That time has not yet come," he scolded, turning to glare at me. "Ewan – not Leander – is Lord of Arvon. I am the one who decides the fates of criminals in this province, not you, at least not until your twenty-first year when you may become Queen."

"But Father...!" I protested as Mithras put his hands on my shoulders, pulling me back.

"This man is responsible for the deaths of several of our people," Father regarded Fawkner with the coldest of gazes as the prisoner put his head down. "He invaded our home and he stole one of the most precious treasures of my life; my daughter."

Fawkner looked up expectantly, waiting to be sentenced. I struggled against Mithras' hands, trying to get back to my father.

"Father, please!" I begged, drawing his gaze to me again. "Show mercy."

"That is not appropriate," my father turned back to Fawkner. "What are you called, mercenary?"

"I am Fawkner of Lorveren," he answered. "And, unlike your daughter, I do not plead for my life."

"If you have violated her virtue..." Father seethed.

"He didn't!" I cried out defensively, more about the suggestion than anything else. "I'm still a virgin!"

"I would have you examined by the physicians, regardless," Father replied to that, then faced Fawkner again. "If what she says is true, it will not grant you a reprieve."

"I did not partake of your daughter's womanhood," Fawkner assured him. "This, however, does not absolve me of my crimes, and I will accept whatever fate you decree, Sire."

"As Aldegaad no longer executes prisoners you will be imprisoned for the rest of your days in the dungeons of Aneuran," Father decided as the soldiers dragged Fawkner to his feet and locked him in heavy chains. "You will be locked in the dungeons of this castle until such time as we can arrange transport to the capital where my brother, our King, will pass the final sentence upon you for what you have done."

"Father!" I screamed angrily, desperately.

"My judgement is passed!" Father snapped back at me. "He is condemned to life in prison!"

"But..."

"Do not test me, Leander!" Father warned me. "Do not. Were it you who had acted in such a way as he, I would not spare you despite being my daughter. So I will not spare him."

I looked to Fawkner hopelessly, feeling that I had failed him. I didn't understand my desire to save him, though it might have stemmed from nothing more than an intention to prove my own compassion. Still, I believed that he deserved a second chance, especially since he could have fled or attacked me at any time during our journey back to Arvon.

I closed my eyes and stopped fighting against Mithras' grasp, relaxing as the soldiers moved to drag Fawkner away. He allowed them to take him, no longer having any urge to fight for his life, but before they could leave Aldwyn intervened.

"Prince Ewan, my Lord," Aldwyn spoke as he stepped forward, gaining Joran's gaze where the giant still bowed before my father. "A moment."

"What would you ask of me, Master Guardian?" Father asked as I opened my eyes and watched.

"This man," Aldwyn gestured to Fawkner, "has made mistakes, I agree. He has murdered for money and threatened the life of your beloved child, a fact *she* has chosen to forgive."

"What is your point?" Father asked too harshly for his character.

"Spare him his life," Aldwyn petitioned, open palmed and standing directly before my father. "Grant him a reprieve."

"This I cannot do," was my father's answer.

"He is a monster!" Mother walked forward, her noble gowns flowing around her, her eyes so deeply intense. "What he has done is *unforgiveable!*"

"I do not suggest forgiveness," Aldwyn told them wisely. "I merely recognise this man's various skills and talents. We witnessed his actions to save your daughter from a Shadow Knight."

There was a sudden chorus of gasps and whimpers throughout the room. I looked around at the people standing there, confused that the words had meant so much.

What is a Shadow Knight, anyway? One of those black knights at Averet?

I turned my gaze back to Aldwyn and my father, seeing the tension between them. If their gazes had been lances they would have been clashing and tearing at each other. And yet, Father's eyes and expression softened as he heard Aldwyn's pleas.

Aldwyn continued: "To waste such talents would be a greater evil than what he has done here. I do not condone his deeds, yet I cannot ignore his actions at Averet."

"What would you ask of me?" Father repeated his earlier question.

"I would invoke the Rite of Recruitment," Aldwyn told him calmly and evenly, his staff passing from his left hand to his right. "He would remain in our custody until our return to the Citadel of Dartaren."

"You would make him a Guardian?" Mother asked incredulously, looking to Father.

"I would rather die!" Fawkner spat maliciously.

"That may very well occur," Tallinn stepped forward, turning her hazel gaze to Father. "My Lord, the Initiation Ritual is very dangerous. It has claimed the lives of so many potentials. In any case, the life of a Guardian is just as hazardous in its own right."

"One way or another," Carden continued from where she left off, his arms crossed, "you will have your corpse, be it by old age's ravages in a dungeon, or death in battle defending innocents as one of us."

"If we free him, he could come back for Leander," Mother said worriedly, eyeing off Fawkner as she held Father's arm. "He could murder her in her sleep."

"The Guardians' Oath would prevent such an act, is that not right?" Father addressed Aldwyn.

Aldwyn nodded. "He would be bound to the end of his days to serve all life, not only in High-Realm, but the entire world."

Father considered this for a few moments, eyeing Fawkner as the Lorveren man struggled against the soldiers that held him. He then turned to me as I looked at him hopefully, my eyes almost unblinking with my silent pleas.

"It would seem that I would be killing two birds with but one stone," Father observed, a little amused by this thought. "I grant my daughter's request to spare him, yet I still condemn him to a life of service."

"I take it that you have made your choice, my Lord," Tallinn assumed.

Father nodded. "Do as you will."

The three Guardians turned to Fawkner, standing there in front of him. The look of terror in his eyes was clear and the fear seemed as if it ran through his body like a coursing river. He glared at them, shaking his head as Joran stood and turned to watch.

I've only ever heard of this rite the Guardians invoke. I wonder what is involved.

Aldwyn held up his right hand after passing his staff to his left, bowing his head to Fawkner, then meeting his gaze once again.

"Fawkner of Lorveren," he spoke clearly, "I hereby enact the duties I possess as a Master Guardian and I invoke the Rite of Recruitment. You have been chosen to become a Guardian. Do you accept?"

"I do not see that I had any choice," Fawkner replied coldly, tensing against the soldiers' grips.

"Then I conscript you as a potential," Aldwyn said solemnly, a strange power filling the air as if a spell were cast. "Until your Initiation you will serve as a Guardian Potential and are now bound by the same oaths we are. You are our charge until you are initiated into the Order."

"Release him," Father stated, seeing Fawkner's defeated stance.

The soldiers released the man and stepped back as he looked to the Guardians dejectedly. I was relieved, glad the man was given his second chance.

Aldwyn placed a welcoming hand on his shoulder, smiled and said: "Welcome, Brother."

Fawkner nodded coldly then looked to me. He strode forward, sweeping his cloak behind him with one hand then dropped to his knee. He bowed his head to me and kept his eyes to the floor. I looked around uneasily, then focused on his scarred and bearded face.

"I solemnly swear my loyalty, Princess Leander," he looked up at me. "For I am now bound as any Guardian and will bring you no harm."

"And you have information about the man that was your employer," Father assumed, drawing Fawkner's reluctant gaze to him. "You will tell us everything."

"As you wish, my Lord," Fawkner said coldly.

Aldwyn directed Carden to stay with me as he and Tallinn moved to follow my father.

"Watch after her, Carden," he instructed. "We have other concerns here and her safety is more than paramount."

"I will," Carden nodded, turning to me, his arms at his sides, his cloak pulled around him.

I flashed him a small smile. There was something about this man that kept drawing me to him.

"Ser Mithras," Father called, catching my attention again. "You will join us."

"As you wish, my Lord," Mithras smiled at me, then moved past my shoulder to follow my father.

Fawkner stood, regarding me with an icy stare. I swallowed hard, nervous as I looked up at him, his eyes cold and severe.

He smirked ironically and shook his head. "It is a strange gift you have given me, girl. A strange gift indeed."

He turned and strode away, leaving me standing there to watch him depart. I felt a new despondency, having thought that I had done the right thing to help this man. Now all I could think was that I had condemned him.

Perhaps it would have been better to let him suffer his fate as he had wanted to.

---

* * * * *

Several days passed in Arvon as preparations were made for the Festival of Light, the town full of activity. This was a time when all of High-Realm celebrated the day when the Age of Shadows was brought to an end, the time when the darkness receded into Gorth'lak and High-Realm was freed.

The castle was no different, filled with activity as garlands were hung, offerings were placed in thanks to the gods and the torches used for the festival were lit upon the battlements. The servants sang happily as they worked, not a care in the world as they stood as equals with the knights and nobles, the one time of the year except for Beltane when no one stood above anyone else.

The sun was setting on the first night of the festival, a seven-day celebration to commemorate High-Realm's liberation from the Shadow Lords, my recognition of that name that I heard at Averet now clear and leaving me uneasy. Bright lights shone as people from all over Aldegaad and other parts of High-Realm made the yearly pilgrimage to stand in the ancestral home of the Great Heroine herself; my ancestor.

I stood on the balcony of my bedroom, looking down over the river, the mountains and what little I could see of Arvon. Music was rising from the town square as bards told the Ballad of the Great Heroine, a song I had heard a thousand times in my childhood.

I'm so glad we're free of the tyrannies of the past, but really, I just want this festival over. I am so tired of having to make an appearance as my ancestor's living likeness. Why must I do this every year?

I looked down at my hands glumly, the wind catching the folds of my flowing dark blue and white dress, its silver and mauve details shimmering as the light hit it. My long brown hair caught behind my bare shoulders, flowing in the breeze as I let out a dejected sigh.

Every year it's the same thing, I thought to myself, shaking my head. *Every year we hold this ball and every year people tell me how like her I am.*

I looked up, running my hand over one of the twin braids flowing from above my ears to meet at the back of my head to hang down as a single braid holding firm amidst the free strands.

I don't want to do this. Not after what I just went through. I want to go into the town and see the people as they celebrate. That's the part of this that I love.

I regarded Tallinn's presence with disdain, resenting the ever-watchful Guardians for standing over me and increasing my security. I had been more or less locked in my rooms for the past week, the Guardians taking turns watching over me as my parents came and went. Even walking in the castle grounds now meant that I had a force of guards surrounding me and at least one Guardian at my back at all times. I felt stifled and I needed my freedom.

What point is there in being home again if I am still a prisoner?

The door to the room opened and Cara entered with Mithras beside her. I looked over my shoulder at them, my blue eyes betraying my feelings as they approached.

"Your Highness," Cara bowed her head, carrying a small box that I knew too well, "your mother bade me to tell you that it is time for the ball."

"I figured as much," I muttered, turning my gaze to the wind once again, one hand knuckling the rail softly.

Cara held the box up. "Princess, your circlet."

I nodded, turning and walking into the room to sit down at the vanity mirror. I remained silent as Cara crossed to me, setting the box down and beginning to apply faint mauve eye shadow to my eyelids.

"There are some three hundred guests out there, your Highness," Mithras told me in his most official tone, looking very honourable in his silver knight's armour and blue cloak, his short, greying hair combed neatly. "Many have come to pay tribute."

"I don't ask for tribute," I said sourly, my stomach turning at the very thought.

Mithras nodded. "I know, Leander, but this is the tradition of the festival. All those of your bloodline are honoured as the descendants of the Great Heroine..."

"I would be so very happy," I said coldly, glaring at my reflection, "to spend just one day and night without hearing about the Great Heroine and how much like her I am. Can I not have my own identity just for once?"

Mithras nodded slowly as Tallinn moved in closer, her black and silver cloak swaying with her movements, her blonde hair hanging freely, but neatly around her shoulders with only a clasp to hold it back.

"I understand your feelings on that subject, Princess," Mithras said gently.

"I don't see how you could," I murmured glumly, eyes on the mirror again. "You don't have the expectations on you that my name has put on me," I sighed. "I mean, even my middle name is hers. If my name is hers and my appearance is hers, then who am I?"

"You are Leander," Mithras told me gently, drawing my gaze as Cara finished and moved to open the small box she had brought. "And you are a truly beautiful and talented young woman, no matter the name you bear."

I looked back at the mirror, my pretty, oval shaped face looking even more beautiful with all of the adornments of make-up that I now wore. I never really liked being made up like this, but I knew it was a requirement of being an Aldrich daughter and an Aldegaadian Princess.

Cara set the silver circlet on my head, allowing it to sit with its coiling designs over my forehead, a single sapphire the crown jewel above my brow. It wasn't heavy, but it felt unnatural in some ways, its touch obvious to my senses. I suppressed a sigh at my reflection.

"When my ancestor was my age she had already fought and won a war," I reflected on my family history as well as my own. "What has my great adventure been? Being kidnapped by mercenaries and spending two weeks terrified that I was going to be violated and killed. Some adventure."

"Yet, here you are," Mithras told me gently.

I shook my head at my reflection. "*She* would never have been kidnapped. My ancestor was too brave for that. I've been trained in swordsmanship and archery since I was eight winters old, and all I could do when faced with danger was cry like a child."

"With respects, your Highness," Tallinn interjected from the corner she stood in, "you were tied up and at the mercy of your captors."

"Then I should have fought harder to free myself," I groaned, hating myself for my lack of action. "I am not worthy of this name, despite my parents' ambitions for me. I could never be like her."

Mithras got down on one knee, drawing my attention. He held my hands as I rested them on my knees, staring into my eyes, his expression more like that of a father than a soldier guarding my home.

"You are *not* your ancestor," he told me softly, comfortingly. "You are you, the girl that I taught for the last ten years to carry a sword, and the young woman that I have watched grow up since she was an infant. You are named Leander, but you are your own Leander, not hers."

I sighed and nodded as he reached up, touching one hand to my cheek.

"Do not be so hard on yourself, child," he advised me, smiling. "You are destined for your own life, not your ancestor's. Do not try to compete with a woman who has long since passed into Azmerath's Kingdom of Death. Make your own legend, not the legend others seek for you."

I nodded, comforted. "You're right, Mithras. I am me, not her. Only our names and blood are the same."

"No, you are completely new," Mithras smiled broader, standing up and looking down at me, his eyes drifting to the other box on the table. "Should you not be wearing this?"

I frowned at him then turned my eyes to the small box, recognising it as the one Uncle Aric had given me.

"The pendant," I realised, opening the box and withdrawing the silver chained necklace. "I completely forgot about it."

"You should wear it and never take it off, Leander," Mithras told me, looking down at the small silver pendant. "It is said that this will protect its wearer."

"Uncle Aric said that when he gave it to me," I recalled, taking it and fastening the chain about my neck.

I let the silver pendant hang gracefully past my collar bones, resting just before my modest cleavage. It seemed to gleam when I touched it with my right hand, my eyes focusing on the purple jewel at its heart. Again, the light seemed to dance through the gem as though it were coming from within the stone rather than the lamps in the room.

There was a knock at the door and my father stepped in, smiling as I looked up.

"Oh, my dear girl," he beamed proudly. "You seem to grow more and more beautiful with every passing moment."

I blushed at his comments. "Father..."

Cara bowed and left the room as I stood up, my long, blue, wide sleeves hanging gracefully from my white clad wrists, my gown trailing on the floor, my shoulders left bare. Father took in every one of my features, studying me intently.

"We must go down to the Great Hall," he told me softly. "All of our guests have arrived. Are you ready?"

I smiled at Mithras, then nodded to my father: "As I'll ever be."

We left the room, joining up with Mother and four royal honour guards at the great staircase. Mother smiled brightly as she saw me, dressed in a royal blue gown with golden trimmings, her hair braided and pulled into two neat coils at the back of her head. She wore the circlet of a Duchess just as Father wore a small gold crown, a minor cousin of Uncle Aric's kingly crown. He wore his ceremonial armour and his long blue and gold cloak.

"You look beautiful, Leander, dear," Mother prided me warmly.

"Thank you, Mother," I smiled as Mithras placed my own blue and gold cloak over my bared shoulders.

We turned and made our way down the stairs in the traditional manor: Father and Mother side by side, her hand resting on top of his as I followed behind them, Mithras at my back as the four honour guards flanked us. This time, though, I walked alone where I had normally walked with Aislinn, my sister most likely enduring her first Festival of Light in Balganis at that same moment. I started to miss her again.

The doors to the Great Hall opened and a herald spoke. "His Lordship, Prince Ewan Garret Aldrich the Third, her Ladyship, Duchess Caralyn Elaina Aldrich, and their daughter, Princess Leander Idona Aldrich the Second," the man called proudly from where he stood.

I cringed at the sound of my full name, hating them calling me *"the Second"*.

It's just yet another reminder that I am the descendant of the Great Heroine. How I wish they would leave that part off my name.

I crushed my annoyance down and forced myself to endure it, following Mother and Father with the poise and decorum that I had been taught to hold.

As we entered the cavernous great hall, the guests – mostly nobles and lords of our district with a few esteemed guests and the commoners from Arvon – bowed their heads respectfully. They stared with proud expressions at us, particularly locking their gazes on me. I shuddered again, managing somehow to hide it.

I wish they wouldn't stare at me like this. It makes me so uncomfortable.

My eyes found Carden, Aldwyn, Joran and Fawkner easily, my smile brightening at the sight of them and becoming real, not played up as it normally was on such occasions.

Fawkner was dressed in his original clothes, though he had been given a black and silver coat under a black cloak with furs across the shoulders, the common style of Lorveren's people. He carried his sword at his hip proudly, looking more like a Guardian even though he did not possess the cloak, clothing or bracers that Aldwyn, Carden and Tallinn wore.

As for Joran, the giant had been given tailor made clothes for the occasion coloured in gold, reds and browns. His long black hair was tied back in a thick plait, a new and strange mark running the entire length of the left side of his face; a golden tattoo of Storvari origins. I imagined that it must have hurt since it looked to be made of real gold.

Father and Mother led the way to the end of the Great Hall, passing by the Sewards among many other Lords and Ladies I knew. I followed close behind them, noting Tallinn joining the other Guardians out of the corner of my eye.

Three thrones stood on the raised dais waiting for us; the central one slightly taller for the Lord of Arvon, on his right the throne of his wife, and on his left the throne of his daughter. Seeing these thrones without the fourth that belonged there dismayed me and it became all the more real to me that my sister wasn't with us.

We took our places, turning to the guests crowding the room's space and tables, but did not sit as a hush fell. The honour guards took their positions behind us, spaced evenly between our thrones.

"With this night," Father spoke clearly, his cloak hanging around him elegantly, "we begin the Festival of Light, the time when we honour the Divine Seven, but more importantly, the moment when all of High-Realm was united and freed from darkness. This festival is the one time a year when all the peoples of High-Realm once again stand united, and all squabbles are forgotten," he held out his hands to the crowd: "We give thanks to the gods for sending the Great Heroine to save our world so many centuries ago, and we thank our ancestors for the roads they have built to bring us all to these days. And we remember the Eldest Ones, those who came before us, though we now no longer see nor hear much of their kind in our world. May their winged souls and their brightly burning hearts stand as the honoured jewels of the Creator, Ankorect, forevermore, just as our ancestors now watch us from the stars above," he looked around and smiled. "I now declare this the start of the Festival of Light."

A great cheer went up as the people rejoiced.

"A moment if you please," Father called again as the people started to celebrate, their cheers silencing as they turned to look at him. "I would like to make a special note this year," he gestured towards the Guardians and Joran. "We have with us tonight the men and the woman who saved my daughter recently, the Guardians from the Citadel of Dartaren. I make special welcome to these, my honoured guests, and hope the Gods and Goddesses will bestow their blessings upon them for their valiant deeds and their chivalrous hearts."

Again, the people cheered, the Guardians bowing their heads in respectful thanks. Fawkner quickly followed their lead, looking a little lost in the movements. Joran simply remained silent as they bowed.

As food was served, the three of us took our seats. I slipped my cloak back to reveal my shoulders, too warm in the well heated room with its many fireplaces. It was at this time that many pilgrims brought their tributes to present to our family. It was one of the parts of the festival that made me most uncomfortable, but I recognised its significance.

Human Lords and Ladies approached with their servants, bringing worldly goods to grant to us as well as gold and silver. They took their turns, smiling brightly just to be there before the descendants of the Great Heroine. I hated it.

I knew that we wouldn't keep most of the riches we were brought, of which I was glad. It was the one thing out of this festival that made me truly proud of my family's heritage, knowing that my ancestor's tradition of giving offerings of wealth to people in need had lived on.

There came Elves from the surrounding lands of Aldegaad, offering woven wreaths and perfumes of the forest along with pelts taken from the most dangerous, yet beautiful creatures. Their beauty as a people had always fascinated me, the Elves a curiously tremulous race possessed of great emotions of both love and violence. I wanted to learn so much of them, but this was the only contact I had ever had with their people.

Dwarven emissaries came from the Dwarf City of Hecturn in the Nartarn'lath Mountains. They brought chests full of precious jewels of all kinds; diamonds, amethysts, emeralds, rubies, opals, sapphires, topazes and many spectacular others. They also brought valuable metals forged from the stone as well as weapons and armour that had been specially made for the Aldrich Royals as tribute.

Mages came with runes, spells, potions and trinkets of magical worth to offer. They gave blessings to us and wished us long lives full of happiness and love. They performed magical displays as offerings as well, not only entertaining our family before them, but also the onlookers spread throughout the Great Hall.

Warriors and hunters, poets and artisans, bards and storytellers, they all came to pay tribute in whatever way they could; with a newly skinned pelt, a beautifully crafted tapestry, or a tale of grand adventure. The stories were the highlight for me, their tributes meaning more than the worldly goods my family was offered.

Then there were the common people who came simply to wish us well and to sit and talk with us. Many drew their attention to me, my name and my so-called beauty of great interest to them. I beared it and smiled, trying to keep up the illusion as I was expected to.

I smiled at children and spoke to them kindly, granted the elderly and enfeebled my touch, while many a young man asked for a kiss from me. I pecked them on the cheek, that in itself enough for them. I was used to all of this, but I grew tired of some of it, though the smiling children were always a welcome sight.

As we sat amidst the activity, an old man approached. He carried a tall, crooked oaken staff with a crystal set into the twisted root-like gathering at its top, a long white beard covering his aging face. He had long white hair and a wide brimmed pointed hat pulled over his eyes. He was dressed in green and brown robes, a grey cloak pulled across his frail looking back, dragging along behind him as he moved with the clicking of his staff. He carried an oval shaped object wrapped in a greyish blue cloth of Elvish silk, his gnarled hand clinging to it tightly and carefully as though he feared to drop it.

He moved forward, bowing his head to my parents respectfully.

"My Lord and Lady, I offer my humble thanks to be granted access to your beautiful home here in Arvon," the old man told them gratefully. "It is a true honour to stand within the ancestral home of your great bloodline."

"And you are well received, my friend," Father smiled warmly at the old man, familiarity on his face.

"Princess," the old man said, turning his hazel eyes to me kindly, "I bring you a gift."

I raised an eyebrow at this, my hands resting on the arms of my throne uneasily. *He brings something for me alone? So strange.*

At my father's bidding, I stood from my throne as the old man looked up at me from beneath his hat. He knelt down to me then bowed his head. I frowned and dropped to my knees before him, ignoring my mother's stare as I just focused on the visitor.

"Your Highness," the old man looked to me, surprised by my action, "you should not be on your knees before a lowly old man."

"I am no different to you," I told him gently, meeting his gaze. "We shall kneel together, or we will stand together. I won't have you kneel before me if I won't kneel before you. Besides, I'm younger, so getting up is easier for me than it must surely be for you."

The man smiled and chuckled, his eyes twinkling brightly. He observed me, watching my movements, studying the facets of my face as though he were viewing a portrait of a long passed loved one. That seemed strange to me, but I pushed it from my mind as I did my strange sense of familiarity towards him, just watching the old man as he stared at me.

"Are you alright, sir?" I asked, wondering what it was he was seeing in me.

"Oh? Sir?" he smiled at me, impressed. "A princess calls *me* sir?"

"As I said, I'm no different from you," I tilted my head at him curiously. "Have we met? I feel like I know you."

"Perhaps from another life, my dear girl," the old man responded softly, still smiling. "You simply remind me of a young woman I once knew."

I nodded solemnly. "I have been told that my whole life."

"Well, perhaps this will entice your interest," the old man took the bundled object from under his arm and settled it on the floor before me.

"What is it?" I asked curiously, looking from the object to the man again.

"A rarity not seen in High-Realm by human eyes in centuries," the kindly man told me and nodded to it. "I thought that it was appropriate for you to take it, my dear girl. I could think of no one better to have this."

Curiously, but cautiously, I unwrapped the object, my slender hands moving slowly across the folds of silk. I pulled the final fold back and stared in astonishment at the object before me.

The entire room was staring, the Guardians' attention on what I now held. Mithras was still standing close by, his dark eyes locked on me and the strange gift, moving forward slightly as if to get a closer look.

Within the silk there lay a beautiful stone that was some forty centimetres long and twenty-five centimetres wide. It was an oval shape, perfectly smooth with the strangest lines and designs running through it, seemingly naturally formed, not manmade. It was a deep mauve colour and looked to be made of thick amethyst, tints of blue, purple and silver running through it and appearing to move as it was disturbed.

I picked it up carefully, holding it in my hands. It was fairly heavy and strange to the touch. It seemed warm, yet it felt cool on my palms. It shimmered as though a trillion diamonds were laced through the stone it was comprised of, a single perfect piece without a scratch on it.

I stared at it in astonishment, completely drawn in by this amazing stone. *It's so beautiful. I've never seen anything like it...*

"You like it, I see," the old man observed as I studied the stone carefully.

"It's the most beautiful thing I have ever seen," I said, turning it over in my hands, then looking to him. "What is it?"

The old man tapped a finger on the smooth surface of the object, meeting my eyes. "This, my girl, is a Dragon Stone."

"A Dragon Stone?" I was quietly excited.

The old man nodded: "Yes. It is a rare thing to find. It has always been believed that when one comes to the world that it is a gift from the Eldest Ones. It is often found by one who never keeps it but is meant to give it to one that it is destined to find."

"What do you mean?" I looked from the stone to him again, his words so strange to me.

The old man smiled: "It chose you, child. And while that seems like a frightening thought in these times, it will not soon enough. She knows what she wants."

I was suddenly very confused by all of this. I looked at the stone, then at the old man again. I couldn't understand anything that he was saying, like he had lost all sense suddenly.

What does he mean "it chose me?" How does that work? Am I the "she" he's talking about?

"I'm sorry," I turned to him again. "I have no idea what you're talking about."

"It is my fault, dear girl," the old man told me gently, waving a hand vaguely. "I have lived many years and I sometimes speak in riddles. But, my point is that only you were the right choice to be the one to take this stone."

"How could you give me something so rare?" I asked, stunned by his generosity. "Its value would be of better use to you, wouldn't it?"

"This stone's worth is not monetary," he told me calmly, but sternly, still very friendly. "It is of greater personal value than anything else. A Dragon Stone fits with its owner, and this one fits perfectly with you. No one else can ever possess *this* stone. It is yours and yours alone, Princess."

I nodded, giving him a gentle smile. "Thank you."

"Never let it go, dear girl," he told me, "for while you carry it with you, you will never be friendless or alone. Even in the darkest of times in your life this stone will light your world with comfort, safety and love."

He pressed a hand to my cheek, smiling as I looked to him from the stone once more.

"And that is something a beautiful young girl with a heart so pure like you deserves more than anything else," he told me kindly.

I nodded and smiled at him again gratefully. I leaned forward and kissed him on the cheek, then with the stone in my arm and the silk cloth in my hand, I helped him to his feet.

"Thank you for this, sir," I said gratefully. "It is more than I deserve."

"Nonsense," he responded. "It is exactly right for you," he winked at me and bowed to my parents before turning to me again. "Take care," he smiled with a strangely familial air to his presence suddenly, "my dear Leander."

His use of my name, not my title, surprised me and left me speechless as he turned from me to walk away.

I watched the old man pass through the Great Hall, reaching the main doors. He looked to me once more, nodded, then disappeared into the night as the celebrations continued around us, leaving me utterly entranced and bewildered.

Chapter Eight
The Festival of Light

I watched the grand ball play out, remaining silent and smiling, though I was utterly bored. I found myself continuously looking to the Dragon Stone that lay near me, resting in a nest made of the blue silken cloth it had been brought in, the strange crystal the only thing interesting me at that moment.

I was fascinated by the colours that ran through it, entranced by the seemingly internal glow that came from the stone's mauve form. The heat that emanated from the cool surface was also strange to me, but just as interesting. I even wondered about the old man who had given it to me.

Breaking my gaze away from the stone, I looked for my parents in the crowd. They were speaking with Lord and Lady Seward, Lord Kalgan of Aldgate, Lord and Lady Howe of Westport, and Lady Garret of Arten, the most well-known of the Arvon Aldrich Family acquaintances.

Mother looked so comfortable, clearly in her element as a lady of social grace, talking with the nobles about various things. Father stood with his hands clasped behind his back at her side, smiling at them and listening intently, but I could see the boredom in his eyes. His years as Prince of the Realm served him well in hiding it, however.

Sighing, I swept my gaze across the room, seeking out the Guardians.

It wasn't hard to find Fawkner, who never seemed to go far from Joran, the Storvari standing out above all others in the room. I could see the exact same boredom in Fawkner's eyes that I felt myself. He clearly had no idea what to do with himself, avoiding anyone other than Joran.

The giant remained silent, a watchful centurion presiding over the ball, seemingly guarding the people with as much dedication as any Aldegaadian Knight, if not more. His gaze occasionally swept to where I sat, and it was clear that he was watching over me.

He nodded to me as he saw me looking at him, his violet eyes clear and calm. I smiled faintly and nodded as Fawkner noticed my gaze. He started to speak to Joran, his lips saying "she's just as bored as I am" from what I could see. This afforded me some small amusement, drawing a broader smile over my face.

Again, I cast my sights through the crowd, finding Aldwyn, who was standing at one end of the hall talking to several mages. He seemed content with his brothers and sisters in magic, all of them carrying staffs of varying designs and woods.

Tallinn stood on the wide steps leading up from the Great Hall and into the main corridors, her black and silver cloak hanging around her comfortably. She carried her sword at her left hip, her eyes surveying the room protectively, her seriousness and dedication astounding. Still, I could see a genuine softness about this golden haired battle maiden. She was a woman of great ferocity and strength, yet there was a caring nature in her as well.

Mithras was now standing with my parents, speaking after being invited by Father to join their discussion at the edge of the dancing couples. He didn't seem uncomfortable in any way at all, his veteran service as an Aldegaadian Knight having lent him to such social niceties as these.

He took it in his stride, and I remembered when I was fifteen how he had told me that socialising could be like doing battle: "Take it one foe at a time and don't rush. You'll succeed eventually." It seemed that his advice was the kind that he himself practiced, both on the field of battle and in the presence of nobility.

I looked for Carden then, wondering where he had gone. It took a few moments, but I found him, the young Guardian walking slowly along the edges of the dance floor, moving towards Fawkner and Joran casually. As he walked, he turned his green eyes towards the dais and to me. He slowed his pace as I watched him, taking in the very sight of me, almost savouring it. There was a gleam in his eyes and he afforded himself a small smile at me.

I smiled back, my greyish blue eyes studying his long, dark hair, his fair skin tone – though it was darker than mine – his green eyes, his masculine, athletic shape and his bright smile. He was unbelievably handsome. I felt a strange sense of connection to him, nothing that I understood, just a calm and safety while he was near me. I had never felt so comfortable in front of a man near my age before.

"My Lady," a voice called to me, drawing my gaze from Carden and to the figure before me.

I had to bite my bottom lip to stop myself from groaning as I saw Tibain Seward standing before me, dressed in his finest clothes and cloak, his arrogant face smirking up at me. He was holding out his hand to me expectantly and I glanced to see my mother watching us like a hawk with Angora Seward.

Why does she keep sending this fool to me? Why?

"Lord Tibain," I forced myself to smile and be sociable towards him. "How... *nice* to see you again so soon," I practically choked on the word "*nice*".

"It has been a month since our last meeting, my beautiful Princess," Tibain told me, a vain attempt to flatter me. "How you grow more and more beautiful with every passing day, even after your little misadventure."

"Uh... thank you," I responded, unsettled.

Tibain pushed on, not noticing my discomfort or disinterest. "May I have the honour of a dance with the woman my heart so desires?"

"Of course," I smiled to myself wryly and looked past him, pretending to search the crowd. "But I don't see her anywhere. Have I met her before?"

Tibain laughed falsely, over exaggerating his mirth at my sarcasm: "Your humour matures as readily as you yourself, my Lady. *You* are the one I desire."

"I... see," I said, frustrated that I hadn't gotten under his skin.

I suppose he's either too stupid or too infatuated with me to be insulted. Damn...

"Now," Tibain insisted with his hand, "that dance, Princess."

I surrendered: "I suppose."

I let Tibain take my hand, though the word *"let"* was a little bit of an overstatement in my mind. I was more taken roughly by the arrogant noble and led down to the dance floor, his overexcitement almost becoming violence as he half dragged me from my seat.

He pulled me into his arms, putting my arm around his shoulder and taking my right hand in his left. He began dancing with me to the soft waltz music that the bards were playing, holding my waist tightly, almost as though he intended never to let me go.

I looked to my left at Carden, Fawkner and Joran. Carden had a very stern expression as he watched the scene before him. Then I caught a new hint of something in his green eyes.

Is that... jealousy? I frowned. *Is Carden jealous of Tibain dancing with me?*

I was stunned by this, stunned that he would be so possessive of me if this was the case. Or perhaps it was simply that he could see how uncomfortable Tibain was making me.

Even with my new Storvari bodyguard and the two Guardians watching me I didn't feel all that comforted while Tibain held me. His arrogance was like a strong odour that made me want to wretch and cough until I was away from it. However, I knew that my mother would never forgive me for making a scene at an event such as this, and I wouldn't risk the honour of my family in such a way. No matter how much I hated this pathetic ass.

I glanced over my shoulder at my parents, my mother talking to Angora Seward and pointing to Tibain and I. The two women were talking excitedly as they saw us dancing, expectations of marriage clearly in their minds once again.

I rolled my eyes, looking to my father.

Father's own blue gaze met mine and I was able to covertly mouth the words "help me" to him. He chuckled at me, shaking his head knowingly, amused by my dislike of Tibain. Still, he could do no more than I could while the festival was in effect.

Tibain drew my face to his, smiling down at me with false gentleness.

"You truly are the fairest of all the maidens in Aldegaad, if not High-Realm itself, Princess," he told me, his tone a futile attempt to mix romance with his arrogance. "I feel that the Gods have blessed your family to have a daughter as beautiful as you."

"Thank you, Tibain," I said softly, trying to maintain my false interest, but struggling.

He lowered his hand to my stomach, touching the fabric of my dress and smiling at me. I felt suddenly very worried and even more uncomfortable with this touch. I flicked my gaze to his hand as we slowed our dance almost to a complete halt and I began to fear the look in his eyes. I gulped hard, trying not to tremble.

"I look forward to seeing the sons you will bear me," he told me smarmily, grinning. "With my looks and skills and your beauty we will have truly god-like progeny."

"Talking about children," I spoke uneasily, a strange shaking in my voice, "is far too premature, don't you think?"

"Why, when I know you will be mine?" he pulled me closer to him.

I pressed my hands to his chest to try and keep myself some distance from his face. I was actually beginning to feel afraid of him and what he was thinking.

"I am not ready for anything like that," I insisted nervously. "I only reached my eighteenth name day a little over a month ago. I'm still too young."

"I have always been attracted to younger women," he told me with a disgusting smirk, my breathing getting harder in panic. "And you are the one I would spend my life with."

"Until I grow too old for you, and you start taking mistresses behind my back," I nodded sarcastically, struggling against him. "Yes, that sounds like a great life..."

"You *will* be mine, Princess," he told me firmly, pulling me closer as I fought a little harder. "And I *will* have the honour of taking your maidenhood and making you a true woman."

"Ugh!" I cried out, staring at him in horror. "You're disgusting!"

He laughed. "You jest once more, Princess. How humorous you are."

"No! That's out of line!" I pushed against him angrily to no avail. "I would never marry you, Tibain! *Never*!"

Then he began to get angry: "You will, girl! You are *mine*!"

"Excuse me," a voice said courteously as I struggled futilely to free myself from Tibain's grasp.

I looked past Tibain as he turned to glance over his shoulder, my relief to see Carden stronger than any anger I had felt with the noble's relentless groping. I let a smile of relief show as I eased my struggles, my heart fluttering at the sight of the Guardian. How chivalrous he was.

"The Princess seems uncomfortable with the way you hold her and the words you speak, friend," Carden said calmly, his left hand resting on the pommel of his sword at his hip. "Perhaps you could let her go now."

"What business is it of yours, whelp?!" Tibain snapped at Carden. "Are you another suitor for my intended?! Well, you're too late, she's marrying me!"

"I am not!" I retorted, glaring at Tibain furiously as he squeezed me closer to him. "Let me go!"

"No, I am not a suitor seeking the Princess' hand," Carden answered, maintaining his calm.

"Then piss off!" Tibain turned to me, grinning as I struggled against him.

I stared at him in utter shock. His vulgarity surprised me for a moment, then I remembered that this was the man who threw his desires for me around blatantly and without poetry.

"I am not her suitor," Carden went on, watching Tibain readily as I saw Tallinn begin to move from her position towards us, gesturing for Fawkner to follow her. "I am a Guardian, sworn to protect her."

Tibain froze, looking to him. "A Guardian? You? Please..."

"I am," Carden said, pulling a medallion bearing the Guardians' Seal from around his neck and showing it to the arrogant noble. "Release her now... *my Lord*," he virtually snarled the last part.

Tibain nodded, letting me go. I thrust myself three steps back and glared at him. A few onlookers were murmuring at the scene that was developing, but I didn't care. His rudeness had offended me beyond caring anymore. Across the room, Tallinn had paused and was watching carefully as Aldwyn was now also directing his gaze towards the situation.

"My apologies, Guardian," Tibain nodded respectfully to Carden, though with contempt. "I will take my leave of you."

"I am not the one you owe an apology to, my Lord," Carden advised him as he hid the medallion again.

Tibain nodded and turned to me. He went to open his mouth, but I slapped him before he could speak, glaring furiously up at him.

"Don't you *ever* touch me again," I seethed, my eyes blazing.

Looking like a simpering dog that had just been punished for being disobedient, Tibain turned and strode away, obnoxiously shoving several people aside and storming towards his entourage. Across from us, Mother looked very disappointed as she watched me, shaking her head disapprovingly, though I wasn't sure it was me she felt that way with.

I let out a sigh of relief, feeling a sense of satisfaction at finally pushing that despicable, filthy, lecherous excuse for a man away from me.

"Thank you, Carden," I turned to the young man who had stepped in on my behalf.

"It was my duty, your Highness," he told me respectfully, bowing his head and turning to go.

I put a hand to his arm, stopping him and drawing his eyes back to me.

"Would you... would you dance with me?" I asked softly, a small smile on my face.

"I shouldn't," Carden looked around uneasily. "I'm not a noble."

"You don't have to be to dance with me," I told him with a half shrug. "I'm a princess, remember? Technically, I can do whatever I want, and that means I can dance with whoever I choose. Especially tonight."

Carden smiled and nodded. "It would be my greatest honour, Princess."

He took me in his arms, and I placed my hands on his shoulders as we began to dance slowly to the peaceful, beautiful string music the bards were playing.

"And that's another thing we have to work on," I said thoughtfully, looking up at him.

"What's that, your Highness?" he asked me, our faces so close.

I looked up into his eyes, lost for a few moments in their deep, green pools. I could feel them staring into mine and I felt that same strange curiosity about him that I'd had before, my heart skipping a few beats.

"The way you refer to me," I said softly, almost shyly.

"I don't refer to you correctly, Princess?" he frowned.

"No, you refer to my title fine," I answered, meeting his gaze again. "But I don't want you to refer to me by that."

"Then how?" he asked.

"Use my name," I responded gently. "Call me Leander. If not in public, then at least in private. Please?"

Carden nodded and smiled softly. "As you wish... Leander."

A smile spread over my lips as I rested my head on his shoulder, feeling unusually comfortable in his embrace. It was a kind of safety and familiarity that I had never felt with anyone before, not even my parents, sister or Mithras. I felt truly safe with him, as if I was always meant to be protected in his arms, like this was destined.

After a while I looked up at him again, our eyes meeting, my lips parted slightly as though I had thought to say something, but the words had escaped me. I could see him watching me, his eyes surveying every aspect of my features, studying my face. It was almost as though he were beholding a treasure of greater worth than gold or silver, an impression that made me feel strangely special for once.

"Carden..." I murmured, meeting his gaze.

"Yes, Leander?" he asked me gently.

I looked at my hands on his chest, then glanced back at him and said: "Can we go outside? I need some fresh air."

He nodded, and we left the dance floor, heading for the doors.

Gratefully, I took my leave. With Carden beside me I doubted that my parents would have an issue with me taking a break from the festivities, at least for a little while.

With my blue and gold cloak draped over my shoulders, I walked with Carden through the outer corridors of the castle, passing above the grounds, the main courtyard alight with torches. Guards passed us by quietly as we walked, making their way through the castle on their patrols.

I led Carden on a slow and mostly quiet walk, our breath materialising as vapour in front of our faces in the cold night air, the breeze catching at us through the stone arches. We moved quietly past the training yards, the archery targets still set up in their places, the dummies and the training course now packed away and dismantled. It all looked very empty, only the slowly meandering figures on the walls indicating any life as the guards watched over the castle's peaceful structures.

We turned down another passage and a set of stairs towards a circular section of the castle, perched high above the river below. Within this enclosed area above the gardens was a circular chamber lined with marble columns and presided over by the statues of helmeted and cloaked knights, their swords held aloft.

On one wall there was a mural painted of a demonic black robed figure with bright glowing eyes, shadows engulfing all the land behind it. Before it stood the image of an armoured girl, a sword in her hand, its blade a brilliant bright white meant to depict glowing steel. Behind her was a dragon; a purple, blue and silver creature with its gigantic magenta wings stretched out as it roared with flames erupting from its jaws into the air. The figures were surrounded by soldiers of the old kingdoms of High-Realm behind the girl, and monsters of the Shadow Dominion behind the hooded figure.

To the far left of it there was another mural showing Arvon, a wizard in a broad brimmed hat carrying an infant. And on the far right of the mural, the victory of the girl over the Daemon, the Scourge fleeing as the dragon took to the skies. Next to this there was the same girl standing before Aldegaadian Knights, a slender, light crown of gold encircling her brunette head, the banner of Aldegaad held high behind her.

Last, in the centre of the room surrounded by the columns there stood a monument, which was a single statue. It was the same girl clad in armour and holding her sword high, her long hair flowing over her shoulders, a dragon towering above her with its wings outstretched and its head gazing down on her protectively.

I walked slowly into the memorial chamber, my eyes on the face of the woman the statue depicted. I knew her well, having heard stories of this woman my entire life. There was no castle in Aldegaad that did not have a version of this statue, and it was known that a few other places throughout High-Realm had similar memorials to her.

I paused to the statue's right, my hands by my sides as I looked up at it, respectful of my great ancestor, but also envious in some ways. Again, I imagined the simple life this woman had lived before her rise against the Daemon and longed for such an existence.

Carden looked around the chamber, stepping past me slowly. I could see he knew it well, probably having seen the same statue before in other cities in his travels.

"The Memorial to the Great Heroine of High-Realm," he said reverently. "The one in Nargilith suddenly seems less impressive compared to this one, though perhaps it is just the fact that we stand in the ancestral home of her line."

"Her line... and mine," I said softly, turning away from the statue and moving to view the four murals on the walls.

Carden watched me as I studied each one, my eyes memorising every detail and every face that I saw.

"Do you know this well?" he asked me, standing close by.

"The story of my ancestor?" I looked to him, nodding vaguely while quietly reflecting. "Too well."

I turned my eyes back to it, starting at the first of the murals. I ran my hand over the baby in the wizard's hands, then stepped back, looking up at it.

I recited from memory as I had been taught: "Almost two thousand years ago, there was a child born in the now long destroyed land of Graphtar. The second child of Richard, Graphtar's second last king, she was chosen by fate as the herald of a new age even before she took her first breaths. They named her Leander, meaning "Fairest Grace" in Elvish and "Great Hero" in the tongues of humanity. Her name would forever be known throughout High-Realm even as she uttered her first cries at birth. But there was darkness over all of High-Realm in those days. It was a time of evil known as the Age of Shadows, and the people feared the greatest evil this world had ever known: the Darkest Shadow, a daemon of ancient times. And this daemon reached out with its immense power, sending forth its most deadly servant, the Shadow Lord known as Morod."

I indicated the darker portion of the mural, the hooded figure standing surrounded by monsters, a black sword in his hand as he stood on the bones of the fallen men and women he had slain.

I shuddered at the sight of him: "He was the most powerful of these corrupt sorcerers, so strong that he was able to craft one of the greatest weapons in existence: the Sword of Darkness, a blade forged in the fires of the Mountain of Dread in the wastes of Gorth'lak. And so, he set out with an army to conquer Graphtar. Less than a week since her birth, Morod destroyed almost all of the girl's family in one night, murdering the Graphtarian King and Queen as they protected their daughter. They knew of the prophecy that she would destroy both Morod and his Master, but so did the Darkest Shadow, and it feared this. And so, it ordered Morod to kill the child immediately. But a faithful wizard named Ranzel saved the baby and took her into hiding in the west to the town of Arvon. For thirteen years, Morod ruled Graphtar, seeking both the Princess and her brother who was now the King. On her thirteenth name day, Leander learned of her destiny and was hunted by the agents of Morod and the Daemon, thus beginning four years of war throughout all of High-Realm."

I moved to the next mural, gazing up at the war scenes, my ancestor and the dragon facing the Darkest Shadow and a figure that was most likely Morod as he carried the same black sword, a large black and crimson dragon standing behind him.

"The War of the Shadow was terrible but lasted only a few months. It began with the death of King Alexander and the razing of Graphtar from the face of Therras. With her brother dead, the Princess was now the last of her line and the only one who could face the Darkest Shadow in combat. She fought alongside the men of Ranhart at the battle of Aged Stone Fortress in the south-east, then journeyed to Nargilith in what was once Nargoth. She joined with the people of High-Realm, uniting them, often seen astride a great dragon, but knowing that the Daemon and its general would not come out of their cursed land, she travelled alone into the howling wilds of Gorth'lak. As the Battle of Nargilith raged on against the Dominion forces, the Great Heroine faced her foes atop the Fortress Tower of Aril'manar. It is said that she plunged the Sword of Light into the heart of the Daemon, vanquishing it and shattering the tower to the ground. As for Morod, he was thrown from the pinnacle of the fortress, falling to his death in the wastes below."

I was now standing before the mural depicting the victory, my ancestor's sword plunging into the Daemon's chest as the Dominion were fleeing from the soldiers.

"The Great Heroine of High-Realm led the combined armies of our land against the Dominion, taking advantage of the confusion that the Daemon's death had caused. They drove them into the depths of Gorth'lak and stood victorious, though Nargilith had almost been destroyed. With her standing before them, the people rejoiced, strengthened with their new leader. But she had thoughts of a quiet life in Arvon, marrying a commoner boy who she had known as a child, the one person who had followed her through every battle."

I loved that part of the story. That my ancestor had fallen in love with a commoner was the reason why I was so determined to stay on equal footing with everyone.

I came at last to the final mural, looking up at the woman surrounded by both blue and gold clad knights and black and silver dressed warriors.

"Knowing that the world needed a guiding hand, Leander built a new kingdom along the previously unclaimed western lands, south of the Nartarn'lath Mountains. She named it Aldegaad and ruled as its first Queen. Still, she knew even as she carried her first son that there would be other threats and that the Dominion may return. So, she recreated the legendary order known as the Guardians, having a great citadel built in the mountains as a neutral point in High-Realm. The Guardians would be the defenders of peace, justice and freedom throughout not only High-Realm, but all of Therras, to serve no kingdom, but all kingdoms, to serve no king, but all kings, no single people, but all."

I turned from the murals and went to face the statue, looking up at it solemnly, studying my ancestor's face.

"Queen Leander ruled over Aldegaad fairly for one hundred years, finally dying as a great-grandmother. She was first entombed in Arvon in the crypts beneath the castle that is the home of her bloodline, but too many pilgrims attempted to open the tomb. It is said that a mysterious order of knights came to Arvon, taking her remains and travelling with them high into the mountains. There have never been any clues as to the whereabouts of the Heroine's Tomb, but it is still believed to exist, guarded and protected by that same secret order that remains unknown to the world even today," I sighed, coming at last to the end. "Her great legacy lives on now, not only in the people of Aldegaad, but in the people of all of High-Realm, forever."

Carden nodded, impressed. "You know it well."

I looked to him, a little sadness in my heart. "I have had to know it. It was expected of me when I reached my ninth name day. As her descendant and namesake, I must know her story."

"That's a lot of pressure to place on a child," he said as I took a seat on a cushioned bench opposite the statue.

I shrugged as he came to sit down beside me, feeling the chilled wind blowing through the memorial chamber. I stared up at the face of the statue again, feeling so little and insignificant next to its grandeur and majesty.

"I am expected to be her," I said glumly, staring at the statue resentfully. "My mother, my father, my uncle, all of Aldegaad... They watch me, waiting for me to take her place, to follow in her footsteps," I sighed sadly, shaking my head. "All because I was named after her."

"That's why you wanted to leave the ball," Carden realised, sitting forward, his hands clasped together, elbows on his knees.

I nodded softly, my eyes forward as I folded my arms, my fingers and palms gripping my upper arms and creasing my gown's sleeves.

"It's been the same every year ever since I can remember," I explained quietly. "People flock from all over High-Realm just to see me, to stand at my feet and ask for blessings or offer tributes. It's all part of the yearly pilgrimage to Arvon."

"Why do they do it?"

I looked to him sharply, but not angrily. "Because they think that I'm the new incarnation of her. They see me as a sign that the Gods have reached out to Therras again, and that I am their divine instrument here in the world," I scoffed, then added quietly: "But I'm not."

"You're right," Carden agreed sympathetically, nodding as he watched me. "What you are is a girl like any other, except that your name and heritage have placed you in the public eye."

"The funny thing is that most people don't even know my name or what I look like. Only the ones who come here do," I said quietly.

I looked back to the statue and sighed disdainfully, feeling so disheartened.

"I even look like her. Is nothing actually mine?" I indicated the pendant around my neck. "Even this was once hers. My uncle says that it was the pendant she wore during all her battles, that it protected her with the power of the dragons," I stared forward again, turning the pendant in my fingers as I shook my head contemptuously. "It obviously didn't work for me."

Carden looked at me curiously. "What makes you say that?"

I shrugged, meeting his gaze. "It didn't help me when Fawkner and his men kidnapped me, or when those... those things attacked us in the ruins."

"I can't recall you wearing it when we rescued you," Carden thought about it carefully as he spoke.

I looked at him, then down at the pendant, shocked as I realised what he was saying.

"You're right," I sounded suddenly stunned, even to myself. "I wasn't wearing it when they abducted me. What does that mean?"

He shrugged. "It could mean nothing at all. Then again, it could mean that whatever power your pendant is supposed to hold might be dependent on you wearing it."

I considered this, nodding as I thought that it was a plausible explanation. "That makes sense, actually."

Having said that, I looked back at the statue of my ancestor, then stood and slowly walked away towards the open part of the chamber. I stood there at the barrier, leaning on the stone banister and looking down at the gardens below. The wind picked up my hair, pushing it past my shoulders, the silver circlet holding it all mostly in place, allowing me to stand without my hair flicking over my eyes. I pulled my cloak further around me, the chill seeming to deepen as the night was wearing on.

"If you are so bothered by your likeness to your ancestor and the name you share," Carden spoke as he walked up behind me, "then why do you come here?"

I glanced over my shoulder at him and shrugged gently. "It's strange, but this place always calms me. It always puts my mind at ease after extremely unpleasant things that I have had to deal with."

He joined me at the banister, resting his hands on it and standing with his back to the landscape, facing me. He watched me as I leaned my elbows there, looking out over the view before us, the three moons high in the sky as faded crescents now at the end of their cycle.

"It is beautiful here," he admitted, casting a cursory glance towards the gardens below. "I can understand why you would come here, I suppose."

"Still, you asked," I looked up at him, observing his handsome features in the pale moonlight.

He smiled and nodded. "Perhaps I was lacking an understanding of you, Leander, not this place."

"You're interested in learning more about me?" I raised an eyebrow curiously.

"I am," he slid a little closer, still smiling warmly.

I shrugged and shook my head, gazing at the gardens for a moment.

I turned my gaze back to him, trying so hard to figure him out. "Why are you so interested in me?"

"Why wouldn't I be?"

"I just... I don't understand this more personal level that I have with you over the other Guardians," I shook my head, lost in that thought.

"I thought maybe," Carden said gently, moving down to my level so he could see my eyes, "that you might need a friend."

I was stunned, those words shocking me so deeply. I turned my gaze down to my hands as I pressed them together on the banister, trying to make my lips work.

"What is it?" he asked, noticing the strange reaction of unease I had given him.

I felt a smile tug at my lips. "I've... I've never really had a friend before."

"Really?" he was taken aback by this. "I find that hard to believe."

"Aside from Mithras and my handmaiden, I haven't. At least, not any my own age," I looked at him. "It's not easy for me to make friends of my own."

"How come?" he leaned one elbow on the banister, holding his hands together as he looked at me.

I shrugged as I stared down at the gardens. "I've never really been left by myself. There have always been guards, knights, servants and my father's advisers around me ever since I was born," I glanced to him morosely: "I can be surrounded by people and be completely alone. That's the price of being a princess."

"And here I thought royals and nobles were the most popular people in High-Realm," Carden commented, shaking away his misconceptions with his head.

"Actually, you're absolutely right. We are, but we're also some of the loneliest people in High-Realm too."

"I think I understand," he said softly, kindly. "Though, I don't know this kind of loneliness."

"What kind do you know?" I asked meekly, looking at him from under my dark locks.

"The kind I would prefer not to relive," he answered simply. "My past was not a good one before joining the Order. It is not something I am proud of."

"I feel that I've spoken so much about myself," I said to him, managing a faint smile. "But I know very little, almost nothing, about you."

"There's not much to say," he told me with a slight shrug. "I'm from Gorvenna, I'm twenty-two years of age, I'm a Guardian and I'm from the ancient city of Nargilith."

"You're from the capital?" I was very curious about him now. "What is it like?"

"It's a beautiful city," Carden answered, reminiscing about his home. "Great white marble structures reaching high up the cliffs of a mountain with the city intertwining through the rocks themselves. Golden spires stand tall and great gardens spread through the commons as far as the eye can see. And at the peak sits the White Palace of Nargilith, a magnificent building that I have only once had the honour of stepping inside."

"Why did you leave?" I questioned.

"I was recruited by the Guardians," he answered with a shrug. "Aldwyn and Tallinn found me there and saw my potential."

"Do you ever get to go back?" I asked softly.

He nodded. "I have from time to time, though my duties as a Guardian do keep me busy. Perhaps not as busy as a princess," he added light heartedly, nudging me with his shoulder.

"Uh... I don't know," I smiled, staring at my hands distractedly. "Being a princess isn't all it appears to be. I wander around aimlessly a lot, you know."

"As do I," he grinned, drawing my gaze.

"Travelling doesn't count."

"Does to me."

We laughed softly and fell silent again, just looking out at the gardens. This felt so good to me, just what I had wanted. Having someone to talk to and understand on my own level was good – even if it was just the very beginnings of learning about each other.

"Do you think...?" I started to ask; our faces closer to each other now.

"Princess," a voice called, the two of us turning to look to the entrance of the chamber.

I felt disappointed at having someone interrupt us, just wanting to be left alone with my companion.

Mithras walked in, his cloak swirling around him, his armour clinking and chainmail rattling. He threw a gaze through the columns, then saw Carden and I. He strode towards us, moving swiftly.

"There you are," he looked to me with relief. "Your father sent me to find you."

"Is this about what happened with Tibain?" I asked tiredly. "That was all his fault. He deserved it."

"I dare say he did," Mithras agreed. "However, that is not the reason why I have come for you. The ball will reach its end soon and you must be there to farewell the guests, as tradition dictates."

"Ugh!" I groaned, rolling my eyes. "Tradition."

"Leander," Mithras scolded lightly, smiling faintly at me.

"I'm going, I'm going," I assured him, walking past him, then looking over my shoulder. "Are you coming, Carden?"

"As you command, Princess," Carden responded, turning and following me with ease.

Chapter Nine
The Last of Her Line

We returned to the Great Hall in plenty of time, entering as the ball was coming to its end. I moved back towards the thrones to join my parents as Carden stood at the main stairs beside Tallinn. The guests – noble and commoner alike – gathered around as the evening came to its end. My father stood from his seat as I reached the dais, Mother on his right, both of them wearing their blue and gold royal cloaks again.

"My friends and esteemed guests," Father said clearly as a hush fell. "It has been a night of great celebration and merrymaking. Alas, it must come to its end, though the Festival of Light continues. And with the lighting of the Guiding Light, we signify the beginning of our festivities here in High-Realm, and our continued belief in those who have passed on."

The guests looked to the large, round ceremonial brazier at the far end of the room near the main doors. This was lit every year at this time, a sacred act to remember all the ancestors of all the High-Realmian Peoples. It was always lit at the end of the grand ball held in Arvon, the pinnacle of the celebration and the start of the Festival of Light itself.

"As she has reached her eighteenth name day," Father turned to me, smiling proudly, "my daughter will now be the one to light the torch."

I nodded to my father, then stepped down from the dais, reaching the honour guard who carried the smaller torch. I took it carefully then walked towards the great brazier, pausing before it. I was afraid I would mess this up somehow, certain that I wouldn't be as graceful or as steady handed as I needed to be.

I took in a breath then gently set the flames to the centre of the dish. Immediately, a new flame caught in the brazier and shed a bright glow through the entire room. As I stepped back and gave the torch to a guard the guests applauded and cheered, the festival now truly begun, though the ball was over.

"We alight this flame to remember those who have passed before," Father recited the customary mantra in its spoken way as I moved back to the dais. "We alight this flame to remind us that they always watch over us. We light this flame so that we do not forget the light that exists in the darkest moments. May the Divine Seven and the Ancestors watch over us. May we make them proud and forever remember the times they lived before us, for never shall we forget the time when Darkness gave way to Light."

Now at the end, Father took Mother's hand and led her forward, side-by-side. I followed on behind them as the honour guard once again surrounded us and escorted us from the room. As we passed through the doors of the Great Hall and left the congregation of guests I felt relief flood through me, the yearly ball now over.

As soon as I was free of my parents and permitted to go off on my own, I went straight to my rooms. I undressed and ran a bath, slipping in and relaxing gratefully amidst the warm waters. I soaked my hair, laying my head back and breathing an easy sigh. Here I lingered until the bath water had cooled significantly, then climbed out and released the water into the drains.

I dried myself then dressed in my silken, silvery-mauve nightgown, the thin straps holding the soft, light dress to my smooth white shoulders. I left my hair untied, turning my gaze to the vanity.

The Dragon Stone that I had been given was sitting there. I had almost forgotten it with all the ceremonial activities as well as the other events of the night. Silently, I studied it, running a hand across the purple, violet, blue and silver surface, once again entranced by it.

There was a knock at the door.

I turned swiftly, my gown flowing around my legs as I moved, my hands finding my silken blue robe and pulling it on as the door opened and my father entered.

"There you are, my girl," he smiled warmly. "I wanted to see how you are now."

"I'm fine, Father," I answered with a gentle smile.

"I only ask because of your absence earlier," he pointed out.

I moved to my bed, sitting down on the edge and nodding, my long dark hair falling over my shoulders smoothly. Father moved over to me, pushing aside the curtains hanging from the high bed posts as he looked down at me. He no longer wore his crown or cloak, dressed only in his best clothes now.

"I know what it was about," he deduced easily.

"You do?" I looked up at him, surprised.

"The Sewards' son," he guessed. "He made his intentions known in a less than charming way. Didn't he?"

I nodded as I rubbed my hand along the inside of my smooth white wrist. "He did."

Father sighed, shaking his head and placing one hand on mine with the other arm around me as he sat. He hugged me closely and I lay my head on his shoulder.

"I understand that it can be frustrating for you, Leander," he told me gently. "Having all these potential suitors propositioning you to be their wife; I know it's not what you want."

"It's not," I agreed glumly. "I'm not ready."

Father nodded, looking down at me. "Not all men are animals, my sweet girl. There truly are some kind and honest ones out there in the world."

"Like Carden," I thought aloud.

Father raised an eyebrow at me. "The Guardian lad?"

"I don't mean it like that, Father," I said quickly, blushing. "I mean, that he is a truly honest man, at least as far as I've seen."

"Indeed?" he smirked broader and broader.

I ran my hand past my face, brushing my hair back gently. "He's become my friend."

"He has?" he smiled and hugged me tighter. "I'm happy for you then, daughter. I believe he is a good man."

"We are nothing more than that," I advised him evenly, though it sounded strange in my head.

Why is that? Why do I think that it sounds so strange forme to say that he is my friend only?

"Well, you will find the right man when the time is right," he told me softly, meeting my gaze and gently touching my cheek.

He seemed to be studying my features, looking at me as though he wouldn't see me again.

"What is it, Father?" I frowned at him, a little confused.

"Oh. Nothing," Father replied. "I'm just so proud of you. You are growing up to be a fine young woman."

I smiled bashfully, blushed and turned away. "Thank you, Father."

"I love you, Leander," he told me gently, drawing my gaze again. "I want you to always remember that."

"I know. I love you too," I studied him curiously, half smiling in confusion. "What's gotten into you?"

"I just felt that I had to say it," he told me with a small shrug. "Goodnight, my sweet girl."

"Goodnight, Father," I let him kiss me on the forehead.

Father stood and walked to the door. He closed it over after looking at me one final time, a strange sheen in his eyes. I furrowed my brow at that strangeness, wondering what it was that was vexing him, though I didn't think on it for too long. I was so very tired and just wanted nothing more than to sleep after the events of that very busy day.

Slowly, I blew out all but one of the lamps in the room, closed the window doors onto the balcony then climbed into bed. I nestled into the pillows and pulled the cotton blankets, furs, and the silken sheets over my body, then closed my eyes, gradually beginning to drift into a fitful sleep, resting comfortably and having happy dreams.

* * * * *

Screams broke through my dreams, snapping me out of my blissful sleep, their echoes shattering the peacefulness that had enwrapped me for so few hours. I sat up in bed, half-awake for only a few moments as the echoes of terror and the roar of fighting rocked the very foundations of my soul and carried through the castle halls. I looked around my room, unsettled by the noises. There was shouting from the walls below the keep, swords clanging loudly as fiery light flickered through the windows and across the walls.

Startled, but curious, I threw back the bedclothes and got to my feet, rushing bare foot across the carpeted stone floor. I pushed open the window doors, running onto the balcony and reaching the barrier, gazing down in horror.

Fire erupted from several wooden structures in the training courtyard, their thatched rooves and timber walls collapsing as the fire spread. On the outer walls the castle soldiers fought against unknown aggressors, too difficult to make out properly from where I stood.

I stared numbly for a moment, wondering if I was dreaming. None of this seemed real to me.

Shouts out in the hall drew my attention, causing me to turn and run back into the bedroom. I stopped in the middle of the room, watching the door in terror, my arms at my sides. The door was shaking, and this all felt like the night Fawkner and his mercenaries had kidnapped me all over again.

In only moments, the door broke open, two broad, muscular men entering my room. They wore heavy studded leather armour, one with a shield and sword, the other with two scimitars. They looked like barbarians standing there in front of me, smirking at me as the most disturbing thoughts of what to do with me were most likely entering their minds.

"No," I staggered backwards as they came towards me. "Please, not this again."

The two of them laughed and growled at me, brandishing their weapons. They said nothing, only drawing closer as a figure wearing a black cloak appeared behind them.

"Get away from her!" Fawkner howled, swinging his blade and slicing the back of the one with the scimitars.

The invader cried out in pain, turning around as the Guardian recruit stabbed him through the chest and tossed him through the door into the hallway. The other invader roared angrily, swinging his sword at the man. Fawkner immediately parried as a third invader ran up behind him.

"Fawkner! Look out!" I cried.

The third invader shrieked in agony, the tip of a sword jammed up through his chest as Mithras appeared, running him through. The old knight threw the man to the wall as he pulled his sword free and took the invader's own weapon, impaling him to the wood and stone with an angry yell.

Fawkner continued fighting the other man through the room as I ducked out of the way. Another two invaders rushed us, one attacking Mithras, the other running at me as he threw a dagger.

With a terrified shriek, I pulled away, the blade missing me as it buried its blade into the wall only inches from my shoulder. I dropped to the floor as Mithras slew the invader attacking him, the one facing me about to hurl another blade.

Seeing my peril, Fawkner kicked the first invader through the windows, shattering them and laying him out on the floor. He snatched a knife from his belt and threw it with deadly accuracy, hitting my attacker in the chest and saving me.

I looked to Fawkner in surprise as the slain man fell to the floor. He turned and walked through the destroyed balcony doors as the invader got to his feet. With one swift kick, Fawkner propelled him over the barrier, the invader's screams ending suddenly a few moments later. I cringed in horror.

"Leander!" Mithras strode into the room, his sword crimson in the moon and firelight. "Are you alright?!"

I nodded breathlessly. "Y-Yes... Mithras, what's happening?!"

"The castle's under attack and has been breached," Mithras explained hurriedly as Fawkner rushed to the door to watch for danger. "I have to get you to safety, now."

"Wait, what about my parents?!" I asked worriedly, standing up before him.

"Other knights are already with your mother," Mithras reassured me. "Your father was in the Great Hall when last I saw him. He ordered me to wake you and take you out of the castle immediately."

"Not without him!" I cried stubbornly.

"This is not a debate, Princess," Mithras argued firmly with me. "We cannot allow you to perish. Your father's orders stand, and we *must* take you to safety."

I nodded then looked to the other man. "Fawkner, where are the others?"

He turned to me, answering: "Joran has gone to the main gates to assist the soldiers in holding them. Aldwyn was in the library ensuring a safe passage for you and your parents. Tallinn and Carden are in the lower halls with the soldiers trying to repel the invaders who have breached the keep."

"And where's my mother?" I demanded of either man.

"She was near the Memorial Chamber, in the gardens," Mithras answered swiftly, reminding me of her tendency to go walking before bed. "Don't worry, our soldiers are protecting her as we speak. Now, you must dress. And pack a bag."

"Who's attacking us?" I asked, frightened, but trying to be strong.

"I do not know," Mithras replied quickly. "Now hurry and do as I say, girl. We'll wait in the hall for you."

I nodded and hurried to the closet as Fawkner left, Mithras pausing and pointing to the vanity.

"Leander, don't leave the Dragon Stone or your pendant here," he said. "Bring them."

"I think our lives are more important than some pretty trinkets, Mithras," I pointed out.

"Just do as I say!" he barked at me. "You'll need them!" and he went out of the room.

Puzzled by this order, I took a backpack from my closet and hurried to the vanity. I grabbed the Dragon Stone, wrapped it in its blue silken cloth and stowed it in the pack. I was already wearing the pendant, deciding to keep it on now no matter what. I grabbed my white dress and folded it quickly, stowing it over the stone then grabbed a few pairs of dark leggings as well as a number of slips and dresses.

I slipped out of my nightgown, throwing it in too, then dressed. I put on dark brown leggings, a very simple grey, long sleeved dress then a dark blue one over it. After lacing up the front, I threw my purple hooded cloak over my shoulders, fastening the cord at my neck and took up my sheathed sword in my left hand. With my hair left long and untied, I ran for the door, slinging the bag over my shoulder.

I stepped out, bewildered by the dead that littered the corridor, many of them soldiers that I had known. I felt nauseous at the sight.

"You have everything?" Mithras asked, my gasp of shock at the scene having made him turn to me.

I nodded, feeling sick from the smell of blood: "Y-yes... I do."

"Good," Mithras nodded. "Let's get to the library and the secret passage."

We ran down the corridor, Fawkner behind me as Mithras led the way. We hurried through the halls and down the back stairs, turning into the corridor that led to the library, a loud explosion suddenly rocking us and throwing us against the walls.

"What was that?!" I cried, Mithras holding my arms to steady me.

We recovered and rushed around the corner to see Aldwyn backing up with two soldiers, casting a spell to send several attackers flying through the destroyed and burning ruins of the library. That entire section of the keep had caved in, timbers burning and scattering flames across the stone floors.

"Aldwyn? What happened here?" Mithras asked, shock registering on his face at the sight of the devastation.

"They entered through the escape tunnel," Aldwyn explained as swiftly as he could. "There were far too many of them. We lost eight soldiers and the knights guarding the library."

"How?" I asked, my eyes wide with horror at the scene before me.

"We think a ballista was fired at the keep, your Highness," one of the soldiers told me. "It tore the walls apart and completely destroyed the library."

"Then our only escape is the main gates or the cliff door," Mithras assessed.

"We should find the others," Aldwyn suggested. "I think we'll need them."

All agreed, we turned and hurried towards the front of the keep. We ran down the main stairs just as a window shattered with arrows flying through. I screamed, Mithras protecting me with his body and shield from the wooden and iron hailstorm as he ran beside me, more explosions rocking the castle around us.

Reaching the main floor, we entered a battle scene, the soldiers immediately swinging their swords into the fray as Mithras pushed me to the floor behind him. Aldwyn unleashed blue orbs of energy from his staff as Mithras and Fawkner began repelling enemies that were charging us, their swords meeting their foes' with clanging, grinding echoes.

From where I crouched, I looked to the main doors of the keep, watching the soldiers fighting to secure them, more enemies trying to force their way in as other soldiers battled those already through. A familiar towering form was holding the great doors shut with both hands, his black hair trailing loosely over his massive shoulders. Joran was trying to assist the soldiers in securing the doors, fighting with all his strength against the attackers' bombardment.

An arrow shot through the air from the Great Hall, Tallinn rushing into view, firing her bow with expert precision, her hair flowing like golden flames as she moved. Carden rushed past her with more soldiers, wielding his sword strongly and meeting the enemy head on, throwing a knife from his belt as he did.

An attacker managed to break the lines, running straight at me with a knife. I drew my sword, swinging it at him and missing as he staggered away from me. I swung again, panicking as the knife wielding maniac slashed at me, catching my shoulder.

I yelped in pain, blood staining the fabric of my dress. I had never been wounded with a sword before, but that didn't stop me as I stabbed forward, managing to score a hit to his hip. The man howled in pain like a wounded animal from my strike, snarling as he glared at me violently.

Suddenly, there was a bright flash and he was thrown into the wall. I looked up at Aldwyn, the Guardian nodding to me before returning to the battle. I kept my sword in my right hand, terrified but ready if another man were to attack me, my shoulder burning with a pain that I had to ignore. Then, my eyes drifted to the throne room doors as I heard my father scream.

"Father!" I cried in terror, jumping to my feet and running towards the doors.

"Leander!" I heard Mithras and Carden shout at once, but I was too focused to really acknowledge them.

I ran into the throne room, a few guards still fighting the remaining invaders. Father was lying beside the four thrones that were set there, propping himself up on one elbow, his hand to his chest as he stared up at one of the most terrifying creatures I have ever seen.

The beast was shaped like a human, but its limbs were grotesquely deformed and longer than normal. It was wrapped almost entirely in black leather armour, even wearing an almost bandage-like mask. It carried dual knives that were horrible jagged chunks of steel that looked as if they had been made by a troll. Tattered robes hung around its lumpy, ugly body as it towered over my father, hissing viciously at him.

"Father!" I cried as I saw him.

"Leander?!" Father looked to me in terror, shaking his head. "Run, sweetheart! RUN!"

The creature turned to look at me, horrible crimson eyes staring at me from the gaps in its mask, a pointed nose and a mouth full of jagged teeth visible. It crouched over my father, shrieking a horribly guttural, high pitched noise. The beast ran at me, leaping through the air and scurrying forward in an almost crouching sideways shuffle. It reached me as I threw down my backpack and held up my sword.

I have to protect my father and kill this thing! I have to!

I blocked the twin blades easily, pushing the unnaturally strong creature sideways awkwardly. I swung my sword, hitting it in the back and causing it to shriek. It swept its blades at me, jumping and kicking me to the ground. Its blades sliced at me again as I fell, missing as I pulled myself away, my cloak falling free from my shoulders.

I got to my feet, striking at it again, the monster attacking me and slashing with its bladed limbs ferociously. I blocked it, slipping and receiving a blow to my right hip, screaming as pain ripped through me. It was only a glancing blow, but it still hurt.

I staggered backwards as it stabbed down, catching a chunk of my dress. I tugged at my skirt helplessly as the thing raised its other blade at me, hissing violently.

Swinging my sword desperately, I managed to knock the knife from its hand then elbowed it in the face. As it swung its head away in pain, I heaved my sword again, cutting through its arm, severing its wrist. Blackish green blood poured from the wound and the creature howled the most horrible, ear splitting shriek of pain.

Ripping my dress loudly, I pulled myself free as the beast turned its eyes back to me and screeched in rage. It pulled a larger blade from its back and slashed at me with its remaining hand, its stringy hair thrashing across its shoulders violently.

I staggered and fell, the beast stomping on my sword and shattering the blade with a splintering cracking. Desperate and afraid, I stabbed the destroyed remains of my sword up just as it struck down at me. A white hot flash of pain devastated my shoulder and I screamed in agony as the creature shrieked again.

The monster's blade had sunk into my right shoulder, my destroyed sword buried into the creature's sternum. It was enough to distract it, the creature staggering back and grasping at the sword hilt, pulling the knife out of my shoulder as it went.

I lay there, turning onto my left side and pressing my hand to the wound, crying out in pain as blood heated my palm. I looked to the creature as it once again screeched and moved towards me, helpless now to do anything. As it raised its blade to strike me it suddenly howled in agony, a sword burying into its back as a paling hand grabbed its shoulder, pressing harder against it. Father was standing behind it, pushing his blade through its torso as he glared at it.

"Stay away... from my daughter, beast!" he coughed at it angrily, blood dripping from his lips.

I stared up in horror as he jammed the sword right through the creature's chest, shedding a great deal of its black blood as it opened and closed its mouth in silence, shuddering violently. It dropped to its knees as Father removed the sword, swiftly swinging the blade and slicing its head from its body with the last of his strength.

I looked from the monster to my father in shock and worry. He could no longer stand, falling to the floor as a section of the ceiling fell in with burning debris, crushing two of the thrones and part of the dais, obliterating the flag and our family crest on the wall behind them. The night invaded the now fire lit room, the lamps mostly out or destroyed, black smoke choking the sky above us.

I crawled to my father's side, my pain and wounds minor compared to his. I dropped to my knees, pressing my hands to his chest as tears streaked my face.

"Father!" I gasped out in a murmur.

"Oh... my-my sweet Leander," Father looked up at me, coughing. "You're... ahem... you're hurt."

"I'm alright," I lied, in a lot of pain. "But you're not. We need a doctor or a mage."

"No, my daughter," Father coughed, struggling to breathe. "I'm... afraid that m-my wounds are too... too great for healing. Even magical h-healing."

"Don't say that!" I insisted firmly, though knowing in my heart that he was right. "You're going to be alright, Father. You will... you will be alright."

I started to cry, tears streaming down my cheeks as I heard footsteps behind me, the fighting outside the room now ended just as the battle within had. Father pressed a hand to my cheek, stroking my silky auburn hair back from my face as I leaned over him, my hands on his chest and shoulder.

"You will!" I sobbed, almost pleading furiously for his survival. "You will be alright, Father! You will!"

"Oh, Leander, my girl," Father said softly, his eyes growing dull as the pain began to vanish from his failing body. "You're so... strong. Were it possible... ahem... I think that your... your will alone would save me. But I am... b-beyond... saving now."

"Don't say that," I whispered, shaking my head, my tears falling to mix with his draining blood.

Father smiled up at me, looking into my eyes proudly. His hand was becoming cold against my cheek as his life was leaving him.

"My youngest daughter," he smiled faintly, his eyes flickering. "I am so... so very... p-proud of you. I-I love you... Leander."

"I love you too, Father," I sobbed softly, looking down at him, my heart cracking inside my chest with each breath that slipped from his body. "Please... don't leave me."

Father stared at me softly and yet aimlessly, holding my hand as his grip began fading. "Don't be afraid, Leander," he spoke his final words.

I stared through my tears at the suddenly lifeless body of my father, his eyes glassed over, his lips parted gently as his last breath left him and his hand fell limp in my fingers. My eyes flowed tears as I shook my head.

"N-no. Father," I called to him softly, then louder again, frantically. "Father! FATHER!"

I began to weep heavily, laying my head on his shoulder, my heart shattering within me, the pain unbearable. I closed my eyes and screamed in grief, his loss beyond my comprehension. I begged him to come back to me, pleaded for him not to leave me, even beseeched Azmerath not to take him, but it was all in vain.

I saw Tallinn standing in the doorway, watching grimly as she slowly took a few steps towards me, stopping to allow me the space to mourn. Behind her the others entered, their faces immediately dropping at the sight before them, even Joran showing sorrow as he bowed his head.

"No... Prince Ewan, Lord of Arvon... is dead?" Mithras said with a shaky, grief stricken, questioning voice. "Gods... no..."

"This truly is a sorrowful outcome," Aldwyn murmured, his staff in both hands as Carden slowly approached me, pausing only a few feet from me.

I could feel my friend's presence as he stood behind me, but I didn't look up, sobbing through heavy tears.

"Vashabaravan Karvarn," Joran bowed his head reverently, his arms crossed, fists closed at his shoulders.

I heard another soldier rush into the room as the echoing of rams against the main doors of the keep continued.

"Ser Mithras," he addressed the Knight-Commander grimly. "I have terrible news."

"I think we all have," Mithras responded numbly, trying to maintain some measure of authority. "What news do you bring?"

"We cannot find the Duchess," the soldier said grimly.

I looked up through my tears, a new horror filling me. "Where is she? Where's my mother?"

The soldier bowed his head regretfully. "Forgive me, your Highness, but there is no sign of Duchess Caralyn."

"No!" I gasped and began to weep even harder as the pain struck me again. "Not her too! Please, gods, not her too!" I trailed off into a continuing sob.

Mithras went silent, watching me as I wept for both of my parents, cuddling into my father's lifeless body. I knew that he was grief stricken just as I was, even the sounds of screams in the night and the echoes of the battle doing nothing to break either of us from our mourning.

"With respects, Ser Mithras," the soldier asked softly, timidly," what do we do now?"

"We still have a member of the Aldrich royal family under our care," Mithras told him calmly, regaining his strength and will to lead. "We must ensure that the Princess escapes the castle."

"There is no way out now," the soldier told him direfully. "We have lost the main grounds and the gardens. It is only a matter of time before they take the keep and slay us all."

"Then we'll have to try something a little more daring," Fawkner suggested.

"You're not thinking we should break through the main doors, then the central courtyard and the main gates?" Tallinn asked in shock. "We can't fight an army *and* protect the Princess. She'll be killed, and all of us with her."

"No, that's not what I had in mind," Fawkner admitted, looking to Mithras. "The north walls are still clear, and the river runs below."

Mithras nodded, understanding him. "Then we go to the north walls."

With a nod from Mithras, Carden turned to me, putting his hands to my shoulders. I tried to shrug him off, becoming more and more violent as he grabbed at me, pulling me back.

At last, Carden lifted me to my feet and I started screaming: "No! No! I won't leave him! Please, I won't!"

"Leander! Leander!" Mithras grabbed my face, holding my cheeks with his palms and looking into my tear-soaked eyes. "We *must* leave. The castle is taken and most of our forces are dead. We have to get you out of here *now*."

"I don't care!" I shouted, struggling in Carden's strong grasp. "My parents... I won't leave them!"

"But you'll die!" Mithras worried.

"Then let me die!" I retorted mournfully.

"You are the heir to the throne! The next Queen of Aldegaad! You know I can't let that happen! And what of your sister?!" he asked me sternly, keeping our gazes locked. "What of Aislinn?! What will she feel if you too are murdered?! Would you wish that she loses her sister as well as her parents tonight?!"

I shook my head, my voice softer now. "N-no..."

"Then we must go," he urged me more gently, taking his hands from my face.

I sighed sadly, tears dropping from my cheeks, gleaming in the flickering fire light.

Mithras stood and turned to the soldier: "Buy as much time as you can to allow us to get her out, then flee."

The soldier nodded and ran to join the others at the main doors to the keep.

"Come," Mithras drew his sword again and took up his shield as Carden grabbed my backpack and grasped my wrist. "To the north wall."

As we hurried from the room, I looked back to my father. I dreaded what my future would now be, tainted with the memories of this tragic night as it had become. I could only wish to wake up, hoping it was all just a horrible nightmare.

We ran out through the outer corridors, dead soldiers and knights scattered over the walkways as the few remaining were being killed in the courtyards. The only way to the wall we needed to get to was straight through the training courtyard. Mithras led the way, killing a few more enemies as we ran, Aldwyn turning as a series of horrific shrieks echoed around us, ready with his staff. I looked back to see three more creatures like the one that had murdered my father scurrying up the walls behind us.

Without hesitating, Tallinn pulled her bow to face them, firing two arrows one after the other. Her shots felled two of the beasts, but the third ducked past and ran straight at me. It avoided Aldwyn's strikes as we reached the wall, Carden managing to knock it down the steps of the battlements with a hard kick to its face.

We ran to the top of the wall, Fawkner rushing towards a spot he had picked out. Aldwyn, Mithras and Tallinn were right behind him, Carden running beside me with Joran at our backs.

"Hurry! Here!" Fawkner shouted as we managed to reach him.

The black leather wrapped creature leaped up from the ground as though it were on springs, knocking Carden and I to the stone walkway of the battlements. It punched Carden in the face, then pinned my wrists down as it bared its teeth and hissed at me.

"Help me!" I screamed, staring into those horrible red eyes. "HELP!"

Mithras was rushing forward as Carden moved to attack the creature, the young man taking a knife to the side and receiving a glancing blow for his trouble. It snapped its jaws at me, drooling and making me scream in terror. Then the creature howled as it was lifted off me, scratching my wrists with its talons. I propped myself up as Carden pulled the blade from his side and followed my gaze.

Joran towered over us, holding the beast above his head. He roared angrily and squeezed hard, breaking the monster's bones and stifling its shrieks before casting it to the rocks below the wall.

The giant looked down at me and nodded.

"Thank you," I said breathlessly, stunned by his strength.

"Come on," Carden grabbed my arm, lifting me to my feet and retrieving my bag again.

We reached the others, Aldwyn taking my bag and casting it into the air, using a spell to guide it to a soft landing across the river along with the bags the others carried too.

"How will this work?" Tallinn asked uncertainly, the wind catching her hair and throwing it around her shoulders.

"We climb down to the river and cross," Fawkner responded simply.

Mithras shook his head. "No. The river is far too deep here. We cannot simply walk across."

"Then we swim," Fawkner answered, compromising.

There was another explosion and shouts echoed through the courtyards. Battle sounds rose from the keep and I knew that the main doors had been breached. We could see invaders running along the walkways and sprinting towards us across the courtyard. In that moment I was certain that the castle had been taken and that I was alone. I was now the last of my line just as my ancestor had been the last of hers.

"We're out of time," Carden observed urgently.

Fawkner looked to Mithras and asked: "Could we survive a fall from the wall to the river?"

Mithras nodded. "Yes, but why?"

"We'll have to jump," Fawkner told us with conviction.

"Jump?" Carden stared at him in shock.

"Either that or die," Fawkner offered the only other alternative, looking around at us.

"Then we jump," Aldwyn agreed, moving into position.

He and Mithras leaped first, dropping from the wall and speeding towards the river. They hit the surface with a loud splash, vanishing from sight into the darkness below. Joran and Fawkner went next, mimicking the dive the Knight and Guardian had taken from the battlements. Again, they vanished from sight.

Tallinn gestured to Carden and I: "Come. We have to move."

"I-I can't jump," I whimpered in fear, shaking my head and bracing against the two of them. "I'm afraid of heights and that's too far."

Carden and Tallinn exchanged worried and urgent glances. Carden was holding onto me tightly as I practically clung to him, digging my nails into his arm. The three of us looked back as the attackers were scaling the walls now and barrelling towards us, their weapons waving violently and their howls growing louder.

"We go together," Carden decided, holding me firmly.

"Agreed," Tallinn nodded decisively.

"What?!" I looked at them in terror.

"Trust us, Princess," Tallinn urged me, locking eyes with me sternly, but encouragingly.

Carden held me close, staring deeply and softly into my eyes as he tilted my face with one hand to gain my gaze. "Just hold onto me, Leander. I won't let you go. I promise."

I stared into his jade eyes, terror rushing through me faster than the stampeding invaders charging us, trying to find my strength. Then I looked past him, my terror peaking as I saw someone I really didn't want to.

The Sorcerer from Averet, the Shadow Lord, was watching us from the shadows nearby, his glowing green eyes locked on me, his jaw set into a scowl. His arms were folded around him, hands beneath them as the icy wind lashed at his black cloak and cowl. His penetrating gaze stared right through me as if I weren't even there, his eyes narrowing as I saw him. He could have done anything to stop us, he was standing so close, yet he did nothing.

"I promise," Carden repeated softly, drawing my frightened eyes back to his handsome face.

Slowly, I nodded, looking up at him again, my heart urging me to trust him.

We moved to the wall, Tallinn putting her arm around my shoulders and holding on tight as Carden kept a firm hold around my waist.

"On the count of three," she instructed us. "One..."

I stared at the water's black surface far below us, terrified of what might happen now, the roar of the river's rapids loud in my ears.

"Two..." Tallinn counted, breathing in and tensing her muscles.

I drew in a few deep breaths, trying to withstand my panic at facing this fear. I was bracing myself, my mind racing with thoughts of what plunging into the freezing waters of the river would feel like.

"Three!" she finally shouted.

I closed my eyes, feeling my feet leave the wall as Carden and Tallinn pulled me with them. I caught one last glimpse of my black hooded nightmare as they took me with them, his glowing gaze never leaving my shape for even a second.

We plunged from the wall, falling towards the river below the castle. I pulled in one last deep breath, closed my eyes again and waited for the crushing cold of the river to hit me...

Chapter Ten
The Uncertain Road

The hard impact of the water was near enough to rattle teeth and shake bones, the cold that accompanied it far worse. Darkness engulfed me as I plunged through the icy depths, the deepest black dominating everything below while the orange light of fires shimmered through the indigo surface above.

I felt myself sinking, my clothing wrapping around me, tangling my limbs and weighing me down. I opened my eyes, the water flooding in and stinging them. I felt insubstantial, lost in an empty nothing.

As I drifted beneath the scintillating surface of the river I thought: *Is there any point? Should I just open my mouth and breathe the water in?*

I looked down into the depths, just barely able to see the deep riverbed below my feet and flowing dress hem. *Why has this happened? Why am I here now?* If I had been fully able to, I would have continued to shed my tears beneath the water. *Please. Just let me go. Just let me disappear. Please.*

Movement caught my eye and I looked to my right. Carden was swimming towards me, holding his breath, his long hair flowing to his shoulders and neck from his face. His clothes swirled around him just as mine did, his eyes focused on me as he reached out his hand.

Suddenly, I felt something grab my shoulders. I panicked and looked behind me, Tallinn staring at me from beneath her billowing blonde mane, her hazel eyes communicating her concern for me. I stared at her in astonishment, unable to really comprehend what was happening.

Carden grabbed my right wrist and slung his arm around my waist, looking to Tallinn as he did. She nodded to him as she shifted, grabbing me in a mirroring hold as Carden drew my eyes to him. He pressed a hand to my cheek in a comforting gesture then turned in unison with Tallinn.

They practically dragged me through the water as I floundered, swimming after the other shapes splashing ahead of us, struggling as we were swept farther downstream. I started to choke, my lungs burning as I began running out of air. I thrashed a little, trying to hold onto the two Guardians, my desire to die now washed away by the fear of achieving such a thought.

It felt like the longest moments in my life, death crawling up on me as life was only inches away. With my heavy clothing I wouldn't have been able to survive the water on my own, surprised that the thickly clothed and heavily cloaked Guardians could swim at all.

We broke the surface, the three of us gasping for air as we struggled and trudged towards the north banks of the river. Joran, Aldwyn, Fawkner and Mithras were ahead of us, pulling themselves onto the shore already, the Storvari looking completely unfazed, the Mage, Mercenary and Knight staggering to their feet.

Coughing as we dragged ourselves onto the shore, the three of us finally left the river and joined them. I collapsed on my knees as Carden dropped to a genuflecting kneel beside me, hands down, breathing heavily. Tallinn was holding my shoulders, her blonde hair hanging in a dark, soaked clump, the water running off her body and clothes in waves.

I gazed up through my drenched hair at the castle a little farther up the river. I hadn't realised the severity of the attack until now, seeing that not only the castle, but the entire town burned. Smoke choked the air and flames shone brightly as they devoured the thatched rooves and the nearest trees. The screams of the frightened people reached my ears as I lay there on the shore, haunting me as I realised that there was nothing I could do.

I felt numb as I sat there on my haunches, only the chilled wind and my soaked clothing drawing any kind of impulse from me. I shivered, my teeth chattering as I watched my home burning, tears sliding free again at the sight.

There was only silence amongst my companions, not one of them thinking of anything to say at a time like this. So, we watched on in a cold hush, the horrific scene playing out before us. Heartbroken, I closed my eyes and dropped my head down, chin to my chest as I sobbed. My hands rested in my lap, my long hair hiding my face from view, my sobs drowned out by the sounds of violence in the distance.

Finally, Aldwyn turned to Mithras, recovering his staff as he went.

"I do not wish to be inconsiderate, Ser Mithras," he said compassionately to the Knight, "but, we cannot linger here. We need safe refuge."

Mithras blinked away his own silent tears, sucked in a gruff breath and nodded. "Yes. You're right. We must make haste to leave this place before the invaders find us."

"Where can we go?" Tallinn looked up at him as she rubbed my upper arms in an attempt to comfort me, my skin numb to her touch.

"The girl's right," Fawkner stated, dragging himself to his feet, clearly aching from the plunge. "Is there anywhere we can go from here?"

"Could we not hide in the hills as we did on our last visit?" Joran suggested stoically.

Fawkner shook his head. "We haven't the supplies we need to go into hiding in the hills to wait for these attackers to leave and give us a clear road."

"Which could take weeks," Aldwyn observed calmly, ringing out his sleeves. "Fawkner is right. We would need shelter and food."

Mithras looked thoughtful: "There's an old guard outpost a mile from here to the north-east. It is a short climb, but it is a welcome place to rest and there's a small stream full of fish nearby. It's deserted and unnoticeable."

"How quickly could we make it there?"Aldwyn asked as Carden got to his feet, breathing easier now.

"Two hours, no more," Mithras replied with a shrug. "If we move swiftly."

"Sounds like a plan," Carden agreed, standing one foot on the sloping riverbed, hands by his sides.

"Then we move," Fawkner consented. "Quickly, before they find us."

Mithras nodded, starting past them with authority again. "We need to find Leander's bag. She has things in it she will need. Get her to her feet."

"Come on, Princess," Tallinn said softly to me, gently guiding me to stand.

"I've got her," Carden told his friend, taking me around the shoulders and walking with me as Tallinn took a step back to follow us.

We walked only a few metres; my bag visible with the Guardians' on the ground near the foothills opposite the castle walls. Tallinn scooped it up with her own, slung it across her back and nodded to Carden as he took the other two. He returned the nod then we continued to follow Mithras through the foothills.

The walk was tiring with drenched clothing, which didn't get any drier as it began to rain. Our cloaks took most of the moisture, but we were still sodden from the river, making our way through the uneven, rocky and muddy hills awkwardly.

After almost two hours we could see it, the ruined, weathered remains of a stone structure. It was nothing more than a small tower with a few dilapidated wooden and stone auxiliary buildings beyond a wrecked fortification wall. Ruins like these were common throughout Therras, the remains of ancient battle structures no longer in service, or temples long forgotten, or even cities left to the wild.

"Here," Mithras said triumphantly, hurrying a little more now as we came up the hidden trail to the ruins.

I snapped out of my near comatose state, looking up at the worn stone and the broken battlements. I felt a small sense of wonder at the sight of this structure, never before knowing of its existence.

We reached the archway that had once been the main gate, Mithras and Fawkner drawing their swords out of caution. We had no idea what might be lurking in the shadows of this long-forgotten ruin. Behind us, Tallinn traced recent footsteps in the dirt with her eyes, studying them carefully.

"This path has been travelled recently," she observed, noticing the depth of the footprints before looking to Aldwyn.

Aldwyn nodded cautiously. "Then we had best be ready for an attack."

"Ease yourselves, friends," Mithras urged them. "I am the owner of those tracks."

"You? Why?" Tallinn asked suspiciously.

Mithras gave her a gentle gaze. "How else do you think I knew of this place? I found it a short time ago. All the same," he then looked at us guardedly, his hand tightening around his sword, "we'd best be on our guard, just in case."

It took us only a short time to survey the ruins properly, the area small and not easily able to conceal enemies. That was perhaps the point of such a location. With the search done, Mithras led us into the only building left undamaged and still boasting a roof. This was the old guard barracks, some beds remaining there, still made as if they had never been slept in.

This building attached to the main tower, the doorway opening into the main hall where a round metal brazier stood, ashes heaped in its centre from the last fire that was set in it. Though one of the pillars had fallen and some of the walls had cracked, the room was sheltered and had a ceiling, the tower above it mostly ruined. The stairs leading up to the watchtower were destroyed, a large portion of stone walling having tumbled down and shattered them years ago.

Mithras stood within the old hall, looking up at the ceiling, checking its stability. Once he was satisfied, he turned to the rest of us and nodded.

The others started to set up immediately, Fawkner and Aldwyn setting the fire while Tallinn climbed as high as she could, checking the surrounding landscape to see if it was safe. Joran closed the damaged doors to the main hall then stood guard, watching the grounds and hills silently. He was an ever-vigilant sentry.

Mithras rummaged around in the old stores while Carden sat me down near the barracks and took my cloak off. He carefully slid me free of my blue over dress, leaving me in my greyish dress, the sleeves ruined, the fabric heavily blood stained.

Tallinn leaped from the ruined stairs, striding over to us. "Carden?" she eyed him carefully.

"I'm just looking at her wounds," he replied honestly, concern in his voice. "She's been hurt."

"How badly?" the blonde woman asked.

Carden shook his head as he slid my shoulder out of my dress. He surveyed the wound and sighed grimly.

"She's been stabbed three times," he reported calmly, but worriedly. "Her shoulder doesn't look very good, but her arm and hip will heal easily."

"Healing magic?" Tallinn suggested and with a nod from Carden, turned and called: "Aldwyn."

Wordlessly, the older Guardian walked from where Fawkner was warming his hands and drying his over clothes by the fire to join us. He took a look at my wounds while I kept my head down.

"Easy to handle," he simply stated, then held out his left hand and touched my shoulder.

I whimpered and looked up at him, then turned my eyes to his hand. There was a light blue shimmer and the dull pain in my shoulder faded away. When Aldwyn withdrew his hand I saw that the skin was healed perfectly, not even a scar remaining. I watched as he repeated this process with my other wounds, healing them completely, again leaving no scar or pain.

"What did you...?" I asked softly, looking up at him.

"I used healing magic on you, Princess," he said evenly, standing tall before me. "It works on most minor wounds. But for the greater wounds like broken bones and sicknesses other more potent spells are required."

"Thank you," I murmured softly, again disappearing into my numbness.

"Tallinn," Aldwyn turned his gaze to the blonde woman. "Could you help clean her up and get her to change into some dry clothes? She might feel better then."

"As would we all," Carden commented sourly.

"There I may be able to help those who do not have their own with them," Mithras told them as he walked in with two bags. "I found some old clothes. They're clean, for the most part. And dry."

"Then we can dry out our own clothes and wear those for the time being," Fawkner said thankfully, shivering.

As they began rummaging through the sacks of clothing, Tallinn took me into the barracks and sat me down. She laid my backpack on the bed then left briefly. She returned after a while with an old bowl filled with water she had heated by the fire and a gathering of clean rags. She set it on the table nearby and started to suds the rag with some soap she'd found.

She walked over to the bed, sitting down beside me with the wet, soapy rag. Almost with the loving care of an elder sister, Tallinn started to clean the blood off me, not only my own, but the blood of my father as well. I stared at my hands as she got me to hold them up and began cleaning them, neither of us speaking.

The sight of my father's blood was unbearable, the pain it caused me merciless. I felt only an inescapable grief, tears returning to streak my face as my soft, short breaths sounded from my lips.

Tallinn wiped the cloth over my chest and neck, cleaning the blood off the silver pendant that still hung there. The blood simply faded away, as if it had never stained my flesh or the pendant, but the grief wouldn't leave me so easily.

* * * * *

For two days it rained continuously, the storm strange, almost refusing to move on from Aldegaad's northern lands as if it had a mind of its own. It raged on high above the old outpost, both sheltering and hindering us with the chill and the dampness. The rain added to the treacherous terrain made it almost impossible for anyone or anything to track us to our temporary haven.

While the others stayed in the main hall, I lay on a bed in the barracks, having been there without uttering a single word since Tallinn had cleaned the blood from my body. I had changed from the ruined dress that I wore to a long sleeved, light-grey dress and a dark forest green over dress, my feet left bare, the pendant remaining around my neck. With a blanket over me, I stayed there in the soft confines of this old bed and the dank stone room it resided in, refusing to leave.

I had seen my face in a mirror and I looked ill now, my skin ashen and my hair hanging limply over my neck and shoulders, my blue eyes no longer as full of life as they had once been. The previous events of the past few days had brought me almost to breaking point and now all that remained for me was my grief; that, and the nightmares that were plaguing me, chief among them the monstrous dragon atop the black fortress with the cowled sorcerer standing behind me.

As I lay there nestled in the bedcovers, there came a knock at the door. I didn't even look up as it opened, Carden stepping inside with a plate of food.

"Leander?" he said softly, walking carefully towards where I lay.

I didn't respond. I simply pulled the blanket tighter around me, staring with silent, dried, teary eyes at the bed next to me. My only thoughts were that I wanted to be left alone.

"I... thought you might be hungry," he spoke softly.

I didn't answer but glanced at him out of the corner of my eye. A small sigh slipped free of my lips softly as I turned my eyes back to the same place that I had been staring at, remaining silent. I could feel him watching me.

Carden was hesitant to make any kind of sudden moves towards me. He was cautious, uncertain how to approach this scenario and deal with it appropriately. I knew this because I felt the same way.

Carefully, he sat down on the bed, his back to me, setting the food on the nearby end table. He hung his arms over his knees and stared at the floor in thought. After a few long moments of silence, he spoke without turning to me, his voice gentle and sympathetic.

"I can't imagine the kind of pain you're feeling right now," he told me without addressing me. "I've never known that kind of pain myself. But I do know how it feels to lose hope, to be alone in the world."

I knew he was looking over his shoulder at me now, that he was watching me out of the corner of his eye. I felt a strange comfort from his presence, as though the mere thought of having him there was enough to ease some of my pain. I felt my muscles releasing their tension, my breathing becoming easier with his closeness.

"I don't know how you feel," he admitted with a glum shrug. "If I did, maybe I could help you now."

As he turned away from me and stared at the floor, I took in a small breath: "I don't know how I feel either."

Carden turned, his green eyes locking onto me as I brought my face around to meet him. I was sure he could see the pain in my eyes, though I wasn't crying anymore.

"That," he said softly, facing me," I can understand."

I sat up slowly, positioning myself so that my back was to the wall, my knees drawn to my chest. I stared out of the curtains of dark auburn hair surrounding my face, my bluish eyes peering up at him. A tear trickled down my cheek as I hugged my knees tightly. I silently cursed it.

"I don't want to be alone," I murmured sorrowfully.

Carden slid closer to me, putting an arm around me and holding me to his chest. I rested my head against him, feeling so lost without my family.

"You're not alone," he told me in a whisper, rubbing my shoulder as he held me. "You've got me, and I'll never leave you."

"Because that's your mission, right?" I murmured glumly, staring at the mattress in front of us. "Protect the Princess..."

"True, that's my mission as a Guardian," Carden agreed, turning my chin with two fingers so that I looked up at him. "But I'm not talking about being a Guardian. I'm talking about being your friend."

"You are?"

He nodded. "Right now you need a friend more than a Guardian. If that's what I can be for you, then that's what I will be."

I nodded at him, grateful for these kind words and thoughts.

"I just... I feel so lost," I said, speaking with confusion and grief. "I don't know what I'm supposed to do now, or how I'm supposed to do it."

He nodded thoughtfully. "The uncertain road is not an easy path to take."

I looked up at him again. "What's that?"

He returned my gaze. "The uncertain road? Not knowing what path to take, which way to go or what to do in times like this. We have a saying where I'm from: Take any path and it will lead you to any destination, but it is the uncertain road that eventually leads to truth of self and purpose; the harder road taken, yet it is the most worthy at the end."

I considered this, nodding thoughtfully. There was a sort of poetry to the words, not in verse or structure, but in ideal. It was strangely comforting in its somewhat frightening concept.

"That's a beautiful saying," I said softly.

Carden nodded with a reminiscent smile. "It always makes me feel better when I'm saddened, and it reminds me of home."

"You lived in Nargilith, didn't you?" I looked up at him, drawing his gaze. "I remember you saying that the night that..." I paused, the pain of that night spiking my heart,"...when we were in the gardens together."

He confirmed: "Yes. I did live in Nargilith."

"You didn't really tell me much about your home," I reminded him. "I mean, you told me about the city, but not you."

Carden looked to me, shaking his head dismissively. "I doubt my story would interest a Princess of Aldegaad."

I shrugged. "It does interest me. I want to get to know you better. You know so much about me and my life, but I know almost nothing about you except your name and the place of your birth."

"Well, alright," Carden agreed with a shrug. "But I am not certain that Nargilith was where I was born."

I frowned. "Really? How can that be?"

He sighed, seeming as though he were facing a difficult memory. I sat up straighter, watching him as he swallowed back and took in a breath.

"I lived in Gorvenna," he confirmed with a cautious air," but I don't know where I was born. Highever is an old term of my people for someone like me."

"Someone like you?" I asked, frowning curiously.

He looked to me solemnly. "An orphan who achieves a greater purpose. When one of us reaches a point where we have potential that is recognised for the right reasons, and we make something of ourselves, we are given the name Highever. It means "*Forever Raised Up*", a term of endearment," he shook his head and glared at the sheets before him, turning from me. "But to me it's a way that I can be forever identified as what I once was. A homeless wretch begging for scraps."

I stared at him, not sure what to say. I felt terrible, almost hating myself for asking him this question. Had I realised that it would cause him such pain I wouldn't ever have asked.

Carden went on venomously and with contempt to himself: "Everywhere I go I am referred to by that name and I despise it. True, it's better outside of Gorvenna, especially here in Aldegaad, because it's just seen as my last name. But it's still a bitterness that I can't wash away and the word is like ash in my mouth."

"I'm... I'm sorry," I murmured honestly, my own pain temporarily pushed to the back of my heart and mind. "I didn't mean to bring up painful memories."

He looked to me, his expression changing to a gentler one.

"No, it's alright," he assured me. "You asked to learn more about me, and if we're to be friends then you have a right to know."

I nodded for a moment, shaking my head then as I stared at my feet in the blankets. "I should have asked what you do for fun."

He smirked at me, a half chuckle slipping past his lips. "I think my hobbies are of far less importance here, especially since I seem to do what we're doing now most of the time."

"Oh really?"

"Really."

I faced him, cautious, but curious. "So... when you said that you can't understand what I'm feeling?"

"I meant it," he replied. "I don't know who my parents are, if they still live or where they are. But I had Varel."

"Varel?" I asked curiously, interested. "Who's that?"

"The man who found me and raised me," he replied, a son's love in his voice for the man he spoke of. "He taught me how to fend for myself, how to use a sword, how to live as part of Nargilith's societies. Varel took me in when anyone else would have left me to the crows."

"Do you mind if I ask," I enquired carefully, "but, how old were you when he found you?"

Carden shrugged. "No older than a few months. I was left in the street, abandoned behind an apothecary."

I was shocked. "That's awful! How could someone do that to a baby?!"

"Believe me," he assured me, "I feel no love towards my parents for leaving me to die like that. The thought of them makes my blood boil."

I tried to urge him on with his story, and change the subject: "So, Varel found you?"

He nodded, smiling. "He was coming out of the apothecary and heard a baby crying. Anyone else would have walked past, but Varel has always been a curious man. He followed the sounds until he found me. I was wrapped in a blanket and lying in the dirt behind the apothecary."

"And he took you with him?"

He smiled fondly. "He did. He always told me that when he saw me his heart insisted that he take me from that place. He was lonely, after all."

"And he raised you?" I repeated his earlier comments.

Again he nodded, shifting to face me more fully where we sat. "He taught me right from wrong and how to survive. When I was fifteen, Aldwyn came to Nargilith with Tallinn. She was nineteen and had just been recruited, but they had not yet performed her Initiation. Aldwyn saw my fighting skills and my abilities that I had learned over the years. He invoked the Rite of Recruitment and I was taken as a recruit that day."

"How did that feel?"

"At first, I felt pretty special," he answered easily, but quietly. "Aldwyn had been looking for recruits and had come during Nargilith's annual jousting tournament. He had already found Tallinn in Dorvana," he started to laugh reminiscently, shaking his head and drawing a smile from me. "Apparently, she had tried to hunt him from the moment he passed the Seraphim."

"The Seraphim?" I asked with a frown.

"You have to know what that is," Carden looked to me dubiously. "Or do they have a different name for it here in Aldegaad? It's the tallest mountain in High-Realm?"

"Oh," I realised. "The Firehorn. Yes, I know it."

"Right," Carden nodded, remembering his histories. "The name Seraphim was given to the mountain by the Northerners. It's still the Firehorn to the Southerners."

I shrugged. "Well, I am a Southerner."

"Yes, I had forgotten," he went on. "Anyway, Aldwyn had apparently been hunted by Tallinn since the Firehorn. He had managed to outsmart her, but she was determined. When he realised that a nineteen-year-old girl had been tracking him for seven and half days without stopping, he recruited her into the Order."

"That's why she was there with him in Nargilith when you met them?" I started to put the pieces together.

He confirmed: "Yes."

"So, how did they meet you?"

"They watched my fight. I took on four men at once while managing to evade them and demonstrated my abilities as a rogue and a fighter. Aldwyn was so impressed by my performance that he recruited me."

"It must have been hard for you, leaving Varel," I guessed, remembering the stories I had heard of the Guardians. "I mean, you had to go to the Citadel of Dartaren, right?"

"That's right," Carden agreed with a saddened sigh. "Leaving Varel was one of the hardest things I have ever had to do. But it's not like I never get to see him. Whenever we go to Nargilith I visit and I'm always sending him money. He needs it."

I figured: "You had a difficult upbringing?"

"We were living in one of the poorer areas," he answered simply. "We had to scrape to get by, but we managed to. We weren't homeless, but we had difficulty getting food and medicines," he looked ashamed. "I... I thought you might think less of me knowing that I was a street urchin."

"Why?" I asked with a shrug. "You really thought that I would have a problem with you being a commoner? Is it because I was a princess?"

"No, it was just shame. And you *are* a princess," Carden corrected me.

I sighed and turned my face from him, pressing my back to the wall again. "I don't feel like one. If anything, it sounds like we're polar opposites. You were a struggling orphan who gained some measure of esteem when you were recruited by the Guardians. I'm a princess who had a very luxurious, if annoyingly privacy deprived life. Now all that's been taken away and I'm... well...," I looked to him sadly. "I'm an orphan too."

"I know," he said sympathetically, pulling me to him again and holding me. "I know it hurts."

"I just want my parents back," I started to sob, the tears flowing fresh. "I just... I can't get rid of the sight of my father dying in front of me, or the feeling of his blood on my hands," I snivelled. "Is it so much to ask to have my life back?"

"Not so much to ask," he told me softly. "Just not possible."

I lay my head against his chest, letting the tears flow as I cried again.

"Please," I whispered to him, trying to push away the terrifying memories of that horrific night. "Don't leave me, Carden. Please?"

"I'm not going anywhere, Leander," he vowed. "I promise."

And so, we lay there for the longest time as I sobbed with no sign of when or how I would stop. Carden kept me close to him, whispering gentle words of kindness and care to me, living up to the promise of being my friend. I soon fell asleep in the comfort of his warm, broad embrace, finally relaxing.

* * * * *

Another four days passed, the storm still not abating as the countryside was drenched in a dismal grey mist. There had been no sign of the rain easing up and though we were safe there in our rundown haven, the dampness, the cold and the lack of food would eventually cause greater damage than the assailants we had evaded.

I sat by the fire, my cloak wrapped around me, my eyes fixated on the dancing flames within the metal dish centring the room. I had recovered enough now that I was able to re-join the group, though my grief still weighed heavily on my heart. I had eaten what I had been given, trying to keep up my strength despite the lack of hunger I felt.

I cast my eyes across the room, studying my companions where they each sat or stood.

Joran was sitting in a corner of the room in a deep state of meditation, his eyes shut, his long hair pulled back from his large featured face, his hands resting palms down on his knees. He looked at peace, possessing an inner control that I had never seen in anyone before. It fascinated me to watch him, though I did worry whether he had noticed by now or not that he had an audience.

Across the room Aldwyn was fiddling with some pouches of herbs he had been gathering over the last few days. All that I could figure was that these were healing potions that the Mage was concocting, though I wasn't sure how well they would work given his limited supplies.

Mithras was standing watch, his chainmail shirt on under his armour plating, his cloak catching in the breeze. He now stood as the single representative of the life that I'd had, my only familial figure left to me in the north of Aldegaad.

We hadn't spoken much since I had emerged from the barracks, but I knew that he was relieved to have me back with them. He had said as much, yet we had remained – for the most part – quiet about any kind of subjects over the last few days.

Then there was Carden, my strongest growing friendship in this new group. While with many of the others I felt that they were only there to protect me, Carden had become much more of a companion in only the last few weeks. Now I watched him as he stood over the fire, his eyes staring at the flames, his palms posed over them to warm up. He seemed contemplative, as if he were analysing some unseen knowledge that only he possessed.

Fawkner and Tallinn had gone out to scout the area and had been absent for the last few hours, day having broken long after they had left. They returned at that moment, pushing through the main entryway, striding in and closing the doors behind them. They dropped their hoods back, the rainwater sprinkling to the floor as they revealed themselves.

"How does it look out there?" Aldwyn asked, standing and turning to them.

"Dismal," Fawkner's response was as dark as the day outside. "I've never known of a weeklong rainstorm."

"Welcome to Aldegaad," Mithras spoke softly, arms crossed as he stared out the gaps in the wall at the land below. "It almost never stops raining here. That's why everything's so green."

"And cold. And muddy," Fawkner scrapped his mud caked boots against the stone floor in frustration.

"The way is clear," Tallinn answered Aldwyn's previously asked question. "There doesn't appear to be any signs of the invaders on the roads. I think they've stayed at Castle Arvon, or turned south, or perhaps headed west down the river."

"Then it would be a good idea to move now," Aldwyn said decisively.

"Yes," Mithras agreed, turning from his guard post and facing the rest of us. "We'd best head out from here today."

"And where are we to go?" Fawkner asked, voicing the concerns that I silently had myself.

"For the moment," Aldwyn spoke evenly, "to the nearest town. I think we could all do with a proper rest and some decent meals."

"That seems wise," a deep voice drew our gazes, Joran standing up and towering above us all. "Though my people are accustomed to harsh conditions, I do not believe that humans are so resilient. My concerns are for the Sarissi, of course."

"Then what?" Carden asked, joining into their discussion. "Should we head to the capital or to the Citadel?"

"I do not think any of us can make that decision," Aldwyn responded. "I think it is up to the Princess."

They all turned to me, expectant looks on their faces, only Carden possessing an expression of care. I glanced up at them from where I sat uncertainly.

"Why are you looking at me?" I asked with confusion.

"It is better to ask your opinion, your Highness," Aldwyn stated, his hands clasped behind him.

I shrugged, shaking my head. "I don't know. I'm not a leader."

"But you *are* a royal," Tallinn reminded me, her arms crossed in front of her ample chest. "It is only right that we ask your opinion."

"I don't know!" I insisted in frustration, Carden walking over to me and dropping to his knee beside me.

"It's okay," he said comfortingly. "You don't have to worry."

I nodded thankfully to him, remaining silent. I really had no idea what to do or how to do it. All I could think was that I wanted to go somewhere warm and safe, somewhere far away from there.

"Alright then," Mithras nodded reluctantly. "We'll make for the town of Unlarta. It's a five-day trip, but there are some old tents and travel kits here we can use. We'll take what food we can, and we'll make for the east. We'll decide what to do when we..."

"Wait," I suddenly spoke up, drawing their gazes back to me. "We should tell my uncles what has happened in Arvon. They have to rally a force to retake the town and rescue any survivors."

"You're sure, your Highness?" Tallinn asked me.

I nodded. "I don't like my Uncle Fane, but he's the closest to us from here. We should send him a message and have him meet us in Unlarta. I mean, there are plenty of soldiers wandering through that town, right? I'm sure they can pass on the message."

"That actually sounds like a good idea," Carden supported me. "Then we can keep her safe until it's done and take her home."

"We still need to go to the council," Tallinn reminded us solemnly. "There's still the matter of the Shadow Lord to attend to."

"Yes, you're right," Aldwyn agreed. "We'll make for Unlarta first, then we'll decide what to do once we're safely within the town's walls."

I was staring down at the floor then, remembering the mysterious cowled sorcerer and the moment I had seen him on the wall in Arvon. I hadn't spoken of this observation aloud or told anyone else in the group, but it continued to haunt me. I couldn't understand why he had been there that night when my family was murdered, and my home destroyed. It was maddening.

"Leander?" Carden was watching me as Mithras was directing the others. "What is it?"

"It's nothing," I told him.

"Leander, Carden," Mithras called to us, drawing our gazes. "You'd best gather your belongings. We leave in half an hour."

With that, we got to our feet and went to do as instructed.

I entered the barracks and went to my backpack. I had left it open, the Dragon Stone sitting there on the bed, visible before me. I had been looking at it earlier, finding a strange comfort in the mysterious object. Now as I stood there studying it I felt a new sensation. I had a strange protectiveness towards it, almost a possessive sense like I wouldn't let anyone else touch it. I ran my hand along its shell, feeling its cool outside and its strange radiating warmth. Cuddling up to it had been a very good idea over the last few nights, the warmth helping me to sleep.

Carefully, I picked it up in its silken cloth and rewrapped it, stowing it in my backpack again. I gathered up my remaining clothes that I had pulled out, then slung the bag over my back and left the room to join the others.

They were gathering in the main hall, all of them dressed in their original clothes and donning their cloaks and hoods.

"Are we ready to move?" Mithras asked, taking the lead.

They all nodded as I moved to stand beside Carden.

"Right. Let's go then," Mithras directed, drawing his hood and leading the way as he hefted his shield onto his back.

I gave Carden a small smile, then pulled my hood up over my head and stayed with him as we walked.

We stepped out into the cold and began our slow march down the mountain's feet, Mithras leading the way, Aldwyn and Tallinn behind him, then Carden and I with Fawkner at our backs and Joran bringing up the rear.

Soon we had climbed down through the foothills and were making our way to the main road heading east towards the town of Unlarta and hopefully safety.

Chapter Eleven
A Conspiracy

The first few hours down from the foothills led our group through the plains outside of Arvon, the tree line of the Scarfold Forest growing clearer and closer in the east and south around us. This would soon lead us to the highway, the cobblestone pathway broad enough for two large carriages to pass each other without slowing down or knocking one another off the road. It became visible as we moved through the underbrush, our group reaching it in less than an hour.

Stepping onto the road, I felt the firm stonework under my boots, somewhat more at ease now that we had left the more difficult path of the uneven, muddy ground. I felt steadier, previously fearing that I would fall into the mud or sink through the ever-moistening earth like quicksand.

We didn't speak, save for Mithras and Aldwyn discussing the path ahead, Fawkner joining them as night began to fall. We were going to have to make camp for the night off the road, our only concern now that we had come to the edge of the Scarfold Forest.

As a child I had been so frightened of this forest, the stories I had heard of horrid creatures ambushing travellers causing me to suffer nightmares and scream in my sleep. I had always been afraid of dire wolves and the dreaded, diseased rat-like creatures called groundmerks that lingered in the underbrush; a fear that remained with me even now.

The others took turns on watch after setting up our camp, carefully guarding against any number of dangerous beasts that prowled the forests. I was the only one allowed to sleep through the night, nestled within the makeshift tent they had erected for me.

With two people on guard at any one time, they watched the camp against the dark forests and listened to the noises of the beasts prowling the night. When morning came, relief flooded the camp as the noises of the night faded away, the most dangerous of the Scarfold creatures slinking back into their burrows for the day.

Again, we set off, travelling along the road that wound through the exterior parts of the forest. We continued on like this throughout the second day, not meeting anyone on the road or seeing any animals, the rains still falling above us lightly. Just as we had the night before, we made camp, two people on guard at all times as the sounds of the forest creatures echoed in the dark. The next two days were much the same.

On the fifth day, we awoke and gathered up the camp, then made our way along the highway again. On this day we came across a group of merchants travelling along the roads towards Westport, the town at the mouth of the Great River Arvon. We paused to speak with the merchants, Mithras warning them of the assailants that had assaulted Arvon.

Concealed beneath my hood, I watched the merchants as their eyes widened in terror at the news. I didn't feel that they were a threat to me, yet Mithras had told me to keep my face hidden, my safety paramount regardless of who it was we spoke to. I thought that he was just being overprotective at this point, but I knew better than to argue with him.

The merchants agreed to take one of the other paths past Arvon to avoid any hostile men that yet lingered there, selling a few vitally needed items to us, then bidding us farewell.

It was sunset when the stone walls of the large town of Unlarta came into view. The rooftops of the buildings rose up before us, the tallest being the watchtower where the local Aldegaadian soldiers stood guard, the next tallest being the roof of a fortress mansion just off the town square.

It looked like a very dismal place compared to Arvon. It seemed as though there was no cheer and no comfort to be found here. It was simply a grey, grim town in the centre of Aldegaad's northern parts. Even the plants that weren't vegetables or fruits were fairly pale looking, mostly just creeping vines and ivies climbing the stone walls.

"This is a gloomy place," I commented softly, gazing up from beneath my hood at the walls.

"It's the last town in Northern Aldegaad before the border with Lorveren," Mithras told me calmly. "That is, it's the last human town. However, we should be able to call to your uncle from here, as you have requested."

"It has been some time since we were here," Fawkner said to himself. "If we had never come to this accursed town..."

"You were here?" I asked, looking up at him.

He met my gaze and nodded, glancing to Carden beside me before responding to my question.

"Yes. This is where Joran, my other companions and I met with the mysterious man who ordered your abduction," he explained. "We stayed at the Last Rest Inn. It is perhaps not the brightest place, but it is comfortable enough."

We reached the western gates, Mithras knocking on the door loudly. We waited only a few seconds before the viewing hatch opened and the face of a middle-aged man stared out at us. He had a pale, milky eye, indicating that it had no sight in it, a scar running up his face, his head covered in a dark blue hood. He eyed us coldly, trying to get a look at our faces in the dimming twilight.

I kept my face down beneath my cowl, feeling very uneasy.

"What do you want?" he demanded coldly.

"We are travellers," Mithras told him, Aldwyn at his side. "We seek to rest in Unlarta for a time."

The man eyed him coldly. "And what are you not telling me?"

"Will you allow us inside?" Mithras asked calmly.

"Who are you?" the guard demanded harshly.

Mithras pushed back his cloak, revealing his armour and the Aldegaadian crest.

"I am a Knight of Aldegaad. I seek refuge for myself and my companions here," he explained coolly and firmly. "Our business is our own."

"My apologies, Ser Knight," the guardsman suddenly sounded as though there was nothing he wouldn't give us. "I just have to ask these questions. There have been strange tidings coming through the roads of roving bandits, and we have to be careful."

"I understand," Mithras nodded to him. "Now, may we pass?"

"Yes. Yes, of course," the guard nodded, shutting the viewing hatch and opening the gates for us. "Go right through, Ser Knight. Welcome to Unlarta."

We passed through the gates, the presence of Aldegaadian soldiers only a mild comfort to me. I wasn't sure why I felt this way, only that it was an unshakable feeling. I watched them from beneath my cloak's hood, trying to stay hidden from sight as my instincts told me to remain silent and cautious.

We made our way through the town slowly, its expanse seeming to be more a city than it had been when it was first built over a thousand years ago. There were larger, better constructed buildings there now, the smaller houses overshadowed by them. The walls were patrolled by the city guards dressed in Aldegaadian cloaks, scale armour and chainmail, archers watching from the highest points of the walls.

There were still people in the streets, men and women making their way home or heading to prayers at the temple, or to the various taverns. They glared at us coldly, giving me the impression that we weren't welcome here, despite the gatekeeper's words.

We passed through the poorer district first, the sight of so many homeless a shock to me. I had walked through Arvon constantly while I was growing up and had never seen a beggar in my life. It was something that didn't exist in our town. I felt the strongest pity for them as I passed by amidst my protective companions, wishing there was something I could do for the poor wretches in the gutters.

Soon, we entered the middle district, which encircled much of the town and met the richer district in the town square. This wasn't devoid of beggars and homeless though, their plight seeming an epidemic in this cursed town. Now I thought that I had come to understand the gloomy disposition of this wayward place.

We entered an alleyway in the middle district, an inn there called *The Last Rest Inn*, the same Fawkner had mentioned. It was a simple grey stone brick building with a dark tiled roof, windows looking out from upstairs, downstairs and the extended parts of the building. Its sign swung in the wind with a slow creaking and a light banging as it hit the post it hung from, a lantern beside it to illuminate its words.

Mithras pushed the door open, and we stepped inside to a warmer atmosphere. The tavern part of the inn was bustling with activity and merrymaking, hornpipe music booming cheerfully through the room. The players sat on the stage performing with their instruments, entertaining the patrons with their continuously cheery music as a few young women were dancing. They were beautiful and wearing outfits that looked more like dancers' costumes than normal clothes. The patrons were clapping at the sight and cheering as others around them ate meals and smoked pipes, laughing and talking.

I was surprised by the activity and fun this room seemed to boast over the original impression Unlarta had given me.

"Stay with Carden and Tallinn," Mithras advised me, then walked to the counter where the bartender – a beautiful older woman – stood talking with a drunken patron.

I looked up at Carden from beneath my hood as he pushed his back. Tallinn was standing beside me, her hood still drawn and her hand resting on her sword. I felt safe with the two Guardians at my side, sensing the mammoth height of Joran behind us as he slouched slightly to avoid a chandelier and roof beam.

Mithras, Fawkner and Aldwyn walked to the bartender and spoke to her quietly. I couldn't hear what they were saying, but she seemed as though she was being very friendly. She reached down behind the counter and gave them a quartet of keys, then assured them of something before they returned to us.

"So? Are we alright to stay here?" Tallinn asked.

Aldwyn nodded, handing a key to her and another to me. "She had four rooms left. They're ours for as long as we wish. She has also said that we can order some food once we've cleaned up and changed."

"We've worked out the sleeping arrangements," Mithras told us calmly. "Leander, you have a room to yourself. I think that would be appropriate. Aldwyn tells me that Carden and Tallinn have shared a room before, so we have given you two that key. Aldwyn and I will take the third room, and Fawkner and Joran have the fourth. Only the room Leander has been given has one bed, the rest have two."

"That seems appropriate," Joran stated evenly.

"Alright," Mithras nodded to us and gestured to the stairs. "Go on up and meet back here in twenty minutes for evening meal. We'll discuss our options then."

Following the others' lead, I went upstairs to the second floor, finding my room easily. I walked inside and locked the door, faced with a simple room that was also quite nice. The bed was a double with curtains of violet cloth hanging around it, the bedclothes matching them.

I undressed, washed and dried myself, then changed into a simple green and gold, wide sleeved dress, leggings and my boots. Keeping my pendant around my neck, I left the room, my bag set on the bed and still packed. I wasn't sure whether to unpack or not at this point.

Reaching the stairs, I returned to the tavern, the music slightly different, but mostly the same cheerful sort of tone, the patrons still laughing and talking as the dancers pranced across the floors.

I could see the others already gathered around a table for eight, two seats remaining cleared. They all looked relaxed, their clothes cleaner and their faces free of sweat and dirt.

Carden looked up as I approached, standing and pulling out one of the two empty chairs. I thanked him and took the seat, allowing him to push it in before he seated himself beside me.

"We've ordered some food already," Aldwyn told me simply. "I hope you like lamb."

"Of course," I responded, smiling at him as I settled into my seat.

The food arrived soon after and we served ourselves, sitting and eating slowly as we watched all the activity around us. For me, this was all a new experience. I hadn't been a guest at an inn before and I found all of this very interesting and exciting. For a time, the activity and cheer of the inn was enough to distract me from the tragedy I had previously suffered, my mind now on the merrymaking locals and patrons all around me. But my thoughts returned to what needed to be done soon enough.

"Alright," I said softly, drawing my companions' eyes to me, then meeting their stares. "So, what exactly are we going to do now?"

"What do you mean, your Highness?" Tallinn asked blatantly.

"Shh," Mithras hissed through his teeth. "Her identity must remain concealed."

"Oh... Uh... Sorry... I mean, Leander," Tallinn corrected herself, looking sheepish.

I sat back with my hands in my lap and shrugged. "How do we get in contact with my uncles?"

"Carrier pigeon?" Carden suggested with a mouth full of food.

"I don't think so, Carden," Aldwyn responded calmly, setting down his mug. "There don't seem to be any message posts available to the public here."

"There aren't," Fawkner agreed. "Messages are delivered by courier, not pigeon."

"Well, that option would be out then," Tallinn muttered grimly, arms folded on the table, her blonde hair hanging about her face.

"Why?" I asked.

"Because we can't afford to take that kind of risk, Prin...Uh... Leander," Aldwyn explained, correcting himself with a glance from Mithras. "There seem to be too many ways that course of action could go wrong. We cannot trust a message to a courier or a pigeon."

"There is another option," Mithras spoke up, drawing our eyes to him.

He was studying the grains in the wooden planks that made up the table, his dark eyes almost seeming to read unseen glyphs or words scratched into the timber. His jaw was set and his body language secretive, his behaviour subtle, but clear enough for the rest of us to know that what he had to say was secret and not for the ears of others around us.

"There is the Baron," Mithras turned his eyes to me.

"The Baron?" I raised a curious eyebrow.

"You've got to be joking," Fawkner rolled his eyes and sat back with his arms crossed, unimpressed.

Mithras ignored him, nodding to me. "Baron Henry Emerton has a reputation for being a very trustworthy man. He could help us make contact with your uncles."

"What would we have to do?" I asked, feeling anxious of this idea.

Mithras shrugged slightly. "Simply go to him and ask for assistance. He could possibly arrange for either your uncles to come here, or for transport to go to one of them."

"That's idiotic," Fawkner snorted, eyeing Mithras coldly. "You want to go to the lord of a backwater town? Might as well throw ourselves to a pack of wolves or dive into shark infested waters."

"This is our best opportunity to call for aid and retake Arvon," Mithras spoke with a very plainly calm attitude, looking to Fawkner sternly. "Not to mention that we could officially gain the protection of the city guards for Leander."

"And you'd trust him with her safety?" the man frowned.

Mithras nodded. "She is a member of the Aldrich Royal Family. Emerton would protect her with his life as any of us would."

"Well, I'd like to hear what the Guardians have to say about this," Fawkner turned to Aldwyn and Tallinn expectantly.

The two exchanged a look that felt like it lasted an eternity to me. Tallinn nodded and Aldwyn turned back, clasping his hands in front of him on the table.

"It seems like a viable option, in all honesty," he consented. "The girl's protection is our first and foremost priority. If Baron Emerton can guarantee her safety then that will aid us considerably."

"I can't believe you're agreeing to this lunacy," Fawkner snorted. "You cannot trust politicians. They're cutthroats."

"Would you have us sit on our hands and do nothing?" Tallinn demanded coldly. "Would you place the girl's life in continued danger just to satisfy your own distrust of nobles?"

"Joran. Help me out here," Fawkner pleaded, looking to his eight-foot friend.

Joran turned his deep eyes around the table, surveying all of our faces before finally settling on mine. I felt him studying me and sensed the thoughts ticking through his towering, silent visage. I could see the turmoil in those violet eyes as the giant was conflicted by both sets of loyalty he felt.

Finally, he turned his eyes to Fawkner and stated: "I am bound to serve the Sarissi, Fawkner. Her safety is my concern before all others."

"I do not believe this!" Fawkner sat back, a stunned look on his face.

"You know," Carden spoke up, drawing our gazes to him, "no one has asked for Leander's opinion. Did we consider that?"

"You're right," Tallinn nodded, then looked back to me evenly. "What would you want to do, Prin... I mean, Leander?"

I regarded the others with a cold, uncertain stare. *I don't want to be asked to make decisions. Not now. Why can't they just let me grieve?*

"I guess, Mithras' idea is a good one," I said very carefully. "We'll go to the Baron and ask for help."

Everyone, except Fawkner, nodded their agreement, the ex-mercenary shaking his head with his arms crossed.

"It's a mistake," he muttered.

I eyed him sternly. "Then it is my mistake."

Fawkner nodded, silently conceding defeat. "As you wish, girl."

There were a few moments of silence between us as we sat there together finishing the food we had left. I just stared at my hands folded together on the table. I felt too broken inside to really care about much right now, yearning to crawl into bed.

At last, Mithras spoke, standing up: "We'd best get some rest. We'll have to go to the Baron's in the morning."

The others nodded and started to head off as I sat there staring blankly into space. When I finally pulled myself away from the table and up to my room only a few patrons remained there, most of them watching me as I sat. If not for Joran's towering presence I might have been an easy target for the drunken men, but I remained safe right up until I closed my door for the night.

* * * * *

Black dreams haunted me as I slept, tossing and turning in the folds of my tavern room bed. I moaned and cried in the night; the death of my father as clear to me then as it was when he had actually died before me. My nightmares scratched and clawed at me, howling as though they yearned for not only my blood but the blood of all those with me.

Then I saw *him*. The black cowled sorcerer towered before me, eyes glowing green as unholy flame swirled around his black and crimson clad form. He stood in front of me, his hand outstretched as if he were reaching for me, his thin, faded lips parted slightly, revealing horrible, pointed teeth behind them...

I woke with a start, propping myself up and turning my eyes to the figure standing beside the bed. Tallinn gazed down at me from beneath the freely flowing blonde mane framing her face, her expression full of concern.

"Princess? Are you alright?"

"Where... where am I?"

"The inn," she responded. "Do you not remember?"

It took me a few moments to remember as I surveyed my unfamiliar surroundings. I cast my vision towards the window, rain running down over the panes in a gently flowing tide, the sky outside the colour of a stormy morning.

"Right. I remember," I confirmed, nodding as I sat up out of bed, dressed in my nightgown.

"Mithras is preparing to head off to see the Baron," Tallinn informed me. "You should get dressed."

I crossed to the basin filled with cool water, dousing my face to wake myself up. There was a knock at the door and I quickly grabbed a quilt from the bed and covered myself as Carden entered. The young man surveyed Tallinn and I for a few seconds, then turned his attention directly to my eyes.

"Forgive my intrusion, Leander," he spoke courteously to me. "Ser Mithras sent me to see if you were ready yet."

"No, she isn't," Tallinn retorted coldly, eyeing Carden with her fiery hazel eyes. "Did the Knight really send you? Or are you simply looking to catch a glimpse of a woman undressing?"

Carden looked offended. "He sent me. He seems rather impatient, to be honest. I think it has to do with the notion that it will be only he and Leander going to the Baron. And you know me better than that, Tallinn."

"What?" I stared at him, stunned. "The rest of you aren't coming?"

Carden shook his head. "Ser Mithras and Aldwyn have been discussing the situation. They both believe that only you and he should go, and that the rest of us should remain here at the inn. They think that the presence of Guardians might draw too much attention to you."

"And what do the two of you think?" I asked, turning my gaze to both of them.

"My experience with the Guardians has taught me to follow my master's orders," Tallinn expressed simply, her voice grave. "However, my own instincts tell me that it is a mistake to leave you without more protection."

"And you, Carden?" I turned my blue gaze to him.

Carden glanced at Tallinn, nodded and turned to me, his eyes burning like a brush fire, his expression one of deep uncertainty.

"I don't like the idea of letting you go to this baron without us," he confessed. "Though Mithras has vouched for him I have my doubts we can trust him. Fawkner had a point last night about politicians, especially backwater town ones."

"Alright," I sighed and nodded. "I'm not going to argue with you, but I don't like the idea of leaving you here while I go with Mithras either," I shrugged and shook my head reluctantly. "All the same, the Baron is my best chance at contacting Uncle Aric and Uncle Fane. I doubt they know what's happened at Arvon yet."

Carden nodded grimly. "If that's your decision, then I'll go and tell Ser Mithras that you'll be right out."

"Thank you, Carden," I nodded to him as he left, then turned to my bag.

A few minutes later I emerged from my room with Tallinn following, dressed in my gold laced blue gown and my purple cloak. After saying our goodbyes, Mithras and I left the tavern and made our way out into the rainy cold of the town, my hood drawn and my cloak pulled around me protectively.

It didn't take long for us to reach the centre of town and find the Baron's residence – the large manor I had seen on the way into the city, as it turned out. We walked along the cobblestone path towards the main gates, two soldiers watching our approach from their posts flanking the gate with stony expressions.

"What can you tell me of Baron Emerton?" I asked of Mithras, glancing out from under my hood as I spoke, droplets of rain sliding off its rim.

"He is a very powerful man in Unlarta and the surrounding estates," Mithras replied begrudgingly. "If anyone in this part of Aldegaad can aid us, it is he."

"Hm," I considered, noting his obvious dislike of the man. "And what is he *really* like?"

"Leander?"

"Do you really expect me to believe that you respect him when you speak in that tone of voice, Mithras?" I asked, locking my gaze with his. "Tell me, what do you really think?"

"Honestly? He is a foul, horrid cretin who is more interested in food, gold and debauchery than altruism," Mithras seethed with disgust. "I'd sooner cover myself in honey and dance before a hungry bear than speak with him. However, our situation requires it, so I forbear."

"What can I expect?" I asked nervously.

He smirked knowingly: "He may try to proposition you. You are an attractive young woman, remember? You are also next in line for the throne and it is not unheard of for a girl younger than you to marry a man of his years."

"Ugh! I'd rather not," I commented, shuddering.

We reached the gate, the guards stepping out before us.

"Halt!" one held out a gloved hand to us. "What business have you with the Baron of Unlarta?"

"I am Ser Mithras of Arvon, commander of the Arvon garrison," Mithras introduced himself. "I come with grim tidings: Prince Ewan and Duchess Caralyn have been murdered, and the town ransacked by unknown brigands. We seek an audience with the Baron and ask for aid."

"If that were true," the second guard said curtly, almost smugly, "then we would have received word by now."

"You do not believe the word of a knight?" Mithras demanded coldly.

"We would need word from Arvon itself," the same guard insisted. "A messenger pigeon at the very least from one of the captains with the royal seal."

"How about a member of the royal family, then?" I asked, tilting my head to reveal my face. "I am Princess Leander Aldrich, Prince Ewan's daughter. What my bodyguard says is true: my father and mother are dead, and Arvon has fallen," my voice cracked with grief saying those last words, my initial strength fading quickly.

"Your Highness!" the first guard stared with wide eyes at me. "Our apologies! We'll alert the Baron at once. Please, pass through."

"See?" I smirked at Mithras as we passed the gates and walked towards the Baron's estate. "Sometimes it pays to have a princess with you."

"Indeed it does," Mithras nodded, smiling at me.

We made our way up the wet steps of the manor, guards saluting us now that they knew the identity of the Knight's smaller, hooded companion. The doors into the estate were opened for us and we stepped into the main hall, passing through a second archway and entering the "*throne*" room, as it was called in the lesser provinces.

It was a garishly furnished room with the Aldegaadian banners littering the high roof beams and the stone walls. There was a grand staircase behind the central dais leading to the second storey and the third storey, the guards as numerous as the flags and banners.

A large, brightly dressed man was standing at the top of the stairs, making his way down clad in blue, purple and gold velvet. He was very overweight with heavy jowls and dark eyes, his face cleanly shaven and his short hair covered by a hideous, billowy hat matching his clothes. He wore an exuberant amount of jewellery, almost every one of his pudgy pork fingers adorned in a large, ugly ring, the heavy chain of the Baron around his generously padded neck.

He smiled a disgusting, greasy grin at the sight of us, his arms out wide.

"Ah! Princess Leander! It is an honour to have you visit my humble little province!" he boomed in a deep, bellowing voice.

I pushed back my hood as the Baron approached, a gaggle of assistants surrounding the disgusting man. Now I saw why Mithras was so callous towards him.

"*I*," he emphasised as he reached us, smiling down at me, "am Baron Henry Emerton, at your service, your most esteemed Highness."

He took my right hand and immediately kissed my knuckles, leaving his lips there a little longer and squeezing a little tighter than I liked. I pulled my hand away and subtly wiped it on the inside of my cloak.

"Thank you for your... uh... warm welcome, Baron Emerton," I forced myself to play the diplomat as my father had taught me.

"It is a great honour to finally receive you, your Highness," Emerton beamed. "I have never heard of you travelling anywhere other than the capital or your own home in Arvon. Are we your first visit?"

"Yes, actually, you are," I admitted, and immediately regretted it.

The Baron lit up as if he had suddenly burst into the whitest of flames, his pride as obvious as the bulbous nose on his ugly face: "Then we of Unlarta are truly privileged! We must hold a banquet in your honour and welcome you properly!"

"No! I..."

"Oh, so modest!" the Baron laughed. "But really," he took my arm and led me towards the stairs, Mithras swiftly falling into step behind us, "you must enjoy the full hospitality of my fine province, Princess!"

"Stop! Listen to me!" I pulled away from him, causing him to turn to face me. "We need your help!"

The Baron stared at me, still smiling, but there was a look of confusion on his malformed face. "Help? What kind of help?"

I ignored his line of gaze directed at my chest and pressed on: "I need to get in contact with my uncle, Prince Fane of Aldilith. I need him to direct his forces to retake Arvon immediately."

"Is this a jest, child?" Emerton chortled, glancing at Mithras as if he expected the very serious knight to be just as astonished by my tale. "How amusing you are, your Highness. Why in all of Therras would you want us to send forces to Arvon?"

"Arvon has been... invaded by-by..." I felt tears swelling behind my eyes, trembling at the thought of relaying the tragedy I had witnessed.

"Unknown invaders have taken control of Arvon and laid siege to the castle," Mithras stepped up, taking over from me as I fought my grief again. "We barely made it away with our lives."

The Baron's expression changed, his joviality replaced by confusion and horror. "You're... serious? Aren't you, Knight?"

"We are," Mithras confirmed.

"How many escaped?" the Baron asked.

"Seven," was the Knight's response. "That we know of."

"Prince Ewan and Duchess Caralyn?"

"Dead. The Princess was the only Aldrich family member we could save."

I looked up at the two men as silence fell between them. I saw the Baron's face and noted the shock in his eyes. He seemed like he was paralysed, his hands rigid at his sides, his eyes unfocused. He stared blankly at nothing for a few moments, almost as though he was processing all of the information he had been told at once.

"How could this... be possible? In this day and age?" he looked to Mithras and I again. "When did this siege take place?"

"The first night of the Festival of Light," Mithras answered bluntly.

"So recently and yet so long ago?"

Mithras nodded in confirmation. "Twelve days ago."

"These are dark tidings. Dark tidings indeed," the Baron nodded grimly. "But at least *you* are safe, Princess."

I sighed and nodded. "Though I don't feel so comforted by that notion."

"I understand, your Highness," the Baron walked towards me. "But perhaps I could offer you something else before I contact your uncle?"

"What's that?" I asked, looking up at him uncertainly.

I didn't like the way he was looking at me, his smile seeming more a deceptive sneer. Then I saw it behind his eyes. There was a lie there, just as my father had taught me to search for, a motive that I didn't trust.

"Perhaps a comforting place to stay where you will be safe?" he suggested. "Safer than that tavern you and your Guardian friends are hiding in?"

I stared at him in shock. "How did you know that my friends are Guardians?"

"You are in *my* domain," the Baron replied, smiling broadly. "I am the law and the lord in this province. You are my guests, your Highness."

"Leander," Mithras stepped closer towards me, his hand on the pommel of his sword. "Step behind me."

I was breathing heavily as I stared at the Baron, seeing the eagerness in his eyes. My fear rose as he reached for me, taking me by the wrist and squeezing tightly. I wasn't able to get free. Then it occurred to me what it was that I was seeing behind the man's eyes. I saw the truth and I knew that my parents' deaths weren't as plain as barbarians invading the fortress that was Castle Arvon.

A cold thought hit me: *How could that rabble have entered the castle without help?*

"You," I gasped. "You were behind it."

"Behind what, your Highness?" the Baron asked sweetly.

I felt my heart heaving inside me just as I felt my stomach churn and threaten to hurl out my last meal. Tears of anger were burning my cheeks as I viewed this disgusting little wretch, his desires as plain to me in his eyes as if they were tattooed across his face.

"The assault on Arvon, the assassination of my mother and father, the attempt on my life, the murder of every man and woman inside the castle," I stared at the human form monster before me in terror. "It was you!"

"Me?" the Baron laughed. "No, no, dear Princess. You have it all wrong. I could never have orchestrated such a masterful stroke."

"Masterful?!" I repeated, wincing at his tightening grip on my wrist.

Emerton nodded to his men as Mithras drew his sword. The guards turned on the old knight, pointing their own weapons at him as Emerton pulled me closer. Mithras looked on in horror, unable to fight off twelve soldiers glaring at him with swords pointed to his throat.

I struggled against Emerton's grasp, helpless to free myself. I stared up at him in horror and anger, hating him even more than when I had first stepped through that door.

"You killed my parents!" I screamed, fighting against him, tears streaming down my face.

"As I said," Emerton held me tightly by both wrists, sneering down at me, "I could not have orchestrated this little coup. I don't have the resources. I merely played my part."

With that, he pushed me backwards, two guards grabbing my arms and holding me tight, my hands suddenly pulled behind my back. I struggled as Mithras was wrestled to his knees, his sword taken away.

"Emerton, you cowardly bastard!" the Knight snarled venomously. "You would betray your own people, your own King?!"

"I was offered fair compensation," Emerton sneered as three more figures emerged from a doorway.

"As were we all," Lord Renton Seward stated, entering with his wife and son.

He rounded on me, smiling at me mockingly.

How could he?! He was one of my father's closest friends!

I stared at the three in terror. "You're responsible for this?!"

Lord Seward smiled coldly. "How else do you think the attackers were able to enter the castle that night? Someone had to give them the best ways to gain entry, did they not?"

"You!" Mithras snarled loudly and poisonously at them. "You are traitors to the Crown and to Aldegaad itself! All of you!"

"Where you see traitors, Ser Mithras, we see loyalists to our nation," Renton Seward remarked, glaring at him.

"Why?! Why did you do this?!" I stared at the four in terrified disbelief.

"For the good of Aldegaad," Renton spoke with a twisted sense of patriotism, facing me again.

"How is murdering my mother and father for the good of Aldegaad?!" I demanded, struggling to stay strong. My heart was twisting in my chest and screaming as though it were burning in a pit of lava.

"Aldegaad is in peril," Renton explained to me as Tibain approached, his son's expression one of intense desire and possession. "There is a threat that lingers on the edge of our nation, haunting us and promising doom for our people. But this is nothing compared to the threat within."

"What are you talking about?" I asked coldly, wishing I could just hurt every last one of them.

"Aldegaad is ruled by a decrepit old man who is too afraid to do what must be done!" Renton spoke passionately, but angrily, glaring at me from his sunken face. "Aric hides in his palace at Aneuran playing the part of a kind and just ruler, unable to address the true threat that plagues this nation!"

"The Ivanstenians are the true barbarians at our gates," Angora Seward spoke up, her aging eyes looking very tired beneath her tightly coiled, grey streaked hair, "They are as dangerous as a herd of wild horses stampeding through a farmer's crop."

"Are you serious?!" I scoffed, struggling against my captors again. "You want to restart the war with Ivansten?! Are you insane?!"

"Idiot girl!" Renton hissed bitterly, glaring at me icily. "You're too young to see what is right before you! We are already at war! Our troops stand in defence of this nation at the fortress of Aldgate! They constantly stand watch against the Ivanstenian filth that waits just on the other side of that ravine!"

He threw his hands up in the air, pacing wildly and furiously. His eyes were blazing as he turned back to me, coming so close that our faces almost touched.

"This cold war between Aldegaad and Ivansten has been going on for far too long! Centuries have been wasted waiting for them to make the first move when they could have been wiped out by now! Is that justice, child?! No! Is it practical?! No!"

"Is what you're suggesting practical, your Lordship?!" Mithras spoke up, drawing their gazes, his eyes fierce. "Murdering half the royal family just to cast away tens of thousands of lives in a fool venture to rid Therras of our northern neighbours?!"

"*Murder* is such a harsh word," Emerton commented, shaking his head.

"So is the word *treason*," Mithras warned icily, glaring at them. "What you and the rest of your conspirators have done, and what you plan to do is an affront to all that Aldegaad stands for. This is *not* what Queen Leander would have expected of her people one thousand years after her reunion with the Gods."

"How do you know, Knight?" Angora asked coldly and bitterly. "Perhaps her royal majesty would have considered this very course of action."

"I doubt it," Mithras hissed.

"How come?" Renton enquired, smirking.

"Because of me," I spoke up, their eyes returning to me. "Everyone always says that I'm like her, after all."

"Perhaps you are more like the Queen Leander that we thought her to be, Princess," Angora commented coolly. "Would you sacrifice your home and your people to a painful and horrible fate? Would you not want to help them in every way you can?"

"I would certainly help them," I agreed. "But..."

"Then you would do as we and our allies have here," she went on, interrupting me. "You would destroy all threats to Aldegaad, both without and within."

"By murdering my family and trying to kill me?!" I demanded coldly.

"Your father, Princess," Renton spoke again, standing over me, "was as dangerous as your uncle. Neither one deserves the throne or the nation's rule. They would both cast Aldegaad to the wolves. So, they must be destroyed."

"And then that leaves *you*, your Highness," Emerton grinned, hands clasped together over his bulging belly.

"Me?" I tensed as I felt the terror and anticipation growing inside me. "What about me?"

"Your uncle announced his intention to make you his heir," he reminded me. "All of Aldegaad now knows that you are next in line for the throne."

"And I suppose you don't like that!" Mithras growled, receiving a sword pommel to the stomach for his troubles.

"On the contrary," Emerton replied, turning back to me. "The Princess is an asset, not a threat."

"An asset?" I raised a concerned and confused eyebrow.

"Think of it, Princess," Tibain reached out, stroking my cheek as I glared at him. "You will be the most powerful woman in all of Aldegaad. Once your uncle passes from this world and into the Beyond, of course. You could correct the mistakes the old fool has made and end your people's suffering."

"How?" I asked calculatingly, meeting his gaze.

"Marshal the armies," Renton instructed, drawing my gaze as his son continued caressing my face, the guards holding me steady, "march into the Ivanstenian Capital and kill their King. Then take command of their lands as they once ruled ours and expand Aldegaad between the north and south of the mountains."

"You mean conquer them? Lead a crusade?" Mithras snorted and shook his head. "Do you really think she'll agree to that?"

"Maybe," Tibain mewed, staring at me, desiring me even as I cringed from him, "she just needs the right incentive."

I turned my gaze to him, his face so close that I could barely see it through more than a blurred haze.

―――――

"We could be so happy, you and I. We could produce a greater bloodline than your ancestor did. Just think of it, my love: Prince Regent Tibain Seward and Queen Leander Aldrich the Second, the great rulers of Aldegaad, uniters of all the lands of Therras."

"You want to be Prince Regent?" I asked softly, staring at him with a hard frown.

Tibain shrugged. "I want to marry you. Being Prince Regent is just a bonus."

"Never," I snarled, glaring at him.

I felt his fingers close around my throat and saw the rage in his eyes appear. I struggled to breathe, but made no sound, keeping my eyes locked on his, daring him to hurt me.

If he's going to kill me, I thought, *then he's going to have to look at me while he does it.*

"You ungrateful little bitch," Tibain hissed softly, glaring at me. "I was trying to save your life. But now," he drew his sword, making me cringe in terror, though I still managed to glare at him.

"Don't harm her!" Mithras cried, then howled in pain as he was slammed to the floor by one guard with the pommel of a sword buried into his back.

"Harm her?" Tibain glared at me as the guards held my struggling body tighter. "I'll do so much worse than that," he turned his eyes to mine, mewing: "I think I could just give you the wedding night without the wedding. Somehow, though, I doubt you'll lie still. I may have to convince you."

"No," I stared at him, terrified, closing my eyes and turning my face from him.

I couldn't hide my fear at the thought of being violated by him, trembling and fighting back tears.

"I have always liked the idea of screwing a girl whilst she is chained to a wall," Tibain laughed. "I think we'll try that. Don't you?"

I tensed up, feeling the cold steel of his sword pressing to my neck. *Please! Not this!* I whimpered as I felt his free hand reaching across my slender body towards my thigh, gripping at my dress. *Don't let this happen to me! Please!*

I could feel his hot breath on my neck, his free hand gripping at my skirts slowly. I couldn't stop myself breathing heavily, trembling just as powerfully in the guards' steel grips. I swallowed hard as I felt his lips on my neck, so frightened that he was going to hurt me right there in front of everyone.

"I cannot wait to feel you, Leander," he whispered, his voice sounding so sharp and coarse, his hand reaching down the collar of my dress now after working its way up my body. "I'm going to show you what a *man* can do."

"You're not a man," I managed in a weak, frightened voice, suddenly aware that I had been shoved away from the guards and up against one of the surrounding pillars.

He chuckled to veil his anger, pressing the sword deeper to my throat.

"You're mine," he hissed venomously into my ear, "and I'm going to make you scream."

Get me out of this! Please, Gods, get me out of this! Do something! Anything! Please!

As if in answer to my plea, I felt a heat coursing through my chest, almost like my heart was burning, but there was no pain. What I felt was a strange power that was radiating out from my core, swirling around me in the safe darkness of my closed eyes.

Something told me to open them.

Tibain's eyes were wide and his face pale, a strange violet light surrounding us. All around us the corrupt nobles, their guards and Mithras were staring with bewildered and terrified expressions as Emerton's servants fled in fear.

I glanced down at my chest, shocked by what I saw. My pendant's stone was glowing with a bright purple light... just like in my dream.

I turned my eyes back to Tibain, staring at him with equal bewilderment.

"What the...?" he didn't finish.

It was like a cool, refreshing rush of air billowed around me, the light exploding from the pendant in some kind of shield. Tibain was thrown backwards, his sword clattering to the floor, the force of his hold releasing and dropping me to my knees...

Chapter Twelve
The Power of The Pendant

I was shaking uncontrollably, stunned. I couldn't even begin to figure out what I had just witnessed, the shock of it too much for my mind to comprehend. There was no explanation that I could find, no reason or sense to what I had just seen.

I took a look around from where I sat on my hands and knees, breathing hard, my heart pounding. I was stunned to see that everyone had been thrown to the floor, all of them dazed. Only the few guards at the farthest edges of the room still stood, two of them holding Mithras.

Slowly, my hand shaking as I reached for it, I turned my attention to my pendant. Its stone was pulsating with that strange glow, the energy rippling from it filling me with both fear and comfort. For a moment I forgot the threat that surrounded me, lost in the marvel of my extraordinary necklace, curious thoughts bringing me to wonder what had just happened.

Noise from ahead of me drew my gaze, the conspirators getting to their feet, still wearing their horrified expressions. I suddenly felt like I was facing a mob of witch hunters rather than a group of traitors. They were speechless, staring wide eyed, Emerton, Renton and Angora trying to keep their distance from me.

Two more helmeted soldiers rushed in, surveying the room with shocked gazes. I could only assume that they had heard the noise inside the entry hall. I was suddenly afraid again, the light from the pendant gone now.

"What was that?!" Tibain demanded, staggering to his feet and looking at me, wobbling unsteadily.

"I-I don't know," I answered honestly, trembling in terror and looking to Mithras. "Mithras?"

"It can't be," Mithras was staring at me in amazement and wonder, a certain awe in his dark eyes that I had never seen before.

"Witch! Whore!" Tibain yelled, regaining his rage and striding towards me.

I pulled back in fear, struggling to get away from him. He grabbed me by the throat and lifted me to my feet, pressing me back into the wall roughly. I stared up in panic as he raised his sword, holding my breath.

"I am going to have you and you're going to like it! Understand, girl?!" he roared, slamming me back harder and grabbing at my clothes to hold me steady.

I fought frantically as the pendant began to shine again, brighter this time, blinding Tibain, but he wasn't going to give up. However, his determination was useless, the pendant launching another blast, casting him down and dropping me from his failed assault.

The three less courageous of the conspirators were being backed up the stairs by their bodyguards; Angora terrified, Renton enraged and Emerton a quivering, cowardly mess.

"Tibain! Don't let her make a fool of you, son!" Renton roared viciously as the guards urged him back.

"I'll kill you for this, girl!" Tibain howled, getting to his feet and glaring at me.

I trembled as I looked up at him, knowing that there was no way this could continue without him eventually overpowering me, even with my pendant's strange behaviour. Then my eyes widened as the two newly arrived guards took their helmets off and came right up behind Tibain.

"Excuse me?" Carden drew Tibain's attention, the young lord stunned to see the disguised Guardian. "I thought we already had this discussion about how to treat a lady."

"You!" Tibain snarled, his face bright red.

Before he could say or do anything else, Carden slammed the pommel of his sword into his skull, knocking Tibain out. Tallinn gave him a little knowing smirk, then turned and aimed her bow around at the guards as Carden pointed his sword at Tibain's throat.

"Carden?! Tallinn?!" I stared at them, amazed and relieved. "What are you doing here?!"

"Saving your lives," Tallinn answered as she rounded with her bow on the guards, making them let Mithras go.

"How did you know we were in trouble?" I asked, unsteadily getting to my feet.

"Fawkner sent his falcon to watch you," she explained succinctly as she kicked a downed guard in the head and knocked him out. "Once he saw you were in trouble we packed up and came to help."

Tibain opened his eyes, his gaze terrified as it locked onto the sword pointed at his throat. He stared up at Carden, visibly trembling as his parents and Emerton looked on worriedly. I felt a little satisfaction at seeing the look of fear replace the smugness he usually wore.

"I wouldn't move if I were you," Carden warned him icily, brandishing the sword expertly.

"You don't know what you've done!" Tibain hissed at us. "Helping her will just get you all killed! Give her to me so I can teach the little bitch her place as my property!"

"Your property?" Carden raised an irritated eyebrow at him, pressing the tip of his sword closer to the other man's throat.

"The only thing she's good for is bending to my will!" Tibain snarled. "She's just like every other woman: a filthy, manipulative little whore!"

"Oh for Gods' sakes, kill him already!" Tallinn rolled her eyes, never once taking them or her arrow from the conspirators.

"No!" I called out, drawing Carden's gaze. "Carden, if you kill him then you're the same as him."

There was a tense moment as Carden considered my words, rage very clearly evident in him. He looked back to Tibain, then to me, almost like he was trying to decide what to do; kill him or show mercy. I watched him, pleading with my eyes at first, knowing Carden was better than this. He was no murderer, not like the smug man-child lying there before him.

"Carden. Please. This isn't for him," I pleaded gently, moving to him and placing a hand on his arm as he looked down at me. "Don't become him."

Carden nodded then withdrew his sword, stepping back and turning his jade eyes to me.

Tibain got to his feet, glaring between the two of us. I turned my eyes to him, then without warning, I kicked him in the groin and punched him in the face, dropping him to the ground once more.

Gods that felt good! But also, ow! I shook my hurting hand, my knuckles burning.

"Is that your idea of mercy?" Carden asked with a smirk as the man groaned and nearly cried where he lay.

I shrugged. "He was planning on raping me. He deserves it."

"Let's get out of here," Tallinn advised, backing up with Mithras to us, neither of them taking their attention from the guards.

"You're *not* going anywhere!" Renton roared as his wife huddled into his arm and Emerton cowered behind him.

The remaining guards turned their weapons on us, blocking us from the way out. Mithras, Tallinn and Carden surrounded me protectively, the four of us looking for any other alternative. There was no way out. We could all see it.

Renton's cold laughter drew my gaze to him, his pale eyes locked squarely on me.

"I think perhaps it's time you surrendered," he told us, a smug look on his face. "You wouldn't want to get the Princess killed. Would you?"

Reluctantly – and to my dismay – my companions lowered their weapons in response. But the truth was that we all knew we couldn't escape. That is until two figures emerged behind the conspirators and their guards.

"This is the shortest escape attempt I have ever seen," Renton laughed obliviously, then gasped in shock as a sword was put to his throat.

Emerton and Angora pulled away in terror as Joran appeared and knocked out the last of their bodyguards with only a couple of swift punches. Renton was frozen as Fawkner held him tightly from behind, keeping his sword level with his throat.

"I think, my Lord, that you'd best release the girl and her companions, or I might have to accidentally...*slip*," he said calmly and clearly, leaning over the older man's shoulder.

"You filth..." Renton went to say, gagging as Fawkner pulled back on the sword.

"Lord Seward," he reiterated, "I am *not* going to repeat myself."

I could see that Renton was calculating his options, but there was only one choice.

"Let them go," he ordered hoarsely to the worried guards. "Let them go, now!"

The guards backed off and we followed Tallinn as she directed us towards the doors into the library. Fawkner dragged Renton with him as Joran followed to join us. We were in the library only seconds later and Fawkner unceremoniously shoved Renton to the ground.

"It's been a pleasure," Mithras bowed his head mockingly to them. "We really *must* do this again."

"Kill them! Get the girl!" Renton shouted, the guards rushing forward but too late to reach us as Joran shut and barricaded the doors.

"So, what's the plan exactly?" I asked them as we moved towards the windows.

"Aldwyn has gotten a carriage and is waiting in the forest," Tallinn explained, opening the window. "We have to get out of the city and meet up with him, then we'll make for the Citadel."

"It's the safest option we have," Carden added, turning his green eyes to me, one hand on my back as he led me forward.

"Definitely after what we've found out here," I agreed, warming at his touch.

"This way," Fawkner urged, leading the way out the windows. "Hurry."

Carden stepped through first then helped me to follow, the hems of my dress making this movement awkward for me. The cold air hit me as I cleared the window and I pulled my hood up, running beside Carden as we made for the side gate. It was open and unguarded, the hidden bodies of several guards indicating to me that it wasn't by mistake.

We hurried through the town, heading towards the east gate of the city. Now we had to be more careful, ducking into cover as soldiers marched the streets in search of us.

"The city guard are on full alert," Mithras observed as we hid just within sight of the east gates.

"Those guards we neutralized must have been found by now," Tallinn guessed in a hushed voice, looking out from under her hood. "And the conspirators will have sounded the alarm."

"So, what do we do now?" I asked in a whisper, my eyes surveying the patrols guarding the gates.

"A distraction," Fawkner suggested.

"What do you have in mind?" Mithras asked, turning to the other man.

"You, Joran and I go out there and draw the soldiers into a fight," Fawkner planned. "We can handle that many. Meanwhile, Carden, Tallinn and Leander make for the gates. They get through, then we can follow them and affect our escape."

"It looks like there are archers in the guard towers," Carden pointed out, his green eyes locked on the figures moving around in the towers over the wall.

"Leave them to me," Tallinn said confidently. "You get the Princess through the gate," and with that she vanished down an alleyway.

"Carden," Fawkner turned to the younger Guardian as we stayed low, "wait for our signal."

"Which is?" Carden asked.

"Us killing guards," he smirked.

Carden pulled me into the cover of an alcove, the two of us watching as the others slowly walked out from the alley. Mithras took the lead, showing his Aldegaadian armour clearly, his right hand at his side, his left resting on the pommel of his sword. Fawkner and Joran followed, flanking him as we watched from the shadows.

A guard captain and some of his men came up to them, stopping them with a raised hand. Mithras was talking to them, but I wasn't sure if he could convince them to let us go.

"Do you think this will work?" I asked Carden, holding his arm and looking up at him uneasily.

At that moment an arrow screeched through the air, catching the captain in the chest. He stared at it for a few seconds, looked to Mithras, then collapsed to the ground.

Carden looked to me uneasily: "I don't think so."

More arrows whizzed through the air, cutting the archers from the towers as Tallinn perched somewhere on a rooftop and began picking off enemies. Mithras, Fawkner and Joran began their attack, the two human men drawing their swords as Joran took men in his hands and tossed them around like ragdolls.

"Come on," Carden grabbed my wrist and led me out into the open.

I ran behind him as the battle really opened up, the city's soldiers fighting desperately against our companions.

I looked up to see Tallinn running along the rooftops, firing her bow to give us cover, heading as fast as she could towards the main gates. Fawkner and

Mithras fought back-to-back as Joran pummelled the soldiers bare handed. They swung their swords, meeting the guards' strikes and throwing them down with far greater skill, giving Carden and I the chance we needed.

Carden drew his sword as he pushed me into cover again. Two guards ran at him near the main gate, the young Guardian engaging them in combat immediately.

"Carden?!" I cried out.

"Leander, open the gate!" he shouted to me, slaying one guard as two more rushed him.

I ran across the length of the wall, reaching the gate. I started unlocking it, struggling since I had never used a city gate before, then moved to the winch and started to work it. It was heavier than I expected, my strength barely enough to even move it. Somehow though, I managed to push the lever down and release the cogs of the gate.

A loud cry alerted me to a guard attacking me and I stepped away, stumbling to the ground, my hood falling back. The soldier came at me with a spear and I quickly pulled back as the point went through my cloak. I kicked him away from me, then pulled the spear from the ground.

He turned to me, sword in hand, leaving me to stare at him as two more rushed towards me. I was outnumbered and unable to fight them all. Their laughing faces stared at me as they moved towards me, the gates opening to our right as Tallinn scrambled down the ladder to help me.

Suddenly, the cry of horses reached my ears and the three guards approaching me were trampled as a carriage and its two horses galloped through into the city. I looked to the driver, breathing hard, relief flooding through me as I saw Aldwyn at the reins.

"Your Highness," he smiled. "Your carriage awaits."

"You were meant to wait in the forest," Tallinn scolded as Carden ran to my side, throwing away the spear and taking me towards the carriage.

Aldwyn shrugged as the blonde climbed up with him. "I heard fighting and knew you would need help."

"Mithras, Fawkner!" Tallinn called clearly to the others. "Let's go!"

Mithras, Fawkner and Joran ran to join us as Carden and I clambered into the carriage. The two men climbed up, flanking us on the doors as Aldwyn turned the carriage back through the gates, Tallinn sending a barrage of arrows at the soldiers chasing us.

With Joran holding onto the back, the carriage charged away from Unlarta and towards the north-east through the Scarfold Forest.

I sat there in the seat, watching through the gaps in the windows as riders charged after us. I swallowed hard in fear. We weren't safe yet.

Arrows shot past us, Fawkner snarling and climbing up to join Tallinn. He took up a bow he had stashed there and aided her in fighting off our enemies, the two of them returning fire as we raced into the forest.

I watched through the back window as Carden and Mithras stood ready in the doors with their swords to fight off any soldiers that might try to jump across onto the carriage. They ducked away from arrows as the soldiers were being hit by Tallinn's and Fawkner's shots.

One soldier got close, reaching out and jumping onto the carriage. Carden launched a powerful kick, striking the man's stomach and dropping him to the ground. Meanwhile, on the other side of the carriage Mithras was engaged in a sword fight with a rider who was galloping beside us. The Knight managed to slip through the soldier's defences and swiped at the horse, the animal reeling and throwing its rider to the ground. Joran dropped from the carriage and threw down two more horses, the Storvari fighting the guards as we kept moving.

There were only a few more guards now, three at most. They were trying to get closer without taking a hit from Fawkner or Tallinn while Carden and Mithras stood ready to throw them back. I trembled, gripping the back cushions of the seat, watching on in terror through the windows.

As they got closer, a large boulder flew from the side, knocking them and their mounts to the ground. Joran jogged up from our right to re-join the carriage, seemingly without effort. I was in shock, his strength and the ease with which he did that unbelievable.

"That's all of them," Carden relayed to me.

I nodded and sighed, slumping back into my seat, relaxing finally as our carriage sped up, Joran now jumping onto the back again and holding on as we fled.

* * * * *

I woke as the carriage hit a bump in the path, startled out of the sleep that I hadn't even realised I had slipped into. I looked around the inside of the carriage, a little dazed, meeting the gazes of Tallinn and Carden as they sat there with me.

"Are you alright, Leander?" Carden asked me gently.

I nodded, propping myself up hazily. "Yes. I'm fine. How long have I been asleep?"

Tallinn shrugged. "Only a couple of hours, although, we think it's night time."

"Or sunset," Carden added.

"You think?" I asked, raising an eyebrow at them, then noticing the poor light around the carriage.

Tallinn nodded. "The Scarfold Forest is too dense for light to really get through. But, it's getting darker which probably means that we're either in the night hours or it's sunset."

"Then shouldn't we stop to make camp?" I asked.

Carden leaned his elbows on his knees, facing me more fully, sitting in the seat opposite me: "The others want to reach a safer place. We're headed to some ruins north of here. We should be there soon."

I nodded and sat back in my seat. I turned my gaze down to the pendant around my neck and held it in my fingers. I began studying it carefully, curious as to why it had acted the way it had.

Is this the magic my uncle told me it possesses?

I felt Carden and Tallinn watching me, curiosity clear on their faces when I looked up.

"How did you do that back there?" Carden asked, drawing my eyes to him. "The light from your pendant, I mean."

I shook my head, my eyes returning to the pendant again in wonderment. "I don't know. I mean, I didn't really *do* anything. It just sort of... happened."

"What do you mean?" he turned his gaze between my face and the pendant in my hands curiously.

Again, I shrugged, meeting his eyes. "It wasn't like I could control it. It was like *the pendant* did it. Like it *knew* I was in danger."

"How can that be?" Tallinn sounded doubtful, and yet astonished by this.

I stared down at the pendant, shaking my head. "I'm not sure."

At that moment, there came a knock on the door, the sudden sound startling me. I looked up as Fawkner opened it, the carriage stopping as he did.

"We're here," he said, the light of night obvious now behind him.

I climbed down from the carriage first and looked around in amazement at the sight around me.

We stood inside the remains of a great silver city, now overgrown by the forest, much of its structures fallen into disrepair and ruin. It held a distinctively Elvish atmosphere to it, almost all of the markings on the walls Elvish. It seemed as if no one had lived here in more than a few hundred years, like the city had been abandoned.

"Where are we?" I asked, gazing around in awe.

"The Ruins of the Elven City of Hintana," Aldwyn replied with a sense of pride and loss at the same time in his voice, "one of the grandest and most beautiful cities ever built by the Elves, abandoned four hundred years ago to nature."

"I've heard of this city," Tallinn said eagerly as she moved away from the carriage. "This was once a haven to any and all who sought safety. This city was one of the places where the Great Heroine and her companions came during the Age of Shadows."

"Great," I sighed, a fresh annoyance filling my heart. "Somewhere else my ancestor went before me."

"You'd be hard pressed to go somewhere she did not, Princess," Aldwyn told me evenly. "Your ancestor travelled all over High-Realm during her lifetime."

"Well," I commented as I looked out over the beautiful, but ruined city, "I'm sure this city was much more beautiful in her time."

We stood admiring the grand Elven city for a short time, all of us standing in awe of the beauty that shone through the vines and the overgrowth from the forest. Even in its ruined state Hintana maintained the humble majesty I assumed it always had, though many of its domed rooves had collapsed or been damaged, and several structures were now little more than rubble on the ground.

Within the shelter of the Elven structures, the others put together a camp as I rested and gazed out at the ruins. Free of their disguises and dressed in their basic dark clothing, Tallinn and Carden were setting up an area for me to sleep near them, most of my belongings sitting there.

"How are we fairing?" Mithras' question drew my gaze as I sat down next to Carden while Tallinn moved to help with the evening meal.

"We don't have enough supplies to make it to the Citadel," Aldwyn informed him grimly. "We barely have enough to make it for another four days."

"That could be a problem," Mithras agreed, crossing his arms and staring at the floor in thought.

"And we can't go back to Unlarta now," Carden pointed out grimly. "Not with the soldiers after us."

"Not to mention the people who want my family dead so they can go to war with Ivansten," I added coldly.

"It certainly seems dire," Aldwyn agreed grimly, shaking his head. "A conspiracy against the King and his line, the murder of the Lord of Arvon and his wife, and now the pursuit of their daughter..."

I took in a slow, painful breath as I thought of the situation before us. Without supplies we wouldn't last long at all.

"So, we can't make it to the Citadel, then?" I asked.

Carden shook his head. "Not without supplies. We'll starve before we get there. Especially considering that it's a trip that will take a couple weeks from here still."

"And that's through the mountains," Fawkner spoke up as he and Tallinn began to serve up the food. "We can't travel by the roads even though they provide us only a third of the time to walk. Not now."

"That certainly is true," Mithras confirmed with a sigh.

"So, what do we do?" I looked around at them uncertainly.

There was an uneasy silence between us then as we all thought about our options. It seemed to me that no one had an answer to give, that all of our choices were limited now and that all we could do was travel into the mountains. I didn't know enough of the Nartarn'lath Mountains to be able to judge this well enough, even the story of the Great Ice Dragon useless to me, despite being set in those mountains.

Finally, Aldwyn turned to us, a new light in his dark eyes. "We could make for the City of Hecturn," he suggested triumphantly. "It is only a four-day journey through the woods from here."

"Yes," Fawkner agreed as I moved to help him and Tallinn with the food, feeling the need to make myself useful suddenly," a four-day journey through the thickest part of the Scarfold Forest. We'd have to be constantly on our guard against attacks from not only groundmerks, wolves and bears, but also from the wilder men."

"Wilder men are not a serious threat," Aldwyn advised him. "They're very cautious around a group like this."

"I've heard of them attacking a group three times this size," Fawkner said darkly. "Would you really risk it? And what of the Dwarves? Do you think they'll just open their doors to us now?"

"The Dwarves have always been a very welcoming people," Aldwyn responded, meeting his gaze.

"They're isolationist," was Fawkner's rebuttal. "And who can blame them after the way things have been since the formation of the seven nations?"

"I agree with Aldwyn," Tallinn spoke up evenly. "Hecturn is the closest and safest place for us to go."

And their discussion continued.

I took a plate of food and moved to where Mithras had taken a seat. I walked to him slowly, standing over him until he looked up and gratefully took the food.

"Thank you, Leander," he smiled and turned his gaze to the plate as I sat down on the floor beside him.

I stayed silent for a few moments as I considered the thoughts in my mind. The events of the day had been swirling around in my head since we had escaped the soldiers, and now I found myself craving answers. Somehow, I had a feeling that it was Mithras who could give light to my questions.

"I want to talk about something," I said, drawing his gaze to me, even as I stared at my hands in my lap.

"Hm?" Mithras turned to me as he ate, Carden handing me some food before sitting down beside me.

"Back in Unlarta when Tibain was going to hurt me," I said, turning my gaze to Mithras, uneasy by the thought of what nearly happened, "what was that light that came from my pendant?"

Mithras merely stared at me, swallowing his food as he considered my words.

I went on: "You know, Mithras. I know you do."

I watched him as he remained silent, his eyes locked on his food as he fell into deep consideration. I could tell that he was trying to decide whether to tell me his secret or not.

At this point all the others in the group had stopped talking and were listening. I didn't care, my curiosity far more powerful than my sense of privacy at that time. I wanted to know what he knew and I wanted to know now. No, I *needed* to.

"You're keeping something from me, Mithras," I observed calmly, but firmly. "What is it?"

Mithras sighed reluctantly and nodded. "You've heard the story of Alura Salu, haven't you?"

I nodded. "He was the wizard who taught dragons to speak."

Mithras shook his head: "He was much more than that. Alura Salu was a very powerful wizard who created several items in his time. One was the Sword of Light, a weapon mystically imbued with the first rays of light to ever touch Therras. The others were talismans he forged with the help of thirteen dragons."

"The Dragon Pendants," I recalled my history lessons. "I remember."

"They were said to possess powers beyond imagining," Mithras recounted, "powers that were of a purely defensive nature designed to protect the wearer. These pendants weren't just simple charms, but the very essence of the Dragons themselves," he shifted in his seat, turning to face me directly. "You see, Leander, the wearer of a Dragon Pendant would first have one gifted to them when no one else could possess it. This is because the Pendants themselves are in fact *alive*."

"Please. They're alive?" Fawkner snorted, though he sounded like he was trying to hide his belief in such things.

Mithras ignored the man's remarks, staying focused on me: "The Pendants *are* living items, though without any true consciousness to speak of. They choose a wearer long before the wearer even knows of the Pendant's existence."

I suddenly remembered something my uncle had told me when he had given me the Pendant: "*I could think that only you should carry this pendant. It has never felt like it could belong to anyone else.*"

Mithras went on with his explanation: "The wearer would often have nightmarish visions of a place where they are left vulnerable. They would face a terrible danger in these nightmares and would be protected by a dragon from the dreamscape, something that barely seemed more than a ghost, but filled them with strength and a sense of safety."

I recalled my nightmares and remembered the spectral dragon that had protected me from the robed man and the black dragon. My heart was racing now as it all fell into place.

"In a time when they are threatened, the Pendant often protects the wearer, provided that he or she is *wearing* it, for it must connect to the magic within their heart, or else it remains inert," he finished.

I looked to him as the others came to the conclusion that I had, their faces showing utter bewilderment. He simply stared at me calmly, saying nothing more, knowing that I had already realised the truth.

"Are... are you saying," I spoke slowly as I indicated my necklace, not sure if I really believed it, "that *this* is one of the Dragon Pendants?"

Mithras nodded, studying it where it hung about my neck. "It looks to be the Amethian Pendant."

"The Amethian Pendant?" I asked, raising an eyebrow.

He explained: "There are many species of dragons in Therras. Amethian Dragons are a purple and blue scaled species that are fairly gentle, but ferociously protective," he nodded to the Pendant: "That looks to be an Amethian Heartstone at the Pendant's centre."

"What's a heartstone?" I held the Pendant and looked at it, studying the purple stone.

I just thought it was an amethyst. I hadn't realised that it's a heartstone, whatever that is.

Mithras went on: "It is a stone taken from the heart of a dragon by the dragon's own will. It links *one* dragon in every generation to the Pendant as a living protector. At least that's how Alura Salu had intended it."

I stared at the Pendant around my neck, holding it in my palms and studying the incredible amethyst-like stone at its core. There was a sheen in the stone's heart that reminded me of gentle purple flames, visible only when I inspected it closely enough, but not at first glance or from a distance.

"So, Leander has a dragon protecting her?" Carden exchanged a look with me, his words gaining my attention back from the stone.

"If that's so," Tallinn said, arms crossed as she sat with her back to a pillar, "then where is this dragon?"

Mithras turned to me with a smile: "Leander, would you bring me the Dragon Stone?"

Confused and suspicious, I crossed to my pack and rummaged around for the silk wrapped stone. It wasn't hard to find, standing out above everything else in my bag. I grasped it and pulled it free, crossing back to Mithras with it in my arms.

Sitting down I unwrapped it, the stone shimmering in the firelight, its purple shell showing its silvery and bluish tints as if they were moving like waves through its surface. As I held it, I felt the cool shell and strange warmth that seemed to emanate from within, this time the stone seeming different.

"This is no stone you hold, Leander," Mithras advised me knowingly. "This is something that has not been seen in Therras for over five hundred years."

"This is a dragon's egg, isn't it?" I asked, surprised and excited at the same time, gazing at the stone in my hands.

The others stared in shock at us, their eyes automatically falling on the egg in my arms. Only Joran remained untouched by this realisation, yet his eyes were focused on the stone just the same. I wondered if he ever showed emotions at all.

"What you hold in your hands is indeed the egg of an Amethian Dragon," Mithras confirmed. "I think you will find that it has been in this world as long as you have, Leander."

"Then why hasn't it hatched?" I asked quietly.

"Dragons can take decades to hatch once their eggs have been laid," Mithras explained calmly. "Now that your pendant has activated, however, it will not be long before the egg hatches and bonds with you. For only *you* alone can control the loyalty of both *this* pendant and *this* dragon."

I stared down at the stone, seeing the shimmering movement inside and realised that it wasn't some mystical light. It was the scales of a baby dragon, the light filtering through the shell to touch it. Suddenly, the warmth of the stone made sense to me.

"It has been so long since a dragon has been seen by anyone in High-Realm in such a way," Mithras went on, more to himself than to us. "Could this be a sign that the Eldest Ones are returning?"

"You seem to know a lot about dragons," Carden said, breaking the egg's hold on me and drawing me back into the conversation.

He stood with his arms crossed and turned to Mithras with an almost demanding gaze in his green eyes, his dark hair looking black in the light of the fire.

"Indeed," Aldwyn spoke up from where he sat, crossing his arms in a gesture of expectation. "It is most curious that you have such knowledge, Ser Knight."

Mithras looked between them, then turned his gaze to me. It was clear to me that the old knight had been keeping far too many secrets for any of this to be a coincidence.

"I admit that I have kept a secret not only from you, Leander, but from your father and uncles as well," he admitted.

I frowned at him, but did not speak, suddenly aware that I was protectively cradling the stone as if it were my newborn child. Well, in a way it was.

"I *am* a knight," Mithras confirmed, standing and moving to stare out at the night as we watched him carefully. "This much is true. But I was merely posing as a Knight of Aldegaad as many others of my order have done before me."

I frowned at him, silently wondering why he would do such a thing.

He turned to me, seeming different as he now admitted who he really was: "I am known as a Dragon Knight of the Order of Draconia, a caretaker of the secret of the Dragons themselves. I – like my brethren – guard the Valley of Dragons, the last sanctuary in High-Realm where the Eldest Ones may dwell without fear of attack. Our order was founded over four thousand years ago alongside the original Order of Guardians; created together to be the protectors of this world. Our purpose was to guard against the darkness and defend all that the Dragons treasured most."

"I've never heard of the Dragon Knights before," I said, staring at him, feeling a little betrayed by his deception.

"We have worked in secret for the generations since our order was founded," Mithras explained calmly. "It was we who originally wielded the Dragon Pendants, gifted to us by the Grand Master of our order, Alura Salu."

"Alura Salu was a Dragon Knight?" Tallinn asked, her shock clear in her voice.

Mithras nodded and went on: "It was our duty to guard the Pendants, but they were ultimately lost to us."

"Because Alura Salu disappeared," I recalled from the legend.

Mithras nodded. "Only one Pendant remained in our sights; the one taken by Shadow Lord Morod, the Darkest Shadow's general. For centuries our order searched for the other Pendants, at last finding one when we heard of a young girl from Arvon possessing the power to call a dragon to her," he looked to me knowingly: "Your ancestor."

"And this is it?" I placed a hand gently to the Pendant around my neck.

Mithras nodded. "The Amethian Pendant has been right under my nose for all these years..."

"Then if you're a Dragon Knight why were you posing as a soldier of Aldegaad?" I asked, confused by this one point now.

"Our order has been spread throughout Therras in search of the Pendants for millennia," Mithras explained to me. "We never approached Queen Leander about her pendant, but simply took up a silent guardianship over her and her bloodline. You see, the Pendant may only pass to the descendants of the original bearers, which means..."

"Which means I'm the descendant of one of the first Dragon Knights," I realised, astonished.

"You are," Mithras confirmed. "You are also the only Aldrich to have learned the secret of our order, for none of us had ever known of your ancestor until her victory over the Darkest Shadow," he met my gaze seriously: "Now, it is *you* who carries the Amethian Pendant and the stone that will soon hatch into a new Amethian Dragon."

"I see," I nodded, looking down at the stone.

Huh, I guess my parents weren't just saying it when they told me that I'm special.

"Now, your protection has become all the more important," Mithras said gently. "There can be no doubt that the activation of your pendant is indeed linked to the rise of this new Shadow Lord."

The mention of him drove a spear of ice through my spine and I felt my stomach knot as a single thought entered my mind. I hesitated to speak it aloud, but I felt compelled to if only to free it from me.

"If the Shadow Lord captures me," I murmured slowly with quiet unease, "what will he do to me?"

Mithras responded grimly: "Some things... are best not contemplated."

I swallowed hard and nodded.

Mithras returned to his meal as the others silently went back to their tasks around the fire.

I sat cuddling the egg to my chest, fearfully wondering what destiny lay ahead of me now that all of this had been revealed, and worrying why the Shadow Lord hunted me so fervently. I just had to hope that whatever power my pendant possessed would be strong enough to fight him back.

Chapter Thirteen
The Dragonling

I woke up to a raining sky, the wind holding a bitter chill and the clouds deeply grey. I was lying on the pile of furs that had been laid out for me, the nearby fire now only smouldering ashes amongst the stones, heat still rising from the remains.

I looked to my right, staring at the purple and silver dragon egg as it lay nestled in the silk nest I had made next to me. It seemed somehow to have taken on a more bluish hue in the morning light, like it had absorbed the rain into the stone sheen of its shell.

As I studied the stone I thought of the night I had been given it. I remembered the old man who had bestowed it upon me, almost as though he had been gifting me an abandoned child. Now, I understood why he had been so cautious with it. In truth this stone *was* a child, small and helpless, needing me to care for it.

"Princess," a voice spoke, drawing my gaze. Aldwyn was standing over me, his staff in hand as the others were packing up to leave around us. "We're leaving now, your Highness. We have a long journey ahead of us."

I nodded, pushing the blankets off me and pulling myself to my feet. I gathered up my belongings and put them into my pack, very carefully setting the egg there at the top so I could see it at all times.

With my purple cloak hanging over my back, my hood drawn and my pack slung over my right shoulder, I made my way down the silvery steps of the ancient Elven ruins to join the others. I found them unhooking the horses from the carriage, the two dark brown animals shaking their heads and whinnying as they stamped their hooves impatiently.

"We'll leave the carriage here and take the horses," Aldwyn was saying as Tallinn gently soothed one of the animals. "They could be of use to us."

"Like perhaps carrying most of the heavier items?" Fawkner suggested.

Aldwyn nodded and looked to me. "And perhaps it would be better for the Princess to ride on one rather than walk."

"I'm fine," I insisted. "I can walk."

"It would be easier to protect you, Princess," Aldwyn stated. "You'll ride with Carden. Then at least he can watch over you."

Reluctantly, I nodded and walked over to the second horse, Carden having found an old saddle in the Elven stables that he was currently putting on the animal. I hated that they thought I needed to be protected so much, but I had no place to argue. This was when being a princess actually made it impossible for me to get my own way.

"It seems a shame your dragon hasn't hatched," Carden commented as he looked over the horse's back at me. "You could have ridden on it."

"I doubt it. I don't think I would handle flying well," I said with a small smile. "I'm afraid of heights, remember?"

"Alright. Well, let's get you up," Carden said, walking around and helping me onto the horse.

I wobbled slightly but managed to steady myself as Carden climbed up and took the reins. I grabbed his waist with both arms, holding on tight, afraid I would fall from the saddle.

Then a thought occurred to me: "Can you even really ride a dragon?"

Carden smirked and laughed, drawing my gaze over his shoulder. "You're a funny girl, Leander. You know that, right?"

"Mm-hm," was my reply. "And you're a strange boy."

"True. But it comes with the territory."

"What territory?"

"Being around you."

"Oh, very funny!" I laughed softly.

Carden nodded, smiling and starting the horse forward as he said: "I thought so."

I hit him in the shoulder with my palm playfully, smiling and shaking my head.

I held on as he led our horse forward behind the others away from Hintana's ruins and east into the Scarfold Forest. As Aldwyn had said, we had a four day trip ahead of us through the thickest eastern part of the forest before the frost touched hillsides where Hecturn lay. Yet, for the first time since I had left Arvon, I felt a sense of certainty and safety despite the awkward journey ahead.

I found that Carden and Tallinn were more friends to me now than just protectors, though I had only known them for two months at this point. My ride with Carden seemed to bring us closer as we were able to speak easily enough on the back of our horse. And whenever I wanted, I walked with him and Tallinn, happy to speak with them about anything, our terrifying journey feeling more like a gentle one now.

Meanwhile, I watched the dragon egg whenever I could, curious to see when the baby dragon inside would hatch, or even if it would at all. In any case, it was a nice diversion from the misery that still clung to me, giving me the much needed peace that I craved.

On the second day out from Hintana I found my curiosity mounting again as I clung to Carden's waist while we rode. The unhatched creature in my pack was far more than a curiosity now. It had become an obsession, but a good one and I found that I wanted to know more, much more.

"Carden?" I tapped him on the shoulder.

"Yes, Leander?" he looked around at me, his hair catching in the wind.

"I want to talk to Mithras," I told him, meeting his gaze, then looking past to where the old knight walked ahead of us.

"Alright," Carden nodded and snapped the reins, guiding the horse forward.

Mithras was walking with Tallinn and Aldwyn, the two Guardians leading the way as Fawkner followed behind Carden and I with the other horse. Joran was at the rear of our group, carrying a few other supplies that the horse had no space for.

"Mithras," I called as Carden and I rode up beside him, the horse slowing to match the Knight's pace.

"Leander?" the man turned his gaze to me, bowing his head. "What can I do for you?"

"I had some questions," I said simply.

"About?"

"Dragons."

Mithras smiled knowingly. "Dragons? It seems that you've gained somewhat more than an interest for these creatures now."

I shrugged. "You said I'm carrying a baby dragon that has not yet hatched. I guess I just want to know as much as I can before it does so that I can take care of it."

"Dragonling," Mithras responded.

"Huh?" I frowned in confusion.

"An infant dragon is called a dragonling, the same as a hatchling," he explained, eyes forward, careful of his path as he walked. "They grow to become dragons, but for a time they are dragonlings. This is not the same as a dragonet, however."

"What's a dragonet?" I asked, Carden now paying close attention, showing this with the occasional glances he gave us while he watched the way ahead of our horse.

"There are several variations on the dragon race as well as species," Mithras explained. "It is like humans have variant nationalities. There are four different dragonkin that I am aware of: Dragons, Drakes, Wyverns and Dragonets. They are all very different, yet the same, as they are cousins, in a sense."

"Alright," I nodded thoughtfully. "Tell me about dragonets."

"Dragonets," Mithras elaborated, "are a small cousin of dragons. They are, in fact, the smallest dragonkin in the world. They are no bigger than a man's forearm," he indicated the length on his right arm as he kept walking beside our horse. "They are very fast and as dangerous as locusts."

"How do you mean?" I asked, frowning.

"Well," he explained, "dragonets are born in larger broods than any other dragonkin, anywhere from forty to one hundred eggs laid at any time by a single female. They are pack hunters and are very ferocious, despite their smaller stature. They swarm their targets and fly in flocks, like birds do. They have the appearance of a dragon, however, they only have hind legs and a pair of wings. The wings serve as their forward limbs, allowing them to walk on all fours. They have sharper teeth and claws than most creatures their size, and are capable of biting through steel."

"They certainly *sound* dangerous," Carden commented calmly.

"Immensely," said Mithras in agreement. "When faced with a swarm, it is best to take cover and wait them out."

"Do they breathe fire?" I asked curiously.

He shook his head. "Only dragons, wyverns and drakes breathe fire, Princess. Dragonets rely on sheer numbers and speed to defeat their prey."

"They're carnivorous obviously," I guessed.

"As are all other dragonkin. They eat meat from the moment they hatch, nothing else sufficing," he stated.

I made a mental note of that fact.

"Tell me about wyverns," I requested evenly, looking directly at the man's eyes.

"Well, some would consider wyverns to be a larger version of a dragonet," Mithras expressed, stepping over a few stray branches on the ground, then recovering his easy pace and continuing. "Others, mistake them for being dragons, which they most certainly are not. Like their smaller cousin, wyverns have only their hind legs and their wings to serve as limbs, lacking arms. Though they are almost identical in appearance, as I've said, wyverns are much larger and have shorter snouts."

"How big are they?" I asked, shifting on the saddle.

"About the size of a large cart if you just count the body and head. The tail adds some greater length. Again, as I've told you already, they *do* breathe fire, but their size is a weapon in itself."

"Out of curiosity," Carden joined the conversation, just as interested as I was, "where would you find these creatures in High-Realm?"

Mithras shrugged. "Well, dragonkin can exist anywhere in the world, from the highest mountain to the darkest of sea caves. Dragonets tend to haunt rocky valleys and canyons with lush vegetation, which gives them a larger amount of prey to hunt. Wyverns are primarily found around the sea cliffs in High-Realm, but have been sighted in the mountains. As for dragons and drakes: well, drakes generally prefer forests near mountains as well as caves and caverns, while dragons prefer the higher mountainous regions. However, dragons have been known to reside in caves in the lowlands as well as on the coasts and islands."

"So, we could walk into any of these creatures in these woods, then?" Carden asked, no hint of fear, though his words could have been interpreted in such a way.

I was a little afraid of coming across one of these creatures, but I tried not to show it.

"It isn't likely," Mithras assured him. "In the last four hundred years there have only been six documented encounters with any kind of dragonkin, and the rest is rumour only."

"I suppose that's good to know," Carden decided, glancing back at me, "unless the thing in your pack turns out to be a killer."

"I doubt it," I rolled my eyes.

"Sorry," he shrugged. "It was just a thought."

"Hm," I nodded and turned back to Mithras, still curious. "So, what about drakes? What can you tell me about them?"

"Ah," Mithras smiled brightly, a deep enthusiasm in his tone and expression. "Drakes are the most unique of the four. Unlike the other dragonkin, drakes are flightless."

"How come?" I asked.

"Drakes have no wings," he responded, keeping pace with our horse. "They have spiny talons on their front elbows instead as an indicator of where wings may have grown. They are quadrupeds, meaning they have four legs. They look the same as most dragons, though they tend to be mostly a greyish-blue colour with mild tints of purple. Drakes are long necked and have the elongated snout that dragonets tend to have. They have feathery spines on the tips of their tails, large claws and teeth. These dragonkin breathe fire, which makes them quite dangerous despite their lack of flight."

"How big are they generally?" I asked.

"About one and a half times bigger than a horse," Mithras explained simply. "They use their size to throw down their prey and gore it to death. They are quite fast and have been known to overwhelm horses and kill both them and their riders easily."

"It sounds like we really wouldn't want to cross paths with any of these drakes," Carden observed. "They could be difficult to fight."

"Difficult," Mithras agreed. "Not impossible. All dragonkin can be slain as any other creature can. You see, the weakest point on all dragonkin is the neck and the top of the head, but those are very hard to reach, especially on the largest ones."

"And what about dragons?" I finally asked about the dragonkin I was most interested in. "Tell me about them."

"Eager, aren't we?" Mithras laughed and nodded, smiling at me then explaining: "Alright. Well, dragons are the largest of all the dragonkin. They were the first ever discovered and, unlike their smaller cousins, are highly intelligent."

"Because they can speak?" I asked.

"They were once known to," he confirmed with a slight nod. "At the very least dragons understand all the different languages of the peoples of Therras. Though they have been seen as monsters that ravage the landscape, dragons are truly beautiful and majestic creatures. They grow to be anywhere from twice the size of a horse to be as tall as a three storey house. They all tend to have long necks and gigantic wings, and are capable of flight. They breathe fire from a gland deep inside their chest near the lungs and are capable of crushing a man with their jaws, breaking him in half."

I couldn't help but cringe at that image.

"In general," he finished, "dragons are quite peaceable unless they are disturbed. They have been known to take up residence in ancient ruins, mountainous terrain or along the coasts, however, their havens can be anywhere with a deep enough place for shelter, plenty of food, water and enough space for the dragon to fly without colliding with the cliffs or rock faces."

"Do dragons ever go near populated areas?" I enquired, the thought purely fascination.

Mithras nodded. "There are cases where dragons have been seen near towns. Generally, this happens when the dragon's lair has been in the region for centuries before the settlement is made, and only after a while when the dragon then awakens to see the people there. The dragon's curiosity usually leads to it venturing near the village and the people then panic. It is very rare for a dragon to attack out of malice."

"I heard stories in Nargilith," Carden spoke up again, recalling his childhood. "It was said that there were some dragons that *did* openly attack villages for no other reason than malice."

"It could be seen that way," Mithras conceded evenly. "However, these attacks are usually the dragon being of a more hostile species and making strikes to drive the people from its territory. Then again, you also get less malicious dragons which simply fear for their safety and attack only after they have been provoked. In either case, it is a very rare occurrence for a dragon to attack a populated area."

"So, do dragons have names?" I wanted to know, my curiosity peaking.

Mithras shook his head: "Not generally. They don't choose names themselves. There are only two ways a dragon is named: either by the peoples living nearby the dragon's lair who are aware of its presence, or dragons are named by the holders of the Pendants as their protectors. But no, most dragons are merely called 'Dragon'."

"So, when this dragon hatches I can name it?" I asked with a twinge of excitement.

Mithras nodded. "You may indeed. Nurture it, keep the egg warm and it should hatch. Also, touching the shell will help you to establish your connection with the dragonling."

"So, it will like me then?" I felt a little uncertain.

Mithras shrugged. "Perhaps. I've never met a Pendant Wearer before, nor a Dragon's Charge. If you are both then the dragonling should attach itself to you. However, when it hatches I would advise care and subtlety."

"And what should I do?"

"Let the dragonling approach you," he explained evenly, stepping over a log and brushing aside a few small branches. "Offer it your hand, palm down, fingers straight. Let it take in your scent as you would a hound, meet its gaze and speak to it. Also, speak to it while it remains in the egg. It should then recognise your voice when it hatches."

I nodded. "Alright. Thank you, Mithras. I think that's all I wanted to know for now."

"You are most welcome, Leander," Mithras bowed his head and turned back to the way ahead.

I pondered on everything the old knight had told me, particularly about how to approach the dragonling when it hatched. I could only hope that the small creature would hear my words and recognise me as a friend when it did.

* * * * *

We made camp again that night and Mithras helped me to warm the egg in the coals by the fire. He explained that the heat would quicken the infant's scaled body and its reptilian blood, urging it to awaken. I think in some way he wanted it to hatch as much as I did.

The night wore on slowly, slower than I would have liked. Lying there in the warmth of my tent, I felt uncomfortable and anxious. I stared up at the folds in the ceiling, studying the shapes they made with the light from the fire coming from outside.

The firelight was enough to illuminate the tent with a gentle glow, distinguishing every detail within easily and bright enough that I could hold out my hands to see the creamy white features of their slender shapes. However, I felt restless lying there in the warm furs and the soft blankets over the bedroll, too much so to sleep easily.

Turning uncomfortably and rolling in an agitated manner, I moved onto my side, my dark hair hanging down my back to meet my right shoulder where it lay against the cushiony makeshift bed. My eyes fell on the purple, blue and silvery dragon's egg that was now nestled amidst the folds of its silken cloth, a fur wrapped up to form an artificial nest accompanying it.

The stone-like oval shaped egg seemed to be a different shade tonight. It was the light, I knew, but I noted that it seemed a deeper purple, almost with a black tint to it. The light from the fire passing through the tent's cloth very gently illuminated the egg, its silvery sheen dancing playfully across the perfectly smooth shell.

I sighed as I looked at it, wishing that it would hatch soon. In my mind it was for curiosity, to see what a dragon actually looked like instead of the images I had seen in old books, on the Aldegaadian banners and the murals of my ancestor. But in my heart I longed for the dragon to come out so that I had something to feel a deeper connection to.

I drank in the silence of the woods, trying to relax as I took in the night tunes. There were, of course, the sounds of crickets and night birds as well as the calls of wolves in the distance, but mostly there was just the wind. That in itself made lying there somewhat peaceful, allowing me to rest my head on a pillow and close my eyes at last.

Then a strange sound pulled me back to the waking world just as I was slipping towards dreaming.

Opening my eyes I looked around the tent, realising that the sound was coming from within. At first I thought something had gotten in and was moving around, but soon my attention was drawn to the egg.

Lying in its fur and silk nest, the egg was moving slightly, wobbling as though it had suddenly sprung to life spontaneously.

Slowly, I propped myself up on one arm and watched the wobbling egg as it made scratching and cracking sounds. There were also other sounds coming from within it; a strange sniffing along with faint, soft, high pitched grunting noises.

With the light from outside the tent I could then see shadowy movements beneath the purple shell. There was the unmistakable shape of a thin, long tail slithering around inside as something that looked like a foot was pushing against the top of the stone.

I gasped, lying on my stomach and watching curiously. "It's hatching?"

There came a louder crack and I saw a tiny purple and silver scaled hand come out. It was tipped in small claws, which immediately began to grip onto the shell's exterior. Another section of the shell fell away and a scaly purple foot emerged, very similar to the hand, but with a longer part to it. The foot kicked away another piece of the shell, a fourth falling free a moment later as a strange, leathery appendage tipped with a hooked claw extended out, catching at the shell ineffectively.

As a fifth piece fell loose I could see a little eye. It was tiny and beautiful with a deep orange iris set into a scaly face of purple and mauve. The eyelids blinked, revealing bluish leathery flesh, the tiny eye flicking around as it looked through the egg's openings, almost seeming to glow with an inner fire.

I heard a strange clicking sound that was akin to a cooing, like from a baby, but with a far more animal tone to it.

A section over the head broke free and a long snout slid loose as the eyes blinked in the light of the world for the first time. The clawed hands pushed and scratched at the egg, the dragonling finally freeing itself, breaking the shell and falling onto the floor in a clumsy pile.

It croaked and squawked, making that same crackling sound as it staggered to its feet and shook itself out, its entire body shuddering as it did.

I was astonished to see it, my eyes wide and my face covered in a huge smile. *Wow... it really **is** a dragon...*

The dragonling was only tiny, no bigger than a year-old kitten, its neck seeming shorter than what I had expected. It had thicker, darker blue and purple scales on its head, down its back, tail, shoulders and legs which looked more like armour plating. There were two horny growths on its crown running parallel to one another and following the length of its head. They were only stubs, really, four other tiny stubs on either side of the infant's jaw right near the neck, a faint leathery layer of skin stretched between them like webbing.

Its limbs were slender, its body sleek, the underbelly a silvery mauve colour. Its feet looked bigger than they should have been, though that was just because it was a newborn. Its long snout was tipped with a tiny horn stub, its nostrils flaring as they sniffed in the scents of the tent. Its wings were folded up but reached back the length of its body to about a third of the way along its thin tail. The tail swayed quickly in a sideways motion as the dragonling looked around the tent curiously.

"Hello, little one," I said softly, smiling at it. "Are you alright?"

The dragonling looked up at me, cocking its head to the side, its large molten orange eyes blinking as it stared at me. It crackled gently, making a gurgling, cooing noise as it slowly edged its face towards me.

Carefully, I reached out my hand, palm down, fingers straight, watching the small creature. The dragonling jerked away for a moment, staring at my hand as if it were some strange thing approaching it. Instinctively, its wings stretched out to make itself appear bigger as it curled its neck back from me like a snake preparing to strike.

I was startled, worrying for a moment that the dragonling might bite me. I flexed my hand back involuntarily, the baby blinking at me curiously. Slowly, I reached out again, making sure I followed Mithras' directions exactly: *fingers straight, palm down, do not move.*

Little by little, watching my hand, the dragonling moved towards me apprehensively, sniffing at my fingers. I watched it quietly, amazed by it as it gurgled and chirped. I felt its nose touch my fingers, its scaly skin rough, but at the same time strangely smooth. It was warm, like the warmth that comes from holding a newborn puppy, its movements softer now as it guided its head under my hand.

"It's alright," I urged it gently. "I won't hurt you. You're safe."

The dragonling looked up at me, cocking its head again with another crackling coo. It seemed like it understood me and it chirped happily as I smiled in response. Then something happened that I never expected and couldn't explain.

A section of scales on the dragonling's chest began to glow with a beautiful purple light. Almost instantly, I felt my pendant grow warm and looked down to see the stone at its centre glowing with the same purple light.

The two lights grew brighter, reaching out to each other and touching. Then I felt a strange warmth in my chest and turned my eyes to my torso. The skin over my heart started to glow purple too as the light reached out and spread to me from my pendant. It didn't hurt, instead filling me with a strange feeling, like a new hope had reached me and enwrapped my heart.

Slowly, the energy faded away, retreating into the Pendant from both of us, leaving me stunned as I sat there on my haunches, staring blankly and touching my chest in bewilderment.

A gentle cooing pulled me out of my disorientation as I felt something nudging into my thigh. I looked down, the dragonling pressing its side into my leg, gazing up at me innocently.

"What does this mean? Huh, little one?" I asked the dragonling. "Are we connected now?"

The dragonling chirped with what seemed like a nod of its small head.

"Can you... understand me?" I stared in amazement.

Again, the dragonling chirped and made the same head tilt.

"Whoa... This is... I mean..." I blinked in shock, slumping back into a sitting position and watching the dragonling, feeling bewildered.

Like a loving little puppy, the dragonling crawled into my lap, chirping and croaking as it looked up at me. It cooed happily, staring at me with what seemed to be a sort of grin. That was enough to make me smile as I slowly began to stroke the infant's smooth scaled back, its wings arching slightly.

The dragonling nuzzled its head into my arm and side gently, cooing at my touch, then chirped happily.

Slowly, I lay back down, the dragonling lying beside me as I gathered up some blankets for it to sleep in. It settled down on its stomach, watching me as I pulled a smaller fur over its back, thinking to keep it warm. The dragonling flattened out its wings, still watching me as I lay down beside it.

"You know, I've only just heard about you a couple of days ago," I told it.

The dragonling chirped loudly, cawing happily. I reached out and started to stroke its back, the little creature seeming very content to lie there with me.

The opening of the tent shifted and moved, Carden sticking his head in.

"Leander? Are you alright? Is something..." he trailed off, his green eyes wide as he stared with an open mouth at me, gazing at the dragonling lying at my side.

I smiled up at him as the dragonling perked its head up, cocking it to the side as it studied him with highly intelligent and oddly experienced eyes.

"It hatched," Carden gasped, crouching down beside me and studying the dragonling. "It actually hatched."

"It did," I nodded, smiling as I caressed a finger under the dragonling's chin, getting it to look at me with a happy cooing.

Carden looked to me, smiling. "You knew. You knew it was going to hatch tonight. That's why you were asking all those questions earlier."

I shrugged with my eyes on the dragonling. "I guess so. I think we need to feed it."

Carden nodded, standing up. "I'll be right back."

He was gone for only a few moments, returning with some pieces of meat on a small plate. He carefully set it down in front of the dragonling, sitting and watching it with fascination. The dragonling pulled itself to its feet and padded over cautiously, sniffing at the meat before snapping its long jaws around a piece. It immediately began chewing and snapping, using its front claws the way a cat does, picking up the meat to eat it.

"This is amazing, Leander," Carden laughed, astonished as he watched the creature. "It really is a dragon."

"Well, a dragonling," I corrected, then smiled up at him happily. "And I know that I'm definitely connected with it."

"How can you tell?" he met my gaze curiously.

I placed my hand to my heart. "Because the Pendant did it."

"How?"

"It did something with the energy it casts. I don't know what, but it connected us with it and now I know we are meant to be together," I smiled down at the dragonling, now understanding the feeling that I had felt during that moment with the energy. "It's strange. It's almost like... well, I'm not sure what it's like."

The dragonling finished eating then padded back to its place beside me. It curled around itself, settling down as it did before and allowed me to put the fur over its back again. It rested its head on the ground, watching the two of us as it softly cooed to itself.

"Have you named it?" Carden asked, looking from the dragonling and back to me.

Watching the dragonling, I smiled and nodded knowingly. "Amethyst," I said softly. "I'm going to call her Amethyst."

"Her?" Carden asked, surprised.

I nodded slowly. "I'm not sure how I know, but I know it's a girl."

"Motherly intuition?" he suggested.

"Or something else," I added with a shrug as I watched the small creature.

We sat for some time, watching her sleep, then Carden left for the night. I didn't want him to go, but I couldn't bring myself to ask him to stay.

I lay down beside the dragonling and stroked her back as I settled my own body.

"Goodnight, Amethyst," I whispered, then closed my eyes and went to sleep.

* * * * *

When morning broke, I woke and began packing up quickly. Amethyst chirped, shaking off the blanket and looking to me as she stood up on her four legs.

"Good morning, Amethyst," I smiled at her. "Are you ready to meet the others?"

She chirped excitedly, enthusiastic.

"Alright," I smiled, kneeling down and scooping her up in my arms. "Come on, then."

Stepping out of the tent, I came to see a sight I wasn't expecting. The others were all seated or standing around the still burning fire waiting for me. Their eyes immediately widened at the sight of the small dragonling in my arms, her wings catching their talons in the cloth of my dress' sleeve and bodice.

"See?" Carden smiled, arms crossed. "Just like I said."

"It cannot be," Aldwyn uttered in disbelief.

"It's real," Fawkner breathed, staring wide eyed at the infant. "It really is a dragon."

"I don't believe it," Tallinn walked up beside me, gazing at the dragonling and receiving a stare from her.

"It's real," I assured them as I cradled Amethyst gently in my arms. "The egg hatched last night while you were sleeping."

They all stared in astonishment, even Joran stunned for once, his expression as clear as day. *Yes! Finally, an expression from him!*

"Never have I see one of the Dragorans," he stated with a tone of amazement. "My people have always believed them to be myth."

"Leander," Mithras spoke up, a warm expression on his face. "Would you bring the dragonling here, please?"

Slowly, I walked to where Mithras sat, taking a seat next to him and allowing him to see Amethyst. She huddled into my arms, staring over her shoulder and wing at him shyly. She buried her head into my chest nervously, crying out a soft croaking howl.

"It's alright," I told her. "He's not going to hurt you. He's my friend."

As if the dragonling believed me, she straightened up and faced Mithras, the Knight nodding his thanks to me and beginning his examination: "Strong legs. A little thin. Wings look good. Hm..."

"What?" I looked to Mithras worriedly.

He smiled. "This is a very healthy dragonling. And it's a girl."

"Huh. Well, what do you know?" Carden murmured, drawing my gaze as he smiled at me.

"How can you tell?" I asked, looking back to Mithras.

Mithras pointed to the back scales: "The scales on the back are a bluish-purple and fairly dark. If this were a male, then there would be a reddish colouring there. This is a female dragon."

"And she's a... um... what did you call it?" I tried to remember the word he had used.

"An Amethian," Mithras confirmed. "Yes."

"Have you named her?" Tallinn asked, coming up next to me and smiling at the dragonling the way someone would a newborn baby.

"Amethyst," I answered. "I don't know why, but it felt like that's her name."

"A good name for a dragon," Mithras smiled and nodded.

Amethyst cooed and looked up at me with her beautiful, large molten orange eyes.

"Is it alright for us to travel with her?" I stroked her head as I looked back to Mithras.

"Dragons are travellers from the moment they hatch," Mithras replied. "I would suggest, however, that you carry her for the time being."

"I think that's a good idea," I agreed, standing up as Amethyst cooed happily.

"We'd best start packing up," Aldwyn stood then, picking up his staff and taking the lead. "We still have quite a way to go."

As the others began packing up I smiled at Amethyst and held her close, the dragonling cooing happily up at me. I was surprised when Carden put my cloak over my shoulders, smiling at the dragonling as if he had just instantly grown to love her as I had. That only made me adore him even more.

My heart pattered at his touch and I suddenly wanted him always near me.

Soon we were leaving our campsite, once again making for the Dwarven City that lay in the distant foothills of the mountains. While I felt a new sense of encouragement with Amethyst in my arms and Carden at my side, I couldn't help wondering if the Dwarves could offer us the safety we so desperately needed.

Chapter Fourteen
The Dwarf City of Hecturn

For three more days we traversed the thick, dark woods, our journey seeming somewhat less perilous, though we still heard the sounds of animals and wilders out there. After all, how many people could feel truly uneasy with a dragon – even a newly born one – on their side?

All the way I played with Amethyst, talking to her just as I would any human baby. It seemed that there in that place where some of the bravest men and women in Aldegaad refused to tread, I found a sense of safety unlike anything I had felt since Arvon.

Once again, night saw us settling in to sleep, two on watch at all times, only Amethyst and I permitted to sleep undisturbed.

As I lay there amidst the blankets of my makeshift bed, I sighed and watched Amethyst. She cooed as she went to sleep, her head resting on her small forearms and wrists, her wings spread to her sides. Her tiny body seemed to grow then shrink beneath the blanket in time with her breathing, her eyelids flickering as she dreamed.

Stroking her back and watching her stir slightly, I smiled and lay down, closing my eyes to go to sleep. A moment of grief hit me again as I felt the death of my parents, but it ultimately faded as I drifted from the world and into my dreams.

I woke up the next morning to a strangely brighter day than the one before and the powdering of snow touching the world. We broke camp fairly quickly, Fawkner sending Farsight on ahead to scout the way before us. Within three hours, the falcon returned with a screeching cry that – to me – resembled a joyous call.

"What does your falcon say?" Aldwyn asked, moving his staff in time with his right step, turning his dark eyes to Fawkner.

"She says the way is clear," Fawkner expressed, seemingly hidden from the neck down under his heavy, fur covered black cloak, "and that the entrance to the Dwarven Halls is not but a few more miles ahead."

"Hecturn awaits us then," Mithras commented to no one in particular, moving easily past the other two men and flashing a smile to me where I sat on the horse.

"Carden?" I looked to the young Guardian as he led the horse on foot in front of me, leaving me alone in the saddle.

"Yes, Leander?" Carden looked up over his shoulder with a smile.

"What do you know about the Dwarf City?" I asked, shifting my hands on the saddle and gaining a better grasp.

He shrugged. "Not much, I must confess. I know that Hecturn was the first Dwarven City built in High-Realm and is one of the oldest in all of Therras. It also has some of the grandest architecture known to the Dwarven underworld. Great stone chambers that seem to go on for miles, fortresses and palaces built from and into the rock as though they were grown, not forged; and vast causeways and commons where the Dwarven people commune with the merchants from both their own world and ours. It is a marvel to behold."

"You sound like you've been there," I observed.

"Not me," he looked back at me, smiling reminiscently. "Varel told me of Hecturn's grandeur when I was a child."

"I've never seen a Dwarven City," I confessed.

"I'm not surprised," he replied. "You said you've only been in either Arvon or Aneuran. That's not a wide travelling repertoire."

"No, you're right. It isn't," I agreed as Amethyst chirped for attention.

I smiled and scratched the dragonling under the chin, her tiny jaws opening as though she were smiling.

"How long until we reach Hecturn?" I asked.

"Six hours," Tallinn spoke before Carden could respond, walking up beside us, her stoic charm having returned to replace her friendlier one as she moved with her bow in hand. "We should be there by sunset."

We travelled on, time passing more slowly than I had remembered experiencing on the previous days. Then again, I just figured that was because of the knowledge that we were so close to our destination now.

As the day wore on, once more the woods began to darken, but soon started to fade. The mountains re-emerged from behind the thick tree canopy and the sky shone through again, a welcome sight to us. The ground here was almost drenched in snow, which still fell now in place of the rain that we had become so accustomed to. The mountains towered above us like monoliths formed of grey stone and rock, their bodies mostly shielded in thick layers of ice and snow.

Feeling the chill, I drew my hood over my long hair, peeking out from beneath the cowl. My companions donned their own cloaks and hid beneath their hoods too, feeling the cold just as much as I did. It seemed that only Amethyst was unaffected, her body running at a higher temperature than the rest of us.

We came to a stone road leading up the mountainside lined with towering pines and flanked with the ruins of great columns that once held archways proudly aloft. Even to me it was clear that these weren't of human make, likely made by the Dwarves themselves.

The road brought our gradually tiring group to a long, wide stone bridge edged with great statues of Dwarven warriors. The stone figures were gigantic, standing some thirty feet tall and holding up symbols of the smith, the warrior and the noble. I felt so tiny and insignificant next to those statues.

Across this bridge was the mountain's face where the great doors into Hecturn stood.

I gasped as we moved towards the gargantuan archway that was left open to the air, serving to shield the main doors from the elements. They were as ornate as the arch before and set within an open hall twice the height of their fifty feet. Like the bridge, the doors were presided over by statues of Dwarven warriors, both welcoming and warning as they stared down at us with their dead stone eyes.

Amethyst warbled softly, huddling her head into my shoulder and staring up at the mountain. I could understand her unease as I felt it just as strongly myself. If the doors and their silent stone guardians were this intimidating, then I could hardly begin to imagine how overwhelmed we would be within the city itself.

Mithras and Aldwyn took the lead as Fawkner called Farsight back to him, the falcon perching on his arm and allowing him to carry her with him. Tallinn and Joran brought up the rear, watchful and guarded while Carden continued to lead the horse that Amethyst and I were riding.

We passed under the great arches, those of us who hadn't come here before gazing up in wonder at the behemoth of a structure that towered over us. Just as I had thought, I felt an overwhelming sense that pressed down on me.

We approached the doors' ornate stone carved forms, the grand stone statues staring down at us with both hammer and axe held high and proud. Our footsteps echoed around the vast entry arches, making it seem as though there were some seventy odd people walking through instead of only seven.

I looked around at my companions, noting their expressions: Carden, Fawkner and Tallinn all looked astonished and bewildered, none of them having been to such a place as this. Aldwyn and Mithras had a look of familiarity on their faces, both of them clearly having travelled here before. Meanwhile, Joran seemed – once again – unaffected by the sights around him, or if he was he didn't show it.

Movement drew my attention and I noticed that the doors were actually open already and had been the entire time we had been approaching. I saw a group of heavily armoured Dwarves marching towards us from the opening, weapons in hand – either axes, hammers or crossbows – swords at their sides. Their armour was unlike anything I had ever seen before, all of it very ornate, but at the same time, functional. It had much squarer shapes than human made armour and the Dwarves were mostly hidden under fully masked helmets.

Out of the five Dwarves approaching, the central most one was different. He wore a helm that was topped with a black plume, a fabric-like chainmail cloak swaying across his left shoulder, leaving his right side free. He carried a battleaxe across his back, his right shoulder bearing a smaller shoulder guard to the one on his left. He was most likely the leader or the captain.

"Halt!" he held out his hand commandingly, standing at only a little over half the height of most of the men in our group. He would have come up just below my sternum if I wasn't on a horse. "State your business here in our domain, humans," the Dwarf commanded, lowering his hand.

"With respect," Mithras bowed his head to the Dwarf reverently, "we are travelling to the Citadel of Dartaren in search of aid from the Guardians. We wish only for accommodation, rest and supplies."

"You are a Knight of Aldegaad, upworlder," the Dwarf captain observed. "It has been many a year since knights have ventured into the depths of our Great Halls."

"I serve the Aldegaadian royal family," Mithras admitted freely, his tone suggesting that he really trusted the Dwarves. "I have been charged with the protection of the youngest niece of our King."

"You bring an upworlder monarch with you?" the Dwarf seemed both surprised and a little suspicious.

"I'm not a monarch," I commented before I could stop myself from speaking, the Dwarves turning their attention to me. "I don't rule Aldegaad. My uncle does."

I noticed the expression on Carden's face and realised that I probably should have kept my mouth shut until Mithras had finished addressing the Dwarves.

The Dwarves, however, seemed strangely humbled and surprised at seeing me. I knew immediately that I had once again been recognised as my ancestor's descendant and that I was facing what could only be considered to be transferred hero worship.

That familiar twinge of annoyance rose up in me and I grimaced to myself.

"You will come with us," the Dwarf directed us clearly, but calmly.

Under Aldwyn's direction while Mithras stood at the door, we made our way into the Dwarven City of Hecturn, the guards watching us carefully.

We were brought into a grand chamber that seemed to stretch out for miles all around us, great pillars of stone carved into ornate shapes standing evenly throughout the expanse, dozens of magnificent statues set all around. The area we had entered into was where the stable was kept, many other horses being cared for there.

I dismounted from my horse, my cloak and dress swirling around me as I set my feet to the stone floor. I gazed around the vast chamber, Amethyst poking her tiny head out of my pack to see. Letting the horse go, I felt an intense sense of awe wash over me, stunned by the immensity of the Dwarven world.

With the horses in the stables, we followed the Dwarven guards into the city itself, passing down the stairs and through the archways into the grand commons. What we came face to face with was unlike anything I had ever imagined could exist beneath the mountains.

The Dwarves had built a grand city beyond imagining, constructed in what seemed like a gigantic, naturally formed cavern, not just carved, but forged into the stone itself. The walls were lined with monolithic columns reaching high into the expanse above us. Molten rock and lava flowed from reservoirs below the commons in waterfall-like streams to pool beneath where the smithies were located. Towering structures rose high up the sloping walls of the cavern, each one connected via stone bridges supported by arches, columns and great steel suspension cables.

The walls of many of the structures seemed to have been overwhelmed by the rock of the caverns where in fact they had been built into the stone. The doors were metal and could only be opened by release levers, great machinery visible, yet disguised to appear as part of the city's facade. The ingenious collection of cogs, wheels and pulleys seemed to operate a vast network of machinery throughout all of Hecturn.

Directly ahead of us stood the grandest part of the city itself; a collection of towers and structures built in multiple tiers up towards the ceiling of the cavern, almost every structure connected by a vast network of walkways and elevators.

At the pinnacle of the city stood the Estate of the High Lord of Hecturn and the Hecturn Hall of Lords where the Dwarven nobility would meet. Both structures were among the grandest, but outdone by the Hall of Ancestors standing the farthest back in the cavern and at the very top of the pinnacle; a place of honour for those who had passed on before.

"This is amazing," I breathed, following Carden.

"It's immense!" Tallinn exclaimed, just as taken aback.

"It's grander than anything I have ever imagined," Carden said in a near whisper, awe struck.

We made our way forward, following the Dwarf captain. All around us in the brightly lit commons Dwarven citizens watched our passing, eyeing us sceptically. Their gazes made me feel a little uneasy, though Hecturn already felt more inviting than any other place we had been so far.

Our Dwarven escorts led us down what I could only assume was the main street of the Hecturn Commons and towards a grand staircase far larger than any human built one. It reached out wide enough to herd a hundred cows easily in rows of ten, and it climbed high towards the towers far above the commons.

We made our way up the stairs, following our escorts. I felt like we were undertaking some great hike to the top, my legs aching a quarter of the way up. But soon enough, we were standing at the highest point of the city, being led towards the estate of Hecturn's High-Lord.

We approached the estate, making our way up the steps at the front of the natural rock-built structure. Two guards flanked the grand doors, their armour bearing the seal of the House of Eilan, the family of the current High-Lord. The guards watched as we were escorted by the soldiers, admitting us through the doors and into the estate.

We were met by a butler, who spoke with the guard captain in Dwarfish before nodding and leading us through the estate. He brought us into the main corridors, and I found myself looking up in amazement. I couldn't understand how the ceilings were so high in Dwarven structures, but all the same I was grateful for it, especially as I looked at Joran.

The butler led us to a set of double doors and instructed us to wait outside before entering himself. He was inside for a few minutes before he returned and directed us to enter.

With our escorts around us, we were brought into a large study that was lit with the warmth of lava jets flowing through specially designed conduits. The stone walls had shelves carved into them, countless books on various subjects filling them. Rugs covered the stone floors and even the furniture was carved from stone. The Eilan Family Seal was also set into the wall above the glowing lava conduit, a place honouring the family itself.

There were four other Dwarves in the room. The first was a fairly young blonde haired Dwarf with no beard, dressed in simple, but fine clothes. He carried a ledger and a quill, his behaviour suggesting that he was the High-Lord's personal aide.

Next was a rather muscular, older Dwarf with dark hair he wore in one long, tight braid. He had a thick dark beard reaching to his belly with two slender braids running through it. He wore Dwarven armour with his blue tunic and coat, and carried a large battleaxe across his back. He had a considerate look to him as he faced us, smiling gently behind his beard.

The third Dwarf beside him looked almost identical, the two likely brothers. Like the first he had the same blackish brown hair and beard, and was dressed similar, but he was a little shorter. His hair was left long with only a clasp pulling it from his face, his beard shorter and twisted into three plaits. He had three scars running down from his right cheekbone, under his beard, over his chin and down part of his neck.

Unlike his brother, he had a less welcoming attitude, snidely smirking at Tallinn and I. He made me feel very uncomfortable.

The last Dwarf was High-Lord Eilan. He was a much older man with shoulder length grey hair and a beard running down to his chest. He was dressed in finer crimson, gold and cream coloured clothes, a medallion around his neck bearing the symbol of his Lordship, a ring on his finger with his family seal. He was a kindly looking man, turning his head up from the paperwork he had been reading to acknowledge us.

"Milord," the butler said to him respectfully. "These are the upworlders."

"Yes, I see that," Lord Eilan then looked to the soldiers escorting us. "Thank you, captain. You are dismissed."

"Yes, milord," the Dwarven captain bowed his head, then turned and led his men from the room.

Lord Eilan turned his attention to us, standing from his desk and smiling.

"Welcome to my home, friends. I am Balfour Eilan, High-Lord of the City of Hecturn," he gestured then to the others in the room, making introductions. "This is my personal aide, Coalan, and these are my trusted messengers and most skilled warriors, Dolin and Holger Axton."

The other three Dwarves nodded to us in turn.

Lord Eilan turned back to us: "My butler informed me that you are representatives of the Aldegaadian Sovereignty."

Mithras took a step forward, placing himself between the Dwarves and myself, my face still shrouded beneath the hood of my cloak.

Mithras bowed his head then addressed the High-Lord respectfully: "Our thanks, Lord Eilan, for your warm welcome. I am Ser Mithras, Knight of Aldegaad and Commander of Arvon's detachment."

"As I suspected," Lord Eilan nodded. "You serve Prince Ewan Aldrich, correct?"

I grimaced at the mention of my father's name, trying to hold back the tears that were already threatening to overwhelm me.

Mithras nodded grimly. "Tragically, Prince Ewan and Duchess Caralyn were murdered more than a fortnight ago."

Lord Eilan stared at him in disbelief. "How?"

"Castle Arvon was attacked and overrun by assailants of an unknown origin," Mithras explained gravely. "We have since learned that this deed was orchestrated by members of the nobility who are conspiring against the Aldrich line."

"Members of the Aldegaadian Nobility are responsible for such a heinous act?" Lord Eilan was shocked. "And what of Lord Ewan's daughters? Were they harmed?"

"Princess Aislinn is married to Prince Sten of Balganis and is currently residing with him," Mithras expressed. "As far as we know, she is safe."

I hope she's safe. I can't lose my sister too.

"And Princess Leander?" Lord Eilan enquired.

"She is alive," Mithras responded, stepping aside, as if giving me a cue.

I pushed my hood back, revealing my face and looking to the Dwarf-Lord. I could see his expression change to a mixture of surprise and relief as he saw me.

Mithras added with a smile: "And she stands here in your presence, my Lord."

It took Lord Eilan a moment to regain his composure, so stunned by my sudden appearance in his halls. He coughed slightly and blinked, then looked back to Mithras.

"Well, that certainly explains the presence of so many Guardians in your company," Lord Eilan commented, then looked to Joran. "Though, I must admit that I have never encountered anything such as you."

"I am a Storvari," Joran expressed, regarding the Dwarf with his intense violet eyes, his voice booming loudly in the rock carved room. "I serve the Sarissi."

"Sarissi?" Lord Eilan raised an eyebrow.

Mithras explained: "He is referring to the Princess. He owes her his life and now serves as her protector."

"I see," Lord Eilan nodded, then smiled warmly and welcomingly. "Then, he is welcome in my home, as are you all."

"Your Lordship," Aldwyn spoke up with a bow of his head, "we seek only a secure place to rest before we continue on our path. We will then make for the Guardian Citadel of Dartaren and leave you to your own affairs."

"You are welcome and safe here for as long as you need," Lord Eilan said, then looked to me.

"Are you sure, your Lordship?" I asked uncertainly.

"I assure you, Princess, that you are in no danger here," Lord Eilan vowed.

I felt extremely ill at ease suddenly, a sharp dread filling me. Perhaps it was the idea that we were deep beneath the mountains, or maybe it was the molten lava running in rivers beneath the city. All the same, I felt that dread growing inside me like a volcano threatening to erupt.

It must have shown on my face because the Dwarf brother with the long plait turned to me with a considerate expression and said: "It is alright, lassie. You have nothing to fear here. Our city is an impenetrable fortress."

Slowly, I nodded, trying to feel at ease.

"We will not burden you any longer, your Lordship," Aldwyn addressed Lord Eilan again. "We will find our way to an inn."

"I will not hear of it," Lord Eilan said, shaking his head. "You are honoured guests in my home and you shall rest here."

"That is certainly a gracious offer, your Lordship," Mithras thanked him. "Yet, we cannot ask..."

"You need not concern yourselves," Lord Eilan dismissed. "My home is open to you. We have an abundance of guest rooms. Besides, I would enjoy your company for dinner tonight," he looked to me as he said this.

I flashed him a small smile and nodded. "Of course, my Lord."

"Wonderful," Lord Eilan smiled brightly then turned to the brothers. "Dolin, would you be as kind as to show our guests to their rooms?"

Dolin, the Dwarf with the long plait, bowed his head graciously. "As you wish, milord."

Lord Eilan then turned back to us. "Enjoy your stay in our city."

* * * * *

Once he had gotten the others settled, Dolin took me to my room, saving me for last. Carden followed on beside me, still protective of me with Joran a short distance behind us, his eyes following the Dwarf as though he were afraid to crush him under foot. I almost had to hold back a laugh from watching him look so uneasy.

"I must say," Dolin confessed as we walked, "I have never met a member of the Aldegaadian Royal Family before."

"Have you never been to Arvon?" I asked him curiously.

He nodded. "Well, yes, I have. But I never had the privilege of entering the castle itself."

"Really?" I looked to him, surprised. "Why not?"

"Well, I was passing through with my brother and an expedition we were on, and only stopped in Arvon for supplies," he explained.

"And your brother? That would be the Dwarf back in Lord Eilan's office?"

"Aye, that is my brother. Holger is his name. We're twins, though we aren't very much alike."

We arrived at a door, Dolin opening it and leading us inside, the room beyond having the same built into a rock face feel as the rest of the estate and city. In the centre back of the room was a large double bed, the frame made of stone, the mattress like any other, possibly imported from human lands rather than homemade. It was dressed with crimson sheets and covers, similar curtains hanging around it for privacy.

There was a set of doors that served as a built-in closet, a heavy wooden box set at the foot of the bed, and a stone desk and chair positioned at an angle in one corner. On the other side of the room was a stone bathtub, pipes leading through the walls from it to supply water. The floor was covered by fine rugs and Dwarven paintings littered the walls along with the specially formed crystal glow lamps.

"This is your room, your Highness," Dolin turned to me as I gazed around the room in amazement. "It has all of the usual amenities such as a bathtub, closet and bed. I hope it is to your liking."

"It's amazing," I gazed around as I set my bag down on the floor. "Do all Dwarven houses cater to human visitors?"

"The Estate of the High-Lord does, milady," Dolin responded, hands clasped at the small of his back.

As we were speaking, the top of my bag opened and Amethyst poked her small head out. The dragonling croaked, then slid free of the bag and rolled onto the floor with the same clumsy flopping of any baby. Amethyst cawed and scrambled onto her clawed feet as I turned to look at her.

"Amethyst, what are you doing?" I crouched and picked her up in my arms, smiling at her.

"Is that a dragon?" Dolin asked, staring at Amethyst.

"It is," I answered, then corrected myself: "Well, actually she's a dragonling. She's still just a baby."

"I have heard only legends of these creatures," Dolin said to no one in particular as he stared at her. "I never thought to look upon one with my own eyes."

"There aren't many left in the world," Carden spoke up from where he stood, leaning against the door, his arms crossed. "Not from what any of us know. She is the first I have ever seen."

"Me too," I agreed, then smiled at Dolin. "Don't worry, she won't harm you. She's too young to even breathe fire yet."

"Amazing," Dolin laughed, smiling brightly at the dragonling. "I'll make sure she is fed. What shall I get her?"

"Meat," I said. "She seems content to eat beef."

Dolin nodded, then made for the door. "I will bring her some food forthwith. Oh, do not forget that dinner will be in less than an hour, Princess. I will come for you soon."

"Alright. Thank you, Dolin," I smiled and nodded to him.

He left the room, passing by Joran's massive form and disappearing down the hallway.

"Well," Carden cleared his throat and stood up straighter as he looked at me. "I will let you settle in."

"I will see you at dinner, right?" I asked him.

He nodded. "Of course, Leander," then he left.

Joran poked his head through the door and looked at me with his stern violet eyes. "If you should have any need of me, Sarissi, I shall be outside."

"You don't have to guard my door all night, Joran," I told him, craning my neck to look up at him.

"It is commanded by the Carethanes," was his answer.

I felt that his response had sounded fairly final, and I just nodded. "Alright."

Joran bowed his head, then turned his back and crossed his arms as I closed the door.

Taking Amethyst to the bed, I set her down then unpacked my bag, fishing out a pale blue, long sleeved linen dress. Amethyst watched me curiously from where she sat on the bed as I moved to the basin and washed my face.

After that, I bathed then dressed myself in a fresh under dress and the blue dress before reaching into my bag again and taking out a beautiful dark teal coloured velvet over dress with gold trims and purple silk lining. I slipped into it, fastening the bodice with its black cord at the front, then pulled on my leggings and boots.

I studied myself in the mirror, my hair flowing neatly, but youthfully unkempt, down my shoulders to where the Pendant's silver shape hung from my neck gracefully. The purple stone glistened as the light danced through it, almost mesmerising me as I watched it.

There was a knock on the door.

"Come in," I called, turning to it.

The door opened and Dolin entered, Joran peering through behind him.

"I am to escort you to the dining hall, your Highness," Dolin told me with a bow of his head.

"Did you bring food for Amethyst?" I asked, worrying about my dragonling.

He indicated the small bowl of diced meat in his left hand: "I did. I hope roasted pork suits."

"It should be fine," I answered, crossing to him and taking the bowl in both hands. "Thank you."

I set the bowl on the floor as I knelt down, Amethyst hopping off the bed and coming to me energetically. She was so like a small kitten, but scaly.

"I'll be back later. Alright, Amethyst?" I told her softly.

Amethyst gurgled, her molten orange eyes large and bright as she looked up at me. I could see the understanding in them, the little creature's intelligence so clearly abundant on her small face. I reached out my hand and stroked her head, feeling the soft, yet sturdy scales and the bony stubs that would soon grow into horns.

"Here's some food for you to eat," I pushed the bowl closer to her.

Amethyst sniffed the meat curiously, then immediately began eating it. I smiled as the tiny dragonling scoffed down a large piece of pork, chomping it three or four times before swallowing it and looking up at me innocently. She burped, gurgled again, then went back to eating.

I stood and turned to Dolin: "Alright, lead the way."

Dolin nodded and gestured for me to exit the room first. He took Joran and I into the centremost chamber of the estate; a large stone room with tapestries across the walls, portraits of all the previous High-Lords of Hecturn hung up, and a large stone table with multiple chairs placed around it. The table was in sections and shaped in an almost horseshoe pattern, some sections much higher along with matching chairs, having been brought in for the human guests visiting.

I entered the room behind Dolin, gazing around in amazement. The others were already gathered, all of them having changed into fresh clothes and were now standing at the table.

"Ah, Princess Leander," Lord Eilan smiled warmly, holding up a goblet in greeting where he stood. "Please, take a seat," he gestured to the one beside Mithras, who sat on his left.

I moved to the seat and sat down, the others all following suit as Joran took up his position behind me with his back against the wall. I looked up at him uncertainly, feeling unsettled seeing him standing over me, though I didn't make mention of it.

Dwarven servants brought out a large assortment of platters with foods from all over High-Realm: fruits, meats, breads and cheeses of all kinds. I was offered some wine, but politely refused it since I had never had it before and never would. I just didn't like the idea of alcohol. Besides, I was much too young.

We were all served according to our personal tastes, then began our meal, Dolin and Holger joining us with Coalan. I noticed another three Dwarves entering behind them, all blonde haired and sharing features with Lord Eilan. I knew immediately that they were Lord Eilan's children, his two sons and his daughter, all dressed in the crimson, gold and cream robes of nobility.

"Ah," Lord Eilan looked up, smiling broadly. "May I present my sons, Hallam and Halvard, and my daughter, Petra," he then turned to his children. "These are our honoured guests."

The eldest, Hallam, looked to me: "You are the Aldegaadian Princess, are you not?"

"I am," I responded, setting my hands together on the table.

Hallam nodded as he took his seat: "Father has often spoken of the Aldrichs of Aldegaad. He has said your line is as the Stone itself; unrelenting to your values and firm against your enemies."

"I don't know about that," I answered with a grievous tone as I turned my attention back to my plate.

I had no idea what the Dwarf-Lord was talking about, not really all that versed in the culture of the Dwarven people. Because of that I had no idea how to take his comment, but I guessed that it was a compliment.

Petra spoke up: "We were grievously sorry to hear of your loss. Your mother and father were truly good people."

"You knew them?" I looked up, surprised.

Petra nodded. "We came to Arvon some seventeen years ago during the Festival of Light. You weren't yet out of swaddling clothes when we last met."

"I truly like Arvon," Hallam said with a smile, "a wonderful city, despite being without a ceiling. I would dearly love to visit it again."

"You can't," I said grimly. "It... it was destroyed."

"The entire city?" Hallam asked. "How?"

"If you don't mind," I looked to Lord Eilan, almost for help, really wanting to avoid this discussion, "I would like to speak of a different subject."

"Perhaps one not so morbid," agreed Fawkner quietly.

"It seems that morbidity," Lord Eilan replied with a narrow glance to Fawkner, "is unfortunately the subject we have the greatest abundance of."

"What do you mean?" asked Mithras after swallowing a mouthful of food, his hands clasped together on the table.

Lord Eilan sighed after taking some wine: "We have had a number of our mining teams go missing in the Under Roads of late. When we sent search groups to find them, we came up with nothing."

"Almost nothing," added Halvard, a warrior's attitude obvious in his demeanour. "We have found half eaten Dwarven remains, weapons and shields of both Dwarven make and unknown manufacture. And, of course, blood everywhere."

I stared at him with a worried frown, that dread I had felt before returning to the pit of my stomach.

Halvard leaned forward on the table gravely, his eyes locked intensely on us. "Something is in the caverns beyond our city's walls and is devouring our kinsmen. And as an added inscrutability, some of our warriors, miners and scholars have seen shadowy figures moving in the tunnels. They have heard demonic whisperings and the howls of animals unlike anything we have yet encountered."

"Do you have any suspicions?" Aldwyn enquired with stern and analytical eyes as he picked at his meal.

"I believe it may be the Scourge," Halvard answered.

"Do not be absurd," Lord Eilan dismissed, turning to his younger son. "The Scourge has not been seen in the Under Roads for nearly twenty years. And what concentration there was appeared near Morthenhas. That is miles from here."

"You think these beasts cannot move, father?" Halvard demanded. "They have legs to walk and eyes to see, they need only choose a direction."

"It is well known the Scourge was driven underground nearly twelve hundred years ago," Hallam added to his brother's case. "It is far beyond a mere possibility that they could be lurking in the tunnels. Many a Dwarf has claimed an encounter."

"Shadows and whispers are not enough to go on, my boys," Lord Eilan retorted and sighed. "How I grow tired of this conspiracy theory."

"With respect, Lord Eilan," Aldwyn spoke up politely, "it was you who engaged this current line of conversation."

Lord Eilan nodded glumly. "Yes. I suppose I did. It seems that there is little mirth to be had at this time, either on or below the surface."

I frowned and bit my lip at his words. It seemed that there was no reprieve to be had from dark musings. My mind once again turned to the conspirators and to the mysterious Shadow Lord. I cringed the thoughts away, determined to be in a lighter mood.

"Still," Lord Eilan stood and raised his wine again to me, "it is a truly grand occasion having a member of one of the upworlder nations' nobility visiting us here in Hecturn, especially the descendant of the Great Heroine herself," he looked to the others. "As it is an honour hosting the esteemed Guardians themselves."

"You are too kind your Lordship," Tallinn bowed her head respectfully.

Lord Eilan turned his gaze back to me. "May you rest well and find safety in our humble halls, Princess Leander, as your ancestor before you once did."

All of the Dwarves raised their goblets and toasted, the others following suit. I watched them silently, dropping into deep thought as Lord Eilan began speaking with Aldwyn with interest about the Guardian Order.

I sighed and continued with my meal, listening to the new lines of conversation that were opening up all around me. Once again, I found myself in a place where my ancestor had been, just as once more I was hiding and hoping for a restful night without nightmares of dragons and demons, though I doubted I would get it.

Chapter Fifteen
Shade Seekers

I was actually glad when dinner had ended. I had gotten so tired of the unwarranted hero worship the Dwarves had been throwing my way all because I shared the same name as my famous ancestor. It was... well, annoying to say the least. Yet I endured it like I had been taught a princess should.

As soon as I was able, I left the dining hall and made my way out to one of the estate's balconies. I stood there looking out over the molten lava lake beneath the monumental city crawling up the cavern walls, finding a strange amount of peace for a short time.

Standing there – in its own way – reminded me of home. I remembered standing on the balcony of my bedroom in Castle Arvon, feeling the cold night air coming down from the mountains. I remembered the sound of the river as it swept by beneath the castle's walls, the smell of fresh water reaching up to greet me where I stood. It all made me grieve.

I can never go home again, I realised sadly, a tear trickling down my cheek.

I turned from the view of Hecturn and made my way back into the stone halls, leaving behind that once good memory that now angled into my heart with a fiery piercing pain. All I wanted now was to crawl into bed and go to sleep, to vanish from the world for just a little while.

"Leander!" a voice called.

I paused, turning where I had been walking in the hall. My eyes fell on Carden, the young Guardian hurrying to catch up with me. Seeing him made me feel a little better and I even smiled slightly, my heart fluttering again and warming me.

"What is it, Carden?" I asked as he reached me, slowing from his steady jog to a stop.

He looked down at me: "I wanted to see if you were alright."

"Why wouldn't I be?"

"Back in the dining hall," he said gently, "the way Lord Eilan spoke to you; I could see it was bothering you."

I sighed and nodded, continuing to walk. He started to walk at my side, watching me with a gentle green gaze.

"I'm getting very tired of people comparing me to my ancestor," I admitted, then added sarcastically: "Oh! Your ancestor visited us over a thousand years ago! Here's the bed *she* slept in! Here's the spoon *she* ate with! Here's the lavatory *she* used!"

Carden frowned with a faint smile. "I do not remember anyone talking about lavatories."

"I'm just making a point," I explained. "It's just that I am never seen as me. I am always seen as someone who is expected to be like her."

"No one expects you to be like her, Leander."

"Oh, really? Most of the last two hours were filled with people saying how like her I am."

As we reached a corner, Carden took me by my arm, stopping me from continuing and making me face him. My breath caught in my chest and I found myself staring helplessly into those incredible jade eyes. His touch was welcome, and I had a deep longing to keep his hand on my skin.

"I don't," he said with a serious, but comforting tone. "To me you are this wonderful girl all her own that I have the privilege to call my friend."

I stared into his green eyes, entranced. His words stunned me, though I already knew how he thought of me. Out of everyone, Carden had been the one to treat me as my own person more than anyone else. He still referred to me by name while most of the others escorting me used my title. Even Mithras still used my title in front of company, using my name only when we were separated from the others. I had often wondered in the last three weeks who among my companions and protectors had thought of me as Leander, and who had thought of me as the Heroine's descendant.

I reached my delicate fingers up to touch Carden's hand, his skin warmer and coarser than mine. Our eyes met with this deep, electric silence that seemed to fill the air and race through us both. My heart fluttered in a way that I had never known it to. My body tingled with an urge to be closer to him, but I didn't understand why.

He really cares for me, more than just as a protector, but as a friend. Is that what this feeling is?

I ended the silence: "You really are a good friend, Carden. Thank you."

"You're welcome," he smiled at me. "Now, may I walk you to your room?"

"I would appreciate it. I actually think I'm a little lost," I admitted, smiling sheepishly as I ran a hand through my hair and brushed it over my ear.

"Don't worry," he assured me. "I know the way."

We made our way down the stone corridors, turning onto the hallway that led to the guest rooms. As we approached, we saw a strange thing that made me frown quizzically.

Mithras was standing outside his room speaking to Dolin and Holger. Holger remained silent, looking a little bored, while Dolin was nodding and taking notes in a leather notebook. Mithras was saying something, though he was too far from us and speaking too softly for me to hear him. Whatever he was saying it was clear to both of us that his words were being meticulously written down by the attentive Dwarf in that strange notebook.

Dolin nodded and said something to Mithras, then turned and made his way towards Carden and I, Holger close behind. The two Dwarves nodded to Carden, then bowed their heads to me.

"Good evening, your Highness," Dolin regarded me respectfully.

Holger just grinned and kept following his brother.

I turned my gaze to Mithras. The Knight looked to me, nodded, then vanished into his room, closing the door.

"He seems to be acting rather strangely," Carden observed, facing me. "What do you think that was about?"

"I'm not sure," I replied. "But you're right. It does seem strange."

We turned away from Mithras' room and continued towards my own, which was made obvious by the eight-foot tall Storvari standing with crossed arms before it. We reached the door, Joran stepping aside to allow me to open it.

I turned to Carden and smiled at him gratefully: "Thank you for walking me to my room and for comforting my thoughts."

"You're welcome," he returned my smile. "That's what friends are for."

"Then I am lucky to have a friend such as you," I commented softly and gave him a small, gentle kiss on the cheek. "Goodnight, Carden."

"Goodnight, Leander," Carden responded, turning away and leaving me for his own room.

I watched him leave, sighing to myself. I was fascinated by him in a way that I had never before been with any person. *Maybe I can spend some more time with Carden. I may not get another chance once we reach the Citadel. Besides, I truly like being with him.*

I watched him until he entered his own room down the hall, then I straightened up from where I had begun resting against the door. I was suddenly very aware of the overwhelming presence of the Storvari standing over me, his piercing violet eyes watching me unflinchingly. I looked up at him, exchanging a stare with him in a moment of strained silence.

I can see why people fear the Storvari, I thought, recalling my first meeting with Joran.

"Why don't you get some rest, Joran?" I suggested kindly to him. "I think you could use it."

"I cannot, Sarissi," Joran responded, staring down at me evenly. "I must ensure your safety."

"At the cost of your own wellbeing?" I asked softly.

"It is as commanded by the Carethanes. My Saris is yours. There is nothing more important than your Cavara, Sarissi."

"Cavara?" I raised a curiously confused eyebrow.

"Yes," Joran nodded.

I frowned. "What does that mean, exactly?"

Joran thought for a moment then said: "I cannot translate a phrase or word in the common human tongue to adequately express the meaning of 'Cavara'. The closest would be 'continued life'."

I smiled gently to him. "Well, I don't think you should be concerned. Not here."

"I have Keravas to you," Joran disputed evenly. "I must ensure your safety, Sarissi."

"I promise you, Joran," I said to him, "I am safe here. Please. Get some rest."

He eyed me coarsely. I could see that he wasn't convinced by my words of care for him.

"Wouldn't it be better for you to restore your energy should the need to protect me arise?" I reasoned, hoping he would take this logic and be convinced to leave me alone.

Reluctant, but obedient, Joran bowed his head: "As my Sarissi commands, so I shall obey."

He turned then and made for his own quarters, passing down the hall.

Gratefully, I entered my room and closed the door. I sighed for a moment, relieved that he had agreed to go, then crossed to my bag and withdrew my nightgown.

Amethyst looked up from where she lay on the floor, a pillow set down there for her. The little dragonling squawked once, getting my attention.

"See? I said I would come back," I smiled down at her.

She arched her back like a cat and settled back down, seeming more relaxed now that I had returned.

I changed into my silver nightgown then turned out most of the lamps, leaving one lit for the night. I moved towards the bed, considering the pendant that lay around my neck. I was deciding whether to take it off or not.

The last time I took this off I ended up in danger. Perhaps I'll just wear it. It seems foolish to cast aside such protection.

With the Pendant still around my neck, I slid under the bed covers and lay back into the pillows. I closed my eyes and took in a few deep breaths, settling in for the night. I needed the rest, feeling the comfort of the smooth sheets pressing on my body, finally relaxing and drifting off...

* * * * *

I stood within a cavernous black iron and stone throne room, the ceiling made of natural formed rock and held up with iron reinforcements. The base of a long flight of stairs reached up behind me to an archway, and before me a long stone bridge led to a circular structure in the centre of the room. Beneath was a cruel void into nothing, the room lit with harsh light coming from blue flamed torches on sinister looking sconces.

Where am I? Am I dreaming?

My eyes then fell on the sinister, black iron, winged throne in the centre of the room. I saw the dark robed figure sitting there, his head down as if he were in contemplation, shadowy misty streaks moving from the darkness all around the rock and iron room as if to form his physical shape there.

I froze, trembling at the sight of him, paralysed with fear. I tried to move, but I couldn't even slide my foot a little.

The figure looked up and once again I was face-to-face with that smooth as marble, monstrous face. The green eyes glowed brightly beneath the brow, the blackened skin around them making them appear as though they were floating in endless black voids.

I staggered as my body unfroze in the monster's presence, my eyes locked on his cruel face as his long hands grasped the edges of the throne. My heart raced and my breathing accelerated, my consciousness threatening to slip away and leave me helpless on the cold floor.

The monster smiled, his thin, grey lips cracking up icily as his eyes brightened maliciously. I could see his pointed teeth through his lips, his strange nostrils flaring with anticipation.

"Princess," the Shadow Lord mewed maliciously. "So, there you are. I was wondering where you had gotten yourself to."

I gasped in terror, turning around fast as the Shadow Lord stood from his throne. I had expected to run for the doors, but instead found myself waking up in bed.

For a split second it was all just a bad dream... then I saw the spectres hovering over my bedside.

They were floating without feet, tattered black robes flowing around them as though they were submerged in water. The cold gleam of icy blue eyes glowing in skeletal sockets shone from beneath their cowls, their ghostly shapes reaching thin, long, bony hands out towards my bed.

I panicked immediately, propping myself up and pulling away from their outstretched corpse-like hands. The two creatures flared up liked angered serpents, the wrappings falling from their faces. They had horrifying visages beneath with glowing blue eyes set into sunken eye sockets, the sight of them making my blood turn cold.

Their jaws opened and elongated with horrible dagger fangs, their mouths exuding the same ghastly light as their eye sockets. The noise that came from them was like a ghoulish high-pitched wailing shriek that echoed through the room as they stretched out their skeletal limbs in rage.

I fell from the bed and scrambled backwards across the floor as the ghostly creatures passed towards me. Their screeching continued as they stalked me, stretching out their ghastly fingers for me again.

Backing into the wall, I screamed, staring up at the monsters helplessly. Then I heard a small howling and saw Amethyst leaping over the bed. The tiny dragonling was surveying the situation with her molten orange eyes, looking between the monsters as they stalked me.

"Amethyst!" I cried out in panic and ducked for her, desperate to reach her.

I narrowly avoided one of the creature's grasps, reaching Amethyst and scooping her up into my arms. I cradled her close to my chest, both of us staring up at the creatures floating towards us. I cringed back away from them, holding Amethyst tightly. I felt like I could cry in terror at the things reaching for me, then I felt a warmth over my chest, almost like a gentle flame that caused no pain.

I looked down, my pendant's stone glowing brightly, surrounding us in a purplish sheen. It was protecting us, I realised, turning my eyes back to the monsters frantically.

As one's hand reached out towards me, it touched the barrier and was cast back, smoke rising from its fingers as it screeched in agony. The other stared at it, then they both turned towards me again, their jaws elongating as they let out another haunting howl. This time they reached towards their left hips, swords appearing from nowhere as if made from shadowy mists.

I cringed down, drawing my knees up and cuddling Amethyst as the pair raised their weapons and reached towards us again.

The door flung open, Carden and Fawkner rushing in, dressed in their pants and shirts, only Fawkner wearing boots. They both carried their swords ready to fight, horror plastering their faces and their eyes widening as they saw the scene they had broken into.

I looked to them in terror and screamed: "NO, RUN!"

My two ethereal assailants turned towards the men with their swords and once again shrieked horribly.

"Get away from her!" Carden shouted, attacking one with his sword, Fawkner following his lead a moment later.

The creatures blocked the two men's attacks with ease, turning their attention to them and forgetting about me for the moment. I watched helplessly, terrified for my friends as they now defended me once again.

"Leander!" Fawkner shoved his attacker away forcefully as he spoke. "Run! Get out of here!"

I didn't hesitate. Immediately, I was up and running for the door with Amethyst still in my arms. As I ran into the hall I collided with a solid shape, crying out as hands grasped my shoulders.

"Leander! Leander, calm yourself! It is I!" Mithras urged, holding me firmly.

I looked up at him, staring for a moment until I heard more shrieks. Mithras pushed me behind him as his eyes settled on the new figures coming out of the deepest shadows at the end of the hall.

I looked past him to see another five of the ethereal monsters approaching, swords drawn, gaunt faces revealed beneath their cowls, eerie blue light glowing from their mouths and eyes. They floated forward menacingly as Carden and Fawkner were forced into the corridor by the first two, backing off to flank Mithras as he drew his own sword.

"What are these things?!" Carden demanded, keeping his eyes on the seven creatures.

"Shade Seekers!" Mithras answered urgently, brandishing his sword. "Ethereal agents of the Shadow Lords!"

"They cannot be killed it seems!" said Fawkner in both frustration and terror, though he still stood ready with his sword.

"Not with any conventional blade!" Mithras agreed.

Carden looked to me sternly. "Stay behind us!"

I nodded frantically, trembling as I cuddled Amethyst close to my chest. We were slowly backing away as the Shade Seekers approached, their whispers seeming to penetrate our minds.

Out of nowhere, Tallinn came running up with her bow, immediately firing two flaming arrows directly into the first two. The flames actually collided with the creatures as the arrows passed through them and hit the wall behind them, splintering upon impact. The two spectres began flailing and shrieking in pain, the fire hurting them as it spread over their black robed forms.

Tallinn took another two arrows and turned to Dolin and Holger, the two Dwarves wielding their own weapons while Dolin was also carrying a torch. Tallinn lit the arrows and fired again, one missing and hitting a wall, the other colliding with a third Shade Seeker.

"Fire hurts them?!" I exclaimed, amazed.

"No!" Tallinn answered as she readied more shots to her bow. "Light hurts them!" she aimed again.

The Shade Seekers turned and flew into the deepest shadows, disappearing.

There was a moment where we were plunged into silence, waiting as Joran joined us with his swords in hand. I was worried, looking around, searching for the next attack. We waited, uncertain if we had won... then came the first volley.

The Shade Seekers began diving out of the shadows as dolphins would through the ocean's surface. They came from all directions, slashing at us as my companions tried to fend them off.

It seemed hopeless to me as I watched the monsters strike again and again before vanishing into their shadowy portals. There didn't seem to be any attack that could fell the wretched monsters.

Then it came. A bright golden light as intense as sunlight shone out, the Shade Seekers staggering and halting their attacks. They raised their hands, howling as they backed away, facing the figure moving towards us. I squinted as I turned towards him, seeing his face.

Aldwyn came forward from the corridor with Lord Eilan behind him, his staff raised, the gem at its top emitting the bright light. He strode towards the Shade Seekers, the light ever brightening, driving them back. Once they were far enough away from us he brought the light to its highest intensity yet.

The Shade Seekers howled, the blue glow of their eyes and mouths turning an ever brightening golden until they simply disintegrated into dust.

I stared in stunned awe at what I had just seen, too afraid to move at first.

Aldwyn lowered his staff, the light fading away as he turned his gaze to us, relief on his face. I relaxed slowly, feeling the tension in my limbs gradually releasing as I calmed down from the attack, my eyes aching from the bright light.

Lord Eilan turned to Dolin and Holger: "Rally the guards; I want the entire estate searched! And send the city soldiers to scour all of Hecturn! I do not want more of those beasts assaulting us again!"

"There will not be any more of them," Aldwyn turned to the Dwarf-Lord. "Shade Seekers always travel in groups of seven, no more, no less. I would not expect another insurgence again so soon."

"I would also illuminate all areas of the estate, my Lord," Tallinn added, bow in hand at her side, her blonde hair hanging to her shoulders messily, "just as a precaution."

"Why would that be necessary?" Lord Eilan asked.

"Shade Seekers move through shadows and darkness," Aldwyn explained evenly. "It is as though they are passing through doorways when they do so. They are vulnerable to any kind of light, their skin burning should they touch it. Sunlight is fatal to them, as is enough concentrated firelight."

"And how does one defeat such monsters?" Lord Eilan demanded.

"You can never really defeat them," Aldwyn replied knowledgably. "You can kill Shade Seekers with enough fire, yet there will always be others to take their place."

"They will never stop coming until they have completed their task," Tallinn finished grimly. "All we have to ascertain is what they were after."

I took in a long, sharp breath, knowing the answer.

"Me," I said, my voice shaking uneasily. "They were after me."

"It certainly seems that way," Fawkner agreed.

I could see the expression on Lord Eilan's face growing darker. I knew that he was deciding whether I was too much of a liability to keep within the walls of Hecturn. To be honest, I wouldn't have blamed him for throwing us out.

"Very well," he said carefully, "then we shall take all the precautions necessary to prevent another attack."

"And I will stand watch over you at all times, Sarissi," Joran convicted, looking down at me severely.

"I'm not sure..." I began to protest.

"Do not argue," Fawkner warned me, drawing my gaze as he sheathed his sword. "He's made up his mind and you need protection."

Mithras nodded his agreement. "At least until we depart."

"And when shall we do that?" Tallinn asked.

"We will need another two days," Aldwyn answered easily, then looked to Lord Eilan. "Will that be acceptable?"

Lord Eilan nodded. "Yes. You are welcome guests as long as you need."

Mithras nodded. "Then we will begin making the preparations in the morning. For now, I believe some rest is of greater benefit to us all."

No one disagreed with his observation, all of us moving off to our rooms, though I completely disapproved of Joran standing outside mine all night. But since I had no choice in the matter, I had to just accept it.

I entered my room again, lit all the lamps and crawled back into bed, huddling down with Amethyst at my feet. I wasn't about to allow those creatures another entrance into my room to attack me again. The thought of them left me terrified until I simply passed out.

* * * * *

For the next two days I was mostly confined to my room. I hated being trapped there under guard at all hours, never permitted to leave the room on my own. This felt suddenly similar to my last few days in Castle Arvon. For the first time in my life I had to allow servants to wait upon me for everything, a prospect that didn't agree with me at all.

Carden spent a lot of time with me, the only saving grace to my situation. He would come and go, but for the most part he stayed with me and tried to keep me entertained, the two of us looking after Amethyst as we sat together.

Dolin often checked in on me more than any other Dwarf, showing a remarkable amount of care towards me. It seemed that most of the other Dwarves now saw me as a jinx rather than the descendant of my revered ancestor. I couldn't decide whether that was a good thing or a bad thing.

At one point, Dolin came with his brother, Holger snickering perversely at the doorway as they delivered a meal to Carden, Amethyst and I. I was unimpressed by the Dwarf, Dolin slapping him and leading him from the room a few moments later.

I slept with all of the lights on each night, suffering from nightmares of the Shade Seekers' attack, seeing their ghoulish visages invading my subconscious every time I closed my eyes. I could never have imagined anything so horrible could truly exist in the real world. It was the stuff of faery tales.

Finally, the last day we spent in Hecturn came.

Dressed in my purple silk lined dark blue and pale blue, long sleeved dress, I followed Joran to the exterior of the estate. I fastened my purple cloak around my shoulders as I walked, Joran carrying my bag with Amethyst sitting upon his gigantic shoulders.

We walked down the front steps of the estate to be greeted by Carden. He was dressed in his dark jacket, shirt and pants, his black and silver cloak hanging from his shoulders, his sword at his hip. He smiled faintly at me as I approached, and I somehow found it in myself to return his smile weakly. We joined to walk side-by-side as we followed Joran down towards the main commons of the city.

Reaching the commons, we didn't move in the direction of the main doors, which surprised me. Instead, we began to move deeper into the cavern to where our companions had gathered with no horses set to journey with us; something else that confused and surprised me.

"What's going on?" I asked as I stopped there, aware of the confusion that was clear on my face. "I thought we were leaving."

"We are," Mithras told me, turning from a Dwarf captain he was speaking with.

I frowned, twisting my hands together in front of my waist. "The way out is behind us."

"We will be travelling via the Under Roads," Aldwyn explained to me calmly, gripping his staff in both hands and leaning on it. "According to Lord Eilan there is a tunnel that leads up to the Lorgath Pass and into the Nartarn'lath Mountains, which is where we want to go."

"A dark journey, if you ask me," Fawkner glowered, trying to settle Farsight, the falcon fidgeting on his gloved hand.

"Are you certain such a path is a sound course?" asked Carden uncertainly, staying at my left shoulder protectively, his green eyes stern. "I have heard of travellers becoming lost down there."

"Which is why you need a guide, lad," a gruff, but proud voice called.

I turned my attention – as the others did – to the two figures moving towards us. Dolin and Holger approached, both dressed in their Dwarven scale shirts, tunics and fur collared cloaks, carrying their weapons over their backs with a backpack each. Dolin looked prepared and determined while Holger looked as though he was just being dragged along for the ride.

"You're coming with us?" Carden asked, surprised.

Dolin nodded, hands on his belt buckle. "Aye. Lord Eilan asked for volunteers to lead your party through the Under Roads, and I decided to follow on to aid you in your journeys."

"You're following us to the Citadel then?" Tallinn enquired, her arms crossed, her hair tied back neatly.

Dolin nodded. "That we are."

"Besides," Holger spoke up gruffly, "it's about time we returned to the surface again."

"If you're certain your presence is not required here in Hecturn," Aldwyn said evenly.

Holger shrugged. "I'd rather fight monsters than hang around the estate all day. I mean, come on, what am I gonna do? Sip tea?"

I had to hide a small smirk at his comment behind my free-flowing dark hair, agreeing with his point of view.

Dolin went on: "And you lot could use a hand. Besides," he pointed to me warmly, "I've got a feeling about you, lassie."

"Me?" I asked, raising an eyebrow quizzically.

Dolin nodded. "Aye. You've got some great future before you. I'd like to know where your journey goes."

Mithras smiled to them: "We would never refuse help. Our thanks."

Both Dwarves nodded to him.

"Are you ready, upworlders?" an armoured Dwarven officer asked us, drawing my eyes to him.

Aldwyn nodded. "Yes. I think we are now."

"Just how many Dwarves are going with us?" I asked Dolin as we made our way forward.

"Only Holger and I follow you to the surface, lassie," he answered in his deep voice. "But the Under Roads are treacherous and this search team is heading in the same direction we are to seek out a lost mining unit. We might as well travel together rather than divide our numbers."

"It makes sense," Carden agreed, walking up beside me.

He flashed me a reassuring smile and I managed to return it before I looked up at the way ahead.

Two monumental iron doors were being pulled open to clear the way, a large number of Dwarven soldiers on guard here. Beyond the doors lay the pathway into the Under Roads, a series of tunnels beneath the mountains, each one a hundred feet tall and wide.

I felt this overwhelming awe wash over me as I saw it, a tunnel far greater than anything I had seen built in my homeland. I could feel my heart pounding rapidly in my chest, instinctively grasping Carden's right hand with my left. We exchanged a glance, Carden nodding his concurrence with my action, then continuing beside me into the tunnels.

We moved through the doors, now numbering nine in our party surrounded by eleven Dwarven warriors on a mission. The doors groaned, drawing our attention as they were sealed again behind us, closing us into the dark depths beneath the mountain halls.

Chapter Sixteen
The Unseen

The journey through the Under Roads was a slow and difficult one that had us wandering through the dark places of the world. On the map of Aldegaad it seemed that Hecturn and the Lorgath Pass were very close, yet in reality the opening to the pass was at least a three-day journey from the city. But the passage would take us even longer to complete.

The Dwarves were tight lipped as we moved through the tunnels, weapons always at the ready as their eyes roved the shadows around the towering pillars. They weren't there to play more than escort with our party, their mission far more important to them. They were a lot less friendly than Dolin and Holger, the two brothers at least willing to show their faces.

Dolin was leading the way for us as the Dwarven commander led the way for his men. Unlike the commander speaking in Dwarfish, Dolin maintained a common speech for those of us who didn't speak their tongue as he read the map and followed the commander's directions.

Holger stayed close to Dolin, though I often caught him glancing at me. He was making me uncomfortable, his stares as unwelcome as the Shade Seekers had been in my room. I was really beginning to distrust him, while his brother gave me a good feeling of security and honesty.

We came to a crossroads in the tunnels, pausing for a while as the Dwarves consulted their maps, Aldwyn looking over Dolin's shoulder curiously. The rest of us waited silently until after about ten to twenty minutes when the Dwarves finally deciphered which path to take. This continued on for the next two days, our group of twenty stopping to make camp each night.

On the third day we came to a downed section of the passages, the Dwarven commander sending four of his troops through a crevice in a wall to search for a way around.

Carden and I set ourselves on a fallen pillar to rest, both of us tired as the others watched all around us for danger. Mithras, Dolin and Aldwyn went up to join the Dwarf commander and his men, Mithras asking a question, too far for me to hear what was being said.

After a short exchange, it became clear that the Dwarf was agitated with Mithras. Mithras and Aldwyn were glancing at each other uncertainly as Dolin began speaking sternly to the commander. After a few moments, the helmeted Dwarf nodded and was saying something to Mithras.

They spoke for a while longer, then Mithras nodded and turned away. He walked to Carden and I, looking down at us and smiling as he saw Amethyst snuggling into my arms.

"Mithras?" I looked up, ill at ease with the darkness of these tunnels. "What is it?"

"We are continuing on, Leander," Mithras informed me.

I sighed. "Alright. I guess we have rested enough already."

"Ah. And I was just getting my legs to stop hurting," Carden joked as he stood, smiling at me.

"The Dwarves have sent scouts on ahead to secure a spot to rest for the night," Mithras explained. "We will not be travelling much farther, I promise you."

Carden helped me to my feet, the two of us beginning to follow Mithras towards the crevice entrance where the rest of our group was already moving.

"How can he even tell what time it is?" Carden asked me. "We're underground."

I simply shrugged, Amethyst stirring and yawning, the dragonling still huddling in my arms.

We reached the opening, its depths dark and unwelcoming. I was hesitant to go through, looking to Mithras uncertainly, but he nodded and gestured for me to proceed. I sighed and turned to Carden as he smiled at me and took my hand, the two of us making our way into the dark.

We joined our companions quickly, Joran following with Mithras close behind us. Up ahead, Aldwyn waved a hand over the crystal set into the top of his staff, the gem emitting a gentle blue glow that illuminated the dark volcanic rock walls all around us. I felt the smallest hint of relief at the light, but it wasn't really enough.

We continued on, moving through the cavern openings carefully, determined not to get caught between rocks and outcroppings. It was a slow trudge through the cavern, our group making its way in silence until we came upon firelight ahead.

We entered into a large space, the scouts that had been sent on ahead already having set a fire and secured the perimeter. With the commander's say so, the Dwarves and our group began unpacking the bags. Within a half hour we had set up camp and posted guards all around the few openings into the cavern, watching for any sign of threats from anything lurking down there in the depths under the world.

I huddled down on a bedroll, cradling Amethyst in my arms as I watched the Dwarves cooking some of the supplies they had brought with them. The others went about setting up their own resting places for the night.

"You would sit with us rather than your own countrymen?" Tallinn asked as Dolin sat down beside her.

Dolin nodded as he settled with his bowl of food. "I am not a part of their group. I am with this one and so with this one I shall travel."

"As will I," agreed Holger, scoffing down his food where he sat hunched over.

I ate quietly, allowing Amethyst to eat her own smaller bowl of food beside me. I was glad to sit with Carden to my right, his presence making this dark and unwelcoming place more comforting. We exchanged a short glance and vague smiles before returning to our meals.

"So," Fawkner spoke up as he carefully fed Farsight, the bird left uneasy underground, "where do we go from here?"

"Yes," Tallinn nodded, resting her elbows on her knees, heels pressed to the floor. "How much farther to the opening to the Lorgath Pass?"

"Holger," Dolin directed his brother, the other Dwarf laying down a map of the tunnels on the ground before them.

I looked down at the map in the firelight, seeing only a series of drawn channels that seemed to form a maze, some symbols I didn't recognise at all – though I knew they were Dwarven – sketched there to indicate the various features. The only thing I did recognise was Hecturn sitting on the far west side of the map.

"These charts only cover the High-Realm Under Roads," Holger explained gruffly, returning to his meal. "We don't have any of the others with us."

"And where is our current position?" asked Aldwyn, cradling his staff between folded arms against his chest as he stood over us.

Dolin indicated on the map: "We are here, inside the walls of this section. We obviously have to mark the collapse for the mapmakers until the passage is clear."

"And the pass?"Aldwyn looked to him again.

"Here," Dolin moved one short, broad finger across the map to a symbol and set of runes. "This passage will lead us up to the Lorgath Pass."

"How long?" Carden spoke up, setting his now empty bowl down.

"Another day," answered Dolin. "Maybe a little less. After that Holger and I will follow you to the Citadel."

"Provided there's better food than this crap," Holger grumbled, tossing aside his last few scraps of food.

Amethyst lifted her head, cocking it to one side curiously. She padded her way over to the bowl and started licking out the meaty remains hungrily, her wings pressed to her small, scaled back. She was so adorable.

"Of course we welcome your companionship," Aldwyn reconfirmed to the two Dwarves, "but what of the others travelling with us?"

Dolin glanced over his shoulder at the Dwarven warriors milling around the cavern, eyeing them off grimly. He then shook his head and turned back to the older Guardian.

"They travel their own path and shall seek out our missing countrymen," he answered. "They will return to Hecturn with whatever they find, whether it be the miners, their corpses or nothing at all."

"A sad journey if either of the latter are the result," said Tallinn grimly, shaking her head.

"As you know, we have been dealing with missing people for some months now," Dolin told her. "We are not sure what it is that has done this, but we have been making every attempt to learn the truth."

"Is there more of that?" Holger asked, pointing to the food then grabbing at the pot before anyone could answer. I could only frown at him with confusion.

Dolin shook his head at his brother then continued on: "There are many dangers in the Under Roads, always have been, same as your topside roads. Beasts attack travellers down here as they do where you come from. It is just part of the life of a Dwarf. Though, the disappearances have been more frequent and more puzzling of late, I am not certain that a beast is responsible."

"Do you suspect the Scourge as Lord Eilan's son suggested?" Carden asked, resting one arm on his raised knee.

"Honestly," Dolin regarded him darkly, "I am not certain what to think."

I felt a great swell of sympathy for the Dwarves. I could never have even begun to understand what their lives were like, only being able to imagine what monsters could lurk beneath the surface of the world.

I sighed as Amethyst returned to me, reaching out one small claw to my knee, cooing softly. I smiled down at her and scooped her up into my lap, stroking her small head with my fingertip.

"Well," Mithras cleared his throat, standing up from his seat, "perhaps we should get some rest. We have a long day ahead of us."

"Are we safe here?" I asked softly, the tunnels unnerving me deeply.

Holger snorted: "What? Ya scared, girly?" he eyed me with an inappropriately suggestive gaze.

"Shut it, Holger," Dolin growled. "Stop having a go at the wee girl."

Mithras shook his head, then turned to me again: "I assure you, Leander, you have nothing to fear. Joran is on guard and we have the Dwarven warriors with us. We are safe."

I drew in an uncertain breath then nodded: "Alright."

"Rest well, child," Mithras smiled, then turned and went to his own bedroll.

I lay back, pulling the blanket made from furs over myself and allowing Amethyst to snuggle in next to me. I stayed there for a few moments listening to the sounds in the cavern until I slowly managed to slip away into sleep while the others settled in around me.

* * * * *

I dreamed of dark caverns and cold abysses, of monsters in the dark and of something lumbering through the depths around us. Six pus yellow eyes opened and glowed as horrible steel crushing teeth parted to release a deep, booming growl, the creature glaring hungrily through the shadows. One gigantic hand reached out, closing over me...

I awoke with a start, my eyes flying open as I sat up suddenly from my resting place. I felt that haunting nightmare still clinging to me, uncertain if I really saw what I thought I had or whether it was just a horrible dream like I hoped.

I looked around me, seeing my companions already awake and packing up to leave.

Carden saw my terrified gaze and moved to me, crouching down at my side as Amethyst squawked worriedly.

"Are you alright?" he asked me gently.

"I-I just had a nightmare," I realised, looking up into his green eyes. "I'm... I'm alright."

He looked concerned. "Are you sure?"

I nodded. "Yes. I'm fine," I got to my feet and looked around at the activity around me. "What's happening?"

"We're moving out now," he informed me, then started to help me pack up. "Here. Let me help you."

"Thank you," I smiled appreciatively.

Within minutes we were packed and, on the move, making our way through the dark tunnels of the Under Roads. As we continued our way through the shadows and the stone halls, I began to feel increasingly strange.

I gazed around at the dark stone walls as I followed the others along our trek, my blue eyes searching the shadows for some sign of the source to my unease. My ears picked up every sound, heard every scrape and cough as the stale scent in the air grew ever stronger with each step I took. Fear and danger were stalking us like predators in the dark, relentless and hungry.

Carden had been studying me for the last hour or so, his green eyes surveying my frowns and winces, taking in every little twitch, every facial gesture, every stare.

After some silent deliberation, he spoke: "Leander, is something wrong?"

I shook my head, still glancing through the shadows. "No, nothing."

He frowned at me. "You're lying. I can tell."

I threw him a stern sideways glance, silently warning him to let it be. Still, I wanted to tell someone what I knew, though I didn't know how. I was afraid of what they might think.

If they knew, they would think I'm losing my mind. I can't allow them to know about my dreams.

Carden prodded: "Something *is* wrong, isn't it?"

I sighed, feeling an ever-growing sense of dread reaching through me, spreading first from my heart then to the rest of my body.

"I have a terrible feeling that we're in danger," I admitted to him, hushed so that the others didn't hear.

"What makes you fearful?" he asked, keeping his tone of voice at the same level as mine.

I shrugged. "I feel like we're being watched."

Carden looked around uncertainly. "By what?" he asked, turning back to me.

I shook my head and chewed my bottom lip. "I don't know, but I feel unseen eyes upon us even now. It worries me."

I looked up at the group ahead of us uneasily. I was beginning to feel a new fear building within my heart and mind, sensing some creature nearby, though I hoped it was only my imagination playing tricks on me.

"I'm beginning to think that Lord Eilan's son was right in his suspicions," I admitted to Carden uneasily. "I think something has been attacking the Dwarves down in these tunnels; something that may now be stalking us."

Carden nodded seriously, his right hand crossing his waist to his left hip and resting on the hilt of his sword. His green eyes were intense, staring out from behind the dark strands of hair framing his handsome face. He surveyed the shadows pressing in on us, as uncertain in his own mind as I was in mine.

"What should we do?" I asked softly, fighting my body's desire to tremble.

"We should tell someone," he decided. "Let me speak with Tallinn."

"I'm not sure about this," I admitted uncertainly.

"It is either that or we stay silent until something attacks us," he offered.

I swallowed hard and nodded. "Fair enough."

He took me by my arm, and we moved up to Tallinn. She was walking beside Fawkner just behind Mithras and Aldwyn, her hand on the bow slung over her shoulder.

"Tallinn," Carden touched her arm, speaking softly. "A word."

"What is it, brother?" Tallinn asked, Fawkner listening in.

"Leander has expressed to me concerns of us being followed. Hunted, to be precise," he said discreetly.

"Have you seen something, your Highness?" Tallinn asked, turning over her shoulder to me.

I shook my head. "No. I've only felt an ever-growing sense of dread, as well as the eyes of some unseen creature prowling behind us."

"Do you fear more Shade Seekers?" she queried, raising one dark, slender eyebrow.

I shrugged. "I feel something more bestial. Something more like a rabid animal rather than one of those phantoms."

"She fears Lord Eilan's son may have been right," Carden said, then admitted, watching the darkness around us: "As I am beginning to. I have seen strange shadows moving amidst the cavern walls within the last few days."

"As have I," Tallinn replied, confirming my fears and compounding her own. "I truly believe some dread thing is stalking us in this dark place. I do not like it."

"I don't either," I said nervously. "But I'm not sure..."

I was cut off midsentence as I felt a sudden rush of heat in my chest. I paused where I stood, letting out a sharp breath, Carden and Tallinn turning to face me. They stared at me, confused by my sudden silence and my obvious discomfort, Joran pausing right behind me.

The giant looked down at me with his violet eyes, frowning: "Sarissi? What is wrong?"

I took in a deep, laboured breath, reaching my right hand to the Pendant around my neck. It felt hot, as though it had been dropped in the fire, then scooped out and thrown against my skin. I shuddered, staring down at its glowing purple stone as Amethyst started squawking wildly like she had been hurt or frightened.

Mithras looked back, most of the others quite far ahead now. Holger cursed and stomped back towards us in a foul mood as two Dwarven warriors stopped behind us.

"What is it?" Mithras called back.

"The Pendant!" I gasped, looking to Carden and Tallinn in mild pain. "It's burning my skin!"

Suddenly, there came the rumbling of stone and the entire tunnel began shaking wildly. We were thrown off our feet to the floor, a horrific cracking echoing all around us. The ground beneath me shook apart and dropped, the stone giving way to collapse. I screamed, grabbing Carden's hand as I slid back, the young man trying to pull me up, but slipping and following me as the ground dropped.

"NO!" I heard Mithras cry out. "LEANDER!"

I felt the air rushing around me for what seemed like an eternity, though it was really only a few seconds before I hit the ground with a hard thud, Carden slamming into the earth right beside me with a groaning yelp. Tallinn hit the floor not far from us, Joran's body colliding with the stone heavily a few feet away, the cavern shaking violently from his impact. Holger fell on top of him, the two Dwarven warriors landing nearby.

Amethyst tumbled from my bag, thrown from Joran's hand when he had fallen. The small dragonling fell hard, yelping and rolling onto her side, waving her limbs, tail and wings mindlessly. She was the first up, scurrying immediately to my side, pawing at my head as I lay there half conscious.

I groaned, squinting as I sat up, coughing out dust that I had breathed in. All around me the others who had fallen were gathering themselves together, trying to recover from the fall.

I looked at the hole above us, seeing that it was some twenty feet up, impossible to reach from where we had fallen and blocked by one of the pillars of the corridor that had collapsed. I could just barely see figures moving around the opening, though I wasn't close enough to see their faces.

My body ached from the fall, a few scratches and bruises all I had to show for it.

"Well... ahem..." Carden coughed, getting to his feet and brushing himself off, "that's something I don't want to do again anytime soon."

"Neither do I," Tallinn agreed, flexing out her arm to test for injury.

"That was most unpleasant," Joran growled, throwing Holger off him, the Dwarf howling as he hit the ground.

"Watch it ya colossal twit!" he roared at Joran.

"You seek to challenge me, small, bearded one?" Joran queried, glaring down at him from where he sat.

"This is not the time!" Tallinn snapped at them both.

"Brother?!" Dolin's voice called from the opening above us, sounding so distant. "Are you injured?!"

"No!" Holger shouted back up. "Just stuck with a big lummox and three bratty kids!"

"Hey!" I exclaimed, throwing him a warning glare.

"We are not kids!" Carden retorted.

"Leander?! Are you alright?!" Mithras called.

I nodded, looking up to the figure I could only assume was him. "Yes! I'm alright! But I don't think we can get out this way!"

"Joran," Mithras called to the Storvari, "could you lift the others out?!"

"Impossible and implausible," responded Joran evenly, surveying the wreckage as I scooped up Amethyst in my arms. "The way is blocked."

"Holger," Dolin called to his brother, "do you know where you are?!"

"How the Void should I know?!" Holger demanded angrily, spitting as he yelled. "We're in a cavern!"

"It looks to be a naturally formed one with a way out," one of the Dwarven warriors observed from behind us, still professional and calm. "There appears to be the remains of a fortress here."

"A fortress?" Tallinn turned to him, recovering her bow.

"How can you tell?" I asked uncertainly.

The Dwarf pointed to stone ruins littering the area. "These are the remains of a Dwarven structure. Possibly one of the bastions our ancestors abandoned two thousand years ago. We had once lived deeper than we do now."

"Is there a way out?" I asked hopefully.

The Dwarf nodded his helmed head. "Yes. The bastions were all linked to the Under Roads. If we can reach the main battlements we can get back to where our companions are."

"It looks like we can get back up to you!" Carden shouted to the others. "One of the Dwarves says there's a way up to the Under Roads from here!"

"That is indeed good news!" called Aldwyn, unseen above us.

"Very well!" Dolin granted. "We'll move towards the most likely entrance we can find and wait for you there! If we are not there, head for the doors to the Lorgath Pass and that's where we will join you!"

"Then we shall meet you on the other side!" called up the Dwarven warrior who seemed to know what we were most likely facing, turning to us then: "Follow me."

Slowly, we continued on through the tunnels of the forgotten underground fortress, the Dwarves lighting torches to lead the way. Carrying Amethyst in my arms, I stayed as close to both Carden and Joran as possible, feeling extremely insecure now that we were separated from the others.

I looked around at my companions worriedly, noting Carden grasping the sword at his hip and Tallinn poised to snatch her bow from her back. I noticed that Holger had drawn his hammer as though he were expecting us to come under attack, both of the Dwarven warriors also carrying their weapons ready for a fight.

We passed through several sealed doors, struggling to open them, then bypassed some collapsed walkways and at last entered a large dungeon-like room; a room which smelled of rotting flesh.

"Ugh! What is that?!" I exclaimed, covering my nose and mouth with my hand.

"I'm not sure," Carden tried not to breathe through his nose as he treaded through the room in a mirror pattern with Tallinn, both Guardians searching our surroundings.

I moved towards a table in the centre of the room, noticing that a darkly stained sheet was set there covering something. I turned my eyes to the smaller table lying beside it, seeing the strange and sinister looking implements resting upon it.

What is this place?

I looked back to my friends, watching them uneasily.

Tallinn crossed to a desk with papers on it and began rustling through them, frowning deeper as she studied them.

"Carden," she called to the other Guardian.

Carden turned from the shelves of strange items he had been staring at and joined Tallinn where she stood. He picked up some of the papers and began trying to read through them as she watched him.

"What do you make of these?" she asked.

He shook his head, frowning: "I've never seen writings like this before."

At the far end of the room, Holger was looking around with the same expression as someone who had entered somewhere unholy and evil.

"This... this is a foul place," he whispered, fear in his dark eyes.

"It reeks of blood and death," commented Joran in his same single toned way. "Kal Vashor. It is an unholy rite that has been invoked here. Varedarak!"

"The more I see here," Tallinn swallowed hard, fear covering her face as she looked around the room, "the more I agree."

"We should leave," Holger insisted grimly.

I was now looking at the shape lying beneath the sheet on the table, Amethyst on the floor after I had set her down so I could use both hands. Slowly, knowing this was a bad idea, I reached out one shaking hand and grasped the cleanest part of the sheet. I drew it back... and screamed.

I threw myself away from the mutilated remains that stared at me with dead white eyes, my screams drawing the others' gazes and bringing out their own cries of terror, only Joran silent as he stared with disgust.

Carden was at my side in an instant, holding me to his chest and cradling me close. I whimpered, feeling hot tears running down my face as I clung to him, the horrific image branded in my mind even with my eyes shut.

Oh Gods! Please! Let me forget that sight! Please! I prayed.

"By the Stone!" Holger staggered back from the sight before him. "It's one of the miners!"

"Some foul creature has brought them here!" one of the Dwarven warriors howled. "What vile beast has done this?!"

"What indeed?" a hissing voice mewed from the shadows, echoing all around us. "What could have done such a thing? What, what, what? Hee ha-ha-ha-ha!"

I looked up, still clinging to Carden, the young Guardian having drawn his sword in his right hand, holding me close with his left. Tallinn had drawn her bow and already laced an arrow to it as Joran had taken up his twin swords, standing closer to me defensively. The three Dwarves brandished their weapons, turning to surround us as Amethyst hid trembling behind my skirt.

The disembodied voice laughed jovially at us, echoing all around the room so that we could not discern where the sound came from.

"Look at the little mice, frantically searching for the cat! Hee ha-ha-ha! Where is it, they ask?! What is it, they ask?! It is... Unseen..."

"Show yourself, coward!" Holger roared violently, brandishing his hammer. "I'll give you the thrashing of your life!"

"Violent little man," the voice mewed from the darkness, "just like all the others who bite with steel and tongue; all bark, no real bite. Hee ha-ha-ha-ha! You'll scream like they did."

"You're the one who's been taking the Dwarves from the city," Tallinn realised, her bow shaking in her frightened hands despite her attempts to stay calm.

"Yes! It is!" the voice chortled. "And not just the rock rats; took from the pointy ears and the menses too. Took them down from the sun and brought them to the dark. Yes, yes, yes, in the dark."

"And you murdered them like you did this poor Dwarf!" Tallinn accused, indicating the dead body on the table.

"The Unseen needed flesh," the voice expressed maniacally. "Yes, yes! Needed flesh! Needed bone! Needed blood! Only works with blood, hee ha-ha-ha!"

"What does? What only works with blood?" Tallinn demanded sounding weaker as her resolve was fading into growing fear, but her courage was still stronger than mine.

"The Experiment," whispered the eerie voice gleefully. "The Master demanded it! Blood is the key!"

"What experiment?" Tallinn forced strength into her voice, her eyes roving continuously.

"The Master's Experiment," the voice hissed excitedly, chuckling to itself, "to crush the mortal world, to burn the lands, to smash the rock rats!"

"Show me your face creature and I'll smash it for you since you like to smash so much!" Holger threatened through his teeth, gripping his hammer firmly.

"You want to see, do you?" the voice asked. "Well then, the Unseen grants your request..."

On the low set of stairs jutting out from the tall archway at the far end of the room a shadowy figure began to appear. At first it seemed like nothing more than a shadow in the dark, but it soon gained a full humanoid form.

The creature stood at about six foot six in height, a broad-shouldered figure in appearance. It resembled a man only in the respect that it had a masculine form and voice, but there was no way to be sure of its actual gender. It was clad in worn looking armour under tattered crimson robes, a tightly fitted wrapping hood set over its head. Its hands were tipped with black taloned fingers and its skin was scaly like a lizard's.

Its face had sharp cheekbones and forehead ridges, wide open slit nostrils visible where a nose would be on a human. Two blood red eyes stared out of the deeply set sockets, no whites at all to the eyes themselves, the pupils like slits. No more could be seen of the creature's face as it wore a crimson scrap of cloak wrapped around the lower half of its face just below its nostrils. In its hand it carried a twisted and sinister mage's staff bearing demonic totems and symbols.

I clung closer to Carden, noticing my companions' expressions of fear as they stared at the horrible creature.

"*What* are you?" challenged Tallinn, struggling to keep her composure.

"It is the Unseen," the creature hissed through its mask, eyes blinking with sidewards lids, "Disciple to the Master. It serves him, the Master of Shadow, just as its brothers and sisters do."

"Who is this '*Master*' of yours?" Carden spoke up, managing to maintain some strength in his voice.

"He created us," the Unseen hissed. "Forged our bones, knitted our flesh and cultivated our blood. In return we serve him as his disciples."

"How many of you are there?" Carden asked clearly.

"We are eight," replied the Unseen, "yet we command legions. And it… it serves the Master by enacting the Experiment."

"What do you want?" my fierce friend growled, holding me tighter to his chest.

"Flesh and blood and bone," was the response, then the Unseen started to stare past the two Guardians.

Its blood coloured eyes locked onto my face as I clung to Carden, studying me for a few moments. It seemed to sniff the air before it began to chortle again.

"You," it pointed to me. "The Unseen knows you. The Master saw you, said you would come to the Unseen. You are the girl he seeks; the Princess..."

I whimpered, Carden's muscles instinctively tensing harder around me at the creature's words.

"You stay away from her!" he yelled, leaping forward with his sword, letting go of me.

"Carden, wait!" Tallinn cried out, trying to stop him and missing.

Carden struck out, swinging his sword at the Unseen, the creature vanishing into thin air and letting the sword pass through nothing but black mist. Carden straightened up, looking around for where it went.

"Hee ha-ha-ha! You try to strike the Unseen!" the voice called from the shadows around us again. "Foolish little Guardian man! The Unseen is a mage, can shift away from you before your little pointy can bite! Hee ha-ha-ha!"

Tallinn caught sight of a shape and fired an arrow, the figure vanishing again before the arrow had even reached him. I had seen the glimmer of a sickly magenta energy appear around the top of the creature's staff. Whatever it was, the Unseen was definitely able to command magic.

"They fight with fist, they fight with sword, and they fight with bow! But nothing can harm it, because it is... Unseen," the monster chortled, mocking us.

"Is this how you fight, creature?!" Carden demanded angrily, sword at the ready and slipping a throwing dagger from his belt. "With parlour tricks?!"

"No tricks," the Unseen mewed from the darkness. "No, no, no. Not the Unseen. But you want a fight? The Unseen wants the girl."

"Never!" Carden snarled, gritting his teeth. "I'll never let you touch her, monster!" he threw the dagger, which clattered as the creature disappeared again.

"Then the Unseen will have to take her from the pathetic little Guardian man," the Unseen hissed.

I looked up to the remains of an old balcony above us, my eyes catching the Unseen as it reappeared there. It looked down at us maliciously, its crimson eyes locked on me. Joran saw it too and pushed me behind him with one hand, making me stagger away as the others caught sight of it too.

"Sad little creatures," the Unseen mused. "Won't give the Unseen the Master's prize. Now you will see... the Experiment!"

The Unseen raised its staff into the air, lighting the room with a horrible magenta glow. The room was illuminated, and we came face-to-face with one of the most terrifying sights. I gasped, shaking and clinging tighter again to Joran as I felt the giant suck in a sharp breath of shock. I had to swallow a hard, painful gulp of my own to keep myself from being sick at the grotesque sight before me.

On the back wall there stood a towering behemoth, some thirteen feet tall. It had an elongated neck with a snubbed head that seemed to be made almost entirely of large jaws. Four huge arms were held with chains, two tree trunk-like legs resting on the ground.

The thing's flesh looked as if it had been patched together by an incompetent tailor, some sections darker than others, but all of it a sickly green colour. The creation wasn't only made of flesh and bones, metal parts forged into its body as well, covering about one third of the creature, implanted into its flesh. Pistons and mechanisms were set at joints on the arms and legs, one leg almost entirely mechanical. Cables reached into the monster's flesh, feeding blood through its systems, steam venting from its neck, side and leg periodically. There were even some stone parts attached to it, mostly covering its massive chest like some great armour plate.

"Varedarak!" Joran cursed, stepping backwards with his weapons at the ready.

I gasped, staggering as I gazed up at the creature in fear, managing to recover myself against a table.

The three Dwarves looked uncertain, shaking as they faced the monstrosity before them as Carden and Tallinn stared wide eyed for a moment, then readied their weapons.

"You like the Unseen's work?" the Unseen asked jovially, proud of its creation. "Flesh and bone and blood with metal and stone and magic. Impressive, yes?"

"I'm sure your Master will be very happy," Carden growled, staring at the dormant creature uneasily, edging back towards me.

"Now, the Experiment will kill pesky Guardians and rock rats, and tall one. Then the Unseen will take the girl to the Master," the Unseen chortled as it reached for a lever and pulled it down.

There came the whirring of gears and the buzz of electricity. Blue energy bolts lanced out from powerful dynamos, reaching down the cables to the creature. The energy coursed through the monster's metal and flesh body, awakening it with a roaring groan that shook the entire fortress.

The monster opened its six eyes, all of them a putrid yellow. It released its lipless jaws and bellowed a mournful howl into the air as it stretched its arms and broke its shackles, shattering the wall behind it. It lowered its head down, staring at us, its four massive hands to its sides.

It sniffed with its gigantic nostrils then bellowed a deafening sound again, laying one foot down with a thundering boom that cracked and buckled the stone floor. Steam was venting violently from its mechanical parts now as it started to stalk towards us, a strange collar around its neck glowing with the same magenta sheen as the Unseen's staff.

"Leave the dark-haired girl alive," the Unseen instructed, the creature looking to it. "Kill the others."

The monster threw its head back and bellowed again, thumping its chest with two hands before turning to us viciously.

"Aw crap!" Holger growled.

Tallinn aimed quickly, loosing an arrow from her bow. The arrow hurtled through the air and slammed into the monster's chest. It bounced off the creature's stone parts, splintering and clattering to the floor uselessly.

The creature sniffed at it, then turned its eyes to us and roared, Tallinn firing another two arrows, one after the other. Again, the arrows hit the monster's stone chest, crumpled and fell uselessly.

"How can we fight that thing?!" she cried out, aiming her bow unsteadily.

Joran stared at the beast with his usual composure: "It is a beast of flesh, though one with metal and stone incorporated. It *will* fall."

"I wish I had your enthusiasm, Joran," Tallinn admitted nervously, stumbling back as she kept her bow aimed at the creature.

Carden grabbed me and pushed me behind him. I couldn't see how such a creature could even have been created, let alone how to defeat it.

I felt something rush by me, looking down to see Amethyst running for cover. I didn't blame the little dragonling as she hid in a crevice in one of the walls. How badly I wished I could hide like she was right now.

One of the Dwarven warriors panicked suddenly, turned and ran for the nearest doorway. Before anyone could do anything, the monster had slammed its hand down, pinning him to the ground. He screamed frantically as the monster lifted him up and crushed him, his cries gurgling out to a strangled end.

I cried out in terror, grabbing Carden's left arm with both hands and looking away, Carden's own fear tensing his muscles near to petrifying.

We all staggered backwards, staring up at the beast as it sniffed the dead Dwarf in its hand. Nostrils flaring, the monster turned its great yellow eyes towards the remaining six of us. It roared again, narrowing its eyes as it cast the mangled corpse of the Dwarf away.

"RUN!" Tallinn screamed.

Carden pushed me away, the two of us ducking for cover as the monster swung one broken chain from its restraints. The massive chain missed us by only a few inches as we hit the floor, the two of us crawling to our feet and running in the opposite direction. Carden pulled me into the cover of a large pillar, holding me close, my breathing as heavy as his.

I looked around the pillar as Tallinn managed to avoid two of the creature's grasping hands, climbing her way up one of the damaged walls to get some height on it. She held her bow ready, rushing over the broken stone pieces as quickly as she could, desperately trying to get a clear shot.

The monster's eyes were on her as she turned to meet its terrifying yellow sextuple gaze. The young ranger trembled as she pressed her back into the wall, trying to make herself as flat as possible on the narrow ledge on which she stood. The monster rose up straighter, snarling as it chomped its unspeakably huge metal jaws with hungry anticipation.

Tallinn struggled to keep her cool, breathing heavily and frantically shuffling along the wall as she reached for an arrow, the monster's hands breaking stone as it grasped for her.

"Tallinn!" I cried out in terror; sure I was about to watch her die.

"No!" Carden screamed, about to run forward, my hands automatically grabbing his arm to stop him.

Tallinn staggered as the monster broke the stone above her, raining it down at her. She screamed in terror, dropping to her knees and nearly sliding into the mammoth metal jaws waiting below her. She recovered, pulling away and saving her right arm just before the jaws slammed shut with a resounding boom.

"Var Lerran Go Var!" a deep voice bellowed suddenly.

Joran rushed the monster with his twin swords, sweeping the unusual blades and cleaving the lowest of the beast's right hands from its arm. Sparks showered from the mechanical inner workings of the arm, the beast howling frantically as it turned from Tallinn.

The monster reeled in pain, swinging the chain on its upper left arm and shattered the floor. Holger and the Dwarven warrior managed to dive out of harm's way just in time, both of them hitting the floor as stone splintered and was thrown into the air. They both scrambled away as the monster turned on Joran, stomping its mechanical left leg down where the Dwarves had lain only a few moments earlier.

Again the Storvari let loose with his war cry: "Var Lerran Go Var!"

He struck out, his swords severing several blood tubes, spraying the near blackened red liquid over the floor. The monster thundered out a terrifying howl and swung its one remaining right hand, throwing Joran from his feet.

The Storvari slammed into the stone wall, tumbling to the ground with a cracking thud, the stones breaking beneath his weight. He slowly pushed himself up as the ground shook, the monster stalking towards him hungrily. His violet eyes locked on the beast's shape and he snarled, grabbing his swords from the floor and readying himself.

I watched on, horrified but somehow studiously too. My eyes searched over the monster's shape, seeking out some way to disable it. Then, I saw them. The vents on its hip and leg were opening and shutting periodically, venting superheated steam into the cold air.

"Tallinn!" I called up to where she was still clinging to the wall. "Its eyes! Go for its eyes!"

Tallinn nodded and aimed an arrow as I turned from Carden and rushed over to one of the walls nearer Joran. Carden followed me, frantically trying to keep up.

"What are you doing?" he demanded.

"Trying to beat this thing," I told him, finding my courage. "I think I've worked it out."

"How?"

"The vents on its body are letting out steam, obviously as a mechanical by-product to its power supply," all my reading came in handy now. "If we can damage the two major vents it won't be able to vent the excess energy from its body and it will be disabled. Then we hit the power source."

"Which is?"

I looked up to the monster, noting the circular metal plating sitting up over the left side of its shielded chest. I could see blue energy bolts flickering behind the casing over some darkened shape beneath. That had to be the horrid thing's heart.

I allowed myself a small smile then looked to Carden: "We go for the heart," I pointed to the chest.

He looked up, following my gaze until he saw it. He studied the structure for a moment as Joran began diving out of the beast's way, then smirked at me and nodded.

"Get Holger," I instructed him. "Go for the left leg. I need that thing down."

"What are you going to do?" he asked worriedly.

"I've got the heart," I replied with quiet determination, then turned and started carefully running towards the door we had entered through, ducking into cover as I went.

Carden ran to Holger, narrowly avoiding one of the monster's flailing left arms. I saw him grab the two Dwarves by the shoulders and quickly explain my plan.

I glanced to the balcony above. Watching on as we fought the monster, the Unseen was looking a little uncertain, getting impatient at the monster's inability to kill my friends. I was actually a little happy to irritate that disgusting creature.

"Forget the tall one!" the Unseen hissed, the monster having grabbed Joran in its remaining right hand, turning its eyes to look at him. "Get the Princess!"

The monster roared and threw Joran aside, the Storvari slamming into a pillar, shattering it with the force of his large body. He rolled across the stone floor and lay still.

Now the monster's eyes were on me, its heavy footsteps breaking stone as it stormed forward. I looked up, only a few meters from the doorway as I saw it coming, trembling as I faced its mammoth size. It slowed, reaching out one hand, determined to grasp me. I backed up against the wall helplessly as it roared victoriously.

Tallinn loosed an arrow, immediately preparing another as the first flew through the air. The arrow went straight through the monster's middle left eye, splattering it in a mess of yellow and crimson. The monster reeled back in agony, flailing its arms, unable to block the next shot as Tallinn fired again. This arrow went through the monster's forward most right eye, destroying it and lodging there in its bleeding remains.

Angry and blinded in two of its six eyes, the monster struck out, Tallinn managing to fire one more arrow that struck it just below its farthest back left eye. It roared and slammed its fists into the wall, shattering it. The wall crumbled, collapsing to the floor and spilling Tallinn into the air. She hit the ground hard, shielding her head as stone pieces rained down over her, breaking into dust and powder on the floor around her. She lay still, not moving as the monster stomped towards her.

"Now!" Carden roared.

He rushed forward, flanked by the two Dwarves, all of them running for the monster's legs. Carden dived between its legs and drew its gaze from Tallinn as Holger ran for its left leg.

The monster slammed its fist into the stone floor, trying to hit Carden, failing as he moved quickly to avoid each strike. He managed to pin its upper left hand as it reached for him, stabbing his sword downwards and through the monster's palm, spilling more blood and sparks.

Holger took his opportunity and rushed forward, swinging his hammer violently. The hammer crushed through the vent in the monster's leg, blocking it with its own debris. He dived away as the other Dwarf slammed his axe into the cables holding the leg together.

The monster snapped and roared, reaching with its right arm for him. The Dwarf ran, slamming to the ground as Carden rushed forward, shouting up at the monster to gain its attention. It swung its arm, hurling the chain after Carden as he ran around a large, sturdy pillar. The chain wrapped around the pillar, tangling there as Carden swiftly took a knife from his belt and plunged it through the links firmly to secure it.

The monster tugged at its chain angrily, its pulling becoming more and more frantic as its body continued venting steam. Then there was a terrifying boom as the building pressure became too much. The metal leg erupted, throwing shrapnel everywhere, burning flesh slapping to the ground as the monster howled unbearably.

I scarcely avoided a piece of metal that buried into the wall behind me, falling to my knees.

The monster collapsed down onto the remains of its shattered knee, blood spilling from all the ruined conduits, sparks showering from its metal skeleton and wires. It pulled its left hand free, Carden's sword clattering to the floor as it reeled its head back once again. It threw its two left hands out, casting chunks of stone at the two Dwarves.

They both barely got out of the way, the ground shattering beneath them and throwing them into the air. They hit the floor hard and laid there stunned.

Now the monster turned its remaining eyes on Carden as he ran for his sword. He reached out, grasping the blade as heavy fingers crushed down on his legs, making him scream in pain. He turned over as the monster lifted him and hurled him to the ground hard.

Winded from the force of his impact with the floor, Carden managed to stab one of its hands again, the same one as before, this time tearing at it with his blade. The monster screeched and dropped him, his sword pulling out of his hands and clattering to the floor. The monster grabbed him with the other hand before he could move and pinned him. It lowered its head, staring him in the face viciously. It roared as it began squeezing, Carden gasping and struggling.

I had been moving carefully to the door during all of this to reach the dual swords the dead Dwarf had dropped. I had them in my hands and was standing with one knee to the floor, my eyes on the scene before me.

Panic filled me and I screamed: "CARDEN! NO!"

I was up, running towards Carden, the world seeming to slow down around me. I ran forward, swinging both blades expertly as I tried not to trip on my long dress, my swordsman training taking over. All that mattered to me was Carden's safety, nothing else. I *had* to save him.

I sliced the monster's thumb with one blade as I spun around backwards, stabbing the other into its wrist with an outstretched lunge. It howled and reeled as I tore its flesh with the dual blades, its monstrous fingers dropping Carden to the floor like a ragdoll, leaving him gasping for air where he lay.

As it reeled, I took my chance, running forward, slamming my right foot into a groove in the monster's knee and leaping up. I plunged the first blade straight through the opening in the heart's casing, pressing down with all my weight from the jump.

The monster lurched again, shattering the stone pillar its arm had been chained to and reducing it to powder. The force nearly threw me off its chest, my fingers tightening on the sword hilts to keep me holding on. With all my strength, I forced the other blade up, jamming it straight through the other side of the casing opposite the first sword.

I felt the blades breaking inside the monster's heart as they shredded through muscle, sinew and tissue. My hands stung with electricity as my last ounce of strength charged through my arms and I pushed the blades harder, securing them in the casing.

As the monster howled frantically and blue lightning struck from its shattering power source, I let go and fell. I hit the ground backwards, grunting hard as the monster staggered on its one good leg. It howled with electricity coursing over the two swords in its chest, reaching for me again. I knew that I hadn't done enough damage to kill the creature. Pressing myself down against the floor, I waited for the monster to seize me in its massive hand, closing my eyes and turning from it.

There came a loud roar and Joran was suddenly in front of me as I opened my eyes, swinging his swords hard. He leaped up to almost be at eye level with the monster in mid-air, his powerful arms slamming his weapons into the blades that I had pierced through the beast's heart. They smashed into the hilts loudly, ploughing the smaller swords almost completely into the creature's chest with an explosive eruption of blood and electricity.

Joran hit the floor as the monster screeched and howled, clutching at its chest.

I threw myself to where Carden lay, covering my face under my cloak as he pulled me into his arms. We shielded ourselves as the monster screamed its last.

Fire erupted from its chest, all the vents in its body belching flame and electricity. The collar on its neck turned a fiery orange and exploded. Its arms went limp and it tumbled backwards, hitting the floor with a resounding boom...

Chapter Seventeen
The Lorgath Pass

Sparks rained down through the smoke that poured from the monster's destroyed shape, the air choked with the smell of burnt metal and flesh. Tallinn recovered, covered in dust, Holger and the other Dwarf staring up in surprise at what they saw before them. Joran stood slowly, swords at the ready while Carden and I peeked up from under our cloaks, still in each other's arms. I glanced to my right as Amethyst came out of hiding from the crevice, then to the scene before me. I couldn't believe we had survived.

I looked back from the smoking flesh wreckage, my gaze falling on Carden's face. Our eyes met – green to blue – our breathing slow, though a little laboured after our ordeal. His hands were softly resting around mine, gently holding my wrists and spreading their warmth onto my slightly cooler flesh.

I felt my heart skip a beat as I stared into those living jades, my breathing staggering as though it were a person tripping on the rubble around us. I had only one thought in my mind as I stared into his eyes, feeling so relieved.

He's safe...

"Are you alright?" I asked him softly.

Slowly, wiping dust from my cheek with one thumb, he answered: "Thanks to you."

We smiled at each other, feeling the warm embrace we shared, the moment tense, but in a good way. It was a moment that I would have lived in, would have revelled in longer if I could have and would never forget. But it ended too soon and too coldly.

A horrifying scream echoed from above us, chilling the air and shaking us to our very cores. We looked up, staring into the darkness.

The Unseen was trembling with rage, shaking its staff in its hands as though it were about to attack us ferociously. It howled in some inaudible language from beneath its hood and mask, screeching like some rabid beast, its talons suddenly very prominent.

"*Stupid* girl! You ruined *all* the Unseen's nice work! Stupid, pretty girl!" it shook its head angrily. "The Master will be very mad! Oh yes!" It jabbed a finger at me accusingly: "We will be coming for you soon, pretty girl! Yes! Very, very soon! The Master will have you! He will!"

Carden got to his feet, reclaiming his sword and pushing me behind him as Tallinn joined us, aiming her bow right at the Unseen's face.

"You won't be able to touch her!" Carden swore venomously. "Not after we've slain you!"

The Unseen laughed: "Not slay it, not the Unseen, no! Foolish little children playing with toys!"

It held up its staff, the top of it glowing as it laughed maniacally. Screeching came from a corridor behind Carden, Tallinn and I, all of us turning to see shambling shadows coming from the doorway.

The Unseen chortled: "You play with the others now. The Unseen goes to the Master," then right before our eyes, it became a black cloud bank of shadowy mist and disappeared.

I faced the corridor with the others, fear gripping me again. "What do we do now?" I asked in a trembling voice.

"We run!" was Carden's answer.

"This way!" shouted Holger, pointing to a clear passage.

I ran as fast as I could, scooping up Amethyst as I went, following the others quickly.

The sounds of the monsters howling and our feet thundering echoed behind us as we ran, the beasts gaining on us. I looked over my shoulder to see strange four foot five tall creatures chasing us, some on all fours some on two legs. They were pale green with large eyes that resembled a cat's, with big pointed ears and skinny limbs, their bodies covered by rags that served as clothing. They carried rusted and discarded weapons that were as dangerous in their savage hands as their pointed yellow teeth.

"Goblins!" Tallinn shouted. "Keep running!"

We ran down another set of corridors, finally reaching a long bridge that stretched out across a great chasm before the fortress. I refused to look over the edge, too afraid to see down into the depths. I just ran behind the others, determined to get to safety.

"There!" Holger yelled, pointing to a large open pair of doors ahead of us. "That's the way!"

We ran faster, Joran following at the rear, cutting down any of the beasts that came up behind us. Tallinn loosed arrow after arrow into the goblin hordes, throwing them back and stunning others.

We sprinted for the doors, the path no longer feeling certain as the goblins gained on us. I was sure that we were about to be overwhelmed, hugging Amethyst tight as she screamed in my arms.

Suddenly, there came the whistling of arrows and crossbow bolts, but not from behind us like I had thought. From in front of us at the doors where a blue glow had appeared came a volley that knocked back the goblins. Fawkner led the way into the opening, flanked by four Dwarves with crossbows. They were firing into the oncoming goblins, dropping the closest ones and saving us as Aldwyn used his magic to give us light. Mithras and Dolin stood ready at the doors, sword and axe drawn as the remaining Dwarves prepared themselves for what was to come.

Tallinn reached them first, turning to join her arrows to the volley being cast into the throng, covering our retreat. Mithras rushed past her, grabbing me as he went, then turned around to guide me through the gap as Carden backed in behind us, sword at the ready. We fell back as Holger, the Dwarven warrior and Joran joined us, Tallinn and Fawkner becoming the last as they fired again and again to discourage the goblins.

They fell back at the last moment, the Dwarves sealing the doors behind them and cutting us off from the screaming goblins now trapped on the other side.

We took a moment to catch our breath.

"Are you alright, Leander?" Mithras asked me worriedly.

I nodded, then said sarcastically: "Oh, please tell me we get to do that again! Giant monsters, daemon mages and goblin armies, I can't wait!"

"Well, I see your sense of humour is unchanged," commented Aldwyn wryly, smiling at me.

I smiled, unable to laugh as I was out of breath, though I was grateful that we had escaped and rejoined our friends safely.

"Come," Mithras directed calmly. "Let us leave this place and make for the pass."

* * * * *

The way from the bastion's entrance was slow, but far less arduous than before. It seemed that there was no longer any threat behind us as we travelled the winding cavernous halls of the Under Roads, but I couldn't be sure of that.

About four hours out from the pass we came to the doors of a second Dwarven bastion, the Dwarf commander ordering us to halt. He called up to the guards inside the bastion and they immediately opened the doors, the Dwarves leading us into the great halls beyond.

Within minutes the garrison commander was summoned, and we were whisked away to the central chamber where we were asked to give full accounts of what we had encountered. We explained about the Unseen and its creature, describing how we had killed it. By the end of our recount, the garrison commander and his captains had decided that they would investigate the bastion in question. They explained that it was one that had been long forgotten, and that they would now deal with the goblins squatting in its boundaries. They would also investigate the Unseen's laboratory and examine the remains of the creature should the need arise to fight more, a sentiment that I didn't want to contemplate.

Aldwyn advised the swiftly rallying Dwarves that we still had our own journey to undertake and expressed a need to leave for the Lorgath Pass. A small contingent of Dwarves was sent with our Citadel bound group, their thanks to us a strong sentiment that followed with extra supplies.

The Dwarves led the nine of us through the Under Roads over the last four hours of the journey, ready to fight at the first sign of the goblins or anything else. Luckily, for all that time we walked without incident, the tunnels echoing only with our own footsteps.

At last, we came to an upward sloping stairway towards another great stone door high up in the mountainside. The air was chilled here from the ice atop the Nartarn'lath Mountains, the frozen winds pressing against the stone doors and slipping through cracks to reach the tunnels below. I looked up at it in anticipation, desperately wanting to get out of those stale aired tunnels.

"This is it," the Dwarven commander indicated, stopping with his men at the foot of the stairs.

"It's very cold," I observed, pulling my cloak further around me and shuddering.

"It *is* snowing up there," Fawkner pointed out, stroking his falcon's neck as she rested on his arm.

"The Lorgath Pass lies beyond these doors?" Mithras enquired.

The Dwarven commander nodded. "Yes. The way through the mountains lies beyond these doors. But be warned; it is a treacherous road to follow."

"We are aware of the path ahead," Aldwyn stated, then turned to the Dwarves. "Our thanks, Dwarf-kin."

"Our thanks are owed to you, Guardians," the commander replied, then bowed to me. "Princess."

"On to the Citadel then?" Tallinn looked to Aldwyn.

He nodded. "To the Citadel," then he said to the Dwarven warriors. "Again, you have our thanks for safe conduct through the Under Roads. Farewell."

The Dwarves bowed their heads and thumped their right fists to their chests. They turned and marched away, returning towards the garrison behind us.

"Shall we then?" Mithras asked us, turning and making his way up the slopping stairway.

I followed with Carden, the way seeming hard due to the stairs' steep angle, but we managed to climb towards the summit. Joran took the lead, pressing his massive hands to the iron doors and forcing them to open, his enormous muscles tensing in his arms. He pushed with half of his might, the old doors that seemed almost never to be used opening slowly with a long, creaking groan.

I felt the cold air hit my face almost immediately, the blinding white of snow filling my vision. The smell of fresh air was surely welcome after a week beneath the mountains. I breathed it in deep.

With Aldwyn leading the way and Mithras close behind him, we started our way out of the Under Roads and onto the white drenched mountain top. The stone ground beneath our feet felt strangely smooth and was lightly dusted with snow powder that soon became deep snow banks.

After a few minutes, I instinctively drew my hood and pulled my cloak around me tightly. The chill began to overwhelm me now as we left the Dwarven Doorway in the side of the mountain and made our way forward towards the Lorgath Pass.

Within an hour we were in sight of it, the pass a long, winding road through the mountains from the north-eastern parts of Aldegaad to the south-eastern reaches of Ivansten. It seemed to be a narrow path through the snowy rocks and crags of the mountains' summits, but this wasn't the highest point by far. To the east we could see the ever-heightening peaks of the Nartarn'lath Mountains climbing into the cloudy grey sky, snow-capped and reaching to the heavens like great white fingers.

Aldwyn led the way, setting foot on the path first, looking out from under his cloak's hood for any sign of trouble. His dark eyes surveyed the way, then he gestured with his free hand for the rest of us to follow, grasping his staff in the other.

Following beside Carden with Joran and Tallinn behind me, I trudged down the slopes to the path, my legs freezing even through my leggings and boots. I trembled uncontrollably, my arms wrapped around my torso and holding my cloak tightly. I turned my eyes back to Joran, locking my sights on my backpack he carried on his shoulder.

Amethyst stuck her small head out, her molten orange eyes surveying the mountains surrounding us. Like the rest of us she had fog vapours appearing before her long snout, but her breath was hotter, causing a rush of heated mist to escape. She snuggled back into the bag, shielding herself from the cold, an act I truly envied.

Carden noted my discomfort, frowning at me as he watched me stumble across the heavily frosted rocky ground. I was studying him fleetingly as we walked, trying to decide whether to cuddle up to him for warmth or not. Snow was falling all around us now and the wind was really beginning to pick up.

"Are you alright, Leander?" Carden drew my gaze as he spoke, his green eyes gentle under his hood.

"It's so cold," I shivered uncontrollably.

He nodded understandingly: "It is."

"How far are we travelling through the pass?" I asked him, peeking out from beneath my hood.

"I'm not sure," he looked ahead of us, calling out to the head of our group over the winds: "Aldwyn!"

Aldwyn turned, wrapped heavily under his cloak and hood. "Yes, Carden?!"

"How far are we travelling through the pass?!" the young man asked loudly, fighting the winds as I staggered in the snow beside him.

"We're heading to the midpoint between Aldegaad and Ivansten!"Aldwyn answered over the winds' howls. "From there we'll take the eastern path through the mountains to the Citadel!"

"How long will that take?!" I shouted against the wind, my hair starting to catch with the currents and brushing over my face.

"Two days by this path!" Aldwyn returned. "We can make it!"

"I hope for all our sakes we do!" Fawkner called, coming up beside Carden and I. "It feels as though a storm is brewing!"

"That's one of the reasons why we decided to take the Lorgath Pass!" Tallinn shouted from the back of the group, the two Dwarves staggering behind her. "It isn't an easy path for anyone to track us through!"

"It will not be an easy path for us to tread if this storm worsens!" Fawkner called back to her.

"The Nartarn'lath Mountains are notorious for foul weather!" Mithras spoke up, calling out so the entire group could hear him. "That is why so few travellers come this way!"

"Then maybe we should seek a better road?!" suggested Dolin, shivering under his cloak, snowflakes powdering his beard. "Perhaps one at a lower altitude?!"

"What?! Scared are ya, brother?!" Holger demanded brashly.

"No!" came Dolin's answer. "I'm practical! This is not a safe path to take!"

"The Lorgath Pass is also one of the most dangerous mountain roads, isn't it?!" Carden asked, grasping me around the shoulders as I staggered and nearly fell.

"Again, this is why we are taking it!" Aldwyn reasoned, ploughing ahead with his staff. "It is also the fastest route to the Citadel! Have faith!"

"Faith will not guard us against such a bitter storm!" Fawkner retorted direly.

We continued on through the ever-growing blizzard as it picked up. It seemed that there was no sign that the storm would dissipate, only deepen and worsen.

I stumbled again; my feet chilled as I struggled through the ever deepening snow. I slipped and fell, hitting the ground hard, my hands hurting from the cold as much as from the impact.

Fawkner reached down and took me by my right arm, helping me to my feet. I looked to him gratefully, the man pulling me close and trying to keep me warm with him under his furred cloak as Carden walked up beside us.

Glancing over my shoulder, I saw that Tallinn and the Dwarves were now struggling too, only Joran managing to overcome the extensive snow banks with his large legs. His sheer size seemed to be of great advantage to him in this harsh white environment.

We were all suffering now as we were overwhelmed by the cold and the blinding snow. The blizzard was defeating us, hindering our progress.

"I can't!" I cried out weakly, my entire body aching as my legs faltered. "Please! I can't!"

"Are you alright?!" Fawkner crouched beside me as I slumped to kneel in the snow.

"My legs hurt too much!" I responded with a shake of my head as Carden joined us. "I'm s-s-so... so cold!"

"As am I!" Carden agreed.

"As are we all!" Tallinn spoke up, standing just behind us, struggling to stay upright. "And this snow is blinding! We cannot hope to pass through this path!"

"We *must* keep moving!" shouted Aldwyn, some way ahead and still going.

"We cannot!" Fawkner shouted back. "Can you not see that the girl can't walk?! None of us can continue along this blighted road!"

"He's right!" Mithras agreed, looking to Aldwyn, his blue cloak furling wildly in the wind. "The way is unsafe! We may as well have taken the main roads!"

"You were as willing to take this road as I, Mithras!" Aldwyn reminded him, stopping and turning. "We cannot risk the main roads! Not now that we know of these conspirators seeking the Princess' capture!"

"We cannot pass into Ivansten, either!" Mithras advised him sternly. "Leander will be seen as a target the moment she sets foot on Ivanstenian soil! They will close in on her so swiftly that she will be unable to escape King Dunmore's wrath!"

Aldwyn shouted over the winds: "We continue on this path!"

"Only if you want to kill her!" Mithras snapped angrily, glaring and rounding on him. "If that is the case then you should have never rescued her from Averet!"

"ENOUGH!" I screamed over their argument, sick of the infighting.

The Knight and the Mage turned their attention to me, stunned by my sudden forcefulness. They both regarded me from beneath their cowls, trembling against the cold themselves.

"This isn't helping any of us!" I told them, shaking in Fawkner's arms. "You two have got to stop fighting! It will just endanger us all further! Don't you see?!"

The two men looked to one another, nodding shamefully. I think they sometimes forgot that I wasn't just a child in their care.

"My apologies, your Highness," Aldwyn said to me gently.

"You are most certainly right, Leander," Mithras acknowledged me. "We must stop this if we hope to survive."

"Exactly," I agreed, shivering hard. "Now, we obviously can't continue on this path."

"We need a safer course," Carden agreed.

"If we make for the Forests of Galvenin we could still reach the Citadel within three days," Tallinn suggested.

"No way!" Holger snapped grumpily, his dark hair billowing around his face like wildfire. "That's Elf territory! There's no way we're going there!"

"We may have no other choice," Tallinn pointed out gravely. "The pass has overwhelmed us. We must make for the forests and head north to the Citadel from there."

"It's just that we Dwarves aren't welcomed fondly by the Elf-kin," Dolin reasoned, agreeing with his brother grimly. "They have very little tolerance for us."

"As it is, we seem to have no choice," Mithras said, his dark eyes focused on a point ahead of us.

I watched Aldwyn as he thought cautiously about our situation, then turned my attention across to the rest of our group.

Tallinn was struggling to stand up to the cold, trembling beneath her cloak. Carden crouched nearer me, his face hidden by his hood from the blizzard, his left hand grasping my arm firmly. Fawkner held onto me tightly, keeping his cloak around me to add extra warmth to my body. I was so grateful to both men for their care and attention.

The Dwarves were forcing themselves to remain standing, using their weapons to rest against. They looked as if they could barely stand up to the frigid winds gusting and billowing across the mountains. Their near four-foot forms were so small in the blinding white snow that they were little more than dark blurs in the blizzard.

Joran was the only one capable of standing against the snowy onslaught, his tough skin and mammoth size seeming to offer him better resistance. He just stood with his arms crossed, violet eyes intensely studying the rest of us, his black hair billowing over his shoulders.

Mithras then turned his attention to Fawkner, his dark blue eyes intense as he tried to force his gaze through the thickening blizzard.

"What of the path ahead, Fawkner? Can your falcon see the way?" the Knight asked.

Fawkner gazed into space, his eyes seeming detached from the world. After a few short moments, he blinked several times then turned his sights to the Knight.

"There has been an avalanche up ahead," he explained, almost as though he had expected this. "The path through the mountains is blocked. We cannot make it along this road."

I turned to Mithras, "What do we do now?"

Mithras looked to Aldwyn and received a reluctant nod. He turned back to me, sighing as he squinted against the snow blowing across his face and hood.

"We take the path through the Forests of Galvenin," he responded.

With a nod of agreement from me, we began making our way down the Lorgath Pass towards the south-east. I huddled under my cloak with Carden wrapping his own around us both. I smiled gratefully at him and we continued on our way down the mountainside, back into Aldegaad's highlands.

Chapter Eighteen
The Forests of Galvenin

The trek down the mountain pass was slow and a little painful, the storm coursing through the peaks showing no signs of abating. It took some four or five hours to journey down the slopes of the Nartarn'lath Mountains to the right point necessary to continue on.

Aldwyn directed us off the road's lightly powdered surface, then through the bushland and trees dotting the mountainside. From there we continued south-east for a short time before turning directly east.

The forests themselves came very close to the Guardian Citadel and the Aldegaadian-Lorveren Border.

The thought of being so close to Lorveren bothered no one in the group, only Fawkner having made mention of it once after sending his falcon up to scout the area ahead. Despite his comments, however, the ex-mercenary – turned Guardian recruit – had nothing ill to speak of.

"I yearn to see Lake Lorver again," he was saying longingly to Carden and I as we journeyed through the uneven terrain. "To stand on her emerald shores and enter the Jade City. To be amongst my kinsmen once more would be a great honour."

"You haven't been back in sometime, then?" I guessed, looking up at him from under my hood, the cold mountain air still chilling my skin.

Fawkner nodded sadly. "It has been some time since I've returned home to my city of Eilath, yet I one day hope to set foot on Lorveren's verdant lands once again and breathe her clear air."

He seemed deeply reminiscent, as if the very thoughts that now shone in his eyes reached into a past long ago. I grew more and more curious about this man whom I had slowly come to call a friend.

"It is not such a bad thing to stand so close to the border between Aldegaad and Lorveren," he went on gently. "There is a strange sense of euphoria to such thoughts."

"I wouldn't know," I murmured, looking at the forest ahead of me.

Fawkner turned to me grimly, realising what thoughts must surely be entering my mind.

"My apologies," he said gently. "I had almost forgotten the events that led us here."

"I never can," I replied softly and sadly, trying to fight back tears once again.

We climbed a new path in silence, obediently following Aldwyn as he referred to the map he carried in his pack. It wasn't a long climb up the slopes of the mountain, but it was an unwelcome one until we breached the tree line and beheld the world before us.

To our left stood the mountains themselves; a foreboding and impenetrable stone wall reaching high into the icy winds and blackening clouds. To our right lay the Great River Arvon snaking through the grasslands below with the expanse of Aldegaad stretching out to the far south. The shapes of the Calian Mountains curving down the eastern reach of Aldegaad and bordering Lorveren were clear ahead of us, though they were a hazy purple compared to the much closer Nartarn'lath Mountains.

I stared at the immensity of it all and felt both wonder and hopelessness. I had never seen a view more spectacular – though I was sure there was one – the vastness of Aldegaad suddenly dropping me into a deep uncertainty.

How can we ever hope to reach the Citadel with so much space before us? It just seems to go on forever.

I turned my eyes south and gazed out across the landscape, catching sight of a glimmering shape on the far horizon near the dark blue haze of the Crestian Sea in the distance. It was the Aldegaadian capital city, Aneuran, the home of the Sovereign Palace and the King.

I wish I could go to Aneuran, to run into my uncle's arms and find safety with him. This past month has been terrible and all I want is to be wrapped in a bed warm and safe behind castle walls with family once more.

"The Forests of Galvenin," Aldwyn's voice brought me back to reality as he surveyed the sight before us. "Our safest route to the Citadel now with the Lorgath Pass blocked."

"Perhaps this is a better option," noted Tallinn as she came up to stand beside him, her hazel eyes roving the forests below. "The Pass is not known for its safety, as we all saw."

"It seems that your journey through the Under Roads was almost a waste," Dolin observed, standing with both hands on his axe as he leaned on it. "Almost."

"Well, they got some great warriors with us, brother," Holger bragged brashly, winking at Tallinn.

Tallinn regarded him with a cold glance, then turned her eyes back to the forests.

"Do you expect trouble from the Elves?" she asked Aldwyn quietly.

I silently listened from where I stood with Carden and Joran. I was wondering the same thing and was just happy not to have to ask the question myself.

"If we move quietly there should not be anything to concern us," replied the Mage evenly.

"We should find a place to make camp," suggested Mithras, standing a few feet away, searching with his eyes for a clearing in the trees, "somewhere flat and dry."

"Within the forests themselves would be the safest option," Aldwyn said, looking to him. "There is plenty of shelter beneath the canopy."

"And far less clear sight should we come under attack," Fawkner advised grimly. "Both a benefit and a hindrance."

"We will not," Mithras told him sternly. "Not here. The Wood Elves are no enemy of ours. They will *not* strike against us."

"It is better to suspect every shadow to be a foe than to hope it to be an ally," Joran spoke evenly, this one sentence his only contribution to the conversation.

I thought it was one of the most foreboding things I had ever heard from him, and it worried me.

"We cannot always believe such things," Tallinn said, then turned to Aldwyn. "To the forests then? Before night?"

"Before night," Aldwyn agreed and started forward down the hillside.

We followed cautiously, Carden, Fawkner and Joran flanking me guardedly. While I resented the extremely protective treatment I was receiving, I also found a sense of security in it. After the events of the past few weeks I was now craving security.

We entered the forests' outer limits without incident, the trees' canopies so thick that the light began to fade much faster. The darkness of the forests crept in and engulfed us, choking all the light from our eyes.

There came a sudden eerie blue light to my sight that blinded me for a few moments. Then I saw the crystal in the top of Aldwyn's staff glowing bright blue, lighting the way as it had in the Under Roads. It was a welcome glow to me, though it made everything about the forest's boughs that much creepier.

After what felt like hours, Mithras called us to stop. We stood in a large opening amidst the trees, the canopy of the forest reaching above us still and blocking the sky from our eyes. I gazed up at the trees, stunned by the immensity of the leaves and tree limbs reaching out above us.

We may as well still be underground considering how dark it is here, I thought.

"We'll make camp here for the night and set out again at daybreak," Mithras said, setting his pack down.

"Can you even tell the difference between day and night here?" I asked, putting my own pack down and opening the flap to let Amethyst out. "I mean, it's just so dark in these forests."

"An unfortunate side effect of the forests' thickness," Aldwyn explained. "However, daylight is quite different to night here as it is anywhere else on the surface of the world. You would have the same affects in the mountains."

"It feels no different to the Lorgath Pass," Fawkner commented as he settled onto the ground. "It's still cold and snow powders the ground and the air."

"We're still in the mountains," Carden pointed out, arms crossed where he stood.

"It's also entering the winter months in Aldegaad," I added as I helped Amethyst from the backpack. "It snows in the northern parts, especially as you get closer to the mountains."

"It certainly snows in Arvon," Mithras said with a sense of loss, looking to me.

I returned his stare glumly.

"Let us make camp," Mithras pulled out of his own grief and pushed on for the sake of the group. "We're going to need food and rest before our journey through the forests continues tomorrow."

The others set about making camp, Carden working with Tallinn to erect the tents they carried in their packs while Fawkner started a fire. Joran watched the perimeter as he had become accustomed to, his Storvari endurance allowing him to go with far less sleep than the rest of us. Meanwhile, the two Dwarves searched for firewood, Mithras and Aldwyn organising the food stores.

Again I felt like the useless member, sitting beneath my newly erected tent's roof and cradling Amethyst as I watched the others work.

Within a half an hour the camp was set and the others were settling in for the night as the fire burned brightly at the centre of everything. Carden and Fawkner were working on cooking up some of the meat we had brought with us from Hecturn into a hearty stew. They were deeply focused on it, their attention shifting to nothing else.

I moved to join them, wrapping myself in a heavy fur blanket to keep warm as I sat on one of the mats surrounding the fire. The warmth from the flames was so inviting, a feeling that brought me a greater measure of comfort on this icy cold night. The flames' light even helped to alleviate my fears of the forests' dark depths around us.

My eyes drifted then to Aldwyn, Tallinn and Mithras crouching together around the large map Aldwyn had been carrying. They were speaking in a hushed manner as they discussed some inaudible topic that made me more and more curious. I could see the unease on Mithras' face and worried what my mentor and old friend was thinking.

Dolin was watching me from where he and Holger sat nearby, both resting on fur mats near the fire as well. Dolin was smoking a clay pipe, which seemed to extend from beneath his thick black beard as though he had no mouth, his right hand grasping it gently as he puffed out grey rings from his lips. Holger was sharpening some daggers he was carrying with a small whetstone, his attitude very suspicious suddenly. It was as though the forests had scared him.

At last, Dolin took the pipe form his mouth and leaned forward. "Is something wrong there, lassie?" he asked, gaining my attention fully.

I looked to him: "Hm? What?"

"I said: Is something wrong there, lassie?" Dolin repeated his question gently. "You seem distracted."

I blinked, stunned that he was even paying attention to me. I felt Amethyst pawing at my arm, cooing gently before cuddling in under the blanket with me. I subconsciously began to stroke her back as she settled into my lap.

"I'm just a little worried," I admitted, snuggling into my blanket and cloak.

"About what, Princess?" Dolin placed his pipe between his lips again.

I shrugged. "The path ahead of us, these forests, everything."

"You have a right to be scared, girly," Holger spoke up gruffly, turning his dark eyes and scarred face to me from beneath his long black mane. "These are dark forests ruled by foul peoples."

"Now, Holger, don't be scaring the girl," Dolin warned his brother, glancing to him.

"She should be scared," Holger waved him away, then looked to me again. "The peoples of these parts don't like strangers invading *their* forests."

"But Mithras said..." I went to say.

"He wasn't telling you the truth, lass," Holger interrupted me swiftly, speaking direly. "The Elves aren't as friendly as he told you, not the ones of Galvenin. They'd sooner cut you up and cast your entrails to the forest floor to let it eat you than be friendly and welcoming."

"Holger, that's enough!" Dolin growled.

"They aren't all sweet like those city Elves you've likely seen," Holger went on. "They don't act *civilized* as we Dwarves and humans do. Even that great behemoth there is more civilized," he indicated Joran.

"You fool yourself, Dwarf," Fawkner spoke, looking up from the fire. "The Elves are no danger, not if we respect them and their culture."

"You're the one who's fooled," Holger retorted then looked to me again, watching my fear grow. "They lurk in the shadows of the forests and wait for travellers, then stalk them for miles. And just when you think you're out of their territory..."

He clapped his hands together, causing me to jump in shock.

"They pounce," he finished, smirking. "They're probably watching us even as we speak."

I was uneasy enough already, but the Dwarf had made this so much worse for me. My heart was racing, and I was afraid of what would come out of the darkness surrounding us.

"And I'm watching a Dwarf who's begging to get slapped in the mouth," Carden warned, annoyed. "Now leave her alone."

"Oh? Defending your girlfriend now are ya?" Holger mocked the young man, standing up.

"Just sit yourself down and be silent!" Dolin scolded, grabbing his brother and shoving him back into his seat. "Not all of us are as dire about these forests as you."

"Well, I know they don't like Dwarves," Holger protested, returning to his original work.

"Don't worry about him, lassie," Dolin told me gently. "He always gets like this when he's drinking."

I frowned. "I didn't see him dr..."

That was when I saw Holger take a skin flask from his pack and begin drinking heavily from it. He put the stopper back in, belched deeply and continued with his work, the scent of ale strong on the air.

"Oh," I nodded. "Now I see."

* * * * *

The rest of the night was fairly calm as we gathered together and ate our meals. I made sure to feed Amethyst before turning in for the night, needing to be certain that she was alright.

I lay in my tent, remaining in my overdress for added comfort against the cold. With fur blankets wrapped around me, a pillow under my head and Amethyst cuddled into my feet, I closed my eyes and managed to slip into a restless sleep.

I dreamed constantly of dark, sinister shadows moving through the trees. I saw the eerie blue glow of ghoulish eyes and heard the howls of the Shade Seekers as they glided through the forests, searching for me. I could feel their icy presence as though they stood over me once again, my fear reaching its tipping point. I felt so sure that I would never escape such horrible things, that they would relentlessly hunt me forever.

Then I heard a soft, beautiful voice in the dark whispering to me: *"Do not fear, child of Aldegaad. You are in no danger here. They cannot reach you within these forests. Only dreams have that power and they come not in dreams."*

Who? What? I was stunned, still turning in my sleep, though I spoke in my mind as if I were actively thinking.

"Awake, child," the voice beckoned. *"Awake and come to me."*

Two turquoise eyes shone behind a milky white face in my dreams, their stare not of anger or cruelty, but of welcome and knowledge.

I woke with a start, looking around me quickly. I still lay in my tent, on my back with one arm over my midriff and the other resting by my head. I stared up into the canopy, surprised to see it there before me as I contemplated my strange dreams.

Suddenly, I felt an overwhelming urge to walk, to move from my resting place. It was so strong, almost like a second nature that I had never known existed. Still, the cold stayed my feet for just a few moments, reminding me to put on my cloak.

Quietly, I pushed aside the flap of my tent and looked out into the night. The camp was silent, Fawkner, Carden and Tallinn on guard, a result of Holger's fear mongering, no doubt. The fire had all but gone out as the three paced the perimeter of the camp, all with their black hoods drawn, Fawkner's fur covered cloak making him stand out compared to the two Guardians.

Quickly and silently, I stepped out of my tent, moving past them and into the forest. I drew my hood over my face and continued forward carefully, my eyes finding a path through the trees, though I didn't know where I was going or why.

There were no thoughts in my mind, no reasons that I could bring to myself that explained my actions. I knew this was extremely foolish, but I couldn't stop myself from walking. There was just this deep, unyielding need to continue on through the forests; a need that brought me into a small clearing some thirty meters from the camp and caused me to stop, though I couldn't understand why.

"Why am I doing this?" I asked myself aloud. "This is insane. I don't know these woods."

I heard a rustling in the underbrush behind me, spinning around quickly. I feared what might come from the shadows, staring back into the darkness with no knowledge of how to fight whatever might come out. My heart skipped a few beats, then proceeded to speed up as I stared between the darkened boughs in cold anticipation.

Two figures emerged from the shadows, their cowled shapes moving swiftly, but humanly through the underbrush. They carried swords and at first felt threatening to me. I held my breath and waited for what was to come.

"Leander?" Carden drew back his hood, Fawkner doing the same.

I felt my body's tense muscles relax and I breathed again. I allowed myself a small, relieved smile as I saw my friends, the fear fading away instantly.

"By the Gods, girl," Fawkner scolded, coming up to me with Carden on his left. "What do you think you're doing?"

"I thought I passed you without you knowing," I said, not answering the question, though this wasn't purposeful, my voice odd to my own ears.

"I caught sight of you and thought you may be a Shade Seeker," Carden admitted, relaxing his stance, his hands now at his sides. "We didn't know it was you until now."

"Oh," I nodded slowly, feeling dazed.

"Now, what are you doing out here?" Fawkner demanded gently.

I stared at the two men for a few moments, trying to find the words to answer them. But I couldn't, the reason eluding my lips and tongue just as the thoughts escaped my mind. In all honesty I had no idea what I was doing, lost even to myself. Finally, I settled on the only thing to say that made any sense to me.

"I don't know."

"You don't know?" Fawkner raised an eyebrow, sheathing his sword.

I shrugged. "I just have to walk," and I turned to continue, knowing this was wrong.

Carden and Fawkner exchanged worried glances, then immediately followed me, staying very close.

"You picked a strange time to go for a walk, girl," Fawkner observed, frowning with puzzlement.

"I'm not going for a walk," I corrected him, feeling very confused by my sudden compulsion. "I'm just... walking."

"And there's a difference?" he asked incredulously.

Carden came up beside me, looking to me from my left and trying to see my eyes under my hood. I glanced to him, his face expressing a new kind of concern unlike any he had previously carried.

"Leander, are you alright?" he asked. "Has something happened?"

I paused and looked at him from under my cowl, frowning. I shook my head slowly as I thought, feeling strangely detached from my companions as they stood there. Then, in a moment of unexpected and sudden clarity, I returned to them from the dazed wakeful sleep that I seemed to have been in.

I looked to Carden, completely scared: "I... I don't know what I'm doing..."

Seeing my fear, Carden reached out compassionately and pulled me into his arms. I rested my head on his chest and closed my eyes, feeling his heartbeat in his broad, masculine torso and the coolness of his teal shirt and black jacket in my hands. It was a soothing feeling that brought me back from my strange trance.

"You were just sleep walking," Carden told me in a gentle whisper. "You're alright now."

"I'm sorry I scared you both," I whispered, my heart once again leaping at his presence.

"Come on," he said, "let's get back to camp."

As we embraced and found a comfort in each other that neither of us had expected to find, Fawkner suddenly and swiftly drew his sword, taking up a defensive position. Carden and I both looked up to him in surprise, then saw what had caused his defensive action.

I stared out at the figures amassing around us, a number of many, but impossible to count in the forests' darkness. They wore cowls and cloaks of green, strange turquoise eyes staring out from angelic faces so beautiful that they seemed unable to be from anything but the Gods. They were clad in leather armour that was unlike anything in any of the Aldegaadian smithies, lightweight garments worn underneath that were close fitting and seemingly useless against the cold.

All of them carried curved, elegant swords and daggers with golden hilts and pommels, strange nature inspired designs carved into the blades themselves. Across their backs they wore quivers filled with eagle feathered arrows, each of the figures aiming an arrow at us with light wood bows bearing the same elegant designs.

None of the figures smiled or flinched as they moved slowly towards us, a mixture of men and women visible in their ranks.

"Verantoth, carshal," one of the figures spoke up, a male's voice, though it was so light and musical.

"That's Elvish," Carden realised, his own sword still in hand as he held me close, positioning me between him and Fawkner for protection.

"They're Elves?" I asked quietly, looking to him nervously.

Carden nodded. "And not too happy to see us."

"Human hating Elves then?" Fawkner muttered, eyeing them off intensely.

Carden nodded again in response, still facing the cloaked Elves cautiously. "Suspicious ones. All of the same clan."

"How can you tell?" I asked nervously.

"The markings on their bows and swords," he answered knowledgably. "Each clan has unique markings on their weapons and armour to distinguish them. These are the Snowleaf Wood Elves, if I'm right."

"Very good human," a single Elf stepped out from the larger group, drawing back his hood.

He was a handsome man with the same turquoise eyes, sharp chin and slender face as the others, his pointed ears suddenly very obvious without his hood. He was blonde, his hair reaching down to his shoulder blades, his eyes severe as he surveyed the three of us before him coldly.

"My clansman has ordered you to relinquish your weapons," he translated the Elvish instructions to us. "You'd best do as you are instructed unless you would rather die with a dozen arrows through your bodies."

"We are not enemies," Carden said, trying to be reassuring while hesitating to drop his weapon. "We mean you no harm."

I clung to him instinctively, watching the Elves uneasily. They were beautiful, but terrifying in their own unique way.

"*You* are intruders," the Elf told him calmly in his coldly sweet voice. "You will relinquish your weapons, come with us, and remain silent, or you shall die. It is your choice."

Carden hesitated for a moment longer, then glanced to me. He looked to Fawkner and nodded, the other man frowning. Slowly, cautiously, the two men lowered their weapons and set them on the ground before raising their hands in surrender. I was relieved and terrified all at the same time, frightened that the Elves would just kill us on principal.

The Elf leader nodded. "Bring them," he turned swiftly on his heel and strode away into the forests as the other Elves moved in and took the two men's weapons.

They surrounded us, grabbing us by our arms and forcing us to move. We didn't resist, obeying diligently as the Elves dragged us forward roughly with stern gazes.

I looked to Carden in fear to receive an uncertain, but strong glance from him as he tried to reassure me that we would be alright.

We were brought slowly from the clearing where we had been surrounded, the Elves beginning a slow march with us through the forests and farther still from our camp and our friends. I could only dread what we would now face under the gaze and care of our intensely beautiful captors.

Chapter Nineteen
The Huntress

I stumbled as I was forced through the darkened nightscape of the forest, hitting the snowy ground as I fell, my hands outstretched before me. My palms were stinging with the strike, my legs hurting at the knees and ankles from where I had tripped. I took a few moments beneath my hood to compose myself, grateful for its protection so as not to show my fear and discomfort in front of the Elves. Unfortunately, it was a reprieve from their coarse treatment that didn't last.

Two Elves slipped through the underbrush and seized my arms again, forcing me back to my feet. Without so much as a kind gaze or even a sound of concern, they pressed me back into our hard march.

I never would have thought people as beautiful as Elves would be so cruel...

I looked to Carden and Fawkner as we were shoved together again, the Elves standing closely around us, bows still trained on our bodies. I could see the concern in Carden's eyes and witnessed the unflinching desire he had to protect me. As for Fawkner, it was clear that he was enraged by the Elves' treatment of me, his disgust worn on his sleeve.

"Move, carshal!" one of the Elves hit Fawkner in the back with her bow, forcing him forward.

I exchanged a worried look with Carden as we were forced to continue on behind them, following slowly, quietly and obediently. He went to put an arm around me, but an Elf snapped at him and caused him to draw back. He looked to me apologetically, his own uncertainty beginning to show, though he remained very calm in our present situation.

It felt like hours as the dozen or so Elves marched us through the forests, the snow falling lighter and lighter as we ventured deeper into the trees. Eventually there was no longer snow on the forest floor, its presence replaced by the lusher green of the trees and the underbrush. It was so dark now that I was stumbling again. I was caught by an Elf that then proceeded to lead me through the deepening darkness. He wasn't particularly kind as he dragged me roughly through the bushes, his movements firm and verging on abusive. The Elf's grasp was firm and vice-like, a grip that would never relinquish my wrist back to me until we were at our determined destination.

All I could see now was blackness, relying on my other senses to tell me about my surroundings. I could hear the whistling of the wind and the creaking of the trees waving in it. Our footsteps reached me in the virtual silence of that dark, but beautiful place, leaves and dirt crunching under foot. The smell of old leaves and newer ones growing were overwhelming, a smoky scent running over the top of these odours and getting stronger. It brought the memory of the campfire to me, warm and bright, a safe place to rest from the shadows of the past weeks. But the cold was all I felt, unrelenting and cruel.

I heard Fawkner grunt as he was struck again, an Elf cursing at him in a coarse but beautiful way. It was an odd sensation to think that something said in violence could sound so appealing in a voice as light and musical as hers. Then I heard Carden groan as he was also struck, the faint staggering movements of a dull shape ahead of me indicating his whereabouts in that black maze of darkness.

After another few minutes, the sight began to return to my eyes as firelight shone through the trees. It was a distant thing at first, a warm glow that permeated the shadows and reached for us like outstretching arms of light. Then, details became clear as the light revealed itself to be a campfire set in the middle of a gentle clearing of forest, small structures erected around it; the smell of smoke I had detected at its strongest now that we were at the source.

As we got closer, the shapes of moving figures could be seen, though not in a large number. There seemed to be another dozen Elves there, maybe two or three individuals more.

The camp was a semi-makeshift set of buildings made from tree bark, leaves, sticks and vines used for twine. Most were set against the trunks of trees, all of them enclosed with cloth flaps serving as doors over the entrances. They all had a semi-circled shape, structured with a strange sense of grace and elegance despite being made from random forest pieces.

Around the campfire was set several small logs and some uprooted stumps to serve as seating, the smell of roasting meat and boiling stew thick in the cold air. There were even a few bedrolls laid out here, sewn from cotton weaves of the forest.

Several Elves sat around this fire, hard at work preparing their meal, their turquoise eyes locking on us as we approached. They watched as Carden, Fawkner and I were forced roughly into the camp, a strange contempt on their fair faces. I stared back in fear, receiving a rough hand on my shoulder and a heavy pull on my wrist to force me forward.

Other Elves patrolled the perimeter, their sharp eyes surveying the black night beyond their camp. They each carried a bow and sword as their brethren did, armoured in the same attire, which I was now able to see more clearly. The Elves wore lightweight leathery armour that seemed to have been laced with faint gold embroidery and made from a single piece of hide. It reached up around their necks and ended at their hips, a pair of bracers of similar make covering their wrists.

Underneath the armour they wore tunics of green and brown that were laced together from furs and cotton weaves just like the bedrolls. Most of the Elves wore only similar leather boots and greaves underneath without leg coverings of any serious length, but they wore tunics with sleeves. Their only other garments were their green hooded cloaks, all of which were clasped with the same cotton weave in a golden braid that fastened across their collars.

The returned Elven party escorting us led us through the camp, passing by the other Elves and bringing us to one of the structures. The leader brushed aside one of the fabric flaps and turned to us sternly.

"Ishvarnael," he directed.

I looked to Carden and Fawkner for answers, completely lost with the Elvish language. Neither of the men spoke or moved, both eying the Elf coldly and defiantly.

Agitation appeared on the blonde Elf's face and he thrust with one hand at the opening.

"Ishvarnael," he repeated coldly, glaring at the stubborn men.

Carden and Fawkner exchanged a look, then eyed him again, remaining defiant.

"Enter here," the Elf said again in common. "Do not make me ask again."

"You're asking, are you?" Fawkner scoffed. "I thought we were prisoners."

"Do not test my patience, carshal," the Elf responded, his eyes icy. "Do as instructed or die; if not for your sake, then for your companions'."

Fawkner looked to Carden and I, seeing the defiance on Carden's face and the fright on mine. I knew that it was my expression that caused him to obey, Carden following grimly as I stayed close to him.

We entered the structure, an open space with only a few slender columns to hold the ceiling, the trunk of the great tree it was connected to serving as a supporting wall. It was strangely warmer inside, the cold seeming to be kept at bay by the apparently flimsy wood and bark walls; a fact that surprised and astounded me as I gazed around the room.

The Elves encircled us again, a few keeping their bows trained on us. I stared back at them, too scared to make even a slight move.

What do these Elves plan to do to us? Are they going to hurt us? Kill us?

They began searching us for any remaining weapons they may have missed. Of course, they found nothing on me, my clothing concealing no weapons at all, Fawkner seeming equally free of weapons since they took his sword and dagger. This was all very intrusive.

Carden was searched, the Elves thumping their hands over his clothing and feeling out anything that may have been concealed. One found a knife hidden in his sleeve, taking it from him. Carden made a silent expression of annoyance as his knife was taken and handed to the leader.

The leader held the knife and looked it over suspiciously, turning his sharp, turquoise eyes to the young man. Carden returned the stare viciously, looking like he would take the knife and run it right up through the Elf's jaw.

"Seat them and bind their wrists," the leader instructed, handing the knife off to another Elf.

I tried to pull away as two Elves grabbed at me, managing to slip my hands free for only a few moments before my wrists were seized. I was forced to the floor, my back pressed up against one of the supporting columns, one of the Elves pulling my hands behind me and crossing my wrists. The other crouched and lashed them together with a length of coarse rope, binding them firmly. He then took a longer length and bound me around my upper arms and waist, pinning me to the column more completely.

As the two Elves stood up, I saw my friends set in the same position, side by side and facing me. Carden struggled against the restraints, gritting his teeth visibly as Fawkner lay his head back and sighed. I just relaxed, my arms and shoulders already hurting from the unnatural position they had been pulled into. I stared at my knees beneath the blue and purple fabrics of my dress, drawing them up a little to regain some measure of comfort.

The lead Elf faced us as the other Elves stood back, his turquoise eyes surveying us proudly. He smirked at the two men, both of them glaring viciously back at him. He allowed himself a small laugh at that, then turned his gaze to me.

I hid beneath my hood, feeling fortunate that it had stayed drawn, shielding my face from his gaze.

The Elf crouched down in front of me and pulled my hood back, freeing my long dark hair to fall across my shoulders. He stared at me, wonder on his face.

"You are Aldegaadian, are you not?" he enquired sharply.

"I... I am," I answered, feeling that I was beginning to gain an understanding of these situations.

The Elf laughed silently, smiling at me and studying every aspect of my shape. "I knew you were. Only Aldegaadian women are so tall and so dark haired. And the eyes: Aldegaadians all have blue eyes," he stroked my cheek, making me cringe. "I must confess that women of your people truly are beautiful... for carshal."

"Leave her alone!" Carden snapped, the Elf suddenly spinning and backhanding him.

I felt the strike as if he had hit me, hating to see Carden get hurt like that.

"Hold your tongue, boy," the Elf leader hissed at him. "It already betrays your homeland through your accent; do not allow it to cost you your life. This is between the Aldegaadian girl and myself."

Carden turned his face slowly back to the Elf, glaring fiercely, his green eyes blazing, his mouth parted harshly as blood coated his bottom lip.

The Elf stared at him for a few moments, then turned his gaze back to me, noting the shock on my face and the pain that seeing Carden hurt had caused me.

"You feel for him, don't you, girl?" the Elf asked me, drawing my eyes as he smirked.

I stared back silently, my breathing staggered and my chest heaving under my bodice.

The Elf nodded and leaned over me cruelly. "We do not take kindly to trespassers entering our territory," he told me harshly. "What are you doing here?"

I swallowed against my fear, meeting his gaze. I focused on my words, levelling my voice, trying to keep my heart rate even and my breathing normal.

"We were passing through on our way to the Guardian Citadel," I answered honestly, my voice shaking a little. "We weren't trespassing."

"I do not believe you," the Elf glared at me.

"I'm... I'm telling the truth," I said, my voice cracking a little and betraying my fear.

The Elf cocked his head at me, suddenly suspicious of my words. He leaned closer towards me, glaring into my eyes and causing me to pull as far back as I could.

"She's telling the truth," Carden said, drawing the Elf's gaze. "I am a Guardian; our friend here is a new recruit yet to be initiated."

"You are a Guardian?" the Elf stared at him doubtingly.

"I wear the medallion of our order around my neck," Carden told him, struggling a little harder. "You can see for yourself."

The Elf moved to him and reached into his shirt. His fair fingers grasped the silver medallion that hung around Carden's firm neck, freeing it from the folds of his shirt. I could just make out the symbol of the Guardians from where I sat.

The Elf turned his turquoise eyes to Carden, both of their stern gazes clashing.

"You may be in possession of such a symbol, and you may in fact be what you claim," the Elf told him harshly, releasing the medallion to fall to Carden's chest," yet, even the Guardians will not enter these forests unless we call to them."

"Does our Order mean nothing to you?" Carden demanded evenly, never once raising his voice.

"When your Order shows us respect, we return such in kind," the Elf said coldly.

He then thought for a few moments and returned from his musings just as suddenly as entering them, his turquoise eyes staring at Carden's handsome, sharp jawed features.

"If you are Guardians," the Elf surmised, turning then to stare down at me as he stood, "then you must be protecting her."

I stared up at the Elf uneasily, my identity in danger of being revealed, not to mention that my body was again in danger of being hurt or violated. I had no reason to trust these Elves after our abduction, and I felt that it was unnecessary for me to reveal my name to them.

"You must be of some great importance if you are being escorted to the Citadel by a Guardian," he prodded with a calmly fervent expression. "I wonder, who are you?"

I shrugged: "No one really. Just... just a girl."

"A very well-dressed girl of Aldegaad by your appearance," the Elf noted. "A noble, perhaps..."

He frowned suddenly and crouched before me again. I stared at him uneasily, seeing his gaze locking onto my chest. I was afraid of his intentions, then I realised that it wasn't my chest that he was staring at, but the Pendant.

With one swift movement he snatched the Pendant from my neck, the clasp seeming to unhook on its own to prevent the chain breaking.

"No!" I cried out.

"You must be of noble blood to wear such a shiny bauble," he mused, studying the simple necklace and its purple stone. He smiled and turned his turquoise gaze back to me, staring into my eyes again. "I am suddenly suspicious of your true intentions here in our forests."

"I swear," I promised softly, trembling, "we're just travelling through."

"With others," the Elf nodded. "And you will tell us where they are so that we can end you all at once."

I shook my head bravely, though fear caused fresh tears to swell in my eyes. I wouldn't betray our friends if he meant them harm. I wouldn't.

The Elf nodded to one of his kindred, the second drawing a blade and putting it to my throat with one swift, liquid movement. I breathed in sharply as I felt the cold dagger against my skin, trembling now as I squeezed my eyes shut, loosing a few forming tears from my eyes.

"Don't!" Carden shouted. "Don't hurt her!"

"She's telling you the truth!" Fawkner yelled.

"You will speak, carshal," the Elf leader murmured to me, my eyes opening to look at him. "You will tell us why you are here."

I whimpered as the other Elf pressed the blade harder into my neck, pricking one drop of blood into existence just below the left side of my jaw. I said nothing, but not out of insolence, my fear paralysing me.

"Then one of you will speak," the Elf leader turned to Carden and Fawkner when I didn't utter a sound.

"We've told you the truth!" Carden insisted, terrified for my safety, his widened eyes flicking to me.

The Elf turned back to me, staring into my frightened eyes cruelly. I shied away, fearing him.

"Then she will die," he hissed.

"No!" Carden screamed desperately, struggling violently against his restraints.

"Leave her alone, for pity's sake!" Fawkner shouted with angry tears in his eyes.

Both men received heavy strikes from our fair faced captors, their grunts loud as they both coughed and wretched from the blows. They bowed their heads for a few moments then turned their eyes back to the scene before them, horror and pain afflicting their expressions.

I tensed, waiting for him to order my throat to be cut, closing my eyes tight.

"Avar'raniel, Beldon," a stern, but harmonious woman's voice spoke from the entrance to the structure.

I managed to glance over my shoulder to the doorway behind me, the Elves stepping away and following the same line of sight that I was.

Before us was another Elf, this one seeming to be the actual leader of the group. She was a tall woman, reaching close to my own height, from what I could tell, and extremely beautiful. She had delicate, pointed features, her turquoise eyes holding a sharp, penetrating gaze as she surveyed the room. Her ears poked up from beneath deep red locks, her hair hanging down to the middle of her back with a few elegant braids framing her slender face.

She was dressed in the same armour as her kindred, a bow of the same make and marking hanging across her back with two curved blades crossing over beneath it. She had a stern, disapproving look on her face as she scanned the room, almost scowling at the scene before her.

Behind her stood a dark-haired male Elf, a little taller than her, probably about five foot eleven, nearly six foot. He shared her look of disgust at the scene playing out in the shelter, his turquoise eyes severe and his expression one of anger.

The blonde haired Elf gestured to his brethren, the blade immediately taken from my throat. He stood as I relaxed, turning to face the red-haired woman and her companion, a shamed, yet aggravated look on his face.

"Viranon, Beldon?" she asked in an amazingly calm voice.

"Mirralas verra'lo, carshal, Ellora," the first Elf responded, defending himself. "Mirras violara avan terrisos; Mirras venna punara."

The Elvish woman glared at him, her rank or position in the group obviously higher as he seemed to be answering to her.

"Mavaren no'ven, breth'ere," she told him gently, but sternly. "Ish varn'a tolor vorn. Co."

The first Elf bowed his head shamefully, then exited the structure, the red-haired woman turning her eyes to the others.

"Loralene," she directed them clearly and strongly.

The Elves inside the structure immediately filed out of the room, obeying their young-looking leader's orders. Once they had all left, she and her companion took one glance at Carden, Fawkner and I, then turned and followed, leaving us alone.

I breathed a sigh of relief, laid my head back against the column behind me and closed my eyes.

There were a few moments of silence as we sat there breathing in our reprieve. None of us spoke at all, still rattled by the events of this night and worried what fate had in store for us.

Suddenly, Fawkner chuckled to himself. I opened my eyes and looked to him, Carden already staring at him.

"What?" I asked, frowning.

"Back in the same position you were in when we first met," Fawkner recalled, facing me with a smile.

I smirked. "Yes, but this time you're tied up too."

He laughed at me, shaking his head as I giggled to myself. We both smiled at each other, finding the irony in the situation humorous, despite the danger. Carden started laughing too as he recalled the events, joining us in our exchange. The laughter lasted a short while, then eased us into an uneasy quiet. It felt like we had really needed the mirth at that moment.

"What do you think made that Elf stop them?" Carden asked, musing over the events that had just played out.

"I would say that she's their leader," Fawkner answered, stretching his bound hands to relieve a cramp. "She's a huntress, and, by the look of things, a high ranking one. She's probably a few centuries old at least."

"How can you tell?" I asked curiously, but softly.

"The way the others responded to her," was his reply. "In Elven culture the oldest warriors are granted leadership."

"But centuries?" I was shocked. "I mean, she looks to be in her twenties. How could that be?"

"Elves are immortal," Fawkner reminded me. "They neither age nor die of natural causes."

"Think of their population growth," Carden chuckled to himself.

There was another moment of silence, then I chose a thought that was swimming around in my head.

"How bad off are we?" I asked, looking around the room for a moment, then back to the two men.

"Tallinn and I were in a situation like this last year," Carden said confidently. "We were captured by an Orc Tribe and tied up in a very similar way."

"How did you escape?" I looked to him.

"Tallinn had managed to conceal a blade in her sleeve then cut us free," he explained, tugging against his restraints again. "After that we just had to sneak out of their camp without getting spotted."

"So?" Fawkner looked to him expectantly. "You have a knife to cut us free, then?"

"I did," Carden turned his green eyes to him coldly. "But the Elves searched me a little better than the Orcs searched Tallinn."

"Perhaps we would have had better luck if she had been captured with us instead," Fawkner commented.

There was the sound of voices and footsteps outside, the three of us looking up as the entry flap was brushed aside again. Anxiety filled me and I sucked in a hard breath apprehensively.

The red haired Elf returned to the room, her turquoise eyes surveying us as she entered alone. She came to stand before us, just to my right as I managed to hide my face behind my long dark hair.

"I must apologise for Beldon's behaviour before," she told us evenly. "My people are not a naturally violent race; however we have suffered greatly at the hands of humans of late. There is great suspicion amongst us."

"But not you," Carden observed, looking her in the eyes as an equal.

The woman shook her head gently: "I do not fear humans as many of my brethren do. I have travelled in the company of humans during the Age of Shadows."

"Then you're over eleven hundred years old at least," Fawkner realised.

The woman nodded: "Fourteen hundred and twelve, to be precise. Now," she looked to Carden, "I was told that you bear the symbol of the Guardians. Is this true?"

Carden confirmed. "I *am* a member of the Guardian Order. My friend here, Fawkner, is a new recruit to be initiated."

"And Beldon said that this girl is an Aldegaadian noble under your protection," she turned to me, my face still down and hidden by my hair. "Who is she?"

"Just a girl," replied Fawkner.

"She seeks refuge with our Order," Carden told her calmly, keeping his eyes on her.

"Then your road is set towards the Citadel of Dartaren," the Elf nodded, crouching down in front of me evenly.

She eyed me with her turquoise eyes, studying my movements and my body structure carefully. I could see her face out of the corner of my eye, her expression a mix of suspicion, confusion and curiosity. It wasn't a look I appreciated receiving from this unknown woman.

"Beldon took this from you," she held up the Pendant, letting it dangle over her hand from its silver chain, its purple stone shimmering in the lantern light of the room.

I saw it, but said nothing, certain that this would lead to a new interrogation that I wasn't prepared to endure.

"How did you come to possess it?" the woman asked.

"It's just a trinket," Fawkner lied, trying to protect my secret, "something her uncle gave her. It's worthless."

"That would have fooled Beldon and the others," the woman eyed him, then stared with a haunted look at the Pendant in her open palm, "but I have seen this pendant before. I know it all too well."

"You know it?" Carden stared at her in shock.

The woman nodded: "It was worn by a friend of mine centuries ago in a time of growing darkness. A time like the one we now find ourselves swept up in."

She turned her turquoise gaze to me, her expression suddenly adamant.

"I *must* know," she insisted, "how you have come to possess it."

"As Fawkner said," Carden answered in my place, "her uncle gave it to her."

The woman nodded slowly, sifting the words through her mind, analysing them.

"You speak the truth," she looked to me again, frowning. "Why do you hide your face from me, girl? I would look upon the one who carries this pendant."

I sighed and slowly turned my face up, letting my hair fall around my shoulders again, looking up through a few stray strands that had drifted over my eyes. I met the Elf's gaze and stared into her beautiful, turquoise eyes, mustering my courage now to face my captor.

The woman stared at me in shock, her jaw dropping and her eyes widening. She wobbled where she crouched, bewilderment plastered across her features.

"It cannot be," she whispered.

I frowned, confused.

"I know your face," she murmured, "yet I know that you could not be her. She died centuries ago."

"You're talking about Leander the First, right?" I asked softly. "The Great Heroine of High-Realm?"

The Elf nodded. "You're the descendant. Aren't you?"

I nodded reluctantly. "I am."

"Please," the woman looked like she had seen a ghost as she faced me, "tell me your name."

"I'm Leander Idona Aldrich," I answered gently and quietly.

"The Aldegaadian Princess?" she asked.

I nodded softly.

The woman quickly pulled a knife. For a moment I was horrified, afraid that she was about to attack, but instead she cut my restraints before freeing my two friends. We all stood and faced each other, my eyes meeting the Elf's gaze again as I rubbed my aching wrists.

"I knew your ancestor well. She was a great friend of mine and I was with her to the very end," she held up the Pendant, smiling: "She never took this off while she lived. It was her greatest power and a symbol of who she was."

Slowly, she took my right hand, placing the Pendant in my palm, returning it to me. I stared at her in disbelief.

"If it has chosen *you*," the Elf said softly, "then it belongs with *you*. Tell me, has the new dragon come to you?"

I nodded slowly, cautious as I took my pendant back.

"Then it is as I always knew," she sighed, seeming suddenly very grim.

"I'm sorry," I refastened the Pendant around my neck, keeping my eyes on her, "but who are you?"

The Elf nodded and smiled. "I am sorry. I did not introduce myself. I am Ellora Snowleaf of the Galvenin Wood Elves. And I will help you where I can."

"You'll help us?" I was stunned.

Ellora nodded. "My people have been waiting for this time to come for nearly twenty years. Your presence here can only mean that what we have feared is now in motion. The Scourge has returned to High-Realm and the Dominion rises once more."

"We're not sure about the Scourge," Carden told her, crossing his arms, "but there have been some sinister events beginning to play out that concern us."

"My parents were murdered several weeks ago when Castle Arvon was attacked," I told Ellora, grief still hanging over me. "My father was killed by some black wrapped creature with blades."

Ellora looked suddenly aggrieved, bowing her head and closing her eyes sadly. She took in a slow breath and let it out just as gradually.

"Such... such tragic tidings come with you, Princess," she murmured, looking to me again. "I know of the creatures of which you speak."

"What are they?" I nearly whispered, half afraid to hear the name of my father's killers.

"They are the Gymphs, creatures from the Scourge, one of the sects of the Shadow Dominion's forces," she looked so silently distressed. "It is as I've feared for nearly twelve centuries."

"Gymphs... I know that name," Carden said thoughtfully.

"Gymphs are the Dominion's assassins," Ellora explained calmly. "They infiltrate and destroy, often silently unless caught in the act, then they shriek and attack with such a frenzy that is unlike anything of the natural world."

"We've been attacked by Shade Seekers too," Fawkner added grimly. "And goblins in the Under Roads."

"Goblins are a common sight in the mountains," Ellora dismissed evenly. "We often catch them on the borders of our forest from where they have breached the mountainside. But Shade Seekers are a threat not seen since the days of the Darkest Shadow."

"You've faced them before?" Carden asked.

Ellora nodded: "Yes. They are hunters of a supernatural and evil nature," then she faced me: "If Shade Seekers are pursuing you, Princess, they will not give up the chase. Not until one of three things happens."

"Which are?" I asked uncertainly, feeling a thrill of fear crawling up my spine.

Gravely, Ellora explained: "They will only stop hunting you if they either succeed in their mission, if their master calls off the hunt," she swallowed hard, "or if you die. Shade Seekers have never given up their hunt even once since they came into existence."

"Oh," was all I could say, twisting my fingers together nervously as I took in all of her words.

Ellora mused, more to herself: "The appearance of Sharveren Shay can mean only one thing: there must be a new Shadow Lord somewhere in the world controlling them, or else they could not exist."

"What do you mean?" Carden frowned at her, his arms crossed firmly.

"The Shade Seekers are created and controlled by the Shadow Lords," she answered grimly. "If there is no Shadow Lord there are no Shade Seekers, so one *must* have come to power."

I glanced up at the two men nervously, watching as they exchanged worried and knowing looks. Ellora was frowning, glancing to me for a moment before realising what we knew.

"You have crossed paths with him," she uttered, a twinge of terror in her voice as she looked at me. "It is the Shadow Lord who hunts you, Princess. Is it not?"

I nodded without speaking.

"That's why we head for the Citadel," Carden told Ellora, drawing her turquoise eyes to him. "The Shadow Lord has revealed himself and seeks to capture Leander, though we don't know why."

"It can be assumed that his purposes are ill natured," Fawkner expressed coldly. "I shudder to think of what cruel things a monster like a Shadow Lord could intend for an innocent young girl."

Ellora nodded slowly, mulling on this, carefully weighing everything that she now knew. Carden came to my side as we watched her, placing an arm around me as I shivered and flashing me a small reassuring look. I forced a weak smile, then turned my eyes back to the Huntress.

"I must take you to the City of Galvenin," she decided after careful deliberation. "The Elders will need to speak with you."

"What about our weapons?" Fawkner asked.

"They will be returned to you immediately," she assured him and moved to the doorway, holding open the flap for us to pass through. "Come, quickly, we must make haste. The Elders must be told of this nightmarish occurrence at once."

"What of Leander's safety?" Carden stared at her sternly, refusing to back down on that point.

"If we go to the city," Ellora explained, "she will be protected by the power of our people. Now, please, do not delay. We must go."

Chapter Twenty
The Words of Illuminil

Ellora led us from the shelter and out into the cold wintry forest air. We were suddenly alerted to a commotion in the camp, Fawkner and Carden immediately closing in on either side of me as they anticipated a fight.

I looked to Ellora, her turquoise eyes narrowing at the activity as she held back a hand to us.

"Wait here a moment," she instructed and took off at a stern walk towards the disturbance.

"What do you think it is?" Carden asked, glancing past me to Fawkner.

Fawkner shrugged. "I'm not sure."

"Avar'raniel!" Ellora shouted loudly as she strode towards the agitated gathering of Elves in front of us. "Avar'raniel!"

It seemed that Ellora's commands were being ignored, yet she remained calm as she stood there, eyeing the Elves that were causing the stir.

"Stop!" she shouted in common. "What is the meaning of this?!"

The Elves stopped their shoving and turned their gazes up to Ellora, the blonde who had threatened us before – Beldon – meeting her gaze and standing out from the others.

"Beldon?" she stood with her arms crossed and her eyes locked on him.

"We came across *these* in the forest," Beldon gestured towards the group, four Elves dragging two figures forward.

Dolin and Holger were thrown to the ground at Ellora's feet, their hands bound in front of them, both Dwarves letting out heavy grunts of pain. They looked so small and squat next to the tall, slender Elves.

"C'mon ya pointy ear bastards!" Holger roared, throwing himself around in the dirt, trying to get back up. "Cut me free and I'll show ya the mettle of a Dwarf! I'll take you all on! Who's first?! Huh?! HUH?!"

"Holger, stop it!" Dolin snapped up at his brother roughly. "You're gonna get us killed!"

"Aye, there'll be some killing tonight," bellowed Holger, snapping at the Elves like a rabid dog, "but it'll be Elf blood on the ground, not Dwarf!"

"Silence, short one," Beldon hit Holger in the back with his bow, the Dwarf slamming face first into the ground, then spinning back to him as the Elf said:

"Your kind knows nothing of self-preservation it seems, let alone respect for one's captors."

"How dare you, forest rat!" Holger howled, glaring at the Elf. "If I had me hammer, I'd drive you into the ground like a tent peg!"

"Brother, enough!" Dolin ordered, pushing himself up with his bound hands to his knees.

"Why?!" Holger was grinning under his thick, matted beard, his hazel eyes sparkling. "I've got them scared! They'll whimper and give in very soon!"

"I doubt it," Dolin grumbled, shaking his head.

I couldn't help agreeing with Dolin's sentiment, the Elves looking rather bored and irritated as they watched Holger throw around his brash attempts at intimidation.

"Dolin, Holger!" I called out.

The two Dwarves turned their eyes towards us, Dolin's jaw dropping as Holger just stared blankly.

"Princess," Dolin breathed in relief. "Oh... you are a sight for sore eyes!"

"How come you three aren't bound like us by these racist, forest dwelling, skin wearing, bough crawling, pointy ear, foul mouthed Elves like we are?!" Holger demanded of us with such a string of profanities.

"It seems," Ellora said coolly, staring down at them, "that you have answered your own question, Dwarf."

"Ah, go drown in the muck ya pointy ear bitch!" Holger spat at her.

Dolin groaned and rolled his eyes: "Ah, by the Stone, sometimes I wish I weren't a twin at all."

"Kill them," Beldon said in a calm, bored tone.

The Elves aimed their arrows directly at the two Dwarves, both of them kneeling upright and looking around with wide eyes.

"Oh!" Holger gulped suddenly.

"Yes, well done, Holger," Dolin shook his head gravely.

"Wait, stop!" I shouted, rushing forward with Fawkner and Carden at my side. "Don't hurt them!"

"Why not?" Beldon demanded, his arms crossed tightly, his sharp eyes glaring at me.

"We know these Dwarves," I turned to Ellora imploringly. "They helped us through the mountains."

"Please," Carden added in the brothers' defence, "they travel with us to the Citadel. They are among our allies."

Ellora considered this, then gestured to the Elves. Two of them moved forward with knives and cut the Dwarves free of their bonds. She turned to us as the Dwarves got to their feet, a knowing look in her turquoise eyes that seemed too old for her young face.

"I have travelled in the company of Dwarves in the past," she said, "and I harbour them no ill will. These two may go free, Princess."

I was relieved.

"You are a wonderful girl, Princess!" Dolin beamed, walking towards me with his arms out wide. "In all my years I have never been so grateful to a human! Bless you lassie!"

He closed his arms around my waist tightly, squeezing me as if he meant never to let go. Holger nearly barrelled into us, grabbing onto me in a mirroring pose that made me yelp in shock, both Dwarves as tall as my sternum.

"Thanks be to you, girly!" Holger nearly cheered as he half hugged me, half groped me. "I'm glad to not be full of arrows! And I'm glad to be hugging *you*!"

"Um... Carden?" I turned to the young man uncertainly as the Dwarves tightened their holds on me. "You're supposed to protect me, right?"

Carden chuckled: "Not from Dwarf hugs I'm not."

I grimaced at him then forced a smile at the two Dwarves, struggling to stay on my feet.

"How touching an image," Aldwyn stated as he, Tallinn, Mithras and Joran were led through the underbrush by more Elves right at that moment. "Would the three of you like to be left alone?"

"Mithras!" I pushed away from the Dwarves and nearly ran straight into the old knight.

"Leander," he smiled brightly, reaching out to me as I threw my arms around his neck.

I gasped as he pulled me to his chest, holding me close and hugging me tight. I stared up at him, the fatherly care that he generated overwhelming me.

"*Never* walk off in the middle of the night like that, Leander," he told me sternly, holding me tightly as if he were afraid to lose me. "Never again."

"I won't," I said, gazing into his dark eyes as he faced me, "I promise."

Mithras smiled at me, brushing my hair from my eyes and placing a hand to my cheek. "I could not bear the thought of losing you, child."

I smiled up at him, then hugged him again, just so glad to see him.

"How the blazes did you get here without being bound like us?!" Holger demanded as Carden greeted Tallinn and Aldwyn.

"Very simple," Mithras smiled as he turned with me to face the Huntress, "I told them that I am a friend of Ellora Snowleaf."

I looked between them in shock, both of them smiling and moving to hug as old friends do.

"It has been a long time, my friend," Mithras said to the Elf warmly. "You haven't aged a day."

"And you've aged terribly, Mithras," Ellora smiled with a half laugh.

"Such is the nature of mortality," Mithras responded kindly.

"You know each other?" I asked, already knowing the answer.

"Ellora and I have been friends since I was a young squire," Mithras turned to me as he answered. "In fact, it was she who accompanied your father, uncle and I when we journeyed across the Crestian Sea to North Storvarkar in our youth."

Joran nodded and bowed his head respectfully to Ellora, who returned the gesture in kind.

I looked to Ellora with surprise: "You knew my father?"

"Well enough to be at his and your mother's wedding, and to come to Arvon when you and your sister were born," Ellora answered with a gentle smile. "Though, I've not seen you since that day until now."

"Huh," I murmured, frowning at that and twisting my hands together again.

"And you must be the Guardians escorting the Princess," Ellora turned to Tallinn and Aldwyn, obviously recognising them now from the black and silver in their clothing. "I doubted that the Order would send only an apprentice and a recruit to be her protectors. A master would be necessary."

"You are right," Aldwyn agreed and respectfully made introductions: "I am Aldwyn Draken, Master Guardian, and this is my junior, Tallinn Landrace. Carden is with us and Fawkner is our newest recruit. We've been with the Princess for some months now as her protectors."

"You must forgive me," Ellora said then, looking around at us, "but further reunions and introductions will have to wait until later."

Joran joined us with Amethyst leaping from his shoulder and into my arms, the dragonling chirping up at me happily. I was grateful to see my tiny friend again, cuddling her closely. Then I noticed the stares from the Elves, all of them shocked to see me holding a baby dragon.

"I do not doubt your motives here in the forests," Ellora addressed the nine of us evenly without halting, though she noted the baby's presence with a brief glance. "If a Shadow Lord truly hunts the Princess, then there is but one place within our borders his Shade Seekers cannot reach; the City of Galvenin itself."

"You want us to go to some pointy eared, forest rat city?!" Holger snorted angrily. "Not bloody likely!"

"*Shut up*, Holger," Dolin warned him, dragging him away from the Elven Huntress. "There are more arrows trained on us here than we can manage."

Ellora rolled her eyes at the Dwarves then turned her attention to Mithras and I. "Mithras, I would not say such things lightly."

Mithras nodded his agreement, keeping an arm around me protectively. "Take us to the city."

I turned my eyes to Ellora and nodded my consent, still cradling Amethyst closely.

"Follow me, then," she directed, turning on her heel and leading the way.

With an Elven escort of about eight archers, the nine of us followed Ellora through the forests, making our way to the north-east. Aldwyn kept his staff's crystal lit, spreading a cool light across the way ahead while he, Carden, Tallinn, Fawkner and Joran watched for any dangers prowling the darkness. The two Dwarves were uncomfortable, shuffling along with wary gazes passing towards each Elf that surrounded them. Dolin was more civil to the Elves than Holger, but I could see the distrust in his hazel eyes all the same.

Apparently, the problems between the Elves and Dwarves aren't as over as history says.

I stayed close to Mithras, feeling unsettled as I walked, cradling Amethyst protectively. The dragonling chirped at me nervously, seeming to understand that we could be in serious danger. I just patted her, trying to soothe her fears, finding that this helped mine as well.

After about a half hour, we stepped through a thick wall of trees, which seemed to be instinctively protecting what lay beyond. The trees groaned as they moved, appearing to change position and open the way for our entourage to pass through. A warm golden light shone through the boughs with an inviting and comforting shine. It seemed to glow from everywhere at once, the trees themselves alive with it.

I stared up in amazement as we came to the feet of the most gigantic trees I had ever seen. They towered up high into the canopy of the forest, the graceful, elegant structures of the Elven City of Galvenin bright with the eerie, yet beautifully comforting light. Stairways curled around the base of the most central tree, reaching up towards the city high above.

Green cloaked sentries watched from both the ground and high up in duck blinds, turquoise eyes trained on us as bows were ready to be strung in defence. They allowed us to pass with a few words from Ellora, the red haired Elf leading our slow march up the great stairway of the central tree.

As we climbed, I could see Elven citizens watching us, coming out from their elegant homes, dressed in simple clothes made from materials of the forests. Many wore furs and clothing weaved from cotton and silk, all of the sentries wearing the same armour that Ellora and her hunters wore.

We came at last to a large walkway that led from the central tree's lower levels and across to the next nearest tree, another curving stairway bringing us to the highest most points of the first. We soon stood before a tall archway leading into a council chamber where dozens of Elves had gathered around the circular floor. They were watching on with hushed whispers, none of their words obvious to me. Then again, I didn't speak Elvish.

Four seats rested at the opposite end of the room from the archway, four Elves dressed in silken robes of gold and emerald seated in them. Their robes had embroidery of silver laced through their golden folds, all of them fairest of complexion and gracefully beautiful.

One was a silver haired woman holding the gaze of a wise grandmother, though she looked no older than her late thirties. The second Elf was dark haired and had a very peaceful look on his young appearing face. He rested with his hands pressed together in his lap. The third man was blonde haired with sharp turquoise eyes, his hands resting firmly on the armrests of his seat. He had a far more severe expression than his counterparts, studying us with distrust, yet showing a strange curiosity too.

Leading them was the most beautiful Elven woman I had ever seen; dark haired, delicate featured and dressed in gold and emerald robes that revealed her neck and arms. She seemed to glow with a strange light that surpassed all others in the forest.

I was entranced by her, feeling as though she were entering my thoughts and grasping my heart with some mysterious unknown power that I couldn't deny.

Ellora bowed her head to them, hands clasped in front of her hips. "Enchantress Illuminil, Grand Elder Eldred, Keeper of History Kirwin, Teacher of Healing Alithia; I come with the travellers who entered our territories this eve."

"Why have you done this, Ellora?" the man in the centre asked coldly, eyeing off the two Dwarves. "Why have you brought outsiders to our city?"

"With respect, Grand Elder," Ellora looked up at him evenly, but reverently, "their coming was foretold by Enchantress Illuminil."

I glanced to Mithras and Carden uncertainly as the Elves around us began speaking hurriedly and excitedly. Neither man could give me any hint of an explanation, seeming just as confused as I was.

Eldred studied our faces calmly, betraying no hint of what he was thinking or feeling: "The prophecy that spoke of the Dominion rising again? Is this the one of which you speak?"

Ellora nodded. "I do, respected Elder."

"The Words of Illuminil spoke of the birth of an Aldegaadian child, a princess born of the Heroine's line," Alithia reminded them, staring from beneath her silvery hair. "The Dominion would not rise again until her life path had crossed tragedy."

"I am aware of the Words of Illuminil," Ellora stated calmly, hands at her sides. "That child has come to our borders this very night."

The Elves started speaking in hushed excitement again, the Elders exchanging significant glances. I knew they were talking about me and I hated it, especially if their prophecy foretold my family's deaths.

My heart instantly ached.

"If this girl has come to us," the dark haired male elder, Kirwin, spoke from where he sat, his voice light and calm, "then let her reveal herself."

Mithras stepped forward, pushing me behind him protectively. I stared at him in disbelief, cradling Amethyst closely as she squirmed under my cloak.

"I am Ser Mithras, Knight-Commander of the Arvon Knight Contingent," he told the Elders evenly and clearly. "I serve the Aldrich Royal Family and I would speak with you."

"We have no interest in speaking with you, Knight," Kirwin proclaimed calmly. "Our interest lies with this girl, if she is truly with you."

"I am her protector," Mithras responded.

"As are we," Aldwyn joined him, standing at his side, meeting their stern gazes unblinkingly. "I am Aldwyn Draken, Mage Master of Safferan and Master Guardian of the Order of High-Realm. My juniors, a recruit and I were commissioned to safeguard her royal Highness by her uncle, King Aric Aldrich, and her father, the late Prince Ewan Aldrich."

"The human names mean nothing to us, Master Guardian," Eldred indicated coolly. "We will respect your order; however, I must remind you that you are in *our* domain."

"I wish only to convey the sincerity of our intentions here," Aldwyn explained, "and ask that the Princess be considered a foreign dignitary."

"The Princess will not be harmed, if that is your concern," Alithia indicated. "We merely wish to see her, to know her."

"You give us your oath?" Mithras demanded, eyeing them off.

Eldred nodded. "An individual under the protection of the Guardians is not under threat from us. She will not be harmed. Now, allow us to speak with her."

Mithras and Aldwyn exchanged worried looks, then stepped slowly back, parting to reveal me to the Elves as I looked up at them nervously.

The Elders stared at me in wonder, their turquoise eyes brightening.

"Do not fear us, child," Alithia beckoned with her right hand. "Come forward. Let us see you."

Hesitantly, I started to walk forward, clinging tightly to Amethyst. I crossed into the centre of the room, my royal blue, purple and pale blue dress, and my dark purple cloak swirling around me with my movements. I stood still, meeting the eyes of the Elders, my heart thundering in my chest as my nerves took over.

"You are the Aldegaadian Princess?" Kirwin questioned me clearly.

I nodded, feeling very small. "Yes, my Lord."

"What is your name?" he went on.

"My name is Leander," I responded softly.

"You do not press your title to us?" Alithia noted in musing. "Why is that?"

"I don't like referring to myself by my title," I answered evenly and honestly. "I prefer to use my name."

"How old are you?" Kirwin asked.

"Eighteen years," I said simply, trembling a little from fear and cold.

"When was your name day?" he urged.

"I turned eighteen a little over two months ago," I replied.

"What is that you carry in your arms, girl?"Alithia leaned forward, trying to see.

Slowly, I nudged Amethyst, the dragonling turning her purple, blue and silver scaled head from my chest. She looked up with her orange eyes, blinking away what little sleep she had begun to slip into and gazing up at the Elders. She gurgled softly, then focused on me with an almost questioning look.

"It cannot be," the woman gasped, staring in surprise.

"You carry an infant dragon with you," Eldred turned his turquoise gaze from the dragonling to me. "How did you come to possess this creature?"

I shrugged. "A stone that was given to me by an old man; it was a dragon egg."

"With respect, Elders," Ellora came up beside me, "she also wears the Pendant of her namesake."

I stared at Ellora worriedly as I heard the gasps of the Elves around me, then turned my eyes back to the Elders to see that they were staring at me. I suddenly felt as if I were naked, my position now seeming very exposed and unsteady.

"Is it truly a Dragon Pendant?" Kirwin asked, almost rhetorically. "Can it be?"

"She *does* wear a pendant," Alithia confirmed sceptically. "But how can we be sure it is one of the Thirteen?"

"She carries a dragonling with her," Kirwin argued softly, facing her. "Is that not proof enough?"

"How did you come by this pendant, child?" Eldred turned his gaze back to me.

"My uncle gave it to me just before my name day," I answered truthfully. "It has protected me since then."

"How has it done this?"

"A strange energy that seems to come from the stone at its heart, though I'm not sure how."

The Grand Elder nodded slowly. "It seems that you are a bearer then. But are you she that Enchantress Illuminil spoke of?"

I swallowed hard, not sure how to respond to anything they were saying.

"What do you say, Enchantress Illuminil?" Eldred enquired of the one Elven Elder who hadn't spoken yet. "Is she the one in your foresights?"

Enchantress Illuminil stood and moved forward slowly as Ellora took Amethyst from my arms. The dragonling leaped from the Elf's grasp and stood at my feet, refusing to leave me.

Illuminil walked leisurely around me as she studied me. This made me very uneasy, my blue eyes meeting with her turquoise ones as she paced. And that is when I recognised them as the same eyes that had been in my dream. A small gasp escaped my lips and I suddenly couldn't take my eyes off hers.

"Princess Leander Idona Aldrich the Second; daughter of Ewan, niece of Aric, descendant of the Great Heroine of High-Realm," Illuminil said in a mystically distant voice, pausing to my left.

She smiled at me as I stared at her in confusion.

"She who possesses the power of dragons," the woman went on dreamily "she who nurtures one of the Eldest Ones' progeny," she paused with a calm, but severe gaze that was unflinchingly locked on my face: "You are she who has been touched by the Hand of the Daemon."

"What?" I stared at her, even more deeply confused. "The Daemon?"

All around me the Elves gasped in fear.

Illuminil went on: "The Shadow Lord seeks you from his black throne beneath the ashen mountains. From the Lair of the Serpent he sends his minions and most loyal disciples in search of you."

"Why?" I asked fearfully. "What does he want from me?"

"You are important to him," she answered in a tranquil tone. "So important that he will not risk you harm. He wants you unspoiled, untouched... He needs you; the doppelganger."

"The doppelganger? What do you mean?"

"You possess the likeness of your ancestor before you," she explained, moving to stand on my right, passing behind me gracefully. "You possess all the power she did and infinitely more."

I frowned, glancing down at Amethyst, the dragonling gazing up at me innocently. I felt stiff, my arms stuck at my sides, my body bolt straight as I listened to the words of the Elven Enchantress, my eyes straying back to her again. It was like she had bewitched me with her graceful voice.

Illuminil frowned. "Gaya shows me your fate. She shows me the path that lies before you; so full of pain, suffering and death. *He* reaches for you from beyond the Void, stretching out his talons, seeking a grasp on you. *Only* the Pendant itself shields you from him."

"What does that mean?" I asked quietly.

"The Shadow Lord is not of flesh and blood as he once was," she explained, standing behind me, her turquoise eyes locked on my slender frame. "He is living spirit, corporeal only in visage, not in substance. His only powers lie in his knowledge of the arcane magical arts and his command over the monsters swarming beneath the skin of the world. He cannot see you while you wear your Pendant. He cannot locate you in the world, though he seeks you. Even those whom you travel with are protected by its stone. The Dragon's Heart is all that shields you from him, for no magic, even his, can touch you while you wear it."

"But it can be taken from me," I pointed out, looking to her worriedly.

———

She nodded: "By hand of flesh and bone, not by dark powers. *He* cannot touch you."

"Then who can?" I asked uneasily, not sure I really wanted to know.

"The Traitors behind the Conspiracy, the Corrupted Gryphon Queen, the Knight-Commander of Wraiths, the Condemned Witch, the Bestial Chieftain, the Dark Kindred, the Children of the Blood, the Disciples," Illuminil answered, staring blankly as she spoke. "They possess living forms and serve the Daemon's General as he once served the Daemon. They seek you out, some for their Master, others for their own ends."

"What do I do?" I was afraid as I asked this.

Illuminil gazed into space, holding up one veiled hand, looking as if she was in a trance.

"Travel to the Cradle of your Ancestor," she replied distantly, "from the Citadel, across the Great Bridge, into the Calian Mountains. Take to the Mountain Falls and seek her out. Only then will you know your path."

"What do you mean *"the Cradle of my Ancestor"*? I don't understand," I murmured, her words only serving to make my headache.

She looked to me grimly: "Death awaits you on your path. It beckons with open palm to you and your companions. Grief has brought you here, yet more grief awaits on the road to the sea in the Cove of Albion. Pain, suffering, death and grief are the legacy you have been given. You have no choice but to follow your path now to its promised end."

"I don't want this," I told the Elf firmly, trying to be calm. "*Any* of it. I never asked for this."

"The Path is set," she turned away from me. "Your journey is long, your quest unseen to you."

"I don't understand!" I cried out, turning around to face the woman again. "There must be more you can tell me! Please!"

Illuminil looked over her shoulder softly: "Three more will die and you will not save them. A man you do not know with an absent heart will seek you out in a time of great need. An Eldest One calls to you from the Coastlands. And you, Leander, will soon become a custodian to a world long since passed... and a victim to an enemy not your own."

"Please. Isn't there something clearer you can tell me?" I pleaded.

"Hold your Pendant to your heart," she advised me in her mystical way. "A time comes where you will face the Serpent in its Lair. This you cannot avoid. Only hope and love will protect you in the years to come. Hold onto these as they are all that yet remain to you."

Years? I don't like the sound of that. How long is this going to go on? How long will I live like this?

Illuminil walked away from me, throwing me a knowing, sympathetic, yet powerful glance, her silken veils and gown trailing around her as she moved. With the grace of a leaf dancing in the gentlest of spring winds she retook her seat with the other Elven Elders, falling silent once more.

I felt a deep sense of bewilderment flowing over me. I wasn't able to comprehend anything that I had been told. All I understood of what had been said was now mixed together into some strange, eerie narrative in my head and breeding anxiety in my breast.

"Illuminil has spoken," Eldred said, drawing my gaze back to him. "She confirms that you *are* the One."

"What does that mean?" Carden asked, coming up to my right as I looked to him, seeking comfort from him instinctively.

"It means that we will aid you as far as we can," Eldred told him, then looked to me. "You and your companions are free to pass through our domain, Princess Leander. You are under the Guardians' protection and shall be conducted to the Citadel itself."

"Respected Elders," Ellora drew their attention, stepping forward and bowing her head again. "I request to follow the Princess and her entourage to the Citadel."

"You would leave us, Ellora?"Alithia raised one silvery eyebrow. "Why?"

"I served her ancestor as a friend and guide," the Huntress answered. "I would do the same for this girl in her time of trial."

"All kindred are free to take their leave," Eldred reminded her. "Should you choose to follow this girl then you must remain with her to the end of her path, not merely her journey to the Citadel. Do you accept this?"

Ellora nodded once, great resolve in her voice: "I accept, Grand Elder."

"Then, Ellora, you shall join this carshal woman-child in her journey to whatever end it brings," Eldred declared solemnly. "So mote it be."

"You don't have to do this," I turned to Ellora, warning her uneasily.

She looked to me knowingly, smiling softly. "We all choose our own paths, Princess. Would I be given another choice I would still follow you."

"But, you don't know me," I said in quiet astonishment.

"I do not need to," she smiled faintly.

The Grand Elder stood, taking his staff from the side of his seat, the Enchantress, the Keeper and the Teacher following suit. Their movements drew my gaze back to them as they addressed the ten of us.

"You shall rest safe within our walls tonight," the Grand Elder welcomed us. "Tomorrow you will set out for the Citadel Keep of the Guardians and we shall gift you what we can to aid in your journey. Go now and rest. You will need your strength for the journey that still lies before you."

Chapter Twenty-One
The Guardians' Citadel

Resting within the silver walls of Galvenin wasn't the easiest prospect for me. My sleep was very disturbed as I lay on the bed that had been provided for me. All night, visions of my parents' deaths plagued my thoughts along with the fall of Castle Arvon. I didn't seem able to shut them.

Mixed in with these images I saw the Unseen bringing its monster to life, the horrible shadowy knights at Averet, the howling faces of the leather-bound assassins and the ghastly visages of the Shade Seekers. All of them haunted me like their Master's sinister desires, pursuing me even into my sleep.

Morning came and I was woken by Mithras, the Knight seeing the visible signs of my restless night. He helped me gather my belongings and we made our way out of our rooms, then towards the outer walkways of the city.

I carried Amethyst in my arms as I followed Mithras down the spiralling staircases surrounding the trees, the dragonling still half asleep. I found a measure of comfort in looking at her, feeling the warmth of her body soothing in the cold air of the forest.

The others were gathered below, the Elves watching them as they prepared to leave Galvenin and continue on our journey to the Citadel. It pleased me to know that our journey was almost over, safety within our grasps at last.

I smiled at Carden and he returned it with his own, putting a hand on my back and pulling my cloak a little closer around my shoulders. I loved it when he touched me in the most casual ways.

We were now nearly ready to depart, Ellora standing in silence as she took one last look at her home. I could see the unease on her face, but also the conviction. She was doing what she thought was right, not for herself, but for the priorities that held strong in her heart.

The Elven Elders joined the large gathering of their people to see us off, the four of them standing with us.

"It is a perilous path that lies before you, Leander, Daughter of Ewan," Eldred said as he stood before me, saying his farewells. "You journey towards safety, however, we can all see the path you must yet travel. Know that while we cannot journey with you that the thoughts of the Elven peoples do. One of our own travels with you now, a protector and guide. She will lead you to the Citadel."

"As I have always been willing to," Ellora bowed her head to the Elders.

The Grand Elder nodded to her. "Go in peace, sister. May Gaya watch over you and one day bring you home."

"Arlatharn varnar, Elsir," Ellora responded respectfully in Elvish.

The Grand Elder turned his gaze back to me, his face seeming softer now.

"We cannot protect you once you leave the Forests of Galvenin," he told me, "yet we may be able to offer you the means to defend yourself."

He gestured off to one side. A young crafter approached with a heavily wrapped package, bringing it to the Grand Elder before taking away the wrapping. Beneath was an elegant recurve bow unlike anything I had ever seen. It was made of the lightest, hardiest of woods, and adorned with graceful golden engravings of Elven origin, a dragon carved above the handle.

Eldred took the bow in his hands and gave it carefully to me.

"We give to you a Forest Heart Bow, the finest bow our crafters can create," he told me. "It carries the very soul of the forest with it and is enchanted to offer protection to you and your companions. No matter your aim, any arrow loosed from this bow will not harm anyone you consider a friend or ally."

I took the bow, the Grand Elder then handing me a hip quiver filled with golden eagle feathered arrows. I stared at the bow in wonderment, studying the extensive carvings in its length.

"May it serve you well, child," Eldred bid me with a bow of his head.

"Thank you," I replied softly, returning his gesture.

Minutes later we were on the move, Aldwyn at the head of the group with Ellora leading the way. Mithras followed with me, Carden and the Dwarves close behind us. Joran trailed on next, Fawkner and Tallinn bringing up the rear.

We passed through the forests, leaving the Elves behind, my eyes catching a glimpse of Illuminil the Enchantress one more time. She stood on a high rock outcropping amongst the trees, a golden veil cloak wrapped around her, a hood drawn over her dark-haired head. She smiled at me then disappeared back into the forests with the rest of the Elves.

* * * * *

The journey through the forests took another day and a half, Ellora finding us a place to make camp, then going to hunt for a meal. We enjoyed a peaceful night before we set back out the next morning.

At midday, the forest gave way as our path turned north-east back up the mountain trails. Daylight shone over us, a welcome sight after the two days spent in the dark depths of the forests, the peaks of the Nartarn'lath Mountains towering above in front of us once again.

The journey slowed as we climbed the mountain trails, dragging ourselves through muddy, snowy grounds towards the main road that led to the Citadel.

Once we had reached the paved road it became an easier trip and I now felt a sense of growing relief.

It won't be long now, I kept thinking as I followed the group. *We'll be there soon. I know it.*

Hours passed by and the sun began to set across the mountainsides. Darkness started to creep back in over the world as night fell, the cold winds filled with gently falling snowflakes.

"How much farther is it?" I asked as I walked alongside Carden, the chill affecting me enough that I had drawn my hood.

"It shouldn't be far now," he told me, pulling his own cloak tighter around him.

"The Citadel is within reach," Aldwyn called back from where he walked. "We should be there in a few minutes."

"Good," Fawkner said, coming up with Tallinn to join us as we walked together now. "The sooner we are out of the cold, the better."

"And the sooner you can begin your initiation into the Order," Tallinn said, reminding him of his fate with a half-smile.

He looked down at her coarsely: "Oh yes. I'd forgotten. Thank you *so* much for reminding me, Tallinn."

"I have to admit that a proper bed and a warm meal would be welcome," Dolin spoke up, a little out of breath from the ever-steepening hike.

"And maybe some wenches to play barmaid with," Holger grinned, laughing sleazily.

"You remind me of a friend I once had," Fawkner told the inappropriate Dwarf. "He was unable to keep it in his pants either."

"It's in my pants!" Holger turned his eyes to me, nudging my elbow and winking. "But I could get it out for you, honey."

"Ugh! That's disgusting," I rolled my eyes and walked a little faster, leaving the Dwarf confused behind me.

I reached Mithras, coming up to his side and smiling at him. He smiled back, moving at an easy pace so as not to waste his energy.

"How are you fairing?" he asked me gently.

I shrugged, Amethyst clawing into my arms tightly as I held her. "I'll feel better once we get to the Citadel."

He nodded. "Our journey is almost at its end. I have accomplished my task and kept you safe."

"Is that all?" I looked back to him curiously. "Were you just protecting me as your duty demands?"

He shook his head. "No, my girl, I was not. Nor is my task truly complete. I was merely expressing my relief at being so close to our destination."

I frowned and glanced away, a little uncertain as to how to take his words.

Mithras saw the unease his words had brought and reached out to me, turning my chin so that I would face him again.

"I do not simply protect you because you are a princess," he assured me. "I would have protected you were you a commoner, but I stay with you as your friend. I have no other motive now."

I smiled. "I know. I just..."

"You fear what is yet to come," he noted, looking at me with an honestly uncertain gaze, "as do I."

I sighed, looking down at the dragonling in my arms. I wanted to be reassured and to reassure him, but I didn't know how. I wanted to show us both that there was hope, that there was a way through this. However, I wasn't sure that I even truly believed it.

"I'm not sure what's..." I was cut off by his cautious wave to me.

I stared at him, seeing the concern growing on his face as he stared up at the darkened mountain before us. He was watching the two figures ahead of us, Aldwyn standing still a few feet away now as we approached him. Ellora had vanished.

"What is it?" I asked uneasily, following his gaze.

"I'm not sure," he responded. "But I want you to stay behind me."

I obeyed, following him slowly as we made our way forward to where Aldwyn stood. The others moved up behind us, all of them knowing that something was wrong. When we reached Aldwyn I could see the dread that was washing over him, his dark eyes locked on the black shapes ahead in the fading twilight.

"What is it, Aldwyn?" Mithras asked, coming up to his right.

"I'm not sure," the Mage answered, still looking forward. "Ellora has gone on ahead to scout out the way."

"Do I smell smoke?" Carden asked as he and Tallinn came to my side, the others close behind them.

"Something's happened," Tallinn realised, fear tinting her voice.

We watched as a figure moved towards us, cloaked and hooded, all of us on edge suddenly at its approach. Ellora reached us, staring out from under her sage green hood with her turquoise eyes, unease showing clearly in their deep pools.

"It isn't good," she stated grimly.

"What did you see?" Aldwyn asked.

Ellora took in a shaky breath: "The Citadel; fires burn within its walls and I saw signs of a battle."

"Someone attacked the Citadel?" Carden stared at her in disbelief. "How can that be?"

"I thought the Citadel was neutral," Fawkner confessed gravely. "No army can lay siege to it."

"It shouldn't have been taken," Tallinn said, recalling all she knew of the defences. "A small contingent of Guardians can hold it against an army for years."

"I saw no movement within," Ellora grimly relayed the sights she had seen. "There was so much devastation within that I am not certain if anyone lives."

"What should we do then?" Carden asked uncertainly, looking to the other Guardians in the group.

Aldwyn answered gravely: "We enter the Citadel cautiously. We'll assess the situation and decide our next course of action."

I felt a growing pain of dread deep inside me as I heard all of this. I could feel that something was wrong, could smell it in the air. I realised that I had smelled this scent before, that the atmosphere was one I had already lived through.

It feels just like it did when Arvon was attacked.

Fear gripped me as I walked with my companions, our path bringing us up to the towering Citadel. The signs of battle were clear before we had even passed the outer walls into the compound.

The walls were charred and broken in places where siege engines had been used, the Citadel Tower itself ripped open like a wounded limb, smoke and flames belching from the destroyed summit. Flames flickered throughout the grounds, smoke choking the cold night air and burning my nostrils as we entered the main gates. Beyond the gates was a terrible scene. Bodies lay strewn about the grounds, all of them clad in the armour, robes and cloaks of the Guardian Order. Weapons were scattered everywhere, broken and useless, blood staining the earth and walls.

Destroyed stone lay where it had fallen from the tower and walls, the trees within the compound now nothing more than ashen husks. What few wooden structures remained were nothing but rubble, their burnt timber ribs sticking up from the earth.

I had never seen such devastation, even after living through the siege on my home. I slowly crouched, setting Amethyst down, the dragonling sniffing the ground cautiously.

The others were moving slowly through the wreckage, all with their weapons at the ready as they trudged over the ruined fortress grounds. They were surveying the unburied bodies with horror, their eyes searching the darkness for some sign of how this had happened.

Deep in my heart, I knew how. The Shadow Lord had countered us. The safe harbour that I had been struggling to reach for weeks now lay destroyed with all its defenders dead, and here I stood, knowing in my heart that it was *Him*.

"This is a cold battle," Dolin was saying as he walked with Carden, the young man looking to him grimly. "No army I ever heard of could have done this."

"None that I have heard of either," Carden agreed, pushing aside ruined wooden rubble with the point of his sword. "Who could have done this?"

I watched my companions gravely as they traversed the ashen boneyard. I couldn't bring myself to move from where I stood, my blue eyes surveying the scene before me. I cringed at the thought of the final moments of life here, feeling only death now inside that compound.

Joran and Fawkner were moving cautiously towards the Citadel itself, Holger shuffling slowly behind them with his war hammer in hand. He looked extremely agitated, like he was expecting something to leap out and attack him.

Heading towards the mountain peak side of the compound, Tallinn and Aldwyn searched the wreckage of what looked like stables. Tallinn had an arrow strung to her bow, cautiously stepping cross footed over the earth as Aldwyn followed behind. The Mage's gaze swept around the area while the Ranger's eyes were fixed on the blackened structure before her.

Ellora walked carefully and gracefully beside Mithras, her hands at her sides, weapons stowed while he carried his sword unsheathed and his shield ready on his arm. They both moved past Carden and Dolin, making their way around the compound in a slow patrol, surveying everything.

Carden crouched down to the corpse of one of the fallen Guardians, checking for a pulse, then the identity. He sighed deeply, stood and started looking around for any other signs of life.

It seemed that there was no safe place for me here, a thought that left me lost and confused.

What do we do now? Where do we go? Is any place safe if the Citadel is not?

I felt a strange breeze push past me and I froze where I stood, feeling a new set of eyes watching me; familiar eyes that promised more pain.

"Magnificent, isn't it?" a cold voice spoke from behind me.

I turned slowly, looking out from beneath my hood at the shape standing there. He stared at me, wrapped in his black and crimson robes, his deep cowl shielding his face as those cold eyes shimmered beneath the rim. His long hands were held together before his chest, his body language so relaxed in the middle of this grim scene as he surveyed the wreckage.

"I have always enjoyed carnage such as this," he mused softly. "It brings me a sense of joy."

The Shadow Lord turned his eyes to me, cracking a closed lipped smile. My wavering step backwards seemed to increase his pleasure.

"You're afraid," he noted coolly. "That's good."

I felt the terror inside me as I faced him, unsure of what to do. I was scared, unable to call out or even speak. Yet, somehow, with my body paralysing at the mere sight of his dark visage, I managed to pull myself free enough to speak.

"Y-you," I managed with a croak. "You did this."

He nodded. "Yes. I did."

"Why?" I rasped out fearfully, my voice nothing but a tiny whisper.

"Did you think I would really allow you a safe refuge to escape to?" he asked calmly.

"But the Guardians are untouchable. No one can attack their fortress," I insisted fearfully, though softly.

"No one among the nations of High-Realm or the entirety of Therras," the Shadow Lord corrected me with a cruel smile. "That does not preclude my forces from striking at them. And so... they have."

I wanted to run, to call out to the others. I felt the desire to scream rising in me as I faced him, knowing that there was no way I could fight him, even with my bow in hand. I betrayed this desire to him without meaning to, the slow backwards steps and the single glance over my shoulder speaking volumes more than my words ever could.

"You want to run to your friends," the Shadow Lord observed, drawing my eyes back to him. "You want them to turn against me, to strike me down and kill me. But they cannot. "He smiled with a mocking sadness. "If only they were to survive the night."

"What?" I stared at him, confused.

I watched his face, seeing his expression change from mocking sadness to a sinister smirk of victory.

I never realised how much I still had to lose, even after everything I already had. My grief had blinded me from really noticing, but in that moment it was all too clear to me. My friends didn't know what was coming, but I did, that knowledge too painful to ignore.

The monster stood before me, his glowing green eyes coldly victorious as that cruel, sinister smile spread over his pale lips. The fear I felt was too real, too tangible as I truly came to understand what he had just said to me.

In that moment I felt an overwhelming warmth and I looked down at my chest. The stone in the core of my pendant was pulsating with violet light, heat radiating out from its centre across my skin and clothing.

I looked to the Shadow Lord, wide eyed as he smirked and began to laugh. I knew what was coming, turning towards my friends with a sudden desperate need to rush forward and save them.

Spinning on my heel, I threw myself into a strong sprint towards the others, my cloak and dress flowing around me wildly as I moved. I heard Amethyst roar her soft howl, the tiny dragonling leaping after me frantically.

"MITHRAS! CARDEN!" I screamed, causing all of the others to turn to me.

Mithras ran towards me with Ellora at his side, Carden reaching me first. The young Guardian grabbed my arms, steadying me as I skidded to a stop, the Knight and Huntress joining us moments later.

"What is it?" Carden asked me. "What's wrong?"

"We're under attack!" I told him urgently, breathing heavily as I looked to him.

Their eyes fell to the glowing pendant at my neck as the others rushed up to us, the howling of monsters having already drawn their gaze. Aldwyn and

Tallinn stood staring at the main gateway, Tallinn ready with her bow before anyone else.

"What is it?!" Fawkner rushed up beside us. "What's happening?!"

"It's the Scourge!" Ellora exclaimed, loosing her bow and lacing an arrow to the string fluidly.

"Prepare to defend yourselves!" Mithras shouted, holding his sword ready in his right hand.

Tallinn and Ellora quickly found higher ground to aim from as Aldwyn, Joran, Carden, Fawkner, Mithras and the Dwarves readied their bladed weapons, all standing in a line with Joran at the centre.

I moved to join Tallinn and Ellora, Mithras catching my arm firmly and stopping me.

"Stay behind us," he ordered me softly.

"I won't stand defenceless this time," I responded with finality in my soft voice. "I'm helping."

Hesitantly, Mithras nodded, allowing me to move. I took my bow from my shoulder, rushing up to the small rise where Tallinn was standing near the collapsed entrance to the Citadel itself. I set an arrow to the string and pulled it back with confidence, standing ready. Briefly, I glanced to where the Shadow Lord had stood, but I found only empty air in his place. Still, I knew he was watching us.

Amethyst found her way to me, managing to hide behind my legs, watching on silently with fear. I could sympathise with the dragonling as I stared at the gates, waiting for what was to come through.

Through the darkness came the howls and barks of many monstrous creatures, their black shadows moving towards the Citadel from the forests beyond its compound walls. Torches glowed as the gleam of swords flashed through the black night, then out of the deep woods came the monsters of the Scourge. I knew them all from my history lessons, terrified to actually be seeing them with my own eyes.

Leading the way were the Gathlorks, all with thick black hair that hung wetly to their shoulders, jagged teeth between their snarling lips, frightening yellow eyes staring out of their skulls. They were muscular and stood between six and six foot five in height, heavily armoured. Four of them wore armour with similar crimson markings and two swords each. A taller one stood out above the rest with scratched white war paint smeared over the left shoulder and chest, a huge great sword clutched in his hand. He was the leader.

Some twenty more of these beasts followed in plain armour with jagged swords, surrounded by the muscular, green skinned, six-foot-tall Orcs, their armour and weapons varying. Mixed through the larger beasts' numbers were the four foot tall, squat bodied, long armed Hurgarks, creeping through the snows viciously. Their mismatched armour and weapons only added to their ferocity, which outweighed their comical appearance. With pointed ears listening in the night and black eyes searching the shadows they shrieked and hissed among their larger allies.

Four black leather wrapped Gymphs leaped up over the front wall of the fortress, sinister blades in hand, their crimson eyes as piercing as their shrilled screams. They joined the numbers, snarling with drooling bloodlust.

I gathered my courage as I stared at the burly Orcs, the squat Hurgarks, the sinister Gymphs and the intimidating Gathlorks, knowing that I had to fight now. I couldn't be the damsel in distress this time, and I was determined that I wouldn't be.

With the Gathlork Field Commander stepping slowly forward surrounded by his four captains and the eight Orc lieutenants, the scene became a stand-off promising a battle. The Field Commander narrowed his yellow eyes on us, studying us coldly. Then he suddenly roared and pointed at me.

"Take the girl! Kill the rest!" he roared in a booming, gurgling echo of a voice.

The monsters roared and charged, the Hurgarks sprinting frantically, the Orcs and Gathlorks moving like the very best of runners.

Aldwyn held out his staff with his left hand while holding his sword in his right. Flames erupted about ten feet from our defensive line, the Mage's magic calling a burning barrier to freeze the monsters in their path. It made those closest to the flames back off while a small percentage were engulfed and sent screaming to their ends.

In unison, Ellora, Tallinn and I loosed our shots, our arrows flying through the flames to strike varying targets and drop them to the earth. Without a moment's pause, the three of us loaded our arrows and fired again.

I focused only on my archery training, seeing a target and firing for the weakest points. I didn't even consider that I was fighting living things, only that I had to hit accurately to survive. I laced another arrow to my bow and struck out, my aim strong as the arrow collided into the shoulder of a Hurgark, dropping it screeching to the dirt. None of my shots were fatal, but they were enough to dissuade my attackers.

Dangerously, ignoring the flames and the arrows flying at them, the Gathlorks charged. They leaped through the fire wall, their athletic, muscular shapes landing heavily on their feet. They turned their attention to the warriors before them, roaring as they swung their swords and blade-like shields into battle.

Mithras let loose a loud cry of rage and power, rushing into the fray with his sword at the ready, taking his shield across his left arm. He slammed into two of the monsters with his shield and engaged a third with his sword. The two Dwarves were right behind him, hammer and axe lashing out violently to crush and cleave at any beast that dared to strike at them. Fawkner and Carden held the line with Aldwyn, the Mage using his sword only if an adversary got too close, magical blue orbs his weapon of choice.

The Orcs were now barging across the flames to join the Gathlorks, howling angrily as they fought beside their equally sapient allies. They were trying to overwhelm our small group; ten against almost fifty. That was without the Hurgarks, some forty from the beginning now reduced closer to thirty, all of them managing somehow to pass the flames and join the battle.

I watched as Joran swung his massive dual blades, taking out scores of Hurgarks, Gathlorks and Orcs as he went, Fawkner and Carden parrying and striking against their foes behind him. The two men were slaying a sizable number of the monsters, but still finding that they were overwhelmed.

Dolin and Holger now fought back-to-back, hammer and axe casting down enemy after enemy, the two crying out through their thick beards and using their sheer strength to their advantage. They would periodically spin around each other, confusing their foes as they forced them back towards the flames.

Mithras was fighting against mostly Gathlorks and Orcs, his sword and shield meeting theirs. He would easily drop one, then block another and start battling a third each time.

Tallinn and Ellora were continuing to fire, turning their attention to the Gymphs, who were now charging into the battle. They easily dispatched two of them while I continued firing into the throng surrounding the others, struggling to thin the herd. The other two Gymphs began ducking and diving quickly, dodging out of harm's way, but were ultimately slain.

"We cannot hope to win this battle!" Aldwyn shouted, slaying another Orc with his sword before casting an energy blast to hurl a myriad of the three species into the flames again. "They overwhelm us!"

Mithras slew another two Gathlorks almost simultaneously, throwing their bodies down as he joined the Mage. "You're right!" he agreed breathlessly, his eyes frantic. "There are too many for the ten of us!"

There came a terrifying bellowing roar from the main gates, all of us turning our attention there. Six seven-foot-tall, muscular beasts lumbered forward with gigantic forearms and hands. Their mouths had upwards pointing tusks, their heads short with inward sloped brows, cold black eyes staring out from underneath. They wore the most basic armour, three unarmed, two with battleaxes and one with a massive hammer. They bellowed as they beat their chests like apes, charging forward violently. Instantly I knew they were the massive Erks of legend.

Ellora was trying to down them without so much as a second thought, managing to slay one with four arrows to its face, neck and chest. It slammed to the ground, dropping its battleaxe, the others still thundering towards us.

"We cannot defeat these beasts!" Fawkner shouted, slaying a Gathlork and kicking it to the ground. "We must retreat!"

"How can we?!" Carden backed up beside him as the others began to climb the front steps to where the other archers and I fired our bows.

I looked around, seeing a gap in the wall behind us large enough for us to escape through. I looked to my friends, then to the wrecked tower, the precarious ruined wall inspiring me.

"Aldwyn!" I called to the Mage. "There's a breach in the wall behind us! We only need to distract these monsters long enough to escape!"

"What are you thinking, Princess?!" he asked.

"The tower," I pointed to the hanging wall, "break it!"

"A bold plan," Fawkner commented.

"It's our only choice," Mithras granted and nodded to Aldwyn. "Retreat!"

I threw my bow over my shoulder, scooping up Amethyst as I turned. The men rushed up the steps from the approaching monsters, Carden reaching me and casting his arms around me as we both ran. We made for the breach as Aldwyn covered our escape. Ellora and Tallinn continued to fire as they backed slowly towards the wall, spacing enough ground between them and the attacking brutes.

As the others reached the wall, I turned to Aldwyn, watching as he sent a powerful magical blast up towards the Citadel. The blue energy shattered the stone and spilled the loose wall from the tower. He moved quickly, a Gathlork reaching out for him easily struck down by his sword with a swift swing of his arm. Suddenly, an arrow injured Gymph dived over the dead beast, stabbing the Mage through the shoulder with its blades and throwing him down to the ground.

I felt my heart sink, time slowing as the ruinous stone came tumbling down with dust and rubble. I watched on with Mithras holding me back as Carden rushed to Aldwyn's side, my struggles useless.

Carden reached Aldwyn, pulling him backwards from the Gymph and staggering it with a strong pommel blow. The creature fell as the two men dived away, the rubble slamming down on several Scourge, crushing them.

The Gathlork Field Commander pulled away, watching on angrily as we escaped the collapsing tower, snarling viscously as he watched the scene. His roar of rage echoed around the ruined compound, the other Gathlorks and Orcs following him and howling into the smoke choked night air.

Carden and Aldwyn joined us, the elder now badly hurt. Fawkner hooked the Mage's arm around his shoulders, helping Carden to carry him as they rushed towards the wall.

Mithras dragged me through the breach as Ellora covered us, giving us the chance to run.

In the few seconds I had, I looked up through the blazing fires and dust to see the Shadow Lord watching on again just as he had at Arvon. He smirked coldly as I turned away, disappearing into the mountain forest and the night with my friends.

We were out of the compound, but we weren't safe yet...

Chapter Twenty-Two
Mountain Falls

The horrific roaring of the Scourge echoed through the mountains, the beasts' heavy footfalls thundering enough to shake the peaks themselves. The flames of torches violated the safety of the night, the monsters hunting us with relentless ferocity. The sound of the brutes breaking through the forest was like some machine of destruction crushing the rocks and trees. Nothing would survive.

We ran as fast as we could, Mithras leading the way as Carden and Fawkner carried Aldwyn. Ellora and Tallinn still covered our escape, turning their bows back as Hurgarks and Orcs caught up to us. They slung arrows into our enemies, dropping them without hesitation, but more followed.

I stumbled in the middle of the group, clutching Amethyst to my chest tightly. I felt her squirming in my arms, frightened squawks escaping her tiny jaws as she cuddled into me.

The Dwarves were amazingly fast on their feet despite their stunted heights and heavy clothes. They sprinted behind me, looking over their shoulders at the two women bringing up the rear. Knowing that danger was flanking us, the two then moved to escort me, running on either side of me and hurrying to keep up with my pace.

Joran was ahead of the three of us, his massive legs allowing him to stride forward to where a shape was now looming through the dark trees. An Erk launched itself forward, roaring like a mountain lion, its oversized hands reaching for me. I screamed, staggering backwards as both Dwarves yelped in shock, but Joran didn't hesitate.

He met the beast head on, slamming his fists into its palms and forcing it back, standing taller by one foot, roaring at it viciously. The Erk snapped at him with its gargantuan jaws, unable to get a good hold on him.

"Varedarak, Hessiik!" the Storvari cursed, his violet eyes blazing into the black eyes of the monster.

The Erk roared angrily into his face, Joran slamming it to the ground, grasping the edges of its jaw and twisting with his powerful forearms. There was a bone shattering crushing sound and the monster fell dead.

I turned my gaze to the Storvari, who simply said in his deep voice: "Come, Sarissi. We must move."

I did as he instructed, jumping up from the ground and running through the forests with him. Now I fully understood what it meant to be a Storvari's Sarissi, and it was something I was extremely grateful for.

Every turn brought us closer to a new enemy, every path bringing us to a battle. Without the day to illuminate our sights there was no way of telling how many beasts hunted us.

We came to a small ditch, hiding as a troop of Orcs and Hurgarks rushed past us led by several Gathlorks. They were following what they believed to be the path we had taken, which thankfully lead them away from us.

"We cannot keep this up forever," Ellora noted breathlessly. "They will surely find us eventually."

"We need a new place to go," Tallinn agreed as she crouched at the edge of the ditch, "a safe house of some kind."

"I thought the Citadel was supposed to be such a place," Fawkner commented grimly. "Where else could we go?"

"There is a monastery on the Calian Passage," Mithras recalled, crouching close to me, one hand on my shoulder as he spoke. "It is not far from where we now stand."

"How far is it?" Carden asked with urgency.

"An hour, maybe two," Mithras responded. "We could easily make it."

"The Void with that!" Holger shouted, brandishing his hammer. "Let's just fight the bastards!"

"No," Dolin shook his head. "We cannot win. We must run, brother."

Ellora turned her sharp eyes to me. "What do you say, Princess?"

I looked at the faces before me, my concern growing as I saw Aldwyn's worsening condition. He was no longer conscious, drooping in the arms of his supporters.

"Can Aldwyn survive if we don't?" I asked.

Tallinn shook her head gravely: "Not from these wounds. We need to seek assistance. The monastery *is* our best option."

I nodded and turned to Mithras: "Then we go to the monastery."

"Very well," Mithras looked to Joran urgently. "Joran, carry Aldwyn and the dragonling; we need to move swiftly."

"As you wish, Knight," the Storvari responded, moving to crouch over Aldwyn, Carden and Fawkner.

I carried Amethyst to the giant as he picked Aldwyn's limp body up in his arms. She obediently leaped onto the Mage's stomach, gurgling at me with a frightened stare. I tried to look reassuring, but it was hard with the monsters chasing us so relentlessly.

Mithras got to his feet and moved to the edge of the ditch, looking up with his sword at the ready. He made sure the way was clear, then nodded to the rest of us. He was over the edge in a moment and sprinting through the trees, cloak and surcoat rushing around him like blue fire.

I ran as fast as I could with Carden at my side, not looking back as I pushed myself forward. I could hear the monsters hunting us crashing through the trees, new, frantic barks indicating that they had caught our scent.

Carden grabbed my arm, dragging me with him as Tallinn and Ellora loosed a barrage of arrows into the trees, killing a few more enemies. I grabbed my skirt hems so I wouldn't trip, half leaping through the snow as I went.

Carden and I ran as fast as we could, separating from the group. We had to split up to keep the monsters confused. So, he led me to Mithras' side, the three of us sprinting along the snowy paths twisting through the mountains.

After a while we managed to reach a bridge passing over a ravine between the Nartarn'lath and Calian Mountains. Below ran the Great River Arvon, snaking through the mountains from Lorveren into Aldegaad.

I stepped onto the bridge as the others began to join us, standing at the edge and looking down. The depth below frightened me, falling from the bridge a certain death. I didn't want that to happen.

I turned my gaze to the way ahead, the wind casting blinding snow into my vision. The bridge reached some twenty to thirty meters to the other cliffs, a long path from one side to the other. Despite the bridge's stable construction, I was certain that I could feel the stone shaking in the high winds.

"Where are the others?!" Tallinn cried as she reached the bridge with Ellora and the Dwarves.

"They haven't reached us yet!" Carden responded, shouting over the howling wind passing through the peaks towering above us.

"They must hurry!" Mithras called from where he stood as I rushed to his side. "We must cross the bridge into the Calian Mountains before the Scourge reaches us!"

"Even though, once we pass the bridge," Carden indicated, gesturing to the structure and squinting against the heavy blizzard, "there is no way to stop those monsters from pursuing us! They can cross too!"

"Then how do we stop them?!" Tallinn asked.

"We destroy the bridge!" Ellora answered. "We get the Storvari to cross and have him bring it down!"

"That's insane!" I shouted, my hair blowing violently across my face.

"It is our only chance!" the Elf responded evenly, shouting against the howling wind coming off the ravine.

"Then we'd best ensure our allies their path!" Mithras was looking to the trees ahead.

I followed his line of sight to see the bulking silhouette of Joran crashing through the trees with Fawkner sprinting beside him. Arrows shot past them and slammed into the stone of the bridge at our feet, causing us to step back. I stumbled quickly, looking up as Ellora and Tallinn took up their bows again.

Orcs, Hurgarks and Gathlorks stood in the trees firing arrows from bows and bolts from crossbows. They weren't only aiming for the retreating giant – since he was the biggest target – but also for the space between the lamps of the bridge.

"Cover them!" Mithras shouted to the archers. "The rest of you begin the crossing!"

I took my bow from my shoulder and strung an arrow to it, firing into the trees as I began backing away. A warning look flashed at Mithras silenced him and I did what I knew I had to, three bows increasing our chances of success more than two. I needed only to aim for the monsters, the knowledge that my fire couldn't harm my allies a great comfort. I wasn't sure that I was hitting anything, but I could hear the monsters' yelps as they were struck by arrows, allowing my friends a clear space to safety.

Joran and Fawkner sprinted between Tallinn and Ellora, rushing over the bridge, the two women turning and running after them. I followed their lead and ran ahead of them, abandoning my defensive fire and sprinting to safety.

I skidded to a halt on the other side, standing between Mithras and Carden, the Dwarves moving in front of me defensively, ready with their weapons. I could see the Scourge rushing from the forest, swarming down the slopes to the bridge, the faster of them already setting foot on stone and making for my fleeing companions.

To my relief the others were across in only a few seconds, Mithras rushing to Joran.

"Destroy the bridge!" the Knight shouted to him. "Quickly, before they cross!"

Joran nodded, setting Aldwyn down in the snow gently. The Storvari then turned his purple eyes back to the Scourge charging over the bridge and took his dual blades from across his back. He rushed forward past me so fast that I felt a cross draft moving against the wind itself.

In one heavy movement, the eight-foot man swung one blade and severed the first of the bridge cables, then turned and cleaved the second from its mount with both blades. He stowed the swords across his back again, reaching for a large boulder that rested nearby. With all his might, Joran heaved the boulder from the ground and cast it high into the air. It slammed into the bridge and a large group of Scourge, crushing bones and stone. The bridge buckled under the weight as the giant hurled another boulder with equal thrust, plunging it through the weakening structure.

There was an awful groaning and crunching, the bridge seeming to heave into the air as if breathing its last. Then, it bowed in the middle and came apart, the stones dropping and hurling the monsters screaming into the ravine below.

I staggered as I lost my footing, the stones under my feet giving way. I felt a pair of hands grasp me swiftly and pull me away just as the bridge crumbled from the mountainside. I turned my eyes to my rescuer, glad to see Fawkner's scarred and concerned face looking down at me. The man cuddled me close to him, pulling me from peril as the bridge shattered on the rocks and riverbanks below with all the monsters that had stood upon it.

Clutched in Fawkner's firm embrace, I looked across the ravine to the far side of the ruined bridge. The howls of the remaining monsters on the other cliffs echoed against the mountains, their sinister silhouettes violently shaking weapons and shields.

"It seems that we're safe now," Dolin breathed a relieved sigh, leaning on his axe, exhausted.

"At least the Scourge cannot pursue us any farther," Ellora agreed, standing beside him and his brother, out of breath.

Mithras looked exhausted as he stood there, bowing his head. He allowed himself a small smile, something only I noticed as I watched him.

"Mithras!" Tallinn called as coughs echoed around us.

I turned in time with Mithras to see Carden and Tallinn crouching beside Aldwyn in the snow. The Mage was pale and sickly, coughing up blood as his wounds seeped profusely. His eyes were sunken now and he looked as if he wouldn't live much longer.

"Aldwyn's heart grows weaker," she looked to the Knight with fear. "We must get him to this monastery quickly."

"Yes," Mithras nodded, pulling what little strength remained in him to his limbs. "It is not far."

Mithras began to lead the way as I looked around frantically for Amethyst. A small croaking caw caught my attention and I saw the dragonling sitting in the snow as comfortably as a puppy would before a fireplace.

She cocked her head to one side, cooing as I drew my hood and reached down to pick her up.

I cast my eyes back towards the far side of the ravine as I cuddled her to my chest, the monsters slowly vanishing into the forests again. Only a lone black robed figure stood on the remaining pieces of the bridge, his cowl and cloak billowing to his right in the wind.

I stared at the Shadow Lord, feeling his untiring gaze burning through me angrily.

He's not finished with me. He never will be.

I sighed grimly, dreading what would come next and what would be thrown at me by that monster as I watched him once again fade away like black smoke in the winter winds.

Fawkner wrapped his cloak around both of us, startling me from my ruminations. He smiled to me gently, giving me a new sense of trust in him.

Holding Amethyst tight, I walked with him as we followed the others, leaving the ruins of the bridge behind.

* * * * *

The way was slow and painful, what would have taken us two hours taking twice as long with our injured companion. Carden and Tallinn supported his weight across their shoulders, struggling as they trudged through the deepening snow on the stone path. They refused to let him fall, fighting against the harsh winds and the blistering cold to get him to safety.

Mithras led the way with Joran, the giant easily striding ahead of us, his stronger eyes able to guide us as Mithras directed him.

Soon enough we came into sight of torch lights on a cliff face high above as the rushing thunder of waterfalls called through the winds. The shape of a second bridge could be seen as we followed the path, crossing over the falls where they dropped repeatedly towards the valley below. The path then curved up the mountain side and back around towards the falls, the shape of a compound appearing before us. Stone walls greeted us as figures moved over the battlements, the so-called monastery seeming more like a fortress.

We passed beyond the main gates and into a winter garden courtyard, the main wooden and stone structure of the monastery standing before us. The large doors opened, and warm light shone out over the courtyard, bathing us in its comforting brilliance and welcoming us in. Several dark robed figures approached, hoods drawn over their faces, their attentions locked squarely on our group.

"Brothers and sisters of the Mountain Falls Monastery," Mithras addressed them respectfully, nodding his head. "Forgive the intrusion, but we require your aid."

"You are travellers," one of the brothers, an older man with greying hair observed, surveying our group carefully. "Travellers who have seen great hardships."

"We do not ask for charity, Brother," Mithras held up his right hand, showing the man the signet ring, he always wore.

I remembered when I was a child how I used to stare at it, marvelling at the gold engraving of a dragon in its black circle on the gold band. I had always wondered why he carried this but had never had the courage to ask.

"Blink not, for you shall miss them," Mithras invoked to the monk with a sense of purpose. "Fear not, for you are guarded by them."

The monk's eyes widened, and he responded: "Come, Knight, we stand the same. Be welcomed in the warmth of their eternal flame."

I frowned, confused by this strange greeting. I glanced from beneath my hood between the two men, noting the expressions on the other monks' faces.

"You are welcome here, Dragon Knight," the monk assured Mithras openly, "as are your companions. But, you are also a Knight of Aldegaad. Yes?"

"I am Ser Mithras," my protector responded, "Knight-Commander of Arvon's contingent; but I am first and foremost a Knight of Draconia."

"It is alright, Percival," an older voice called as a figure approached from the doors. "I know this man."

The monks – who I now realised were actually knights in disguise – stepped aside, allowing the man to come forward. He was dressed in black, blue and gold robes over his gold armour, a black and gold cloak swirling behind him. He had short white hair, bright blue eyes and a stern, yet friendly face.

Mithras bowed his head respectfully to the man, clearly his superior. He then smiled warmly and reached out his right hand, the other knight mirroring him, the two embracing each other's forearms respectfully.

"It is good to see you, old friend," the Knight smiled at Mithras warmly.

"And you," Mithras replied.

"I feared for your safety, Mithras," the Knight admitted to him. "News of Arvon's fall has travelled far, and we are greatly disturbed by the rumours of a new Shadow Lord arising in High-Realm."

"The news is grave indeed," Mithras agreed grimly, "and it appears to be all true."

"Are the family all dead as the rumours say?" the Knight asked gravely.

"No, Grand Master," Mithras shook his head solemnly. "Princess Aislinn was still in Balganis when last we heard. Her sister travels under my protection."

"I would see this girl," the Grand Master said.

Mithras turned to me, beckoning me forward.

I moved slowly, Fawkner staying guarded at my side, clearly suspicious of these monks. I cradled Amethyst tightly, refusing to reveal her until I knew for sure that we were safe. I looked out from under my hood, my face now clear to the man's bright eyes as he studied me.

"Princess Leander," he bowed his head reverently and straightened up. "I am Ser Callenhad, Grand Master of the Knights of Draconia. It is an honour to receive you here in Mountain Falls Keep."

"Keep?" I frowned. "Mithras said that this was a monastery."

"So it appears," Callenhad answered me gently. "It was always decided that the Order of Draconia would appear to be a religious sect that worships the Eldest Ones and the goddess Ankorect. But this can be discussed at a later time. You are all in need of rest and shelter."

"Our friend is hurt," I told him, indicating Aldwyn as Carden and Tallinn held him up.

Callenhad nodded and turned to one of the knights posing as a monk: "He will get the attention he needs," he directed him with a wave of his hand.

<hr>

The young knight pushed back his hood and beckoned to Tallinn and Carden to follow. The two Guardians carried Aldwyn through the doors, following the Knight into the apparent monastery, disappearing from sight.

I watched them worriedly, unaware that I was no longer hiding as well as I had chosen to. I was too distracted by my concern for Aldwyn, the Grand Master's eyes turning from my face to the necklace hanging about my neck. I turned back to catch his staring gaze, my own eyes following his to the Pendant. Unease filled me and I stared at him nervously.

"It cannot be," Callenhad gasped. "Is that one of the Draconian Hearts?"

I frowned. "Huh? What?"

"The Pendant around your neck, Princess," he clarified with a sense of urgency. "It is yours?"

I nodded. "Since my last name day. It was a gift from my uncle."

Callenhad then noticed the movement under my cloak, both of us looking down as Amethyst poked her tiny head out from beneath the folds. The knights gasped in awe as they saw the infant in my arms.

"You also carry an Eldest One Hatchling," Callenhad looked to me in amazement. "This... is astonishing," he straightened up, looking to Mithras, then back to me. "Follow me."

He turned and strode back inside. I began following uncertainly with Mithras at my side, not really knowing what to think of all of this.

We entered the monastery with the others at our heels, the knights closing the doors and sealing us inside the main hall. It was here that Callenhad turned to me once again, very calm, though clearly perturbed.

"We will give you safe harbour in which to rest as long as you and your companions need it," he told me evenly. "You are under our protection now, Princess, and I must ask that you not leave the keep. Rooms will be prepared for you and your companions."

"Thank you," I said gratefully, though uneasily.

Callenhad turned to Mithras. "A word if I may, my Brother Knight."

Mithras nodded and followed, leaving me standing there with Fawkner, Joran, Ellora and the Dwarves.

"A strange reaction to your pendant and dragon," Fawkner noted in a murmur so only I could hear him.

It was an observation that I had already noticed myself, one that left me deeply uneasy. But at least, for the moment, we were away from the Scourge and safe inside from the blizzards. I just couldn't help but wonder if that safety would last long.

Chapter Twenty-Three
The Knights' Charge

I was taken from the main hall by a knight and brought to a rather palatial room, leaving my companions behind. I frowned at its grandeur, telling the Knight that it wasn't necessary for me to be treated with such prestige. The Knight simply commented that I was their most honoured guest, then left me.

I shrugged out of my cloak, glad to be free of the wintry chill of the mountains and back in the warmth of an actual bedroom. I slipped out of my overdress then took to the basin, filling it from the spigot and washing my face with warm water. I turned my blue eyes to the mirror, studying the brown flecks that dotted my irises, distracting myself for a short time.

I wasn't at ease as I stood there, wondering about the knights, confused by their sudden desire to separate me from my friends. This was worrying as only Amethyst was still with me, the dragonling hungrily gnawing on a large boar bone they had given her in the corner, stripping it of all its flesh. I had never seen the small creature eat so much.

The Pendant caught my eye, drawing me to gaze down at it. The more I thought about it, the more I realised that it made perfect sense for the Order of Draconia to know about the Pendant. Its presence around my neck and the fact that I carried a newly born dragonling made the truth obvious to any who knew the legends.

The Pendant could be a very dangerous thing to carry, but I can't discard it either. That would be a stupid thing to do.

I sighed and looked to Amethyst from the mirror, a little frustrated by everything. "Is this as unsettling for you as it is for me?"

Amethyst looked up from her meal, pausing only to coo softly, her hands clawing into the bone. She turned back to the meat, wrenching another piece away and gulping it down hungrily.

I sighed, crossing to the bed and sitting down as I slid my boots off.

"I wish you could understand me, Amethyst," I said, more to myself than to her. "I wish you could talk. You might know more about all of this than I do."

Slowly, I dropped under the covers of the large bed, grateful for the heavy fur blankets and rested my head on the pillows. I lay there for a short time, watching the dragonling eat her food, then slowly faded away from the world, disappearing into a deep, sound sleep.

I dreamed, lost in a strange world that made no sense. At first it was just unusual images that weren't frightening and barely worth remembering. Then they became progressively more realistic.

I found myself in the walkways of Castle Arvon, making my way to the gardens. The sun shone through the arches and windows brightly, a warm, sunny day outside. I felt safe, finding myself at a happier time in my life.

I came to the memorial chamber, the marble columns standing strong beside the proud statues of helmeted knights encircling the room's edge. My eyes fell on the murals over the far walls, all exactly as I remembered them, the great battles painted there echoing soundlessly in the past.

I turned to the statue in the centre of the room, beholding my ancestor once again. I studied the face more closely now, finding a new feeling there in her likeness. I could see how much like my ancestor I was, a sense of pride seeming to touch me gently. My eyes fell on the Pendant hanging around her neck, a stone replica of my own. Now it all seemed to make sense.

I watched as the stone in the heart of the statue's pendant shimmered with purple light, which grew brighter with every moment. It engulfed me and left me lost in its brilliance...

I woke to the sound of someone knocking at the door as I lay there in bed, one arm up under the pillow, the other across my stomach. I was a little confused by my surroundings, a feeling that had become all too common for me of late.

This only lasted a few moments and I was able to speak: "Come in."

The door opened slowly, Mithras entering wearing the same cloak and robe over his own version of the gold armour that Callenhad wore the night before. He turned his gaze to me, smiling as he saw me laying there.

"Still in bed at this hour?" he shook his head, smirking at me. "I've never known you to be capable of such sloth, my girl."

"What time is it?" I asked.

"Past noon," was his answer. "You obviously needed the rest."

I nodded, propping myself up in a sitting position. "I haven't slept so well since we left Arvon."

"I am glad," Mithras smiled, standing over my bed, his arms crossed. "Do you feel able to meet with Callenhad and the Council today?"

I shrugged as I hugged one of my knees through the covers, my hair hanging a little messily around my bare shoulders, this place letting me finally feel like an ordinary girl again.

"I suppose," I answered. "Has this got something to do with my pendant?"

Mithras nodded evenly: "It does."

I sighed and looked down at the foot of the bed. I felt very uneasy about that knowledge, not certain how to proceed from there.

"Do not be afraid," he told me gently, sitting on the end of the bed and smiling as I looked to him through my hair. "You are in no danger here. You're safe."

"To be honest," I said, feeling a lot older than I really was," I'm not sure anywhere is safe for me now."

"I promise you," he placed a hand on my back, rubbing it gently, "that the Shadow Lord cannot harm you here."

I felt as if I were about to cry.

"I keep seeing him," I whispered. "Every time something horrible happens, in my dreams... even with my waking eyes... I see him."

He frowned, worry painting his face. "When did you last see him?"

"Last night when Joran destroyed the bridge. He was standing on the other side, staring at me," I took in a hard, shaking breath. "And he spoke to me... be... before the attack at the Citadel. He was there, Mithras..."

Mithras was silent for a few moments, mentally chewing on my confession. I watched him, fear creeping through me and entering every pore I had. It was seeping out of me as sweat would, coating me in its film and overwhelming my skin. There was no way to escape it, as inevitable a thing as my own breath.

"We will address this with the Council then," he decided. "Callenhad and the others may know what to do."

I said nothing, simply nodding my head as I remained where I sat. He stood and turned to me, his eyes locking onto my concerned expression instantly.

"You should dress," he advised me. "And bring Amethyst. The other knights wish to see her just as they wish to see you."

I nodded and looked up from the covers I had been staring at: "Where is she?"

There came a caw from the edge of the bed, this time louder and deeper. I turned my eyes there as a purple shape leaped up onto the bed, shaking it heavily. I found myself facing Amethyst, but not as she had been the night before.

The dragonling had grown overnight, no longer as small as a kitten, but now as large as a tall hunting dog. Her cranial horns were no longer stubs, having grown about half their previous size, the smallest horn set between the two that ran parallel from the back of her skull. The smaller horns at the back of her jaw had sprouted out and had obvious webbing now, just as her wings were larger and well developed.

Her legs were thinner than before and her body a little sleeker, though the baby fat was still evident. Her tail seemed longer and a feathery barb had begun forming, coloured with a shade of blue and violet. Her back scales were stronger looking and larger, and her talons were beginning to curve. Finally, her snout had grown, the small horn at its tip beginning to lengthen.

Amethyst barked at me happily, sitting there on her hind legs, forehands curled up at her silvery-mauve chest. She craned her neck, which had become longer, her molten orange eyes brighter as she looked at me.

"She grew overnight," I gasped. "How?"

"Rapid metabolism and a speedy gestation," was Mithras' answer. "When Pendant linked dragons eat a great deal, they grow faster. Once this first change occurs the dragon will then grow very quickly."

"How quickly?" I asked, looking up at him from the small dragon.

"She'll be fully grown in a little over a year," he responded. "She won't breathe fire until her fourth year, however."

"How big will she get?"

"A little over the size of a horse in another three months, twice that size after that," he explained knowledgeably. "Amethian Dragons are one of the smaller breeds."

"So, she won't be a hundred feet tall?"

He shook his head. "No. About... oh... say... thirteen feet or so."

I turned back to Amethyst, smiling. "This is amazing."

"Enough distractions," the old knight ordered me, heading for the door. "Dress and bring her. We'll go to the main hall together."

I nodded. "Alright."

* * * * *

Once I had donned my clothes and boots, I brushed my hair, then took Amethyst and went to the corridor where Mithras waited. The three of us made our way together, Amethyst walking beside me, too big to be carried now.

We entered the main hall's high-ceilinged structure, a fireplace inviting us in. We were greeted by a pair of gold armoured knights who then escorted us through another corridor to a set of heavy wooden doors. They opened them and allowed us in as they stared at my dragon with wonder.

There was a polished round table in the centre of the circular room made from a dozen smaller curved tables, a large gap left in the middle. A fire burned in the centre of a large brazier on a metal stand in the gap, torches glimmering all around the room on columns that separated the knights' flags. The flags were a black colour with gold and silver lining, the likeness of a dragon set there, very similar to the Aldegaadian motif.

Some two dozen chairs were set around the table, the majority of them hosting a gold armoured knight, but several were left empty. Each knight had laid his or her sword on the table, displaying it with honour.

I noticed then that the Knights, unlike the Guardians, were all humans, not one among them from the Dwarves, Elves or Orcs. That surprised me.

Callenhad stood at the side opposite the door we had entered, smiling as he saw us. Mithras stayed at my side, guiding me to a seat where I then stood, Amethyst cocking her head curiously.

Mithras took the seat to my left, flashing me a comforting smile. It wasn't enough to ease me however, and I found myself growing more apprehensive with each passing moment.

"Brothers and Sisters of Draconia," Callenhad raised his hands, addressing the other knights in the room. "Let us speak our oath to the Eldest Ones as laid out in centuries past."

All the knights – including Mithras and Callenhad – then spoke in unison: "To serve those who came before. To hold true to the teachings they bestowed. To guard them as they guard us; to see them not as gods, but as creatures of flesh and bone. To believe in their hearts, to honour their might, so we stand, Protectors of the Eldest Ones for all time."

Callenhad lowered his hands as he nodded to all gathered there. "Be seated."

The Knights moved and took their seats as I looked to Mithras for guidance. He placed a hand on my shoulder, having me seat myself before he did the same. I felt all eyes on me as a knight pulled the chair beside me out, Amethyst leaping up to perch there with a sense of awareness I hadn't seen in her before.

"Princess Leander," Callenhad addressed me clearly, but kindly. "No doubt you wonder why we have summoned you here."

I nodded, not sure what to say. I knew my unease was obvious, all of the knights seeing it clearly.

"Do not fear, girl," Callenhad advised me. "You are safe here in our halls."

"Forgive me, Ser Callenhad," I disagreed respectfully," but I don't really believe that I am. Everywhere my companions and I have travelled we have been attacked by demons and monsters, at times, even men of my own country. I just don't see how you can guarantee my safety."

"Mountain Falls Keep is guarded by powerful warding magic," Ser Callenhad explained. "No omniscient sight may fall upon it or the mountains surrounding it. You have no need to fear Shade Seekers entering these walls."

"You know about them?" I was surprised.

"Ser Mithras informed us of the events that led to your journey here," a dark-haired woman spoke. "We are aware of the number of unnatural creatures that you and your party have faced in recent months."

"It is troubling," a blonde-haired man spoke from where he sat, his hands resting on the table before him. "The re-emergence of the Scourge and the Undead Legions is a dire thing. They have not been seen in some five hundred years."

"Then the rumours of another Shadow Lord rising must be true," Ser Percival sounded worried. "This could mean another Age of Shadows... or worse."

"There is little to concern ourselves with right now," Callenhad said, silently calling for them to settle. "These *are* ill omens, however, we *must* be certain that such a thing has come to be."

"With respects," Mithras spoke up calmly and clearly, "but it appears this fear of ours *is* a reality."

"You have proof, Mithras?" Callenhad asked.

To my dismay, Mithras looked to me: "The Princess only just now brought to my attention the Shadow Lord's appearance to her in both dreams and waking sight. It seems that he has attempted to make contact beyond his failed abduction of her several months past."

There was a sudden cacophony of fearful and angry discussion among the knights. I cringed at their agitation, worried about the conversations erupting all around me. I could see the outrage on their faces as their fears were now confirmed.

"Silence!" Callenhad boomed, the room falling quiet once again. He spoke with a calm voice, his hands clasped in front of him as he leaned forward on the table, his blue eyes piercing and intense: "We must not get ahead of ourselves. The Princess has merely confirmed what we all suspected," with a more sympathetic gaze, he turned and faced me: "Tell me, child, what did this man look like?"

Seeing that I had no way of escaping this, I sighed and nodded to myself. *Tell them. You have to.*

I chose my words slowly: "He...he was very tall, and dressed in black, grey and crimson robes beneath a black hood. His hands were long and slender, his face... was like a monster's."

"Describe it," Callenhad urged.

I shrugged and shook my head, the fear showing ardently in my eyes as cold rippled through my body. I felt tears trying to break free as I tried to bring the memory of his sinister features to description.

"It was sunken and sallow," I answered, a cold dread flowing through me. "His skin was a horrible grey colour, his nose more like gashes in his flesh, his lips thin and hiding pointed teeth. There were strange, bony ridges on his forehead, and he looked more like a demonic corpse than a human being." I paused, staring blankly, my breathing shallow and heaving: "And his eyes... They were set back in deep sockets, the skin around them blackened as if it had been burned. And they glowed at the centre with an eerie green light like demonic flame. I've never seen anything so terrifying," I trembled, my breath shaking, my eyes burning.

"Was there anything else you can recall about him?" Callenhad asked gently, the other knights listening intently.

I thought for a moment, frowning as I concentrated. *There's something, but what? I can't remember...*

I shook my head and sighed. "I'm sorry, but that's all I remember of him. I don't really want to think about him anymore, if that's alright."

"Of course," Callenhad nodded understandingly.

"Why is he after me?" I asked, wanting an answer to this all-consuming mystery that was still pursuing me.

"We cannot be certain," Callenhad responded evenly, sitting back in his seat. "Until this Shadow Lord openly reveals himself there is no way to determine his motives or his designs for you."

"Did you learn his name, your Highness?" the dark-haired female knight asked softly.

I shook my head. "He never mentioned his name. He spoke of my ancestor a few times and he even noticed my pendant as well, but I don't recall him ever introducing himself. Our encounters weren't so... civil."

"It is a shame that he did not," Callenhad commented. "Such knowledge could have been of greater use. It is unfortunate that you do not have more information of use to the Order."

I sighed glumly. "Is that why you wanted to speak to me? Because I might have useful information?"

"You come before us with the Pendant carried by your ancestor and with firsthand knowledge of our enemy," he explained severely. "Under normal circumstances we would have taken the Pendant from you and placed it under guard. However, it has called a dragon-child to you as your kindred companion and bonded with you itself. The Pendant is yours and yours alone until your final breath."

"But why *me*?" I demanded, frustrated with all of this. "Why is this happening to *me*?"

"Because the Draconian Heart at the Pendant's centre chose you," was Callenhad's answer. "And as such, our Order is now sworn to protect you, both as the descendant of the last bearer to wield it, and as a bearer yourself."

"I don't understand," I murmured, staring at him grimly with growing agitation. "*Why* did it choose me?"

"You obviously have some connection to this Shadow Lord," he told me bluntly, "a foe that you will one day have to face. To whatever end."

I stared at him with anger and bewilderment. I couldn't believe what I was hearing.

"You're telling me that you think I'm like my ancestor?" I spoke harshly.

Callenhad nodded. "Yes. It is very likely. And if that is so, you must embrace this as your destiny and be what you are expected to be: a Pendant Bearer and hero."

I stood up abruptly, staring across the table at him angrily, though I knew that it was the only way to hide and resist my near paralysing fear.

"You're wrong," I insisted, my chest heaving as my upset grew. "I may hold a pendant but I am no hero."

"You have been called by a Dragon Pendant, Princess Leander," Callenhad informed me sternly. "This is not something you can merely turn from through choice. You, like your ancestor, have a destined purpose in this conflict and *must* embrace it."

"I'm not like her," I said softly, then loudly added with rage: "I am *nothing* like her!"

I turned and hurried from the room, leaving them behind angrily. As I broke into a slow run, I heard chairs scrapping back against the floor and the murmurs of the people behind me.

"Leander!" Mithras called out to me, but I refused to turn. "Leander, come back!"

I heard Callenhad gently say: "Let her be, Mithras. Let her be."

I ran from the meeting room and through the corridors towards a set of doors, rushing out onto one of the balconies of the keep's wooden and stone structures. I slammed my hands to the wooden railing, my hair and my gown's sleeves and skirts swirling behind me with my angry movements.

I stood there, resting against the railing, fighting the urge to cry, my anger so great that it burned inside me. I let the cold mountain air wash over me, trying to give in to the cooling effect, hoping my anger and fear would fade away with it. The thoughts of my ancestor, the Shadow Lord, and this situation plagued me violently. I hated it, hated the journey that had been forced on me, hated everything that had happened to me, especially the knights' belief that I had a destined calling in all of this. It made me sick, my mouth feeling dry with the thought's taint.

I'm not like her... I'm not anything like what they want me to be... I'm not...

Slowly, I took in deep, soothing breaths of fresh air, opening my eyes as I calmed down. The azure sky was clear except for a few fluffy white clouds. I wanted to be like that sky, free of anything dark and cold, only clear and bright. But the truth weighed on me and such thoughts faded quickly.

I rested my hands there clasped together, staring at my thumbs grimly. That was when I noticed something past my hands in the gardens below me, my attentions drawn inexorably towards it. There was a strange stone structure, the archway clear, the doors open with the statue of a guardian angel watching over it, a blue flame flickering in a bowl held in its hands. I grew curious, moving across the balcony and making my way down the stone steps into the garden.

Cautiously, I entered the archway, making my way down the steps and into a circular chamber. I let my eyes scan the room automatically, taking in its dull grey interior. There were marble columns reaching up to the ceiling, proud knight statues similar to the ones in the memorial chamber in Arvon set between them.

My eyes fell on the shape in the centre of the room flanked by continuously burning bowl torches. At the feet of the statue of an Amethian

Dragon was a tomb, the stone carving of a body resting over the remains that surely lay on the slab beneath.

Hesitantly, reverently, I edged towards it, standing there and looking down at the face of a woman, beautiful in her advanced years, her long hair splayed out behind her head and shoulders. She lay there wrapped in an elegant, but simple gown and over robe, her hands together resting on her abdomen. A sword was laid out across her legs, its point to her feet, its pommel pressed into her palms.

I stared at her in wonder, drawn to this woman like no other person I had ever been drawn to. I studied the familiar features, turning my eyes to the inscription on the tablet in the dragon's clawed hands.

It read:

Here lies Leander Idona Aldrich, the Great Heroine of High-Realm, Last Princess of Graphtar, First Queen of Aldegaad. Let her rest eternally in the gods' loving embrace.

I stood there staring in astonishment at the face before me. I had found the resting place of my ancestor; a place lost to the world since she had been moved centuries ago from Arvon.

"It really is you. Isn't it?" I murmured, not expecting a response as I stared at her.

I sighed, feeling tears run down my cheeks as I studied her features, looking away for a few moments to try to compose myself. Rage and hurt rose in me and I glared back at the stone face.

"It's all because of you," I grumbled sadly, glaring as I leaned my hands on the edges of the slate. "I was named for you, I look exactly like you... I even carry *your* pendant. Is it any wonder people expect me to be just like you?"

I studied her stone features again, closing my eyes for a moment as my rage and hurt built inside until they exploded out of me.

"Nothing is mine!" I shouted angrily. "Everything about me is about you! I'm sick of it! I'm sick of living in your shadow!" I shook my head sadly, crying: "My name isn't even mine. It's yours, and because of that everyone expects me to be like you. But *I'm* not..."

I sighed, sitting down on my knees at the side of the tomb, the cold floor barely registering to me.

"I'm not," I said quietly, staring at my hands. "I've never been like the rest of my family. I didn't like hearing your story every day. I wasn't proud; I just hated you for so many expectations being put on me."

I looked up at the tomb sadly.

"I used to dream about having an adventure," I said in a calmer, but sadder voice, tears flowing hard now. "The stories about your life made me want more than debutant balls and days in the royal court. I wanted to explore the world, or at least more of Aldegaad," then I laughed faintly to myself: "I've done all of that, but not the way I'd hoped. I didn't want to lose my mother and father or my home. I didn't want monsters to be real. Now there's a Shadow Lord chasing me, some of our own nobility are trying to kill me, and all I can do," I locked my eyes on the stone face, "is blame *you*."

I looked down at my hands in my lap, my chest shuddering with my sobbing breaths.

I sighed sadly, feeling the heat fading from my tears as they slid down my cheeks. "I know it's not really your fault, but I don't want your life... I want my own."

"So did she," a voice said softly.

I looked up to see Ellora in the doorway, the Elf's eyes locked on the tomb as she entered the room. I didn't stand as she approached, her eyes gazing down at the stone face with loving respect.

"Leander never wanted to be a warrior," Ellora recalled, her hands clasped in front of her. "She did not wish to be a princess or a queen, either. She was a simple girl from a mountain town. I think that is what the stories often forget. They speak so much of her heroism against the Scourge, Lord Morod and the Shadow Lords; of how she killed the Darkest Shadow and ended the Age of Shadows, but so few tell the truth of who *she* really was: a very sensitive girl who was not as headstrong and battle hardened as they describe."

I sniffed against my sobs quietly, listening to her gentle words. Her love for my ancestor was clear.

She smiled reminiscently at the tomb: "She was so quiet, always looking to others to lead. She was so afraid of what was to come, so sure that there was no way to survive. Then she and Jaryn Hatch fell in love, and he gave her the strength she needed. He was there with her in that final battle, the only one of us to follow her into Gorth'lak to face the Darkest Shadow. I believe it was their love that brought them through the nightmare of that day, *not* her skills as a warrior or an archer, or even her destiny as a great champion," Ellora turned to me and smiled: "She once dreamed of adventures too."

"Like me, right?" I grumbled, still sitting on the floor. "Because I am *so* like her..."

She shook her head. "No. In that you are *nothing* alike. She never once regretted the journeys she embarked upon. And unlike you, she did not know the pain of losing her parents, only the pain of never knowing them at all."

"She was stronger than me," I said sadly, feeling ashamed as my tears continued to flow. "I just want to run and hide. I'm a coward."

Ellora crouched down and pressed a hand to my face, drawing my eyes to meet hers. She regarded me with a nurturing gaze, running her hand across my forehead and brushing my auburn hair from my eyes.

"You are no coward, child," she told me softly. "A coward would not even seek aid, nor would they join into a battle while those protecting them tell them to hide. You are even braver than your ancestor, not because you are a warrior, but because you *are* you. Your name *is* yours. You only have the honour of being named for a woman who would now stand here if she were able and tell you how very proud she is of you."

"You don't know that," I murmured, staring into her turquoise eyes.

"I know she would have loved you very much," she responded, "and that she would have wanted to stand with you through this. You are so very strong, and you do not even see it."

"I'm... I'm just so scared," I admitted, trembling.

"I know you are," Ellora nodded, stroking my forehead the way a mother would. "And that is what makes you so much stronger than your ancestor in many ways. She was not as afraid as you, yet here you are, fighting to survive it. I admire you for that, Princess, as would she."

I felt calmer as I heard those words, turning my eyes back to the tomb and staring at my ancestor. I felt a sense of peace flow through me and I lost all the unreasonable hatred for her that had once been in my heart. I stared at her face and felt only love, knowing that my centuries' distant grandmother would have been proud of me, no matter what. It was strangely comforting to have that knowledge.

"I don't know what to do next, Ellora" I whispered through quiet tears.

She smiled at me, pulling me into a hug, stroking my hair and allowing me to just let out all of my fear and hurt on her armoured shoulder: "It is something you do not have to discover alone."

I closed my eyes and wept quietly, clinging to the woman firmly. I longed for my mother to be the one holding me, letting all of that grief join with all the fear that I felt and flow out of me in my soft, snivelling sobs. And for just a little while I was able to not think about what lay ahead, to not be focused on being strong, able to just let go.

As I sat there in the Elvish woman's arms, for once I was not a princess holding fast against the tide of responsibility and heritage, but just a normal girl being human.

Chapter Twenty-Four
Aneuran

I spent the next few days in deeply quiet reflection on my own, considering everything I had learned since my arrival at Mountain Falls. The only companion I permitted to stay by my side was Amethyst, the dragon moving beside my shins wherever I went. I was in no way ready to speak to either the knights or my friends, finding that the solitude of only my dragon and I was enough for now. My heart still hurt too much as it was.

I stood on the battlements overlooking the waterfalls, contemplating my path ahead. The sound of the thundering water was enough to help me ease the tension inside me as I considered all that I needed to. Resting my arms there on the stones of the wall, I watched the sun setting over the majesty of the Nartarn'lath and Calian Mountains. This view was enough to calm me, allowing me to take in the truest beauty of the world.

I felt strangely safe there in the mountains, almost as though there was no way I could ever be harmed. Perhaps it was the heights of the peaks, the inhospitality of the blizzards or the natural walls that offered such strong protection that made me feel that way. Either way my heart was at ease and my mind was no longer burdened with fear.

I turned my eyes from the golden-orange sunset and looked to Amethyst. She was curled up on the ground beside me, her snout resting on her scaled arms. She glanced up at me with those molten orange eyes, making no sound at all, seeming to understand me without words.

I turned my eyes back to the world around the stronghold and gazed out over its expanse. My sights spread from the mountains around me and towards the Coastlands in the south-west. Far in the distance I saw the shimmering gleam of Aneuran, a glistening jewel at the edge of the Crestian Sea. The wide expanse of the Knolling Plains and the deep greens of the many forests stood between the capital and the mountains, its many spires seeming like the tiniest of twigs from where I stood.

I thought of my uncle and the grief that must have plagued his mind. He had lost his brother and his sister-in-law, and he probably believed that I was dead too, especially if the conspirators arrayed against us were plotting as fervently as they seemed to be.

Suddenly, realisation rushed through me as these thoughts dived and swam through my mind. The faces of the Sewards and Baron Emerton emerged from my memories, along with the words Renton Seward had said to me in the Baron's residence.

"Aldegaad is ruled by a decrepit old man who is too afraid to do what must be done! Aric hides in his palace at Aneuran playing the part of a kind and just ruler, but he does not address the true threat that plagues this nation..."

"Uncle Aric..." I whispered in fear. "They're going to kill him!"

I turned and ran from where I stood, Amethyst leaping to her feet and following. The dragon and I rushed along the walkways and into the monastery keep, passing by the gold-plated knights on guard. We made for the main hall as quickly as we could, my feelings telling me that Amethyst had registered what I had.

I won't let them do this! I won't let those monsters hurt what's left of my family!

I slowed my pace as I reached the main hall, walking in past a knight as he left. My eyes surveyed the room where the knights were sitting down to their evening meal, my companions all gathered around a table together to one side near a fireplace.

Aldwyn looked much better, the knights' herbal medicines and healing magic clearly having helped. He was favouring his arm a little, but otherwise he seemed unhurt as he sat with Carden and Tallinn.

Fawkner sat beside Dolin, Farsight perched on his left arm as he fed her meat from his plate. Dolin was drinking a large mug of meed while Holger was gobbling down a big plate of salted pork greedily, snatching his own pint in between gulps.

Ellora was calm as she ate her meal, her movements graceful and delicate. Beside her, Mithras sat eating a little slower, preoccupied by something while Joran stood silently by one of the pillars, watching on stoically as always.

I approached my friends, Amethyst at my heels, instantly gaining their attention as I stopped by the table.

"Leander," Fawkner smiled, greeting me. "Come, join us."

I forced a smile to him then looked to Aldwyn: "You look better, Aldwyn."

"I feel much better, Your Highness," Aldwyn responded with a gentle smile. "The knights' healer works wonders with her herbs and spells."

I nodded. "I'm glad you're still with us."

Mithras studied my face, frowning as he saw my unease. "What is it that bothers you, Leander?" he asked.

"I've been thinking about what we should do next," I told them, hesitating slightly.

"We have you in a safe place," Fawkner pointed out distractedly as he ate and drank. "Was that not the objective of this journey?"

"I don't think we can just hide here," I told him grimly, twisting my hands together nervously. "Not yet, anyway."

Holger and Dolin exchanged quizzical looks, then turned their eyes to me.

"You look like you're fixing to do something mightily stupid there, lassie," Dolin observed gravely, pointing at me with his clay pipe.

"What is it?" Mithras stood up, looking down at me worriedly, a full half a foot taller than me.

I met his gaze, the pain and worry in my eyes like fire burning through us both. I didn't know how to say what was in my mind, but knew I had to.

"It's Uncle Aric," I told him. "He's in danger."

Mithras' eyes widened as he realised what I meant: "The conspirators."

I nodded, crossing my arms and pressing my palms to my elbows. "Lord Seward said that Uncle Aric is a weak king. I think they're going to kill him. He and Aunt Evangeline have to be warned."

Mithras nodded his agreement with conviction. "You're right, they must be. What would you do?"

I felt a deep certainty in me and knew what needed to be done: "We have to go to Aneuran. We have to get to them before the conspirators do."

"These conspirators," Carden noted, speaking up and drawing our attention, "may be of greater numbers than we first thought. Caution must be taken."

"They are most likely already within the city itself," Fawkner added grimly. "We cannot hope to enter the palace undetected. This is a foolish endeavour to embark on when we have already reached safe harbour."

I nodded, turning front on to my friends, looking down at them where they sat. I stepped forward, gazing into each of their faces, studying their features carefully.

"I don't disagree with you, Fawkner," I spoke with a strength that I had never felt before. "There are many enemies out there against us, many who would kill all of you to reach me, and I still don't really know why. But it isn't the Shadow Lord that we face now. It is men and women, human beings who seek to steal power from the rightful King of Aldegaad," I shook my head, prepared for the worst. "Only Mithras and I are Aldegaadians, so I don't expect the rest of you to follow us to Aneuran. It's your choice, but I won't sacrifice what's left of my family to those murderers just so that they can start a new war with Ivansten."

They all looked like they were contemplating my words, each of them deciding what they would do. I took in a slow breath, drawing in my courage to do what I needed to do next, letting my hands drop to my sides as I looked at my companions in turn.

"So, I'll just ask: who will come with us?" I said. "Ellora?"

The Elf bowed her red-haired head gently, smiling faintly at me. "As I followed her, so too shall I follow you."

"Joran?" I turned to the giant, gazing up at him.

"You are my Sarissi," he placed his right forearm across his chest and bowed his head. "As demanded by the Carethanes and the honour of my Jaaktar, I will go with you."

"Dolin?" I looked to the elder Dwarf.

"Aye, lassie," he nodded. "All the way, axe in hand."

"Me too, sweetie," Holger raised his mug strongly and winked at me. "I'm just hoping those bastards try something, then I'll give 'em a taste of my hammer. Ha-ha!"

I smiled at that then turned to the Guardians: "Aldwyn, are you able?"

He nodded. "I am, your Highness. And I can speak for both Tallinn and Carden when I say we will follow."

"It is our duty," Tallinn added. "We were bidden to protect you. So we shall."

"Carden?" I turned my eyes to my closest friend hopefully.

Carden stood and came to me, standing at my side and gazing down at me. How I adored this handsome man with all of my heart and soul.

"I will follow you as a Guardian, commanded by my oath," he told me, then smiled away the severity of his words, "but as your friend, you need not ask. I will *always* follow you, Leander."

I smiled brightly at him: "Thank you, Carden."

"Always," he promised, placing an arm around me and squeezing my shoulders gently.

I felt myself blush.

Fawkner downed the last of his drink and stood with a shrug, drawing everyone's eyes to him.

"Well, it seems that everyone here is determined to be stupid, so what the Void?" he nodded to me. "Count me in."

"And what about you Amethyst?" I looked down to her, already knowing the answer.

Amethyst sat on her hind legs, threw her head back and let out the loudest, most awe-inspiring roar any of us had ever heard. The hall shook with the ferocity of the dragon's call, all of the knights jumping up and looking to us in shock.

Mithras smiled as the dragon stretched out her wings powerfully. "Alright then. Let us save our King..."

* * * * *

It took us so very little time to pack for our journey, all of us resting up for the dash we were going to have to make the next morning. Mithras spoke with Callenhad and arranged for our transport, the way ahead decided that night. The next morning the keep was abuzz with activity as the knights rallied around to watch us depart.

I hurried down the front steps into the main courtyard to find that the knights had arranged horses for us. Aldwyn was already atop his mount, Fawkner the same with Holger holding onto his waist, the Lorveren man grumbling as the Dwarf did the same. I hid a small laugh at seeing the two of them like that.

Ellora was stroking the head of a beautiful white mare, turning her turquoise eyes to me as I approached.

"She is a good horse," she told me as if she had been conversing with the animal. "She will not let you fall."

"I'm glad," I smiled and started stroking the horse's mane.

Callenhad was walking with Mithras, the two knights moving to stand with me as Ellora turned to her own horse. She climbed up into the saddle, taking Dolin with her as the two knights approached. Mithras was dressed in his Aldegaadian armour once again, pausing there as Carden guided a black stallion by the reins to stand with my white mare.

"I cannot say that I approve of this action, Mithras," Callenhad was saying. "I would prefer that she stay here for her own protection."

"Yes, well," Mithras chuckled to himself, "she is like her ancestor, is she not? Stubborn to the end."

"Indeed. Princess," Callenhad drew my gaze, "I do not condone this course you are taking, yet I will not condemn it. I wish you luck."

"Thank you for all your help, Ser Callenhad," I thanked him.

"You are welcome back here at any time," he told me, smiling faintly, his blue eyes so bright. "In fact, I would ask that you *do* return. We can protect you here."

I climbed up onto my horse, taking the reins as I adjusted my cloak so it didn't catch around me.

"Once the rest of my family is safe," I promised him honestly, "then I'll come back and let you do whatever you feel is necessary to protect me."

"Then, may the Eldest Ones watch over you, Princess Leander," Callenhad bowed his head. "I wish you safe travels and great success on your path."

The others had mounted their horses by now, Joran driving a cart with all of our supplies, a work horse set into the bridle. Carden came up beside me on his black horse, Mithras riding an identical one.

With Mithras in the lead, Aldwyn behind him, Carden and I close to them and the others following, we left Mountain Falls behind, the knights watching on worriedly. Leaping from the wall, Amethyst took flight at last, spreading her magenta skinned wings majestically and following Farsight, the dragon and the falcon flying together over us as we rode.

The path we chose took us down the western slopes of the Calian Mountains and led us towards the edge of the Alstan Forest. It was a journey that would take us a little over two weeks but was made so much easier with the horses. Alstan Castle was visible in the distance and I suppressed my unease at being so close to the Sewards' home. I just had to push my fear of them - especially Tibain - from my mind and just focus on the task at hand.

We broke the edge of the forest and charged over the Knolling Plains' grassy expanse. The Ruins of Averet appeared on the horizon, making me cringe at the thought of that place. I was glad to pass it without getting any closer, the memories of that night still too coarse in my mind.

The town of Varlen on the banks of Lake Varlen was the first place we were able to stop and resupply, allowing us two days to rest before continuing on. Our next port of call would be the small town of Arten, a day south on the southern banks of Lake Varlen.

In the final day of our journey we increased our speed, managing to avoid a single Aldegaadian cavalry patrol as they came from Aneuran. The city itself grew larger on the horizon as we made for it, rushing ahead at our horses' full speeds.

We came to the city outskirts after dusk, a dark night lying before us where the three moons hung in the sky only as faded crescents, black clouds looming over the lush greenery and the grey and white stone of the city. The palace itself was set on the north side of the cove, built there in the cliffs with a grand view over all that lay beneath.

Dismounting from our horses, Mithras and I walked to the edge of a cliff overlooking the city in the bay. The three Guardians came up behind us as Ellora leaped up and perched on a higher cliff, her eyes gazing down at the way below.

"How do we plan to enter the city?" Tallinn asked, uncertain as she hid beneath her hood and cloak from the cold coming off the ocean.

"We could just walk through the front doors, right?" I asked, looking to Mithras.

"Into the city, yes," Mithras nodded, surveying the scene before us, "but not the palace. I think we may have a greater set of problems before us."

"But you sent a messenger pigeon to Knight-Commander Tavish, didn't you?" I recalled. "You said he would help us reach the palace."

"He said he could only open the way into the city for a few of us," he explained. "He has had suspicions about the possibility of a conspiracy for some time, and he cannot guarantee that entry into the palace would be safe for you. Not via the main entrance."

"How do you suggest we proceed, Mithras?"Aldwyn enquired, leaning on his staff for support.

"Myself, Leander and two others could go via the Aneuran Basilica of the Divine Seven," Mithras determined, studying the city below cautiously. "There is a secret passage within which leads directly to the King and Queen's bedchambers inside the palace."

"I never knew about this," I stated, surprised.

"These things are best kept secret until needed," Mithras said, looking at me. "It is primarily an escape tunnel, however we can use it to reach the King before it is too late."

"And you don't think this looks a little suspicious?" Fawkner commented coldly, his arms crossed, right hand ready to snatch up his sword from his hip. "Sneaking into the palace?"

"Do we have any choice?" Dolin asked him, leaning one hand on his large battleaxe.

"I've got one," Holger snorted, twisting his head to the sides and making his neck crack, "fight."

"We *aren't* killing anyone," I scolded him, then turned to my protector. "We'll do it your way, Mithras."

"Then choose who else you would have join us, Leander," he advised me. "Only two more can accompany us."

"Carden and Tallinn," I said easily. "The presence of the Guardians should put my uncle's mind at ease."

"We're with you," Carden assured me, putting a comforting hand on my shoulder briefly.

"Good. Aldwyn," I turned to the Mage, "watch Amethyst for me, please. Keep her safe."

"I will," he promised with a nod.

The dragon growled sourly at me, and I crouched down to stroke her head.

"It's alright, Amethyst," I cooed. "I'll be back soon. Just stay with the others. Alright?"

Sulkily, the dragon snorted and nodded as I stood and turned to Mithras.

"Let's go," I authorised.

With our hoods drawn and our bodies wrapped in our cloaks, Tallinn, Carden, Mithras and I made our way down the cliffs and to one of the entrances into the city. Mithras was able to get us past the checkpoint, several knights there loyal to him and prepared to fight for their King if there really was a threat.

The way to the basilica was easily made, our small group reaching it less than twenty minutes after entering the city. We soon passed through the cavernous chapels, pushing our hoods back and turning down into one of the groves set there. Mithras pressed his hands into two particular stones on the floor near the statue, gears turning somewhere beneath us, and a passage opened in the wall.

He led the way, lighting a torch that had been set there on the passage wall and illuminating our darkened path ahead. I followed close behind him, realising that all three of my companions weren't happy about me being unarmed, but I didn't think it was necessary to carry a weapon. Not with Uncle Aric.

I felt secure with Carden and Tallinn behind me, that security even more important to me as the passage sealed us inside itself and left us with only the dark way ahead. It was a claustrophobic path that led us up a long road. I reminded myself to breath deep and not panic, trying not to give in to my fear of small, tight spaces.

With no lights or any changes in the dark stone walls, the way seemed unending, condemning us to walk until we at last came to a spiral staircase.

A bad feeling soon filled me as we climbed through the secret tunnels, passing by the sewers and catacombs of the ancient city. I began to worry as dread grew within me, fearing what I might come face to face with down in those forgotten depths.

My mind began playing tricks on me and I thought for a few moments that I had seen the Shadow Lord standing there in the dark. I ignored what my eyes showed me, thinking to myself: *It's only the darkness of these tunnels. He's not here. I'm safe.*

"Here," Mithras' voice snapped me back to reality as we came to a dead end. "This is it," he placed the torch in a sconce on the wall and searched for the release.

His gloved hand grasped a lever and with a few grunts he managed to force it to open. The door clicked loudly and groaned as it moved out into the palace bedchambers.

Light shone through and I breathed the fresher air in deeply, relieved to be free of those tunnels. That's when the sickening smell overwhelmed me, like heavy copper burning my nostrils. My heart sank and I felt terror rising in me anew as I beheld the scene beyond the secret door.

"No," I gasped and stepped into the room swiftly.

"Leander, wait!" Mithras exclaimed, reaching for me, but missing as I pulled my arm away from him and entered the doorway with a frantic heart...

Epilogue
Assassination

I threw myself out of the secret door built into the grey stone walls of the royal bedchamber, the majesty of the palatial room's blue and gold hues lost on me. Only one sight filled my vision, the one that I had dreaded for too long and raced here to try to prevent.

Uncle Aric lay on the floor dressed in his blue, gold and dark grey finery, his crown cast on the rug near his right hand. Blood stained the chest of his jacket and tunic, a slender, elegant knife buried through his sternum.

Aunt Evangeline lay at his left side, her right hand in his left. She was face down, her eyes shut, her dark blue, gold and white gown stained with crimson as she rested in a pool of her own blood. Even in death she remained so beautiful.

Uncle Aric was coughing up blood, still breathing as he held her hand tightly. He turned his blue steel eyes towards the opening in the wall, his greying beard stained with blood and spit. Seeing us, he reached out his shaking right hand towards me.

"L-Leander," he called weakly, barely more than a whisper.

"Uncle Aric!" I rushed to him, dropping to my knees at his side.

Behind me Carden and Tallinn moved to the double doors of the room, the two Guardians watching out for any sign of trouble. Meanwhile, Mithras came to crouch beside Aunt Evangeline, checking for her vital signs though I already knew her fate.

Uncle Aric touched my cheek, smiling up at me as I pressed my hands to his wrist, my long dark auburn hair hanging like two curtains around my face and shoulders. Tears filled my eyes as I stared down at my dying uncle, wishing to save him from this fate.

"My d-dear niece," Aric coughed weakly, happiness flowing through him. "You're alive. I thought for certain that... that you were dead."

"Mithras and the Guardians saved me, Uncle Aric," I explained, struggling against imminent sobs, feeling the warmth leaving his hand already.

"Sire," Mithras spoke to the King, genuflecting near us, "how badly are you injured?"

"M-Mortally I-I fear," the King responded, his eyes fluttering weakly.

"Who did this to you?" I demanded so softly and tearfully that it sounded more like a plea.

"It was... F-Fane," Uncle Aric managed slowly.

"Uncle Fane?!" I was taken aback. "*He* did this?!"

"He has al-always wanted to be K-King," Uncle Aric struggled. "He orchestrated a-all of-of this. Evangeline: my sweet wife, m-murdered before my eyes by my own b-brother..."

"We're going to help you, Uncle Aric," I tried to sound strong, losing my composure as the memory of my father's death paralysed me once again. "We'll take you to Aldwyn; he can heal you"

"I'm... I'm sorry, my sweet Leander," he apologised slowly. "I-I will not survive much longer, I think."

"No!" I began to sob despairingly, closing my eyes against my tears as my heart tore apart once again.

"M-Mithras," Uncle Aric turned to the Knight. "I-I want you to prom-promise me something."

"Of course, Sire. Anything," Mithras agreed with a nod.

Uncle Aric swallowed hard against the blood rising in his throat. "I want you to pro-protect Leander, no matter the cost. Give me... your... your word that she will l-live."

"By my honour as a knight, I swear to you that I will protect her until my dying breath," Mithras swore honestly, "and then beyond."

Uncle Aric nodded and looked to me. "Leander..."

"No. Please, Uncle Aric. Don't," I pleaded hoarsely, looking down at him through hot tears.

"I have always l-loved you, my dear girl," he told me, fading fast, grasping my right hand tightly. "You are like a daughter to me. I would have you and your sister survive this treachery. Please, Leander. Run... Go..."

He closed his eyes and let out one last breath.

I began to cry heavily, Mithras moving to me and pulling me from Uncle Aric's body. He held me in his arms, cradling me and stroking my back soothingly. I clung to him, devastated as I once again endured the pain of losing a loved one to a murderous end.

"We were too late," I heard Tallinn murmur sadly.

"Leander," Mithras tilted my chin to look into my eyes as I opened them, his own hurt clear. "We cannot linger. We must leave."

Slowly, teary eyed, I nodded, letting him help me up, staggering a little as I tried to force strength back into my legs.

Suddenly, the dull sound of hands slowly, deliberately and mockingly clapping drew our attention. I looked up to the secret passage to see Fane stepping through with the tall, white haired Knight-Commander Tavish behind him. Fane wore a sword sheathed at his left side and a cruel sneer branded over his darkly bearded face, his eyes cold as he regarded me sinisterly.

"A wonderful performance," he commented, lowering his hands to his sides as several blue and gold surcoat wearing soldiers followed from the tunnel.

I stared at him, horrified and feeling hatred rising up in me at the sight of him, but I remained quiet, clinging to Mithras tightly.

"Honestly, I don't think there has ever been a play written better than this little tragedy," he continued smugly. "What do you think, Leander?"

Mithras snarled, his eyes burning with rage as he shoved me behind him to protect me.

"You have no right to address her, traitor!" he hissed venomously, his right hand to his sword, though he didn't draw it.

"Traitor?" Fane chuckled to himself, amused. "Really? Because, Ser Mithras, it seems to me that the deranged Knight-Commander who slew the Lord and Lady of Arvon has recruited conspirators, assassinated the King and now holds the Princess hostage."

"What?!" I exclaimed as Carden came swiftly to my side. "You can't be serious!"

Fane went on maliciously: "The Knight and the so-called Guardians are locked in a dungeon while I, the Regent of Aneuran, decide their fate. Meanwhile, the Princess, stricken with grief and trauma after all she has endured, is incarcerated for her own safety."

I felt numb as Carden pushed me behind him, clinging to his arm as he drew his sword. Mithras had his sword at the ready, Tallinn prepared with hers as well. The doors opened behind us, more soldiers standing ready as Farah stood with them, a sword in hand.

"Surrender peacefully," Tavish advised us evenly and arrogantly, "and there will be no need for bloodshed."

"Do you still worry about us spilling blood?" Carden asked me in a hushed voice.

"No," was my frightened response.

"Good!" Carden swung his elbow back and threw down a soldier hard, knocking him out.

Mithras slung his shield from his back and slammed it across Tavish's face, throwing the white-haired younger knight into Fane and the soldiers. He then turned and rushed for the doors as Tallinn engaged a pair of soldiers. He bowled through them with his shield, throwing Farah against a wall as Tallinn followed him.

I grabbed the nearest downed soldier's sword, running beside Carden as Fane got to his feet furiously.

"Stop them! I want the girl alive!" he screamed.

"Move!" Mithras shouted, clashing swords with a soldier briefly and dropping him quickly.

"Which way?!" I cried out, my heart frantic in my chest.

"To the mezzanine!" Mithras directed me.

We began a fighting retreat, sprinting through the golden hallways of the palace with the soldiers chasing us. Tallinn switched from sword to bow, hurling arrows back at the soldiers as we ran, determined to discourage them.

I ran through the large doors out onto the mezzanine, the icy bay air gusting up at me as the dark night exploded through my senses. I found myself staring down into the ocean below, my heart pounding in my chest and my lungs burning.

I turned as a soldier launched himself past Carden and straight at me. I let out a yelp and blocked his strike with my sword, the clang of metal resounding around me. I parried and ducked, slamming him in the face with the pommel as the two Guardians rushed to help me.

A second soldier was on me, his hand reaching for my neck. I pulled back in panic, the man's fingers grasping my pendant, rending it away with the harmless snap of its silver chain. I felt it tear from my neck, swinging my sword and catching his shoulder. He screamed, the necklace clattering to the ground at Carden's feet as he was fighting back another soldier.

I rushed for the Pendant, seized by my arm suddenly by a soldier as Tavish and Mithras stumbled backwards through the mezzanine doors, fighting fiercely. The two men swung and slashed with their swords and shields, Mithras seeing me struggling as my sword was forced from my hand. He tried to reach me, but Tavish kept him engaged in their battle, relentless and cruel.

"CARDEN!" I screamed, trying to free my wrist from the soldier's hard fingers.

"LEANDER!" Carden turned to me, terror in his green eyes.

"The Pendant!" I cried, fighting as I was dragged backwards towards the doors. "Get it! Please!"

Looking down, Carden scooped the necklace up and turned to run after me. I wanted him to reach me, to pull me into the safety of his strong arms, but the soldiers were overwhelming the Guardians' position, and I was now stuck behind them as they rushed the mezzanine.

"Go, you two! Go!" Mithras shouted to the Guardians. "Alert the others! Quickly, before... oomph!"

He was struck in the head with Tavish's sword, his sentence cut short as he dropped to the ground.

I screamed as I saw him fall, struggling to break free as two soldiers held me tightly, pinning my arms against their chests. I looked to Carden desperately, my heart breaking at seeing him in such terror.

Carden rushed forward to help me, but Tallinn grabbed his arm and pulled him back.

"No, Carden, we cannot!" she cried out fervently.

They looked into my frightened eyes, then faced Tavish and his soldiers as they drove them back towards the edge of the mezzanine. Taking one look down, then flashing a glance at each other, the two Guardians knew they had only one choice.

Carden threw a longingly painful glance back at me, our eyes meeting desperately. I wanted him to save me and he wanted to do it, but we both knew that it couldn't be done. Not yet.

Clutching the Pendant in his hand, Carden followed Tallinn, the two of them throwing themselves over the barrier of the mezzanine and diving into the dark waters of the cove below. A small relief filled me as twin splashes reached up from the sea, my friends safely away. At least that was something.

I was dragged to the side, looking down at Mithras' unmoving body, relieved at seeing that he was still alive. I struggled against the two soldiers passionately, desperate to reach my friend, but their holds were too tight, hurting my arms.

Fane and Farah stormed up, Fane glancing at me, then Mithras respectively before turning his eyes to Tavish.

"Where are the other two, Knight-Commander?" he demanded.

"They dived off into the waters below," Tavish reported coldly. "Shall I have my men search the bay?"

Fane nodded his head, turning with a cruel, cold smile to me. "Find them, whether they live or not. Regardless, we've got what we wanted."

He stood over me and eyed me off with a cold sneer. I glared up at him as the soldiers held my arms out to my sides, closed lipped and gritting my teeth.

"You didn't help yourself by coming here, Leander," Fane snarled coldly. "It would have been better for you to have stayed in whatever hole you crawled into."

"You're a murderer, Fane," I hissed, my arms aching, the soldiers jerking me back painfully.

"All for the greater good, my girl," he tried to justify, stroking my face.

I pulled away hard, glaring up at him furiously, fighting the urge to let loose more tears and show my fear. I was determined not to give in and appear weak before these monsters.

"Take Ser Mithras and Princess Leander to the dungeons," he commanded. "I want it made certain they cannot escape."

"Yes Regent," was the soldiers' responses, two of them picking up Mithras and dragging him away.

Fane paused the guards holding me as he stood up close to me, glaring into my eyes and coldly smiling. All I could do was stare back with all the hatred that I had for him. If my stare were a sword he would have been impaled by the ferocity of my strike.

"I hope we can come to an understanding," he said mockingly. "I would hate for you to remain in those dark cells indefinitely."

I remained silent, refusing to beg or make any sound that might satisfy his foul mind.

Fane nodded to the soldiers and I was dragged away, still struggling.

The thought of Aneuran's dungeons distressed me, a place I had always feared as a child. Now I was being condemned to those dank confines below the palace by my own uncle, the man who had been systematically murdering my family. Both thoughts were daunting to endure.

Knowing that Carden and Tallinn had escaped gave me hope though. I was sure they had survived, imagining them standing on the shore looking back at the palace, Carden holding the Pendant in his large, strong hands.

They could reach the others and mount a rescue, I knew it. I just knew it in my heart. Carden wouldn't leave me trapped like this. He just wouldn't.

As I was forced down towards the darkness of the dungeons, that hope from my friends was my shining light. It was the only thing I had left to hold onto. They would free me. I was sure of it...

The Story Continues in Book 2...

Pendant of Dragons
Custodians of The Past

Excerpt from Custodians of The Past

Once we all had our cloaks on again and the two men had donned their armour as well as taken all of their equipment, we passed through the door. Like the two before it, the door sealed as soon as we had passed, and we had no choice but to continue onwards through the Gauntlet's tunnels.

Carden now carried the only torch we had between us and lit our path in that dark place. I was thankful for it until we found a charred and broken body slumped against a wall. I stayed back beside Fawkner as Carden crouched over the body with his light and inspected the damage.

"This was a challenger," he guessed, still studying the armour and the body. "The apprentice judging by the seal on the armour. The bones and clothing are heavily burnt."

"A hint of the test still to come?" Fawkner suggested gravely.

I swallowed hard against the lump in my throat but kept my hands at my sides as I looked past Carden at the corpse.

Carden looked up at us from where he crouched with a calmly worried expression: "Or there's something else down here. Something *not* part of the tests."

"Another Fire Golem?" Fawkner offered.

"I don't know, but you'd better take this," Carden took the long sword lying on the ground and passed it to Fawkner as he stood. "Stay on your guard, Fawkner," the young man then looked to me. "And you stay close to us, Leander."

I nodded uneasily. "Alright."

We started forward again, making our way slowly through the tunnels and their twists and turns. They led us down to another stairway opening up beneath the island and into a great drop into darkness. I could hear the ocean crashing on the rocks below, knowing that there had to be a break in the cliffs somewhere to let the water in.

The stairway brought us to a narrow walkway that had the three of us pressing ourselves against the stone wall. The two men were obsessively protective of me as we crossed this and wouldn't let up until we were at last safely across the drop. We then had to climb another steeper and more awkward stairway. We had to crawl on our stomachs up the incline and once again I found myself relentlessly cared for by my two companions.

At last we made it to the top, Fawkner reaching the landing first and turning to help me. He grasped my wrist and pulled me up as Carden supported my back. My feet touched the flat ground of the ancient stone landing and I gazed around at the cavernous ruins we had found ourselves in. They were the remains of castle towers and battlements sunken beneath the rocks, almost like the Dragon's Crest had swallowed up a fortress and dropped it down into its depths.

"This place is ancient," Fawkner noted as we walked through archways of human make and natural formation. "How old must it be to have been swallowed by the earth like this?"

"I'll bet Ellora would know of other places like this," Carden said as he stared in wonder at the ruins. "How much must she have seen in fourteen hundred plus years of life?"

We continued through the ruins and up into another series of caverns. It was so intensely dark that Carden had to take the lead with the torch now, the flames struggling to light the way.

As our passage curved around a corner, there suddenly came a light through the parts in the rocks; a dull glow of a yellowish sheen. It was not intense light, but warm and beckoning to us as we silently turned the last corner.

"By the gods..." Fawkner gasped in wonderment as his grey eyes widened at the bewildering sight.

"Incredible," Carden whispered in astonishment.

I could say nothing, just walking between the two men as we traversed the steps down to the main floor of the gigantic cavern. My breath caught in my chest for a moment as I stared at the immensity of it all.

High above in the central ceiling of the cavern there shone the light of night down through a great hole that was too high to reach. With it and the torches set on the many natural columns surrounding us, the chamber was so brilliantly illuminated. But this wasn't what drew our wonder.

Piles upon mountainous piles of treasure clogged the arteries of this great natural chamber; chests laid open to bare their riches as vast fields of gold and jewels stretched on seemingly forever. The immensity of it all would drive many a greedy man to insanity as his eyes set upon such unadulterated wealth.

I just stood still at the edge of the great sea of precious gems and metals, staring and silently wondering why it was there.

Suddenly, a low growl echoed in the depths around us and our wonder faded away.

"What was that?" Fawkner drew his sword, looking around nervously as Carden did the same.

They pushed me between them as the growl reverberated off the cavern walls again, this time louder. I froze, listening and waiting. Then I heard the clinking of a wave of coins, my eyes finding the source of the sound as something seemed to swim beneath the great hoard's surface.

The two men turned to follow my gaze as the shape began to rise from the golden seas, horns and scales appearing out of the great mass of coins. Two enormous wings spread up into the air, raining coins and jewels down all around as clawed hands of brown, teal and pale blue scale clutched at the piles.

The men took a few steps back, pushing me behind them further as they went, their eyes locked on the behemoth rising before us. All I could do was stare up into the long snouted face of scales and its vibrant molten eyes.

The golden rain of coins settled with the trickling of metal on metal as the great tail swayed back and forth a few times, then coiled around one of the piles. We were face-to-face with an enormous brown and green scaled dragon, six great horns rising from its head, spines jutting up with large scaly plates across its shoulders and back. It was twice the size of Amethyst.

The Dragon locked its eyes on us, the irises looking like they were glowing in the shadows of the cavern. Its nostrils flared and its wings arched as it grimaced with razor sharp pointed teeth peering from beneath its great lips.

Wonder drew me to it as it sniffed at us, and I slowly slipped past my protectors.

Carden seized my arm to stop me, making me turn my face to him. "Leander?! What are you doing?!"

"It's alright... trust me," I urged him, placing my hand on his and gently unhooking his fingers from my arm.

I approached the great being and stood before it, looking up at its majesty and grace. The Dragon lowered its face to me so that our eyes met. I had never felt smaller in my life before its immense greatness. It sniffed deeply, pulling in my scent, my hair and clothes being sucked towards its face so forcefully that I had to plant my feet to save myself from falling into its snout.

"Hm..." a low, rumbling, deep voice spoke as the Dragon moved its mouth. "You are the first in many a century to approach me with wonder and not fear, human woman-child."